THE BLUE PENCIL

David Lowther

Sacristy
Press

Sacristy Press
PO Box 612, Durham, DH1 9HT

www.sacristy.co.uk

First published in 2012 by Sacristy Press, Durham

Sacristy Limited, registered in England & Wales, number 7565667

British Library Cataloguing-in-Publication Data
A catalogue record for the book is available from the British Library

ISBN 978-1-908381-07-1

London, October 1939

I'm standing on the concourse of King's Cross Station. With me are most, but not all, of the people I love; my mother, my father, and my girlfriend Jane. The one person missing is my nineteen-year-old brother John who's been spirited away from his studies at Cambridge to some hush-hush establishment to plot the downfall of Nazi Germany, with whom we have been at war for just over a month.

I've enlisted in the Army. Conscription hadn't swallowed me up yet but it would do so sooner rather than later. Besides, I'd decided long ago that I would fight. What would have been the point in waiting to be called up?

My mother fussed over me. Had I got everything? Did I have enough food for the long journey? I was heading north to undertake six months of basic training. After that, who knows? I'd been treated like everyone else when I signed up at the Ministry of Labour but a close friend had told me I was likely to be sent for officer training and, after that, perhaps to serve in the Intelligence Corps.

A loudspeaker announces that my train will be leaving in fifteen minutes. My father shakes my hand warmly, a hint of pride in his eyes. My mother wraps her arms around me and holds me for a moment or two. Then Jane kisses me and, with a smile, reminds me that time will fly and we'll soon be together when I come home on leave.

I'm not sure whether I will ever see them again and this fills me with sadness as I join the huge throng of young men who, like me, are heading north to an uncertain future. I settle into a seat by the window and soon the train is slowly pulling its way out of London. I'm reminded of a similar journey I'd taken in very different circumstances less than a year ago.

I'm watching the houses of suburban London speed by and thinking back over the past three years and the circumstances that have brought me here. I'm going to fight in a war that might have been avoided but, once it became inevitable, had to be fought.

It had all begun for me a little over three and a half years ago.

CHAPTER ONE

The Red Flag

"City of perspiring dreams"
FREDERICK RAPHAEL

The menace of Nazi Germany didn't hit me until Hitler sent troops marching into the Rhineland in March 1936. The Treaty of Versailles had also told Germany not to build an air force or conscript civilians into military service, but Hitler didn't bother with that either. I'd spent almost three years at Cambridge University pretending to be a socialist while everyone around me was screaming about the threat of Fascism. I just hadn't noticed.

"But they're only taking back what's rightly theirs."

"You're right Roger, but it's the way they're doing it that worries us."

I was sitting in a restaurant on King's Parade, a short walk from Trinity College where I had spent the last two and half years studying and trying to work out what to do with my life. Sitting opposite me was my tutor Maurice Dobb, a charming and handsome man a little over ten years older than me. He had offered to buy me lunch so that we could talk over my future. He was an Economics lecturer and a Marxist and it was he who had persuaded me to change from Modern Languages to Economics.

He was hardly an establishment figure in that most traditional of English educational institutions but was at least a Cambridge man himself. He had been an undergraduate at Pembroke College before two years of research at the London School of Economics.

Dobb was already a member of the Communist Party when he had returned to Cambridge as a lecturer in 1924. For the past twelve years he had been developing his theories of Marxist Economics and had attracted a growing number of disciples not by coercion but by reason—including, I have to admit, me. He was a towering intellect and I liked him immensely. He was quietly persuasive but not to everyone's liking, particularly amongst the university hierarchy who viewed him as an outsider, and this meant that, especially in terms of his relationships with his colleagues, he was, at times, rather lonely. His revolutionary ideas were at odds with the conventional academic world and, to cap it all, he was a divorcee who had married his second wife Barbara five years ago. Nevertheless I found him fascinating, loyal to his students, over whom he took endless trouble, and a real gentleman.

"The man's a complete lunatic and he'll drag us into war. Even before he seized power in Germany that buffoon Churchill was warning parliament about the threat he poses."

The speaker, and third man at our table, was Anthony Blunt. He had joined us uninvited, spotting us through the restaurant window as he walked down King's Parade. I disliked Blunt almost as much as I admired Dobb. He was a Fellow of my college, Trinity, and had graduated six years earlier. He'd stayed on after graduation before going to London to work as Art Critic for *The Spectator* magazine.

I had no interest whatsoever in either Art or Art History but that wasn't why I disliked him. Blunt was arrogant and supercilious, and had no time for people like me who didn't share his public school background. He was also an Apostle; a secret society of the self-appointed Cambridge elite who discussed heaven knows what cloistered in rooms around the city.

Neither Dobb nor I were Apostles, nor ever would be; we were far too ordinary. I'd come across Blunt at meetings of the University Socialist Club. He too was a Marxist but whether out of conviction or because of his obsession with another Trinity man, Guy Burgess, I couldn't say. Burgess wasn't about any more. He had been carrying out some kind of History research after graduation but had left Cambridge to get a 'proper' job. There was gossip that he and Blunt had had a brief affair. Frankly this didn't bother me at all but Burgess' outrageous behaviour, especially when he was drunk, left me cold.

My main objection to Blunt, and his acolytes like Burgess, was the way in which they'd bullied the University Socialist Society towards adopting Communism. Where Dobb got his point over through thoughtful and quiet reasoning, others chose loud and forceful argument and action. Burgess had even persuaded the college waiters to strike for better wages and conditions and was a frequent noisy participant in anti-establishment gatherings.

"The fact is," Dobb added, "that Hitler is using the alliance between France and the Soviet Union as a reason for putting armed troops into the Rhineland. He feels he needs to strengthen his western flank against attack from France."

"Sounds reasonable enough to me," I replied. "The French have played a big part in preventing German recovery since 1918 so he must have reason to fear his neighbours. Besides, Hitler hates the Communists, the Soviet Union in particular, so he must provide Germany with some security."

"There, you've said it," said Blunt. "That word hate. Hitler hates Communists and he hates Jews and, wherever there's been hate throughout history, there have been wars. The whole wretched Nazi regime reeks of evil. Of course, Hitler can kick the Jews out of Germany and lock up the Communists, but which country in the world has the most Communists?"

"The Soviet Union," I replied.

"So you see, in order to destroy Communism he'll have to wipe out Russia. Everything Hitler does from now on will be a step towards war with the Soviet Union. Seizing the Rhineland was just the start. He's begun to secure his western flank. Next he'll turn his attention to the east."

"Yes I can see that," said Dobb. "I suppose he'll start to look at Austria and Czechoslovakia. Plenty of Germans there and a couple of other pieces of Versailles he'd like to dismantle."

"How will he go about that?" I asked.

Blunt raised his voice.

"By force of course."

"Surely we won't stand by and let him," I said.

"You must be joking," replied Blunt, "Baldwin's government and the French have done nothing to force Germany's troops out of the Rhineland. Sure the French made a fuss for a day or two, but they soon backed down. Baldwin has made a commitment to peace and you can work out our government's attitude to the whole business from reading that *Times* leader of three weeks ago."

"Yes, I read that too," said Dobb, "blaming the Franco-Soviet Pact for upsetting the Germans and recognising their fears of being surrounded by enemies. They then told the government that they should be seeking peace with Germany."

"Pah," said Blunt. "Hitler's not interested in peace. He'll stamp and shout and try to get everything he wants. If he fails, he'll go to war. But if we sit back and let him have his way, like we did over the Rhineland, he'll have won without firing a shot and he won't have touched our precious Empire."

"But that's *The Times* not the government." I replied.

"You're very naïve, Martin."

Unlike Dobb, Blunt always called me by my surname.

"*The Times* is the government," continued Blunt. "Dawson, the Editor, is bosom pals with half the cabinet and he prints what they tell him."

Blunt was, of course, right about me. I was naïve. I understood little about foreign affairs. I knew about Hitler and his persecution of the Jews in Germany but paid scant attention to his rantings about the injustices of Versailles and, anyway, I believed the situation of the German Jews was mostly newspaper talk.

In truth I became interested in politics at Cambridge when my chief concern was the gap between rich and poor, unemployment, housing and poverty. Unlike many in the University Socialist Society, I believed that the Labour Party would remedy the ills of the country in due course. I suppose I was what some Communists might disparagingly call a Social Democrat.

True, the present Parliamentary Labour Party were a pretty feeble bunch and had yet to recover from the collapse of the previous Labour government in 1931 when their leader, and then Prime Minister, Ramsay MacDonald had betrayed the party and set up a National Government of predominantly Tory MPs, with him staying on as Prime Minister.

"So do you think there'll be war?" asked Dobb.

"Quite possibly," replied Blunt, "but when I couldn't say. What will you do, Maurice, if there is?

"I'm totally against war. I knew I hated war even when I was too young to be called up in 1914, but I am a patriot and if, heaven forbid, we do go to war with Germany, I would want to make my contribution, but I won't fight. For now I must be off. I have a lecture to give at four o'clock. Thank you, Anthony, for sharing your views with us. I just hope you're wrong. Roger, call on me next week and we'll talk some more about your future. I'll pay the bill on my way out."

With that he was gone, closely followed by Blunt. Our little chat about my future had been hijacked by Blunt but, much as I disliked the art historian, I found his views interesting. I was no nearer to knowing what I wanted to do but Blunt's assertions about *The Times* and his mistrust of Hitler and Germany had stirred something in me. At the time though, I wasn't sure what it was.

CHAPTER TWO

The Shape of Things to Come

"It is well that war is terrible. We
should grow too fond of it."
ROBERT E. LEE

I did have several more chats with Maurice Dobb but we came to few conclusions about my future. I knew he wanted me to join the Communist Party but, while I felt myself to be a committed socialist, I was certain that the best way to achieve social justice and equality was through the ballot box. From the little I knew of what was going on in the Soviet Union, they had chosen another route and I wasn't sure that I liked it.

Dobb, of course, wasn't the kind of person to force his ideas on me, or anyone else. His chief concern, and mine, was that I should do well in my final exams. In the late spring and early summer I was well on course to do just that. I knew I wouldn't get a First but felt I had done enough to get a good degree.

I was at home during the Easter vacation and my parents more or less left me alone to study and to spend time with my girlfriend, Jane.

Neither my father, Reg, nor my mother, Mary, had been lucky enough to benefit from a university education. They had grown up locally. Reg had worked in a small general store and had become manager by his mid-twenties. His growing success attracted the attention of the owner of Howell's, south-west London's best known department store, and by

1930 he was its manager.

My mother had worked in the first of father's shops. They had married in the spring of 1914 and I was born in the following year. My father had fought on the western front during the war but was lucky to return largely unscathed, albeit with many unpleasant memories.

So here was I, twenty-one years of age, the son of reasonably prosperous parents, about to graduate from one of the world's great universities but without a clue as to what I was going to do with my life.

My younger brother John was sixteen and tall like me, but still growing. He was in the final two years of the same local Grammar School that I had attended. He was keen to follow me to Cambridge, but, where I'd been interested in languages and later Economics, he was totally committed to studying Science. He was much cleverer than me. I had achieved good results in education through hard work but he was, right from the first year at the Grammar School, a high flier and seemed destined for great things—yet, despite our differences in outlook, we got on well together. He'd probably have made a good sportsman but wasn't showing much interest in it. He was too tied up with his pursuit of Science.

I had been very happy at school, just as I was at Cambridge. I had worked hard and played hard. I was a member of the school rugby, hockey and cricket teams and held the school record for the quarter mile run. When I went up to Cambridge I carried on playing sport, mostly rugby, for my college and athletics in inter-college competitions, but I never came even close to winning a Blue in either sport.

Games played an important part in student life at Cambridge and the annual matches in various sports with arch rivals Oxford were fiercely contested. I was just under six foot, weighed twelve stone and was quick on the rugby field, but nowhere near fast enough to cope with brilliant Cambridge players like the giant Wilfred Wooler or the mercurial Cliff Jones. Both were Welshmen and had played for their country with great distinction while they were still students.

The main man in the Cambridge University Athletics Club that summer was Godfrey Brown. He, like me, was a quarter miler, but while I would struggle round the distance in around 52 seconds, he was more than five seconds faster. Brown was Britain's number one at the event and there were high hopes at Cambridge, and throughout the country, that he would excel at the Olympic Games in Berlin later that summer.

I met my girlfriend Jane during my final year at school, at a dance at her school in a nearby town. She was a good looking dark haired girl, quite tall and with a vibrant personality that was great fun. She played hockey and tennis for her school, but the two things we shared were a passion for dancing and a love of the cinema.

Our relationship was on-off; on in the sense that we spent a lot of time together when I was at home, and off when I was at Cambridge. Jane hoped to become an accountant and had spent three years as an articled clerk at a practice in the town. Female accountants were scarce in England in 1936 but I had little doubt that Jane would soon be joining that select band. She had a mind of her own and wanted to find her own way in life, not follow the traditional path of shop girl, wife, mother and housewife. She would be qualified in a couple of years and I had secret hopes that my father would persuade his store owner to give her a job working alongside him. Spending more time with Jane after I'd come down from Cambridge was something that I was really looking forward to.

All in all I was pretty well set up for life—or so I thought—when my father sat me down for a chat shortly before my return to Cambridge for my final term.

I loved and admired my father. He had worked incredibly hard to establish himself as a successful businessman and had given my mother, my brother and me very comfortable lives. In return he had expected my brother and me to work hard at school and university. I felt that we had both repaid him, so I was always anxious to listen to his advice.

"I hope you don't mind, Roger, but this seems to be the right time to look at your future. I know you're preoccupied with your exams but you'll need to be making some big decisions about the next stage of your life when they're over."

"Of course, Dad. I've been giving it a lot of thought and have talked to friends and tutors at university about it."

"Come up with any ideas?"

"Well, not really. What do you think?"

"All I want is for you to be happy and successful doing something you want to do."

This was typical of my father. He loved his family passionately and wanted his sons to grow up with minds of their own, but I wanted him to help me and point me in the right direction, so I said, "OK you're not going to tell me what to do, I know that, but how do you think I should go about reaching the right decision?"

He thought for a moment then, looking me straight in the eye, said, "The first thing is to ask yourself what you're good at, then think if you would enjoy using those skills as a career. So what are you good at?"

"Well I enjoy working hard and playing and watching sport. I'm good at languages and I have a decent understanding of Economics."

"Any other interests?"

"Yes, well you might not approve of this, but I've been a member of the University Socialist Club for a couple of years and I've started taking an interest in foreign policy."

My father, the self-made man, was a dyed in the wool traditionalist and, as far as I knew, voted Conservative at General Elections. He looked at me closely and said, "Good, you're thinking for yourself, not just blindly following what the older generations are preaching. And another thing I've spotted is you have a passion for something. What it is I'm not sure, but it's there. Use that with your skills and interests and see where that takes you. Just one thing though: make sure it pays well."

I laughed. "Of course I will."

"If either you or John wanted to come into my business you'd be welcomed with open arms but it's something you both must want. Don't do it just to please me. You'll probably need some help with money at first and you can count on me, but not forever. You have to learn to stand on your own two feet."

"Thanks Dad. My exams finish in mid-June and I'll really give it some serious thought then. It might help if I had a little bit of time to sort myself out so would you mind if I spent a couple of days a week working with you till I find a job I want?"

"Of course you can, Roger, and I'll look forward to that a lot."

"Thanks again, Dad."

I'd promised Jane I'd take her for a day out in London before I returned to Cambridge. I thought she might like to see a film then have tea at Lyons Corner House in the Strand.

She was as keen as I was on the outing and I suggested we see *Things to Come* at Studio One in Oxford Street. The film had created quite a stir amongst some of my friends at Cambridge when they had seen it and I wanted to know what all the fuss was about. So did Jane.

We took a train to London and as it was a fine late April day we walked to the cinema. We strolled across the tired old Waterloo Bridge, down the Strand along the edge of Trafalgar Square and up to Charing Cross Road before turning left down Oxford Street at the junction with Tottenham Court Road.

My mother and father had taken my brother and me into the West End many times but it was only now that I realised what a busy city London was. The pavements were crowded with pedestrians, all of whom seemed to be in a hurry. The roads were jammed with vehicles of all shapes and sizes; cars, vans, lorries, buses, bicycles and even the odd horse-drawn cart. The noise was deafening and not at all what we were used to.

We eventually settled in our seats to watch the film about which we had heard so much.

The first half hour was very disturbing. The film was adapted from H.G. Wells' novel *The Shape of Things to Come* and evidently Wells himself had had some small involvement with the production. The story started in a nameless city, presumably London, with newspaper banners predicting war and it continued with pictures of mobilisation, silhouettes of soldiers marching to war and calls of 'stand to arms.' There followed warnings of air raids, people racing down the underground for shelter, threats of gas and skies filled with bombers and fighter planes engaged in dog fights. It was chilling stuff and I could feel Jane shifting uncomfortably in the seat next to me. Silently, I shared her discomfort as I remembered reading about the Japanese bombing Manchuria.

The rest of the film was a letdown. While the first 30 minutes dealt with a situation that might become reality in the near future, the rest was pure science fiction. It dealt with the aftermath of war with scenes of devastation, the rise of dictatorships and the growth of a world peace force.

We walked out into the late afternoon sunshine, had tea at Lyons and talked about the film.

"Now you know why there's such a great yearning for peace in England," said Jane. "Everybody knows about the bombing by the Japanese in Manchuria and what the Italians did to the Abyssinians with their bombers. Now they've seen what it might be like for themselves."

"I'd no idea you were interested," I replied.

"While you've been lounging in your ivory tower in Cambridge," Jane said, her voice rising, "the rest of us have been worrying about the prospect of war. You can see why there have been marches and ballots calling for peace. You probably don't know this, but I went on a peace march while you were at university. There's tens of thousands, maybe hundreds of thousands, who feel just like me and the government know it. Why do you think Baldwin promised he wouldn't allow the government to spend millions on armaments? He'd already lost one by-election to the peace lobby. He wasn't going to risk losing the General Election."

I sat in silence for a short while to collect my thoughts.

"There's plenty at Cambridge afraid of war and some who think it's inevitable given the noises coming out of Germany."

"What people are really frightened of is being bombed," Jane observed.

"Not surprising really. Do you think the opening scenes were just propaganda to show what'll happen if we don't bolster up our air defences?"

"Could be. Churchill is forever warning the government that the German air force and army will soon overtake ours."

"But not our navy," I added.

"The next war, if there is one, will be won in the air, not on the sea," continued an increasingly exasperated Jane. "What happened when Zeppelins bombed London in 1916 was nothing compared with the havoc a fleet of bombers will do. We must be ready to face up to that."

Jane's understanding and passion astonished me. I walked her home from our local station and I told her I wouldn't see her for about six weeks; not until after I'd finished my exams. I said I hoped there wouldn't be a war in the meantime. She laughed and kissed me goodnight.

That night I lay awake thinking about what Jane had said as well as Dobb's and Blunt's concerns but I decided to put everything about war and Germany out of my mind and concentrate on my exams. When they were over, I'd think again.

CHAPTER THREE

Death Walks in Spain

"I have seen war . . . I hate war"
FRANKLIN D. ROOSEVELT

I went back to Cambridge and prepared for my exams. I studied furiously, anxious not to let my parents or my tutors down.

Dobb told me in mid-May that however hard I worked I wasn't going to get a First. He told me to relax and enjoy my final few weeks at Cambridge, so I did.

I revised, watched cricket at Fenners, and drank in the town pubs with my friends. I went home for a weekend. My father left me to myself. Jane and I went to the Regal in town and saw *A Night at the Opera* with the Marx Brothers at their best. The Regal was a huge cinema with more than two thousand seats and a giant organ playing music in the interval between films. Before the film we had tea in one of the cafeterias in the cinema. We talked about films, accountancy, the weather and our feelings for one another—anything except war and my exams.

Back at Cambridge, I listened while my friends told of their plans to become lawyers, accountants, diplomats, civil servants, academics and teachers. What was I going to do, they asked. "I haven't a clue," I replied. I couldn't see myself in any of those professions and I wasn't sure what was left for a Cambridge graduate, always assuming that I would graduate.

The weather was fine and warm in early May but turned cooler and wetter as the exams approached. Apart from a short spell at the start of June, it stayed like that until the exams were over. They went very well and my optimism was well placed because, by the time I left Cambridge, I had been awarded the good degree expected of me.

I felt a mixture of pride and relief. I hadn't let anyone down, and graduating from Cambridge alongside the sons and daughters of wealthy people who had been educated at our most famous public schools, gave me an immense sense of satisfaction.

With my life as a Cambridge undergraduate over, I went to work part time for my father. Before I decided what to do next, there was still plenty to look forward to: dancing and films with Jane, cricket at Lords and the Oval, and the Berlin Olympic Games to listen to. There was no talk of war even from the only active European warmonger, Benito Mussolini, the dictator of Italy.

I watched some of the first Test match against India at Lords (England won comfortably) and was back there three weeks later to see Cambridge trounce Oxford in the annual Varsity match.

During those three days my friends and I ate, drank, cheered, but not too loudly because this was Lords after all, and talked about our happy years at Cambridge. These were our final days as students and we were going to enjoy them.

Back at home, I worked in the busy office of my father's store, went dancing with Jane and took her to see Bette Davis and Franchot Tone in *Dangerous*. Davis was a rising Hollywood star and her portrayal of a washed out alcoholic stage actress who would stop at nothing to achieve what she wanted was utterly convincing. She obviously had a great future. I was, I suppose, being a bit irresponsible, drifting along with no real purpose, but all that that was to change for me, less than three weeks later, with the outbreak of the Spanish Civil War.

I knew little of Spain. As far as I was concerned, it was a backward country whose main preoccupation was bull fighting. I'd never been there and had no wish to visit it. I'd never met a Spaniard, as far as I knew, and hadn't a clue what the conflict was about.

It was Jane who first sparked my interest. A couple of days after the civil war had begun we were having a meal in a local café when, out of the blue, she said:

"Nasty business in Spain."

"Oh?"

"Haven't you been keeping up with it?"

"Not really but I knew civil war had broken out."

"For heaven's sake, Roger, this could affect us all," Jane said, with a hint of anger.

"Really, how?"

"Have you any idea what's going on?"

"Not really. Tell me about it."

"The Spanish government has been attacked by the army."

"So what's that got to do with us?"

"I'll tell you what it's got to do with us. The Spanish government was elected by the people of Spain. They're mostly Socialists, some Communists and a few Anarchists, though none in the cabinet. Those who don't like the government are trying to overthrow it by military might. If they succeed there'll be three countries in Western Europe governed by force rather than the wishes of the people. You're a socialist, Roger. Can't you see that this is another threat to Parliamentary democracy after Mussolini and Hitler seized power in their countries? Where will it all end?"

I must confess that I felt ashamed of myself. I had been so wrapped up in my own insignificant world that I wasn't paying attention to the real world at all.

Having said as much to Jane, I promised her I would follow the progress of the war more closely. Perhaps the best way to do this was by reading my father's *Times* every day.

I remembered Blunt's cynicism about *The Times* but it still seemed to me to give the most accurate and complete accounts of what was going on in the world. So I read it avidly. My father was quite surprised and told me he was pleased to see me taking an interest in the wider world.

It soon became clear that the war in Spain was going to be a thoroughly unpleasant business. Reports suggested that no quarter would be given on either side. When the army captured government troops, they shot them. Government forces were accused of burning churches, monasteries and convents. By now the government were being called Republicans and the army the rebels, with a general called Franco emerging as the rebel leader.

There was an enormous amount of coverage of the war both in the newspapers and the cinema newsreels. At the end of July, Jane and I went to see *Fury*, an American film directed by the German Fritz Lang. The film was about the dangers of mob rule and lynching and got us thinking, but it wasn't the film that left us with a lasting impression. It was the Movietone newsreel that was shown before it.

I'd always thought the purpose of cinema newsreels was to report the news not to comment on it. The item *Death Walks in Spain* on Movietone that evening certainly gave the impression of being on the side of the rebels, not so much in its support of the army, but rather its attitude towards the Spanish Republicans whom they described as Socialists and Communists despite the fact that I knew there were no Communists in the government. I felt that, by including Communists in their description of the Spanish government, Movietone were trying to discredit the Republicans.

After the film I said as much to Jane and she agreed with me. The conflict, less than two weeks old, appeared to be escalating. The Nazi press in Berlin came out in full support of the rebels whom they portrayed as fighting against Bolshevism. Shortly afterwards, the Republicans accused Italy of supplying aeroplanes to the rebels and a few days later Germany accused the Soviet Union of giving moral and material support to the Republicans.

The lines of battle were being drawn up with the democratically elected Spanish government on one side supported by Russia, and the rebels supported by Italy on the other. How long would it be, I asked myself, before France, which itself had a popular front left wing government, came in on the side of the Republicans? And if France intervened, where would that leave its closest ally Great Britain? There was little doubt in my mind that Germany would support the rebels and that full scale European war was not far off.

I read exhaustively about the conflict from every newspaper I could get my hands on. *The Times* seemed fairly neutral whilst others applauded the rebels' stand against Communism. Left wing or liberal papers like *The Daily News* took the side of the Spanish government. As least someone was standing up for them.

The Spanish Civil War, and the interest in it from newsreels and newspapers, changed my life. For the first time I became aware that there was life away from Cambridge and that greedy men wanted to seize power for themselves without caring two hoots about the quality of life for the majority of citizens. My sympathies were firmly on the side of the Republic: I could finally see some purpose in my life.

I gradually grew more and more angry. I was furious with the rebels, who were, by now, calling themselves Nationalists, for attempting to overthrow by force the government that the majority of the Spanish people had chosen. I was livid with much of the newspaper coverage, which supported Franco, who, they said, was making a stand against the evils of Communism.

But what could I do about it? Demonstrate, Burgess fashion, outside the Houses of Parliament? Fat lot of good that would do. I felt that I needed to have my say and the best way of doing that was to write about it. Where lies were told, I wanted people to read the truth. Where corruption existed, I wanted to expose it. Could I become a journalist? Plenty of Cambridge graduates were. So I headed back to my old university to talk to Maurice Dobb and seek his advice.

CHAPTER FOUR

The Fourth Estate

"I'm with you on the free press. It's
the newspapers I can't stand."
TOM STOPPARD

I went to see Dobb on a Wednesday in early August. Shortly after lunch I was treading the familiar path from the railway station to the town. It was a cool and cloudy day, but at least it was dry.

Dobb seemed pleased to see me. We met in his rooms in college. He offered me a scotch but I chose a coffee instead. He was dressed, as he often was, in a sports jacket and slacks with his dark hair brushed back. He looked at me kindly through his black horn rimmed spectacles.

"Good to see you, Roger. How are things going?"

"OK I suppose. I've been working for my father part-time, watching cricket and dancing and going to the pictures with my girlfriend Jane. However, before you admonish me about wasting my time, I'm here to ask your advice about a job."

"Not at all, it's no more than six weeks since you went down. It's still early days. Many of your contemporaries are in the same boat. So what have you got in mind?"

"Well," I began, "you know I mentioned my girlfriend Jane. She's the same age as me and training to be an accountant. We go to the cinema a lot and, after seeing *Things to Come* a few weeks back, she started talking

20

about the threat of war, Fascism and concern over air raids and so on. It came as quite a shock to me. She was far more in touch with international politics than I was."

"You must have dozed through Socialist Club meetings."

"Well, yes, but I didn't take them all that seriously; please don't be offended, it was just a student thing really."

"I'm not at all offended. I think I'd prefer your quiet introspective view of things to the way the militants behaved with their marches and demonstrations. Sorry, I interrupted you, please go on."

"Thanks. Well the next thing that really got me going was the outbreak of the Spanish Civil War."

"Ahh," said Dobb.

I told him about the Movietone news Jane and I had seen, how I had avidly devoured the press coverage of events and my concerns about the interpretation of events, especially in the right wing press, and then I told him I wanted to be part of all this. I wanted to write, not just about the war in Spain, but other things as well, especially international affairs.

"Well as you might imagine, I'm very concerned about what's going on in Spain and so are many of my colleagues and I'm certain it's going to be a very big issue amongst the students when they return in October. Some former students are even thinking about going to Spain to fight for the Republicans. Julian Bell for instance."

"What about Communists like Blunt and Burgess?" I asked.

Dobb laughed.

"Oh no, I can't see Anthony with a rifle in his hand. Funny thing though, Burgess appears to have changed sides."

"Changed sides?"

"Mmm, he was always one of those who seemed to fully embrace Marxism but he's packed up his research here and gone to work for the Anglo German Fellowship."

"Who on earth are they?" I interrupted.

"I don't know a great deal about them but they seem to be a group of aristocrats, politicians and businessmen keen to be friends with Hitler."

"Good heavens."

"You'd be amazed how many people in this country think Hitler is a good thing. Anyway, another for whom I had great hopes has jumped ship and gone to work with Burgess."

"Who's that?"

"Kim Philby. Bit before your time but very promising. A man seemingly totally committed to the cause. He'd seen the evils of Fascism at first hand when he visited Austria a year or two back. I'm amazed that a man who seemed so convinced about the threat of totalitarianism would have anything to do with Germany. Still, he must have his reasons. Anyhow, enough of disappointments. What's your view of events in Spain?"

"That's simple. I'm for the Republicans. They're the democratically elected government. I believe in democracy and I'm a Socialist and this government in Spain seems to be trying to put those things right that will help Spain become a modern European state, divide the country's wealth more fairly and stop the rich landowners and industrialists from keeping the mass of Spanish people in poverty."

"Well spoken," said Dobb, "but I do think it's far more dangerous than that."

Dobb then talked for twenty minutes or more. He opened my eyes to the political divisions that existed amongst the Republicans and said that he had a very reliable source who had told him that the Italians were already supporting Franco. Hitler, he believed, was bound to come in on the side of the Nationalists since he couldn't stomach the idea of a Marxist state in Western Europe. Dobb spoke of non-intervention, a plan being suggested by France and Great Britain to prevent the conflict spreading beyond Spain's, borders but above all he talked of his sorrow for the Spanish people who would suffer intolerable hardship in what he was sure would be a long and brutal conflict.

"Anyhow, that's my take on things. It's a very complex business. So you want to write?" Dobb asked.

"I think so yes."

"Books, magazines, newspapers?"

"Newspapers."

"Daily, weekly, evening?"

"Most days of the week, so a daily or evening."

"You'll need to find a paper that matches your political aspirations. No point in writing for some right-wing rag. Before you write to editors asking for a job, check them out. Read their papers and look into the background of the owners."

"The owners?" I asked.

Dobb then explained to me how some newspapers reflected the owners' views. He made special mention of *The Times* and its Editor Geoffrey Dawson, who was a close friend of more than one Cabinet Minister and used his position to promote government policies.

"*The Times* does provide a pretty comprehensive picture of what's going on in the world but, you're right, I don't much like the tone of some of their leading articles," I said.

Dobb nodded and continued.

"*The Times* is the most influential of our newspapers. Despite its low circulation it has more influence in Berlin, Rome, Tokyo and Washington than any of the others. But you're not ready to catch the ear of foreign governments. You need to reach the ordinary British citizen. So you need a paper with liberal views that has a decent circulation. No point in trying to join *The Daily Worker*, nobody reads it, and the other quality papers are right wing, apart from *The Manchester Guardian* which has a low circulation. Not a bad paper though."

"What about the popular papers?"

"Avoid *The Daily Express*. The owner, Beaverbrook, is an out and out imperialist and would happily see the rest of the world go to the dogs as long as Britain and its precious Empire were OK. And avoid *The Daily Mail* and *The Evening News* like the plague. The man who owns them, Lord Rothermere, is, if not a Fascist, certainly a Fascist sympathizer. You probably don't remember but a couple of years ago *The Daily Mail* headed a story "Youth Triumphant in Germany" in support of Hitler, then a little later "Hurrah for the Blackshirts" backing Moseley and his bunch of Fascist anti-Semites. And what's more, Rothermere part owns Movietone News so you're extremely unlikely to get an unbiased view of things from that source. No, avoid Rothermere's rags at all costs."

"That's really helpful, Mr Dobb,"

"Maurice please."

"I'll think over everything you've said, then write to some editors."

"Please let me know how things go."

"Of course I will, er, Maurice."

"Good to see you Roger."

"Thank you very much. I'll keep in touch, I promise."

CHAPTER FIVE

An Idle Summer

"Sure, winning isn't everything.
It's the only thing."
HENRY RED SAUNDERS

My mother and father were waiting for me when I reached home just after eight that evening. They were listening to the radio when I walked in but immediately switched it off. My brother was nowhere to be seen, probably upstairs working on some life-changing invention.

"How did it go?" my father asked.

"Very well. Maurice was really helpful."

"So what are you going to do?" my mother asked.

I looked at the two people whom I loved most in the world. They were sitting side by side on the settee waiting for their eldest son to tell them what he was going to do with his life, their boy who had just graduated from one of the world's finest universities and for whom they had worked so hard. For both of their children they wanted only the best.

"I'm going to try to get a job as a journalist," I said confidently so that they knew I had made up my mind.

"Good heavens!" exclaimed my father, clearly surprised. "Which paper?"

"A London-based paper. Then I could carry on living here, if that's OK with you?"

"Of course it is," my mother replied, "this is your home for as long as you want it to be."

"Thanks. I don't suppose I'll get paid much at first anyway so that'll be really helpful, and besides I like living here. I'm not ready to leave home yet."

"Good," my father said, "but one day you will want to leave home and start a family of your own. Until then you're most welcome here."

My mother and father had got my life mapped out not in specific, but rather in general terms; school, university, job, marriage and family. How I was going to get there they would leave up to me.

"I think you know my political views so I'm going to be careful about which newspaper I approach. There's no point in working for a paper full of rampant Tories so I'll be writing to four or five daily and evening papers to see if they'll give me an interview. It may be that none of them will want me, in which case I'll have to think again. Anyway, that's what I intend to do for the rest of this month."

"Fine," my father said. "Tomorrow it's the 400 metre semi-finals and final at the Olympic Games. I expect you'll be looking forward to seeing how Godfrey Brown goes on."

"Let's hope for a medal, maybe even gold!" I replied. "And thanks—for everything."

I knew from friends at Cambridge that there wasn't a single route into journalism and that writing to editors of bigger papers was just as likely to be successful as starting at the bottom writing obituaries and reporting on council meetings for the local paper.

I was up early next morning writing the first of my letters addressed to the Editor of what I thought to be a liberal, if not left-wing, national daily. The letter took me all morning. I started several times, scrapping half a dozen attempts before settling on one. I told them about my education, my home background, my interests in sport and the cinema, my willingness to work hard and my commitment to finding out and writing about the truth. I told them about my politics but made sure I didn't come across as a troublemaker. Satisfied, I took the letter to the post box and settled down to listen to the Olympic Games on the radio.

The Games were in full swing. There had been an enormous amount of newspaper coverage, not just because it was the biggest sports event in the world but because it was were being held in Berlin in the heart of Nazi Germany. Some had tried to get the Games cancelled, or transferred elsewhere, because of the German treatment of the Jews. Other countries had threatened to boycott the games for the same reason. As it turned out the Games went ahead unhindered and newspaper reports from Berlin suggested there were no indications that German Jews were being ill-treated.

The Germans had prepared tirelessly for the Games and were expected to be the dominant nation. Athletics was the most important sport but the person in whom the press was most interested was not a German but an American Negro, Jesse Owens, who had set several world records during one afternoon in 1935. Reporters, especially in the English speaking press, were making much of the fact that Owens, racially inferior according to the Nazi doctrine, was likely to wipe the floor with the so-called master race of Aryan Germany.

Brown reached the 400 metre Final and was narrowly beaten by Archie Williams of America. I listened to the race on the radio with Jane, my brother and my parents. He'd won a silver medal and kept up the great Cambridge tradition at the Olympics.

One of my earliest sporting memories was Harold Abrahams winning the 100 metres in Paris in 1924. Lord Burghley had been 400 metres hurdles Gold Medalist in Amsterdam in 1928 and although he had been beaten into third place in defence of his title in Los Angeles in 1932, another Cambridge man, Robert Tisdall, had won the Gold, although he had been running for Ireland. Now we had to wait for the last day of the Athletics at the Games when Britain would take on the USA in the 4×400 metres relay with every chance of success.

In the meantime I sent out the remaining letters to the newspaper editors.

The first letter had been tough but now, with practice, I was getting better and felt I was doing myself justice. I anxiously waited for the first reply.

On the final day of the Olympic athletics, expectations were high for the men in our 4 × 400 metre relay team. The omens were good for Brown, as his sister Audrey had already won a silver medal for Britain in the women's sprint relay.

The men's long relay was a wonderful affair with Godfrey Brown combining with another Godfrey, Rampling, Bill Roberts and Freddie Wolff to produce a brilliant gold medal performance and finish ahead of our arch rivals the United States.

Meanwhile Jesse Owens had been collecting gold medals on a daily basis, much to Hitler's evident displeasure. He followed up victories in the 100 metre and 200 metre races with a win in the long jump where he had the added bonus of beating a German, Luz Long, into second place. He brought his gold medal tally to four in the 4 × 100 metre relay. He was truly the man of the Games.

My first rejection came shortly after. A national newspaper had no vacancies. I was disappointed at first but, on reflection, accepted that I wasn't going to get the first job for which I applied.

That weekend I took Jane to her first cricket match. It was the third Test Match between England and India at Kennington Oval. England were already two up in the series, having followed up their win at Lords with victory at Old Trafford Manchester. Although there wasn't a lot to play for, the final Test at the Oval was one of the high spots of the English summer.

There was a good crowd and the weather, which had been cool during the first part of the month, had picked up and it was warm and dry.

Jane enjoyed it immensely. We sat at the Vauxhall End, ate our packed lunches, chatted about just about everything and watched the famous gas holders empty and fill as Londoners boiled their kettles and cooked their meals.

England played well and this, along with Jane's obvious enjoyment, helped to lift my mood because, despite telling myself that although I could hardly expect to walk into the first job for which I applied, I did feel a keen sense of disappointment.

The second day was a Monday so Jane missed the game to go to work. Before I set off for the Oval I received another rejection from a daily, but I was determined not to let this spoil my enjoyment of the day. England won the match easily and I spent the rest of the week working with my father.

Then, on the following Monday, came an invitation to come to see Ben Rogers, News Editor of *The London Evening Globe*. Even though I was not seeing the Editor, I guessed my luck was turning and I began to plan what I would say when I met him the following week.

CHAPTER SIX

Fleet Street

"We tell the public which way the cat is
jumping. The public will take care of the cat."
ARTHUR HAYS SULZBERGER

My appointment was for half past ten as Mr Rogers wanted me to see the
paper in action before interviewing me. I left home just after half past eight,
walked to the station then joined a train crammed full of city workers
and shoppers on their way into 'town' as everyone called London. I had
to stand all the way but the train was fast, not stopping at every station,
and I was soon part of the herd emptying itself onto the packed platform
at Waterloo.

Most of the passengers seemed to be heading for the Underground so
I decided to join the walkers on Waterloo Bridge. It was a decent day and
plenty seemed to choose the same route as me. I was wearing a dark grey
suit and, apart from the lack of an umbrella and briefcase, I looked much
the same as everyone else on the bridge that morning but I felt a bit of a
fraud. I hadn't even got a job. Not yet anyway.

I reached the end of the bridge and glanced down the Strand. It was
packed with traffic and scores of workers and shoppers were pouring out of
Aldwych Underground station. I turned right, strolled past King's College
with Bush House on my left then past the Temples with their multitude
of law offices. Opposite these were the law courts and I glanced at them

before hurrying into Fleet Street.

Here I was then, at the heart of the British newspaper industry and I felt a rush of excitement and a fair bit of apprehension. What would they make of a Cambridge boy in Fleet Street? Would they like me? Could I do the job? I was very nervous.

My first port of call was the building in which I had my appointment. The *Globe* shared a building with its sister paper *The Daily News*, just off Fleet Street, on Bouverie Street. I had plenty of time to spare and, thinking it was just as rude to turn up early as it was to turn up late, decided to explore. On the front of every tall building were emblazoned the names of many of the world's famous newspapers. I had written to some of these and had received either letters of rejection or no reply at all. Still that wasn't bothering me now and, having glanced at *The Times* building in Printing House Square, I nervously made my way back to my appointment.

I arrived five minutes early and asked the receptionist to let Mr Rogers know that I was at reception.

"He's busy," she said.

I explained I had an appointment for half past ten, so she picked up the phone, dialed a number, muttered into the receiver for a few seconds, listened for a few more, looked at me and said:

"Newsroom's first floor. Lift's just round the corner or you can take the stairs."

I thanked her and climbed the stairs to the first floor. In front of me stood a pair of double doors with "NEWSROOM please come in" written above them.

I pushed the door open and entered a room the like of which I had never seen before. There were more than two dozen desks, on each of which was a typewriter and a telephone. Most were occupied, mainly by men but a few by women.

Everybody in the room seemed either to be talking into the phone or typing, and those phones not in use seemed to be ringing. The air was thick with smoke and most desks seemed littered with ashtrays, piled high to overflowing, and cups and saucers. It was warm and every man in the office was in shirt sleeves with the women in summer blouses. I felt horribly overdressed and uncomfortable but I was quickly rescued from my embarrassment by a middle aged man, a little shorter than me with dark hair thinning on top.

"Mr Martin, Ben Rogers. I'm the News Editor." He shook my hand warmly. "Welcome to the lunatic asylum. It's a bit hectic at the moment but I wanted you to see the paper in action before we talked about a job. Let's be honest, it's not exactly Cambridge University and you might not like it here. Cup of tea?"

"Yes, please."

"OK take a pew in my office and I'll have one brought through. I'll be with you in about five minutes."

I sat in his office, which was no more than a corner partitioned off with glass. There was just about room for a desk and a couple of chairs. The desk was covered in scraps of paper, newspapers, teacups and the obligatory ash tray, full of cigarette ends. I sat in the corner facing the desk. A few minutes later a smart looking youth in a suit with a cheeky grin came in carrying my tea.

I watched the action in the news room through the office window. The pace seemed to be slowing as the journalists pulled typescript from their machines and gave them to another group of men in the far side of the room. Then they returned to their desks, pulled on their jackets from the backs of their chairs, some put on hats and lit a cigarette, then left the room. Far from being put off by what I was seeing, I was energised. The intensity of everything was just what I needed to shake me out of my post-Cambridge lethargy. This was the real world of news making and I was desperate to be part of it.

I had just finished my tea when Ben Rogers walked in. He took my cup, somehow found space on his desk for it, looked at me, smiled, and said, "So what do you make of all that?"

"Well I was pretty amazed when I walked in but the atmosphere really appeals to me."

"The atmosphere? You mean the smoke?"

I laughed. "No the nonstop action, the speed of things, the need to get work done, I like it."

"Not exactly punting up and down the river at Cambridge is it?"

"I wasn't interested in that. I was at Cambridge to study hard, pass exams and play sport. I owed it to my parents to do well."

"Hmm," he said, "but it was still a pretty cushy life, wasn't it?"

"It was enjoyable," I replied, "but not cushy. I was always under pressure to succeed, to pass exams, and hand in essays on time."

"Working to deadlines, eh? If you work here you'll get plenty of that. Why choose this paper?"

"I didn't. It was one of five I wrote to."

"What were the others?"

I told him and said that I'd had a couple of rejections and was still waiting to hear from two more.

"I see you have no liking for the establishment," he said. "Red, are you?"

"I believe in fairness and equality and democratic government. There were plenty of Communists at Cambridge but I wasn't one of them."

"So you don't want to overthrow the government?"

"I'd like to see a change of government but not through revolution like in Russia or through brute force like in Germany. I'd like the Labour Party to win the next General Election."

He pulled a packet of cigarettes from his pocket and offered me one. I said no thanks and he lit up, and then continued.

"Not likely to happen though is it?"

"Not in the next year or two. They haven't fully recovered from MacDonald's betrayal and can't make their minds up about rearmament, but they are growing stronger. I reckon in a year or two they'll be an effective opposition to the government."

He clasped his hands behind his head and leant back in his chair. "I can see why you chose the papers you did. Wouldn't exactly fit in at *The Daily Mail*, would you?"

I laughed. "Definitely not."

He then told me what the paper stood for. The owners, the editors and those journalists who had political views were liberals with a small

L. The most important people were the readers because if they didn't like what the paper printed, they'd stop reading it and the paper would go out of business. On the other hand, the paper had more or less full editorial independence from the owners, and the journalists were encouraged to say what they thought.

"But always remember," he continued, "our job is to report the news and to comment on it. We've got a great deal of influence and a lot of responsibility to give our readers the truth. No cover-ups. Just report the news as you see it happen.

"So, that's what we're about. Now more about you. Can you write in clear and concise English without using those long Cambridge words that none of our readers can understand?"

"I'm sure I can," I replied.

"And what would you like to write about?"

"Foreign affairs and politics, maybe some sport and the cinema."

"That's good; obviously we've got senior staff covering all of those areas and you might get a chance to work with them from time to time but you'll have to prove yourself before you get anything really 'big time'. You'll not be going off to Spain just yet. Besides, we've got a good bloke over there. He always seems to be in the right place at the right time."

"I understand that," I replied. "I'd expect to start at the bottom."

"Not quite at the bottom, that's Jeremy the lad who fetched your tea, he's the bottom of the ladder: tea boy and messenger. But if I give you a job it'll be as a Junior Reporter covering the stuff that nobody else wants; small police court cases, firemen rescuing cats from trees, lower league football, bad films and so on. Can you type?"

"A bit. We've got an old machine at home and I've used the ones in my father's office."

"Good. You'll cope all right. Half of that lot," he said pointing towards the now almost empty news room, "are fully paid up members of the two finger brigade."

He went on. "A lot of the people here started right at the bottom like Jeremy or came to us from reporting on flower shows and Women's Institute meetings for their local rags. None of them got here via Cambridge

University or any other university come to that. They'll probably take the mickey out of you at first and call you 'Prof' or 'snooty' or something. That's a good idea. I think I'll call you 'Prof'."

"Does that mean I've got the job?"

"The pay's lousy, the hours long and you'll be writing about a lot of trivia. Do you want it?"

"I do."

"Then the job's yours. When can you start?"

"Any time you like."

"Good. Let's say Monday week at eight in the morning. I'll get a letter of appointment off to you in tonight's post."

"Thanks. I'm really looking forward to it. I won't let you down."

"I don't think you will. In fact, I think you'll cause a few ripples here. Just as long as they increase circulation and don't upset the owners or the Editor. Right then Prof, see you on Monday week."

He shook my hand and I made my way back to Waterloo. I walked into the house gave my mother the news, called Jane, then told my father when he came in from work. My brother said he would give me some Science scoops when I told him. Everyone seemed delighted. In fact, I was pretty pleased myself. Jane arrived, smiled at me, patted my hand and said "Well done". My father beamed at me and shook my hand, my mother kissed me and John had a grin from ear to ear. Ben Rogers had given me my chance and I was determined not to let him down.

CHAPTER SEVEN

Marking Time

> "Journalism largely consists in saying
> 'Lord Jones dead' to people who never
> knew that Lord Jones was alive."
> G.K. CHESTERTON

For the last four months of 1936 I put heart and soul into becoming a competent junior reporter. I spoke only when I was spoken to and I listened to, and learned from, those around me. Ben Rogers was, of course, quite right. I was a bit of an oddity. There were no other Cambridge graduates, or indeed any other graduates in sight. Most of the other journalists had learnt their craft through years of experience on a variety of different types of publications and some were professionally qualified through college and night school courses. The nickname 'Prof' soon stuck but the respect that I showed to my colleagues meant that I quickly became part of the team.

Naturally there was some frustration in not being involved with great events at home or the growing threat from abroad. The Spanish Civil War seemed to escalate day by day and the big issue of the late summer and autumn was non-intervention. Our government, and the French, were keen to let the Spanish get on with it but the Germans and Italians, it seemed, were not. A Non-Intervention Committee was set up in London with Hitler and Mussolini's people, the Russians and the Portuguese as well as ourselves and the French promising not to intervene, although it was already obvious that the dictators had not the slightest intention of keeping their noses out of what was happening in Spain. The Spanish Republicans were desperate to buy arms from Britain but our Foreign Secretary, Anthony Eden, put a stop to this.

Soon it became apparent that while we were sticking to the rules, others were not. The Spanish government produced photographic evidence at the League of Nations in Geneva of a seized German Junkers bomber and a declaration from a captured Italian airman who admitted he had fought for the Nationalists at Seville. The Germans and Italians denied it but the Soviet Union said that they had sufficient evidence to prove that both powers were involved and that if this did not stop, they themselves would feel free to intervene and support the Republicans. The thing that everybody was keen to avoid was, in fact, happening: the conflict was escalating.

My paper, and its sister daily, supported the Spanish government and their views strengthened when both Germany and Italy declared that Franco's Nationalists were the legitimate Spanish government. But although this was of great concern to me, I got on with my task as a junior reporter.

At first this consisted of writing up small columns on such earth shattering events as the huge increase in London traffic, the gradual replacement of electric trams by motor and trolley buses, the construction of a large new cinema in Leicester Square, outbreaks of drunk and disorderly behaviour outside pubs and minor thefts from garden sheds. Ben kept me busy chasing up and writing small stories.

From time to time I was loaned out to other departments. The Sports Editor needed help with football match coverage so I was dispatched to Lea Bridge Ground in north-east London to report on Clapton Orient's 3-2 victory over Reading in the Third Division South of the Football League. Then I started doing the rounds of London's other football grounds; Selhurst Park, Southend and even Plough Lane in Wimbledon for a non-league match.

I covered some rugby games including seeing my old University beat Harlequins at a half-empty Twickenham and my Cambridge heroes Wilf

Wooler and Cliff Jones wipe the floor with Blackheath when they turned out for Cardiff at the Rectory Field.

I must have done something right, or perhaps nobody else was available, because I reported on a First Division game at Griffin Park Brentford where the home team beat Birmingham in a mud bath. It was like that in a packed Twickenham in early December when, much to my delight, Cambridge had a narrow win over Oxford.

In between further visits to Griffin Park and to some new venues, White Hart Lane and Craven Cottage, I wrote my local stories. Occasionally the Crime Correspondent called on my services and I was at the Old Bailey to see two policemen acquitted of a charge of falsely arresting a burglar. On another visit to the Old Bailey three men were convicted of an insurance fraud (setting fire to their own premises).

I was at Marlborough Street Police Court where a woman was convicted of shoplifting and for a dangerous driving case at the Bow Street Police Court; these stories didn't seem like desperately important news to me but Ben assured me that this was just the kind of stuff the public like to read about after their evening meal.

There were so many films to cover one week in early December that I was even sent to review Alfred Hitchcock's new film *Sabotage*, a cracking thriller about bombs being set off in Central London. It seemed that the villain had a suspiciously German accent. I watched it in a screening cinema with an audience that consisted of film correspondents from other papers and I noticed every one of them was pale in complexion and most were wearing spectacles. They were obviously spending too much time in the dark.

Ben called me in during the following week. He was busy with the abdication crisis. The King was trying to persuade the government to let him marry a twice divorced American woman, Wallis Simpson, but Ben took time out from dealing with this story of the year to speak to me. He told me how well I was doing but felt it was time for me to find a big story of my own and suggested I gave it some thought over the Christmas break.

Over the Christmas holiday I either stayed at home or spent time with Jane. I'd not seen a lot of her because I'd been so busy with the football and rugby reporting on Saturday afternoons that we'd only really been together on Sundays. She continued to be uptight about the war in Spain and sensed that I was sharing her concern. Then, on the Friday after Christmas, my father hosted a dinner party. Mysteriously, my father had earlier promised us an interesting evening but I wasn't prepared for the devastating revelations which followed the meal.

CHAPTER EIGHT

German Awakening

"Wickedness is the root of despotism"
MAXIMILIAN ROBESPIERRE

It was probably the largest dinner party my parents had ever hosted. As well as my mother, my father, my brother, Jane and me, the other family of four were a man and his wife, both appearing to be a little younger than my father, and their two children, both boys and in their early teens. Introductions were made. Our guests were Richard and Inge Walker and their children Paul, the elder at fourteen, and Michael who was thirteen.

Our house was spacious with a decent sized lounge and dining room and a smallish kitchen downstairs, with three bedrooms and a bathroom upstairs. Even so it was a bit cramped with nine around the dining table but we managed alright and the meal passed pleasantly and quite quickly.

Conversation during the meal was mostly small talk with information about school, work and university. The Walker family had recently arrived in England from Germany and planned on settling here. Richard was English and his wife Inge German. She, and both of their boys, spoke excellent English although the two youngsters spoke little during the meal.

After we had finished our meal, my brother John, responding from a heavy hint from my mother, took the two Walker boys to his room, no doubt to introduce them to the scientific wonders of the modern world.

We settled in the lounge with coffees, then my father began.

"Richard has been working for a shipping company in Hamburg. For how long Richard?"

"Since the early twenties. Your father and I have been business associates for six or seven years. I've been shipping German goods for him to sell in the store. I've had to pop over to England from time to time to discuss arrangements and that's how we met and became friends."

"We read a lot about what's going on in Germany," said Jane, "but what are things really like?"

"Awful," said Richard, "in fact that's why we're here."

"Go on," my father said.

"Well, to start with we couldn't be having this conversation in Germany in case somebody overheard us and reported us to the authorities, but we'll come back to that later. I hope you don't mind Reg, or indeed you Mary, but I've been waiting to get a lot off my chest for ages. I don't want to abuse your hospitality."

"Don't be ridiculous, you're among friends here. Please carry on."

"Thanks Reg. The fact is we're refugees from Germany. We got out before we were thrown out or worse."

"Had you committed a crime or something?" my mother asked. "You certainly don't seem the criminal type to me."

Richard gave a small laugh. "Of course not but Inge, according to that maniac Hitler, is the worst type of criminal; she's Jewish. Before Hitler hijacked the government almost four years ago, being Jewish was no worse in Germany than in most other places, perhaps with the exception of Poland. But now the Jews live every day in fear of what the Nazis will do next."

"Just how bad is it?" I asked.

Richard then gave us a long description of the ugly details of the Nazi persecution of the Jews. At first, he told us, Hitler and his henchmen were just as anxious to get rid of the Communists since he saw them as a political threat. Now with the Communist party banned and most of their leaders in exile or in prison, he was giving his undivided attention to what he called the 'Jewish Problem'.

He told us about the boycott of Jewish shops in 1933 and Jews being

thrown out of the professions, the civil service and so on later in the same
year. Some towns and streets put up placards "Jews not wanted here, Jews
enter this locality at their peril". Richard had actually witnessed Jews being
beaten up by Nazi thugs but, as far as he and his family were concerned,
it was the Nuremberg Laws of the previous year that threatened them the
most. Inter-racial marriages and sexual relationships were forbidden by
these laws and Jews were no longer citizens of the Third Reich but merely
subjects. Jews, Richard explained, were no longer regarded or treated as
human beings in Nazi Germany.

Yet again my own naivety was being brutally exposed. Of course I knew
Hitler despised the Jews but thought that the situation was little worse
than in England. Here a very small minority of people disliked the Jews
and anti-Semitic idiots like Oswald Moseley and his Blackshirts were
taken seriously only by a small band of extremists who posed no threat
to the state. I knew there had been some grumbling in the East End of
London that Jewish families, who had fled from the pogroms in Russia
at the end of the nineteenth century, were taking too many jobs during a
time of high unemployment but again, this was just a minority. I'd heard
that some wealthier Jews had been refused admission to golf clubs but that
just told me how stupid the golf clubs were. I had assumed it was only a
little worse than this in Germany and, until this evening, I thought there
wasn't a great difference between our society and the Germans, but, of
course, I was terribly wrong.

"Inge and I are already falling foul of the Nuremberg Laws, but even if
I, as a non-Jewish British citizen, could escape their clutches, Inge and the
boys will not. They're protected at the moment because Inge is married to
a non-Jewish foreigner but how long that'll last is anybody's guess. Anyway
we're not waiting to find out."

"But the boys are only half Jewish." said Jane.

"Doesn't make a scrap of difference. They'd trace your ancestry back to
the nineteenth century and, if they found a drop of Jewish blood, you'd
lose your rights as a German citizen and become a target of their hatred,"
Richard replied, a slight tremble in his voice.

"Many of our Jewish friends have either left Germany, or are planning to, but those are the better off families. Those who are worse off just have to stay and God knows what will happen to them. Jews are being expelled from sports clubs and the works of great German-Jewish musicians and artists, Mendelssohn for instance, are banned."

My mother asked, "But how do Paul and Michael feel about being taken away from their home and school?"

"Very relieved I think. They're old enough to feel the fear that Inge and I have been experiencing for the past couple of years and, as for the schools, they're the real places of horror."

At this time in Germany every classroom had a picture of Hitler displayed on the wall, and each day began not with prayers but with the German greeting 'Heil Hitler'. Political speeches from party leaders would be relayed to the listening pupils in school halls. The whole school curriculum was in the process of being 'Nazified'. History text books were being re-written, Science lessons were devoted to ballistics and aerodynamics, Geography lessons to examining those lands in which the Germans might find living space and Biology lessons to theories of race. Even in Maths lessons age old questions like how long does it take to fill a bath if only one tap is running were replaced with puzzles like how much it would cost to keep a mentally defective person in an asylum?

There was a huge amount of Physical Education, taught not for pleasure but so that all youngsters became fit to serve the state. School notice boards were covered in Nazi propaganda and anti-Jewish insults. I couldn't even begin to imagine the uncertainty and terror that these poor children must have felt.

"Have you heard of a publication called *The Stormer*?" Richard asked. None of us had.

"It's a Nazi rag that's violently anti-Jewish. People are asked to contribute to it, even children. One youngster recently had a statement published: 'The Jews are God's creatures but so are vermin and we exterminate them.' I've seen a children's book with a Jew lurking behind a tree ready to pounce on a young German girl. Then there's the Hitler Youth."

I'd heard of the Hitler Youth and assumed they were the equivalent of our Boy Scouts. Evidently not. They were Germany's future, according to

Hitler. Jews were not, of course, admitted to membership and Richard's boys hadn't bothered to apply, not, he added, that they would have wanted to. On evenings after school, and at weekends, young German boys were taught the basics of war—map reading, Morse code and drill—and went on long hikes to improve their physical fitness. Those who chose not to join the Hitler Youth, Richard told us, were seriously disadvantaged. They were refused school leaving certificates and found it impossible to get a job in competition with Hitler Youth members, and use of sports facilities was restricted to Hitler Youth members.

There was no stopping Richard now.

"There's no free press, all the newspapers and radio are censored, and the theatre, cinema, music and art are either censored or banned. Many shops won't serve Jews, including pharmacies, so Jewish families often can't get medicine. I'm sorry I really am abusing your hospitality."

"Nonsense," said my father, "you must finish telling us everything. We all need to hear what you have to say."

"Thanks Reg. I'll finish where I started. We couldn't be having this conversation in Germany. Eavesdroppers are everywhere and denunciation is virtually a national sport. Every citizen of the Reich is told that he or she must report anything they hear that is critical of the state to the authorities. Where the working people live in apartment blocks there are wardens who snoop on the families. Everyone's at it: ordinary people in the street, school caretakers, doctors, dentists, tax office officials, railway staff and on it goes. The walls in some apartments are so thin folk daren't pass any comment for fear of being reported by their neighbours."

"What happens to them when they're reported?" Jane asked.

"At the very least they'll get a visit from the Gestapo. They might be warned, arrested or even imprisoned. A man was jailed for criticizing the regime last year, another found himself locked up for listening to Radio Moscow. The Nazis hate the churches and I did hear that a pastor was executed recently for telling an anti-Hitler joke. I'm not sure whether or not that's true, but I wouldn't be surprised."

"Children denounce their parents and their teachers. In Paul and Michael's school the parents of one boy were arrested when their son defended the Jews in the classroom. If you don't report what you hear you're not a decent German citizen, according to the Nazis."

"Workers denounce their Jewish bosses in the hope of gaining promotion. So-called enemies of the state: Jews, Communists, and so on, are thrown into the concentration camp at Dachau, near Munich, without trial, and probably some will never be seen again. And they're building another of the wretched camps near Berlin. They'll soon have them all over the country."

"But there must be something good in Germany," I said.

"Well, there's a lot less unemployment but most of the workforce are either building new roads, Autobahns, or working in the armaments industry. Hitler's preparing for war, you mark my words. Even these new roads are being built to move troops about quickly I reckon. The workers get paid a pittance. There are no Trade Unions. Hitler got rid of them."

Jane asked, "But what do the ordinary Germans think of all this?"

"Who knows? Nobody dares to breathe a word. You can tell when you're in Germany; all the people in the streets look over their shoulders before they speak. I will tell you one thing though. All this indoctrination is getting the young people on the Nazis' side, for the time being at least."

We sat in silence. Inge had tears streaming down her cheeks, Jane's eyes were moist and my mother and father seemed stunned. I was completely shocked and ashamed and felt a deep sense of revulsion. I had no idea until that evening just how desperate the plight of the German Jews was. Few of the newspapers and none of the cinema newsreels had bothered to report on Hitler's treatment of the Jews. Some of the papers even suggested that how the Germans treated the Jews was their own business. To someone like me, and all those in my father's house that night, who believed in the essential decency of all human beings, the whole thing was sickening. The Nazis were treating the Jews as sub-humans but it was they, Hitler's henchmen, who appeared to be behaving like animals.

"Thank you Richard," said my father. "Please let me know in a day or two if you're coming to work with me. You and your family are welcome in this house at any time and I know you will be made to feel at home in my store and please, don't apologise again. It's us who should thank you for shaking us out of our ignorant lethargy over what's happening in Germany."

"I'd like to write about it," I said. "Can I come and talk to you again one evening?"

"Of course, Roger, and the sooner the better."

CHAPTER NINE

Blue Pencil but no Spike

"The power of the press is very great, but
not so great as the power of suppress."
LORD NORTHCLIFFE

I was back in the office early in the New Year, and as soon as the chance arose I went to see Ben.

"Happy New Year Prof. What can I do for you?"

"And the same to you. Have you got a few minutes?"

Ben looked refreshed after his short Christmas break. He smiled and offered me a seat.

"Certainly. What's up?"

I told him about the evening spent with Richard and how we'd all been stunned by what he'd told us. I said that I wanted to write about both the Walker family's experiences in Germany and the horrifying picture that Richard had painted of life there.

Ben sat in silence throughout and seemed deep in thought for some time after I'd finished. At last he moved in his chair, leant forward and looked at me.

"This is pretty hot stuff," he began, "and although I knew the Nazis were giving the Jews a hard time I'd no idea it was as bad as this. Our sports people were in Berlin for the Olympics and seemed to think things were settling down over there."

"Well evidently the Nazis were on their best behaviour during the Games, with all those visitors, athletes, judges and press. They wouldn't want to create a bad impression, would they?"

"Mmm. Perhaps not."

"They made damn sure there wasn't any evidence of Jewish persecution, warning signs about boycotting Jewish shops and other anti-Jewish notices were all removed."

"OK. Go back and see your source then bung together a thousand words or so and I'll take it upstairs and see where we go from there. I'm not promising anything mind you. Of course our papers are liberal and don't like the Fascist dictators; we reckon they're a threat and we support rearmament, but this is a step further: accusing the Germans of terrorising a whole load of their citizens. Most folk in England think the Germans are not much different from us. They're going to have a nasty shock when they read this."

"Subjects, not citizens," I said, reminding him of the Nuremberg Laws.

"Right, Prof, let's have it by the end of the week."

I was pretty excited by this. Although my work was enjoyable, I was itching to get my teeth into something really substantial. This might be my chance.

I telephoned Richard from the office. Inge answered the phone and told me he had gone to work with my father. I thanked her, rang off, and then called the store. Eventually I got through to Richard and repeated my conversation with Ben. He asked me to drop in on my way home that evening.

Richard answered the door just after six. He looked totally relaxed in his baggy green cardigan, dark brown corduroy trousers and slippers. He was as tall as me and looked in good shape although his fair hair was obviously receding.

"Come in Roger. Good to see you," he said as he showed me into his lounge. Inge got up and walked towards me smiling as she offered me her hand. She was a fine looking dark haired woman about six inches shorter than her husband.

"Hello Roger, please take a seat. Would you like something to eat?"

"No thank you. My mother is expecting me for dinner at home. A cup of tea would be nice though."

"Of course. Richard?"

"Yes please." Inge left to make the tea.

Richard and I sat down and I repeated the details of my conversation with Ben. I pulled out my note book and told him I had tried to jot down everything he'd told us after the dinner party but was sure I'd missed something and would be grateful if he would help me fill in the gaps.

While he was doing this Inge returned with the tea and the three of us continued checking my scribbling. After a quarter of an hour or so Richard said, "You'll make a good journalist Roger. You've remembered just about everything I said pretty accurately."

"Thanks," I replied, "but that doesn't mean they'll print it without chopping bits out or even print it at all."

"I realize that."

Inge then looked at me.

"There is one other thing. For the time being we'd like to remain anonymous. The boys have just started at school and we don't really want them to become the centre of attention. I expect they'll find it difficult enough settling in a new school as well as a new country."

"And anyway there's some pretty nasty Germans in England. Heaven knows how they might react to bad publicity like this," added Richard.

"OK. If it's published, it will be without mentioning your names or not at all. I'll make that clear to my boss. I'm sure he'll understand."

"Thank you," said Inge and Richard more or less simultaneously.

"Right, I must be off or else my mother will be complaining that I've let my dinner go cold. Thank you very much. That's been really helpful."

"Before you go would you mind letting me have your telephone number at the office? You never know, I could come up with something interesting."

"Certainly." I gave it to him. "There is just one other thing I'd like to ask if I may."

"What is it?"

"Well I was wondering, Inge, if I you had any relatives left in Germany?"

"No," she said. "My father died four years ago and my mother and brother left to live in America at the beginning of last year. He's a doctor and has set up a practice in New York."

"OK. Thanks very much and thank you for the tea. I must be off."

"Goodbye Roger," said Richard. "The freedom of the press is a great thing. It's such a pity that such freedom doesn't exist in Germany."

My parents were anxious to hear about my chat with the Walker family. I told them whilst eating my dinner, then telephoned Jane. She was almost as excited as I was and wished me luck. We arranged to go to the cinema that Saturday night.

The next day I told Ben that Richard, now officially called my source, wanted anonymity for his family and himself. I told him why and he agreed that this would be for the best.

It took me a while to write the article. I don't suppose I'd ever written more than 400 words, and that was for First Division football matches, so more than twice that amount was proving tricky. It wasn't so much filling out the thousand words but keeping it down to the thousand. I knew that if I went well over the limit the subs would hack it to pieces and the whole thing might become meaningless.

As well as the challenge of writing my first feature, there was my day-to-day news reporting to fit in, so it was late on Friday afternoon before I passed the complete job to Ben. He said he'd let me know. It wasn't as though rival papers would get hold of the story, so time wasn't that important, he told me.

The following week passed slowly though there was plenty going on in the world. The situation in Spain was growing worse as accusations and counter-accusations were made by the Germans, Italians and Russians. It was clear that those foreign powers were totally committed to providing military support to the two sides in the war in Spain. Russia was keen to see a Republican victory, Germany wanted Franco to win in order to prevent a communist regime in Western Europe and Italy supported the Nationalists in the hope that triumph for them would enable Mussolini to increase his power in the Mediterranean.

Meanwhile our government and the French did nothing but threaten to rap the knuckles of the three in the Non-Intervention Committee. Stanley Baldwin seemed worn out after dealing with the abdication crisis but at least allowed the Chancellor of the Exchequer, Neville Chamberlain, to find money for an increase in our armaments. Chamberlain started poking his nose into foreign policy and, in a speech in Birmingham, he praised the Foreign Secretary, Anthony Eden, for his efforts in appeasing the dictators. Meanwhile the war in Spain dragged on towards what appeared to be an inevitable, sickening conclusion.

On the Thursday afternoon Ben called me in.

"The good news is that it's going in tomorrow night's paper."

"Thanks."

"The bad news is that it's been chopped to pieces."

He threw down my article on the table for me to see. There were crossings out and alterations everywhere. The subs had been at work with the dreaded blue pencil.

"Now before you start," said Ben, "the subs weren't responsible for this. I read it and thought it was brilliant. I showed the Editor and he agreed, but he felt that it was such a hot potato he'd need to speak with the owners. Evidently at a black tie bash one of the owners had been buttonholed by some government press bloke and had been asked to hold back on having a go at Hitler and Mussolini while the powers that be were trying to reach some accommodation with the jackboot brigade over Spain."

"Well we agreed for the time being but our owners did tell the Number 10 guy that we weren't going to be the government's mouthpiece like in Nazi land."

"I see."

"So the next time you write a feature, and there will be a next time, we'll see what the response to that will be up top. Meanwhile type up the revised version this afternoon and let's get it out tomorrow. We'll sort out a headline and you'll have a byline. The story will go in under your name."

I suppose I should have been over the moon. My first feature in my own name in one of the country's leading evening papers. What more could I want? But I wasn't pleased at all. In fact I was a little bit depressed. I felt I was letting the Walker family down, and all the Jewish people in Germany. Still, I did as I was told, typed it up and handed it back. I trusted Ben and, through him, that trust extended to the Editor and the owners. I would get another chance, I was sure.

My parents caught my mood as soon as I got home and left me to ring Jane. Although she shared my disappointment, she said there was a lot of encouragement for me. I told my parents, who were pleased too, and then I telephoned Richard. He said he understood why the story had been tampered with but he was still looking forward to reading it. He said he'd call me again soon. He had something else to tell me.

CHAPTER TEN

Harry

"I thank heaven for a man like Adolf
Hitler, who built a front line of defence
against the anti-Christ of Communism."
FRANK BUCHANAN

Jane and I spent Saturday afternoon talking and worrying. She did most
of the talking and once again amazed me with her depth of understanding
of what was going on.

The early edition of my article had been read by some of her colleagues,
two of whom were Jewish. They'd read the story but said it hadn't gone
far enough, but that hadn't surprised them. Jane had defended me, telling
them that the piece had been severely edited, according to her boyfriend
who, she explained to her colleagues, had written the article. An intense
discussion had followed about being a Jew in England. Most of our papers,
they told her, wouldn't have even bothered to print such an article. So at
least mine was a step in the right direction.

"Why did they believe that most papers wouldn't print a story like that?"
I asked. "Surely any journalist worth his salt would jump at it."

"They think that a lot of English people don't believe the stories about
the treatment of the Jews in Germany. Those who do know what's going
on, think we should mind our own business and let the Germans get on
with their own affairs."

"You're joking."

"My friends told me that there are plenty of our people who actually approve of Hitler's treatment of the Jews."

"Why on earth would they do that?"

"They think that all Jews are Bolsheviks and Hitler is the world's best chance of keeping what he calls 'the red menace' at bay."

"Yes, there's plenty in the office who reckon some of our top people prefer Hitler to Stalin because he poses less of a threat to us. Baldwin and his cronies are terrified of communism. Some say Stalin's calling for world revolution whereas Hitler is only trying to restore Germany to Europe's top table. I'm not so sure. It strikes me that Hitler's got more up his sleeve than just domestic bliss. Anyway, go on."

"There's quite a bit of prejudice against Jews in our country, you know, not like Germany, of course, but the guys in the office think that there's plenty of it here. Businessmen are jealous of successful Jews and ordinary workers blame Jewish refugees for taking jobs from them. They call them refu-jews," Jane said.

"Yeah. That's one of Moseley's chief gripes."

"Plenty of people actually blame the Jews for the economic depression."

"But it's still nothing like Germany."

"No, they accept that. They'd rather be here than there. Some feel uncomfortable but nobody actually feels threatened. You had the guts to stand up for the German Jews. OK, it didn't quite end up as you'd hoped, but it's a start."

"Thanks."

"And another thing: you and I have been going to the cinema together for more than three years; when in those wretched newsreels have you seen film of Jews being ill-treated in Germany?"

"I do remember once a report on the boycott of Jewish shops soon after Hitler came on the scene."

"And since then?"

"You're right. I can't remember one."

"And do you know why?"

"Not wanting to upset the audience? They've come to be entertained by the likes of Charlie Chaplin, not made to feel depressed by watching scenes of Jews being persecuted."

"That's one reason."

"What's the other?"

"Cover up. The people who own the newsreels don't want to upset the Germans and Italians because they know the government wants to be friends with the dictators so we won't have to fight them."

She was right on the ball and her conviction made me feel a growing admiration for her.

"You should have been a journalist you know."

Jane laughed. "No thanks. The pay's not good enough."

Richard's call came early in February. He was going to be in town on business and asked if we could meet for a lunchtime drink and suggested that I should choose the place for our get together, although he did stress it should be a fairly inconspicuous spot.

I thought the Coal Hole in the Strand, underneath the Savoy Hotel, would be ideal. Intrigued, I set off to meet him.

Although I arrived on time, Richard was already there when I walked in, sitting in a corner with a glass of beer on the table in front of him. He got up, shook my hand, and then asked me what I was having. I thanked him and said I'd have the same as him.

We made small talk for a while. He asked how my work was going and I asked about his family and working with my father. He told me everybody was happy and he was doing well. Then he got down to business.

"As you can imagine," he began, "I have lots of German friends and most of them hate Hitler, and those who don't are becoming increasingly nervous about his motives. Nearly all of them believe that war is inevitable within the next three or four years. They reckon that the only chance of stopping this is for strong countries like the United States, France, Russia and Great Britain to gang up on Germany and make it clear to them that any aggression on their part will be met with overwhelming force."

"I wouldn't disagree with that. The trouble is that we mistrust the

Russians and it could be difficult to convince other countries."

"Quite. So our government has to be convinced that, without some form of alliance with Russia, war is inevitable. At the moment they appear to want to 'appease', to use the current in word, rather than stand up to Hitler. Nor do they fully appreciate the threat that Nazi Germany really poses."

"OK, but we do seem to be making some efforts to get Italy on our side."

"Waste of time," said Richard. "Italy poses no military threat to us or France. Mussolini is just a bully and he only picks on people half his size like Abyssinia and Republican Spain. Italy would be no use to either side in any war. Anyway, back to my German friends. When I was working in Hamburg I had a bit to do with the German government, organizing exports and so on. I became very friendly with a civil servant, let's call him 'Harry', who later got posted to the German Embassy in London. He hates Hitler and the Nazis and this led to him getting the sack when he refused to join the party. He had some money so he bought a small art gallery in Bloomsbury and is now applying for British citizenship, which he'll probably get."

Richard sipped his beer and paused before continuing.

"Harry is doing well with his gallery by the way. But he has kept in touch with one of the consular staff at the German Embassy who has been feeding tit-bits of information to him and he's been passing these on to the Foreign Office, particularly their head man Vansittart, so you can see now why Harry is likely to get British citizenship."

"Yes, I've heard of Vansittart. People on our papers rate him."

"So they should, but the trouble is the politicians like Baldwin, Chamberlain, even Eden, turn a deaf ear to this intelligence. They either don't believe it or don't want to. Vansittart is certain that Germany means war but the politicians won't go along with that."

"So where do I come in?" I asked

"Your paper seems very liberal and I think recognizes the threat from Hitler. Others, especially *The Daily Mail*, appear to believe that Hitler is doing a good job. *The Times* as well seems to be backing away from confronting Germany. Through me, Harry would be happy to pass on information he gets from the German Embassy which he, and I, believe would be in the public interest.

If you could persuade your paper to print this information, you'd be performing a great service to the real anti-war effort whose aim would be to oppose Hitler through alliances, not appease him through concessions."

I was both excited and apprehensive, and had good reason to be as Richard warned me that I would most likely be making enemies on both sides. The Germans would want to trace the source of the leaks and plug them and our government wouldn't want their pursuit of friendship with Germany interfered with.

He went on to say that the Germans had an organization in England called the Landesgruppe whose main job, along with a number of Gestapo agents in London, was to keep an eye on German citizens living abroad. He explained that the Landesgruppe's official duty was to promote Anglo-German friendship and organize social and other events for German citizens living in England, but, he told me, this was just a cover for their more sinister activities.

"The new German Ambassador, Ribbentrop, is a rabid Nazi and will do almost anything to stifle anti-German feeling in England," Richard continued. "He calls himself Von Ribbentrop but he added the von himself to pretend he had an aristocratic background; he's just a former wine salesman who's attached himself to the Nazis. A revolting specimen. So what do you think?"

"Well first thanks for thinking of me," I began. "I'm really interested, but I will have to run it past my boss first. I'm sure you understand that."

"Of course. Let me know what he says, but it may be some time before anything much happens. Hitler and Mussolini seem pre-occupied with Spain at the moment. As soon as Harry gets something which he thinks will be of interest to the newspapers, he'll get it to you through me."

"Thanks again, Richard. I'll wait to hear from you."

I didn't catch Ben that afternoon but told him more or less everything the following morning. I told him that Richard would act as a link between us and an unnamed source who was getting information from the German

Embassy. Ben, not surprisingly, thought this opened up all sorts of possibilities and was very enthusiastic. He told me to give my source the go ahead, which I did.

Back in the office, I settled down to the usual routine. In Spain there were stories about the bombing of civilians by Franco's forces, Madrid being regularly targeted, and then a particularly nasty air raid on Durango in Northern Spain. The Sports Editor asked me, towards the end of March, if I would cover some cricket in the summer but just as the cricket season started, news arrived from Spain of the most appalling atrocity.

CHAPTER ELEVEN

Guernica

"The sky is darkening like a stain;
Something is going to fall like rain,
And it won't be flowers"
W.H. AUDEN

The newsroom was always buzzing with activity but that morning, Tuesday April 27th 1937, was like no other day I'd experienced in my short time there. Apart from the constant clattering of typewriters and the shrill ringing of phones, there were at least a dozen highly animated conversations taking place, some of them quite heated.

"What's happening?" I asked the reporter whose desk was next to mine.

"Haven't you heard, Prof? That bastard Franco's really upped the ante in Northern Spain."

"How?"

"He's blown Guernica off the face of the map."

Over the next hour or so I pieced together what had happened. My first task was to find out where Guernica was.

I was told it was a small town in the Basque territory in Northern Spain. It was highly symbolic in Basque history and, on that day, April 26th, the town was packed because it was a feast day.

The Globe correspondent was actually present when, at five o'clock that afternoon, the bombers came. He had watched from a nearby hilltop when the first planes pounded the defenceless town with incendiary and other high explosive devices. Then came the fighters, machine gunning the citizens of Guernica as they fled from the fires and the explosions. Our man identified the aircraft as German and said the raid lasted for three hours, during which time up to a thousand bombs were dropped and countless innocent people were slaughtered.

When he left Guernica at four on the following morning, the town was still ablaze and the red sky above it was visible for miles. As the only British journalist present during the raid, he had a scoop. It was a triumph for *The London Evening Globe* but even in the hard world of journalism there was an underlying feeling in the office that this was some sort of turning point towards a terrible future.

I spent the rest of the day chasing up small stories and getting my assignments for the week. I was late home, tired and very depressed. Jane was at my house when I got there. Both she and my parents had read the exclusive and were horrified. I slept poorly that night. When the Japanese had bombed Manchuria and the Italians gassed the Abyssinians, it all seemed far away. This was almost on our doorstep and it was impossible for me not to recall the images of *Things to Come*.

Over the next few days, the full extent of the rebels' monstrous act was revealed. Our daily ran the story under the headline "FRANCO BOMBS TOWN" and reported that the Basque President Aguirre identified that German fliers and planes were responsible for the barbarous acts.

Even a flock of sheep had been machine gunned. Not a single newspaper failed to condemn the Germans and the Nationalists and there were protests throughout Britain and around the world.

Although we had had the exclusive on Guernica, it was *The Times* which, initially at least, gave the most complete description of events. On that Wednesday, April 28th, their correspondent in Northern Spain had been having dinner in nearby Bilbao when news of the air raid reached him. Earlier in the day he had spotted a fleet of German Heinkel 51 bombers heading towards Guernica as he returned to Bilbao from the front. By the time he went back to Guernica, the raid was over but, by speaking to survivors, he was able to piece together an accurate picture of events. Apart from Heinkels, there were Junker and Dornier bombers and Heinkel and Messerschmitt fighters attacking the town. They flew in waves, returning to the rebel airfield at Vittoria to refuel.

The Times man had seen several twenty-five-foot-deep bomb craters, the ruins of a hospital in which all forty two patients had been killed, houses completely destroyed in Guernica and the surrounding villages.

Bodies riddled with bullets lay in every street. Many more had probably been buried alive beneath the collapsed buildings. The numbers of those who died in the attack were thought to be more than eight thousand.

The story was headed "THE TRAGEDY OF GUERNICA" and, to its credit, The Times condemned the attacks in its editorial on the same day. What happened next, however, filled me with dismay.

Three days after the raid on Guernica, Franco's government issued a statement denying that they had been responsible and accused the Basques themselves of setting fire to the town, pouring petrol on the buildings before setting them alight. I was very unsettled by this. Our man and The Times correspondent had seen German planes on their way to Guernica. What on earth was going on? Surely no one would believe Franco's denials?

The Times itself then joined in the cover up, publishing a letter from a Hugh Pollard in which he claimed that Guernica, which had an arms and munitions factory, was a legitimate target and that arms manufactured there had been used by terrorists against British citizens in India and Egypt. The Times correspondent in Nationalist Spain reported that Franco, who by now had occupied Guernica, had used a team of engineers to prove that the destruction of Guernica had been caused by fire setting not bombing.

On top of all this, our own government refused to condemn the bombing of Guernica. The Foreign Secretary, Anthony Eden, said that there was insufficient evidence to prove German involvement. Various right wingers claimed that the Germans were only in Spain as technical advisors despite the fact that, at the last count, there were 18,000 of them in Spain fighting for Franco.

I became increasingly unhappy about the whole business. Not only, it seemed were the Nationalists telling lies but there were people of influence in our own country prepared to accept these lies. Was there anything that the dictators could do which would make our government stand up to them? I began to lose faith in the whole rotten system.

Towards the end of the first week in May, Ben called me in.

"Got much on at the moment, Prof?"

Not wishing to appear underemployed, I replied: "I'm quite busy; cricket, some film reviews and some court work."

"Drop that lot for the time being. The Editor's anxious to put that Guernica stuff in perspective. The government's backing off from confronting the Nazis about it and their mouthpiece, *The Times*, is running scared after Steer's article caused all that fuss."

"Who's Steer?"

"George Steer, their man in Northern Spain, a right fireball. He wrote that *Tragedy of Guernica* piece the day after our scoop. Hell of a bloke by all accounts; always seems to be on the spot. Mussolini kicked him out of Abyssinia and Franco out of Nationalist Spain. Not a popular fellow with our Fascist friends."

"Sounds like I should meet him. He seems like a man after my own heart."

"He's in Bilbao so you can forget that. The paper isn't going to pay you to traipse over there just to get your balls shot off. Just put together what evidence you can and point a few fingers. The great British public is beginning to see just what a shit Franco is so just try and confirm their suspicions about the Fascists and try to persuade our government to pull its finger out."

"Right boss. I'll get on with it straight away."

The good thing about writing a feature, as opposed to hot news, was that I wasn't trying to beat anybody in a race to publication. So I took my time. I read everything I could about Guernica and the aftermath and tried to find as many answers as I could to the unanswered questions.

The first of these questions was, why Guernica? I spoke to a number of colleagues and one recommended that the MP Philip Noel Baker would be worth talking to. He had spoken out strongly against non-intervention, and for the Spanish Republic, both in the House and in the letters column of *The Times*.

Noel Baker was a Quaker and a Cambridge man, and silver medalist in the 1,500 metres in the Antwerp Olympics of 1920. Although a pacifist, he had distinguished himself in the war in France with the ambulance service.

I arranged to meet him at the Commons and, as he strode to meet me, it was easy to see he'd once been a great athlete. In fact he looked as if he could still run the mile in four and a half minutes although I knew he was in his late forties. He was tall and slim and his greying hair was receding. He smiled at me from beneath his horn-rimmed spectacles and offered me a firm handshake.

Noel Baker was the Labour MP for Derby. His father had also been a Member, but was a Liberal. The son felt that Labour matched more closely his political views than the Liberals who, by this time, were in a state of total disarray. He explained the conflict in Northern Spain. He told me that the Basque territory was heavily industrialized and that Bilbao was Spain's third city after Madrid and Barcelona. Iron and steel were the main industries and both were desperately needed by all sides in the race to build bigger and better armaments. Noel Baker reckoned the bombing of Guernica was carried out to terrify the inhabitants into early capitulation of the Basque country, leaving the Fascists to grab the valuable minerals and wipe out potential resistance.

I'd struck up an instant rapport with him and realised how lucky I was to meet a man who had already had so much international experience, having been part of the World Disarmament Conference earlier in the decade. Besides, he was a nice man, charming, courteous and bright, and I liked him very much.

I read Steer's earlier dispatches from Spain and his criticism of our government for failing to protect British merchant ships bringing essential non-military supplies into Bilbao.

Meetings followed with people who had been with Steer in Bilbao and they told me that Steer had shown them spent bomb tubes stamped with the German eagle that had been recovered from Guernica. They also told me of a German pilot who had been shot down and captured near Bilbao who admitted he had taken part in the raid.

I sought opinion on the Spanish conflict from experienced colleagues as well as Noel Baker. All agreed that it was a total mess on the government side, split by various factions, helped by the Russians, and with the Nationalists seemingly in the pockets of the dictators. The Italians were there because Mussolini saw himself as a new all-conquering Roman Emperor and the Germans were there to prevent the spread of Communism into Western Europe and to practise for the war which many thought inevitable.

I put the article together, gave it to Ben and waited. A couple of days later he called me in and congratulated me. It would appear in the next day's edition. The blue pencil, he told me, hadn't been used as often as on my previous effort but my criticism of the government had been toned down. It was published the next day and my parents, Jane, and Richard and Inge Walker were all delighted.

A week or so later I was at home, discussing with my parents Neville Chamberlain replacing Stanley Baldwin as Prime Minister, when the phone rang. My father answered it, hesitated for a moment then chatted briefly to a colleague at the store. After he had finished he said: "I'm sure there's something wrong with the phone. Every time I use it there's a clicking sound."

I thought no more about this until a couple of men approached me one evening at Waterloo when I was waiting for a train home.

CHAPTER TWELVE

Threat

"No, when the fight begins within himself,
A man's worth something."
ROBERT BROWNING

Both men were shorter than me and were dressed in sports jackets and slacks. One was black haired with a small moustache while the other was thinning on top with fair hair. Both appeared to be in their late thirties or early forties.

"Mr Martin?" said the one with a moustache, who was much shorter than me and looked overweight. His nose and cheeks were a kind of washed-out red and his chin and neck were covered in dark stubble, as if he hadn't shaved properly that morning.

"Yes."

"We'd like to have a word with you."

"Why?"

"It's nothing much. It won't take more than a couple of minutes," again from the moustachioed man who stared at me from his small, black, piercing eyes.

"Go on then."

"Well sir, it seems you've been upsetting the applecart."

The black haired man with the moustache seemed to be the spokesman for the pair. His colleague stood silent and fixed another unpleasant stare on me.

"How have I been doing that?" I asked.

It's not every day that two strangers approach you on the platform at Waterloo Station and I was just a bit shaken, especially since they knew my name.

"Anyway who the hell are you?"

"Let's just say we represent people who are a damn sight more important than you."

"That wouldn't be difficult and you still haven't answered my question."

The only thing that prevented me from panicking was the fact that I was one of hundreds of people milling about a busy station, so it was unlikely that I'd come to any physical harm. Nevertheless, my heart was beating furiously and I was more than a little worried by this sinister pair.

"You don't need to know who we are, just that we're giving you an important message and offering you some advice, which you'll do well to heed sir."

This sir business made me think they might well be policemen and, though my conscience was clear on that score, they still disturbed me.

Moustache went on. "There's a few people that don't like the stuff you've been writing in your newspaper."

I was beginning to get an inkling of what they were talking about but I put a brave face on it and said "Oh, now I see. My football reports. Your powers that be don't like the things I've said about their favourite football teams."

"Yes, very funny sir, you know we're talking about the rubbish you wrote about Spain and the government's attitude to Guernica."

"What I wrote was the truth."

"That may be your opinion, but the fact is, by criticizing the government, you're upsetting Number Ten."

I was beginning to get angry.

"What on earth are you talking about?"

"You see, sir, the PM wants to stay on the right side of Hitler and Mussolini. If he rubs those mad bastards up the wrong way, there's no telling what they might do."

I was furious by now.

"Don't talk nonsense. Most of the papers said much the same thing."

"Someone will be having a word with them as well."

"This is ridiculous. How on earth is an article I wrote in a London evening newspaper going to affect the PM's relationship with Germany and Italy?"

"Oh you'd be surprised sir, there's a nasty little man in Berlin called Goebbels who reads all the English and French papers and if he sees something he doesn't like he runs off and tells Adolf."

"So?" I said.

"We've said what we came to say. After that Guernica stuff we checked up on you and found that last year you wrote some nonsense about how the Jews were being treated in Germany. That didn't go down well either."

"Why not?"

"What the Germans do to their Jews is their business not ours. Keep your nose out. Good day sir."

They walked off. I was absolutely stunned. Here were a couple of, I assume, London coppers, telling a junior reporter on an evening newspaper what he should or should not write.

The train was crowded but I found myself a seat. People were chatting to one another and others were reading their evening papers. I didn't hear a word of what was said. My mind was going round in circles. I tried to calm down, and then asked myself how on earth they knew who I was? Of course, they'd followed me from the office. Someone had pointed me out to them as I left. But who?

Probably they'd shown their police credentials to the receptionist and she'd given them the nod when I left. But how? I never spotted them. Still, that didn't really matter. The important thing was that they knew who I was and had followed me to the station.

I'd more or less recovered from my ordeal by the time I reached home. I was a bit later than usual and explained to my parents that I'd had a busy day. The four of us sat down to the evening meal. Not much was said, mostly small talk. Towards the end my father mentioned again the noises on the phone. I shrugged my shoulders. My brother said that the telephone was quite a new thing in family homes but he was sure the scientists would soon bring about big improvements.

I settled down to read the previous Sunday's *Reynolds News*. It was a paper I enjoyed reading and it disliked Hitler, Mussolini and Franco. I wondered if their reporters had been approached by those unpleasant men. I supposed they had, but it hadn't stopped them printing the truth and their views on foreign affairs and I was damned sure it wasn't going to stop me either.

Jane should know about this, I thought, and I was about to pick up the phone and call her when the penny dropped. Of course, the clicking noise my father had talked about. The sods had tapped our line.

I knew something about phone tapping. Some of my left wing friends at Cambridge told me that the police or the security services, or both, were tapping the phones at the headquarters of the Communist Party of Great Britain more than ten years ago. They'd even put an undercover agent to work in the offices of Odham's Press where the Trade Union left wing newspaper, *The Daily Herald*, was printed.

Was I becoming paranoid? At the time I didn't know. I thought of calls made to and from our phone over the past couple of weeks and reckoned that none of my calls would have created any difficulties. Then I remembered Richard. If they intercepted any conversations we might have in the future, it could land us both in real trouble.

My father told me that Richard would be working in the store on the following day so I asked if I could accompany him to work so I could have a brief chat with him. I explained that I was thinking about doing a follow up on my earlier piece on the Jews in Germany and would prefer to speak with him face to face.

The next morning I took Richard to a quiet corner and recounted the previous day's events at Waterloo to him. I also told him I thought our line might be tapped and, if that was the case, perhaps they might also be listening in on both my father's business and my office phones.

Richard told me he hadn't heard from his contact 'Harry' for a while but, if he did get hold of anything he thought might be of use to me, he'd send me a note through my father. He thought I should explain to my father what was going on. I thanked him then told my father about the possible phone tapping. He was livid and threatened to write to his MP, the papers and anyone else he thought might be interested. I told him I didn't think that would do any of us any good and he agreed to the clandestine passing of notes.

When I left for the paper, I spent a great deal of time looking over my shoulder. Hadn't Richard said that's how it was in Germany, with ordinary people worried that if they said the slightest uncomplimentary thing about the regime they'd be arrested and taken to Gestapo Headquarters for questioning? Of course, even the mildest criticism of Hitler and his Nazi sidekicks would certainly lead to imprisonment or even worse. Surely that couldn't happen here? Or could it?

Ben called me in as soon as I reached the office.

"What's up Prof? Later than usual today. Anything interesting going on?"

I explained that I had been seeing a contact but nothing had come of it, so far anyway. Then I told him about the business at Waterloo on the previous day and how I thought my home phone might be tapped.

He was in shirt sleeves and braces and seemed concerned but not totally surprised: as always he looked hot, but not really bothered.

"Are you sure it wasn't a couple of comedians taking the piss?"

"Of course I'm bloody well sure. They knew all about me."

"All right, Prof, keep yer hair on. I wondered when this sort of thing might start."

He went on to tell me that the Editor had been talking to the paper's owners and that they, the owners, had been asked by government people to show restraint, in their words, in reporting on events in Spain and the involvement there of Italy and Germany.

"Like that slimy pair said to you, we don't want to be upsetting Adolf."

Ben reminded me of Chamberlain's speech when he had become Prime Minister at the end of the previous month.

"Chamberlain seems to be setting himself up as the saviour of Europe. He believes that, unless we can appease Hitler and Musso, there'll be another shooting match. It was bad enough last time but this time it'll be much worse. The Nazis gave us a hint of what it might be like when they flattened Guernica. So Neville thinks it's his job to save us from all that."

"So we pal up with Hitler so he won't attack us?" I said.

"More or less."

"So we don't tell the truth about what we know and what we think?"

"Yes, we bloody well do. It's not Nazi Germany, we don't have press censorship and the owners will back us all the way. But," Ben continued, "it ain't going to be easy as you've already found out. Now's the time to be a real reporter and you'll have to show some guts if you want to be able to look at yourself in the mirror in the morning."

"Just how shit scared Chamberlain and his cronies are," Ben went on, "you could tell from last Friday's debate in the House on Spain. Everybody in the Commons knows non-intervention in Spain isn't working. The Labour Party said we should pack it in and at least start sending arms to the Spanish Government. Then that horrible man, Archibald Sinclair, shouted out his support for Franco and called for an understanding with Germany.

How the hell can we have an understanding with a bunch of cutthroats who persecute the Jews and bomb women and children? Then Chamberlain calls for press restraint! Well he's getting no restraint from us. We'll go on telling it as we see it."

"I'm glad to hear it," was all I could think of saying in response to Ben's outburst.

"And I reckon it'll get worse. Like I said, we're all going to need plenty of guts. No doubt *The Times* will continue to toe the party line, but hardly anybody reads it in this country, so the rest of us can concentrate on telling the truth. Anyhow this little business of yours has come at the right time. How do you fancy a paid holiday?"

"Sounds good."

"We need you to go over to Paris for a week to cover the Exhibition. You know the sort of thing, look at a few pavilions; ours, the Germans, the Russians, get some views from the visitors then tell our readers what you make of it all. How's your French?"

"Pretty good. I studied Modern Languages before Economics. My French and German are both OK."

"Right, we'll fix you up with train tickets and a decent hotel. Look after yourself while you're there but don't dine in the very best restaurants. Oh yes, and that bloke Steer who wrote all that good stuff about Guernica; he's in Paris writing up his experiences of the Basque country. See if you can track him down and get him to give you the low-down on the Spanish War. He sounds like an interesting character."

CHAPTER THIRTEEN

Picasso and George Steer

"Paris is a movable feast"
ERNEST HEMINGWAY

A week or so before I left for Paris I put in motion my search for Steer. Ben told me that the best way of doing this was to speak to his colleagues on *The Times*, not all of whom, he explained, were in the Editor's pockets.

Unlike lots of journalists, I wasn't yet in the habit of being a lunchtime drinker so I started by trying the new milk bar in Fleet Street. I went a couple of times but had no luck. Milk bars didn't seem to be much of an attraction to hardened members of the fourth estate.

I tried a few more of the traditional watering holes without success then struck lucky one evening in the Wellington at the top of the Strand. A noisy gang of obvious-looking correspondents were chatting at the bar and I joined them. I told them I worked for *The Globe* and having introduced myself I was flattered to discover that they knew me from my Jewish piece of last year and my more recent Guernica stuff.

I explained that I was off to Paris to cover the Exhibition and that George Steer was in the city and I hoped I'd get a chance to talk to him. One told me he was holed up in a flat of another newspaper man called Tom Cadett.

We chatted a bit more, mostly about the Exhibition and how they'd heard that the British pavilion in Paris compared unfavourably with those of the

Germans and Russians. Then, thanking them and armed with Cadett's Paris address, I left for home.

The next day I sent a note to Cadett, explaining who I was, when and why I was going to be in Paris and asking him to let Steer know that I'd like to meet and talk with him. I gave him my hotel address in Paris, saying that Steer could leave a message for me there if he was willing to meet me.

Leaving Victoria Station on the boat train at eleven o'clock on a bright July morning, I guessed my friends from the unpleasant encounter at Waterloo wouldn't bother following me to France. Having done nothing to upset them since they'd issued their warning, I felt fairly relaxed, although every time I stepped outside the office I did feel some trepidation, a bit of an innocent abroad. I had promised Jane to bring back something exotically French for her. Whilst I had never been to Paris, my father had taken us on a couple of trips to northern France and I spoke the language pretty well. I was confident I could cope with my first foreign assignment.

My mother had packed me some sandwiches and I had a couple of books for the journey; Orwell's *Keep the Aspidistra Flying* and *The ABC Murders* by Agatha Christie, featuring my favourite sleuth, the Belgian Hercule Poirot.

The journey to Dover was uneventful and the Channel crossing smooth. Ben said the paper couldn't run to first class so I was travelling second. I started reading the Orwell book as the train sped across the dull, flat landscape of northern France and, just before six, it reached Gare du Nord in the French capital. I thought I'd be at the hotel not long after but I seriously overestimated my ability to navigate the Paris Metro. The London Underground was very familiar to me but the Parisian equivalent was most certainly not. Their map was a confusing crisscross of coloured lines and I had great difficulty in identifying my destination. I knew I needed to be at the Rue Pierre Charon, not far from the Champs Elysees, so I eventually made my way to a train to take me to Chatelet where I would change.

At Chatelet there was further confusion, with this being, I could see, an important interchange. The train from the Gare du Nord had been pretty full but this station was incredibly busy, with Parisians of all shapes and

sizes either rushing home or heading for a night out. I got on the wrong
train, managed to arrive at the Champs Elysees, but nowhere near my
hotel, and decided to test out my French by asking for directions. To my
delight, my French held up well and I got precise instructions. It was a
warm evening and I was carrying my suitcase, leaving me rather tired
when I reached my hotel a little after seven.

Le Chateau Fontenac turned out, surprisingly, to be a very smart hotel
and I was amazed that the paper could afford such a posh place. Many of
the rooms had baths but I soon found that Ben, with one eye on the budget,
had arranged for me to have a room without one. Still, it was clean and
comfortable and, after an excellent meal in the hotel restaurant and some
more of George Orwell, I had an early night after a long and tiring day.

I had two jobs to do. One was to write about the Exhibition and the
other to interview George Steer. I decided to deal with the Exhibition first
while waiting for Steer to get in touch.

Luckily the Exhibition site was a reasonable walking distance from the
hotel so I wasn't forced to test my navigational skills again on the Metro.
The various national pavilions were spread along the banks of the Seine.
Paris had hosted a similar event in 1900 but had erected the Palais de
Chaillot especially for this Exhibition. It was, I thought, a fairly ordinary
building behind the Trocadero Fountains. I wasn't here, however, to judge
the architecture so I kept my thoughts to myself.

The area round the Eiffel Tower was teaming with visitors because here,
menacingly placed facing each other with Paris' most famous feature in
between, were the pavilions of the Soviet Union and Germany.

I discovered that the German pavilion had been designed by Albert
Speer. Above the entrance to the pavilion was a five hundred foot high
tower topped with an eagle and a Swastika. Inside were several huge halls,
each packed with visitors and many imposing exhibits glorifying the
achievements of Hitler's Reich. There was a mightily impressive Mercedes
car, a number of motor engines, examples of new electronics, optical
equipment, toys, glass, ceramics, art, furniture, musical instruments and
so on. Here was Germany, a country on the brink of total ruin less than
ten years ago, showing itself to be a world leader in modern technology

and export goods. All this was, of course, because of the leadership of the Nazi Party in Hitler's new Germany, or so I was told by the blonde female guide.

I spent the next day in the Russian pavilion. A gigantic statue of worker and peasant towered over the impressive entrance. The statue was of a male worker and a female peasant, their hands thrusting upwards holding a hammer and sickle together in a symbol of communist union.

Inside the halls were tractors, cars, models of dams, of giant industrial complexes and a plan of the newly completed Moscow Metro. There was a huge jeweled map of Russia and examples of socialist art. Everywhere there were display boards showing statistics on economic growth and social welfare provision, but there were few consumer goods on display.

The entire pavilion was a monument to Communist achievement and testament to the resounding success of Stalin's Five Year Plan.

I hated Hitler's Germany and believed all that I had heard about Stalin's tyrannical rule in the Soviet Union. Who could say which posed the greater threat to world peace if that is, as some would have it, either was committed to plunging Europe into another war? Of one thing I was certain: the pavilions represented two entirely different ideologies.

This was the substance of the article I began to write back at the hotel. I still had not heard from either Steer or Cadett and was able to spend the next day at the British pavilion. This hadn't received a very good press and letters had appeared in *The Times* and elsewhere criticising our contribution to the Exhibition. There'd even been questions in the House of Commons, mostly from the Labour Party, about the British contribution. So, when I set out the following morning I was prepared to be disappointed.

The first criticism of our pavilion was that it was difficult to find. To an extent that was true, but it wasn't that difficult. It didn't have the commanding position of either the Russian or German pavilions but was tucked up against the banks of the Seine, very handy if you were arriving by boat. Then there was the look of the building, variously described as resembling a factory on London's Great West Road or a riding school. Perhaps this was fitting. After all, JB Priestly, in his book *English Journey*,

d read the previous year, described the factories on the Great
l as looking like exhibition halls.

I must confess that the interior of the British pavilion was a disappointment. On entering, the first things to strike you were models of people hunting and shooting then a large picture of Prime Minister Neville Chamberlain fishing. Further inside there were other sports exhibits including cricket and darts, both quintessentially English. There was some rather poorly designed furniture, various posters covering the walls, a display of women's dresses, which compared very badly with those of our French hosts, and cheap drapes, badly hung. It was all a bit of a shambles. There were few visitors, compared with the Russian and German pavilions, and plenty of people walked past without bothering to come in.

On my way back to the hotel I thought that it was the British way of doing things simply, cricket, a game of darts, and a pint of beer and that was infinitely better than shouting their glory from the rooftops like the Russians and Germans. True, we could have done it better, but what would have been the point? We didn't feel the same need to impress.

There was a note from Steer when I got back from the hotel. He suggested we meet on the following morning outside the Spanish pavilion.

Waiting for me when I arrived the following day was a small red-headed man. He smiled, walked towards me and warmly shook my hand.

"Roger, it had to be you. Dressed like a true Englishman."

I was wearing a blue blazer and grey trousers while Steer had on a light green jumper over an open necked white shirt and dark brown trousers. He had a small ginger moustache.

"Before we chat there's something you must see. Ever heard of Picasso?" Steer continued.

"I have, yes," I replied.

"Right then, come and look at this."

Taking up an enormous amount of space on one wall in the Pavilion's main hall was a painting, no, a mural, in black and white and various shades of grey. It was more than twenty feet from end to end and almost ten feet deep.

"That's Picasso's work," Steer said, "it's called Guernica. What do you think?"

I stayed silent for a moment, and then slowly strolled the length of Guernica. It depicted suffering, death, destruction, fire and terror in a way that no photograph could have achieved. The fear of obliteration was brilliantly portrayed in the victim's eyes and even those of the animals. I didn't have a great understanding of art but I was immensely moved by Picasso's masterpiece.

"It's absolutely incredible Mr Steer."

"Please call me George. Yes, you're right, it's incredible and it shows the atrocities of Guernica as the world should see them. Once you've looked at it, you can never forget it.

Of course the Germans don't think much of it. One of their critics called it a hodgepodge of body parts that any four-year-old could have painted. Then they would say that, wouldn't they? OK, let's find a quiet corner where we can get a drink and I'll tell you all about Spain and Abyssinia."

We found a spot, grabbed a couple of coffees and then George began.

"The first thing you need to accept, Roger, is that the government can't win the Spanish Civil War. There are too many factions: Socialists, Communists, Anarchists, all arguing and sometimes fighting amongst themselves. Franco's lot, on the other hand, are totally united in their determination to win, and they've got German muscle and thousands of Italians on their side."

"Surely the Russians can make a difference?" I asked.

"In theory yes but they lack the commitment of the Germans and Italians. They came into the war much later than Hitler and Mussolini. Stalin isn't interested in helping to create a Communist Spain. He just doesn't want to see a fascist Spain. Besides he's got problems of his own. He's a bit of a mad bastard and seems to think his general staff and half the country supports Trotsky, so he's busy getting rid of them. Oh yes that's another faction on the government side in Spain: the Trotskyites. It's a real mess."

I could see he was warming to the task and, like many redheads, he was passionate so I said nothing and let him carry on.

"Hitler will do anything to prevent a Communist Spain and Mussolini just wants more clout in the Mediterranean."

"But that's a threat to us surely?" I asked.

"In theory, yes," he answered, "but at the end of the day Mussolini's just a glory hunter and his army's pretty useless. We've seen that already in Spain."

"How did you get involved in all this?" I asked.

"Well, I was born in South Africa went to school in England then Christ Church College in Oxford. What about you?"

"Local grammar, then Trinity College Cambridge."

"Ah! Did you know Kim Philby?"

"Of him, yes, but he was a bit before my time. How do you know him?"

"I don't, but he's just taken over as *Times* Correspondent in Nationalist Spain. He's a big mate of Franco's by all accounts."

"Odd that," I replied, "he had a reputation at Cambridge as a rampant socialist, probably even Communist. He was a sidekick of Guy Burgess who's also jumped the party ship and has got some kind of job with the Anglo German Fellowship."

Steer responded: "Yeah I've heard of Burgess but from what I've heard he's more interested in the Hitler Youth than politics."

I laughed, then asked, "So what happened after Oxford?"

George told me how he returned to South Africa, became a junior reporter on the *Cape Argus* then came back to England to work on the London desk of *The Yorkshire Post*.

"Anyway, to answer your question I got a job with *The Times* reporting from Abyssinia. I did some extra stuff for *The New York Times* which bumped my salary up. Met my wife there, a French journalist, but she died in childbirth in London at the start of the year."

George suddenly looked sad and sat in silence looking down at the table for a few minutes. I waited for him to continue.

He then went on to tell me about the Abyssinian war, how he developed a close friendship with the Emperor Haile Selassie, about the Italian bombing of innocent people and their use of poison gas.

"Of course the Italians won as you know. They weren't keen on the things

I'd been saying about them in the papers so they booted me out."

After a brief spell back in England, he'd gone to Spain and filed reports for *The Times* from the Nationalist side in the north.

"But Franco soon got wind of my presence from the Italians and I got kicked out from there as well. Then I got involved with the Basques. I quickly grew to love the Basques. They were decent and hardworking and had a really strong tradition of family life."

He told me about his time in Bilbao; how the city was regularly bombed, the siege of Bilbao with the Royal Navy refusing to escort relief ships into the harbour because they said the waters were mined, though this wasn't true. He had evidence that the Germans bombed Durango, killing 248 innocent people, and so on through Guernica, the fall of Bilbao then Santander, and the end of Basque resistance.

"It was dangerous work. Eventually I decided to carry a pistol, though, thank God, I never had to use it. My heart bled when the Basque Republic was forced to surrender."

He was getting quite emotional by now.

"What really pissed me off was the attempted cover up of the business at Guernica by my own bloody newspaper, printing rubbish about anarchists being responsible or even the Basques themselves. Of course, there are plenty of Tory MPs and *Times* readers who've got business interests in Northern Spain. They wouldn't want a Republican win. And the papers are still at it; not so much *The Times* but that awful Geraghty of *The Daily Mail*. He described the Spanish as victims of a Communist plot, inspired by Jews and international agitators. Anyway, that's what I'm doing now. Writing the truth as it happened in the Basque war."

I reflected on what he'd said, then told him about my articles and the threats I'd received on the platform at Waterloo Station.

"Not surprised," he said, "Chamberlain will do anything to avoid upsetting Hitler. Those guys who warned you were maybe MI5 or more likely Special Branch."

"But surely Chamberlain won't muzzle the newspapers? We've got a free press not like Germany."

He laughed. "Don't you believe it. When did the great British public hear about the ex-King and Mrs Simpson?"

"Last December I think."

"Quite. The rest of the world knew about Edward carrying on with that tart for months. Your papers were asked to keep it quiet. And what's more, articles about Edward and Mrs Simpson in American papers that reached England were cut out before the public could see them."

"Look," he continued, "you need to stand up for what you believe in. If you want to be a good journalist, write the truth; tell the readers how it is. Don't be put off by bullying coppers or cowardly editors. If your paper won't print your stuff, find one that will."

"My paper's been pretty good so far."

"Good, let's hope it stays that way but remember, stick to your guns whatever the provocation."

I shook his hand and thanked him and made my way back to the hotel. He wasn't much older than me but, in terms of achievement and experience, he was light years ahead. George Steer was just the kind of correspondent I hoped I'd become.

The next day I was on my way home. I left Gare du Nord at half past ten and was back not long after six thirty. My parents were pleased to see me. They'd invited Jane for the evening and over dinner I told them all about the Paris Exhibition and the remarkable George Steer. Jane was delighted with the exotic perfume I'd brought her from Paris.

On the following day at the office I wrote up the two articles; one a report on the Exhibition and the other my interview with Steer. I gave them to Ben then went home. I wasn't followed, as far as I could see. Back home my father told me that Richard wanted to see me. I told my father that I couldn't manage it the following day as I was too busy, but that the day after was fine. My father said he would find a reason for Richard to go up to town and he would let me know when and where the meeting would take place.

CHAPTER FOURTEEN

The Smell of Treason

"When a stupid man is doing something
he is ashamed of, he always declares
that it is his duty."
GEORGE BERNARD SHAW

When I got home the following evening my father gave me a note from Richard agreeing to a lunchtime meeting the next day. I was a little apprehensive, thinking back to the earlier confrontation on Waterloo Station. Richard had asked for the meeting, so I assumed he had something important to tell me, which added to the tension.

However, I was determined not to back off. My trip to Paris had hardened my resolve. Seeing the German Pavilion illustrated that this was a regime intent on causing serious trouble, if not throughout the world, then certainly in Europe. Coupled with the long discussion I'd had with George Steer, I felt certain that the Nazis posed a real threat to peace and I'd decided that I would do my tiny part to make our readers aware of this threat.

When I reached the office, Ben called me in and told me that my articles were fine and both would be printed over the next few days. I let him know that I was meeting my contact that lunchtime and he asked me to drop in later in the day and let him know what had gone on.

The rendezvous was in a pub in Brewer Street, just behind the Regent

Palace Hotel and a stone's throw from Piccadilly Circus. I set off in good time on foot and took a roundabout route. Whether I was being followed or not, I'd no idea but I wasn't taking any risks. I went in and out of the Aldwych Tube Station and Charing Cross Station, and spent a short time in Lyons Corner House on the Strand and tried to get lost in the crowds in Trafalgar Square before heading up through Coventry Street to Piccadilly Circus. Then I cut into Brewer Street via Regent Street. It was all rather amateurish and would have probably raised suspicion in any tail. I hung around the corner of Brewer Street then, reasonably satisfied that I hadn't been followed, went into the pub.

Richard was already there, sitting at a corner table sipping a pint of beer. He stood up and greeted me then bought me a pint. We had a good view of the entrance, so if any suspicious characters came in, we'd see them straight away. He asked me about Paris and I gave him a full account of my trip. He listened attentively, then began.

"Roger, I've nothing for you just yet but, from what I've heard, something's brewing. Our source in the German Embassy is fairly certain that Chamberlain becoming Prime Minister has upped the stakes in the appeasement game."

Richard then told me that it had all started about a year ago when Ribbentrop became German Ambassador in Britain. It seems he was under orders from Hitler to get Britain to join the Nazis and Japan in their anti-Communist agreement. Hitler, by all accounts, was terrified of encirclement, having the Soviet Union and their ally Czechoslovakia on his eastern front and the left-wing French, who had also concluded a treaty with the Russians, on his western side.

"Anyway," Richard continued, "he's got nowhere so far. Baldwin wasn't keen on the Communists and Chamberlain doesn't trust them either but neither of them sees the Soviet Union as a threat. The British communists may rightly kick up a stink about poverty and unemployment but they're hardly equipped to start up a Russian-style revolution and there's no way they're going to win a General Election; maybe a seat or two."

I sipped my beer then asked,

"So if he's getting nowhere, what's the problem?"

"Chamberlain may mistrust the Russians but he's terrified of the Germans and he'll do almost anything to keep on their good side. He doesn't want our cities bombed like Guernica."

"So where does Ribbentrop come in?"

"He doesn't. He's failed to get us to join Hitler's anti-Communist club. Chamberlain won't wash that, so he's no use to the Nazis. Ribbentrop's a complete idiot anyway. Evidently, when he went to present his credentials to the King, he clicked his heels and gave the Nazi salute. He tried to get close to King Edward before he jumped ship in December. He told Hitler that Edward was very friendly towards Germany. There's even the odd rumour that he had an affair with the Simpson woman."

I laughed. "Three husbands and heaven knows how many lovers. She's got some stamina that woman."

"Maybe, but they're gone now so that's another of Ribbentrop's crazy schemes scuppered. Hopefully it'll not be long before he goes. Everybody in the diplomatic community thinks he's a complete fool; official cars flying swastikas, black uniformed SS guards outside the embassy and so on. I had to laugh last week when our man in the embassy told Harry that the idiot had had the whole place re-decorated."

"The staff there knew exactly what he was up to, installing hidden microphones so he could listen to anti-Hitler chat, so they regularly have conversations proclaiming Ribbentrop to be the greatest German statesman since Bismarck. He's too dim to realise they're taking the piss."

"He does sound like a complete prat."

"He is, but now he's starting a new campaign that could be far more threatening to us."

"What's that?"

"Getting Germany back her African colonies. You know how the government thinks Britain has the greatest Empire on the planet. Well, they're not about to start giving bits of it back to the Germans or having the Nazis setting up a rival empire. I'm not sure how badly Hitler wants his colonies back. It might be just another part of the Versailles Treaty he wants to show the German people he can overturn.

"You know how horrible living in Germany is and not just if you're

Jewish. Ordinary citizens are under constant threat of being denounced, wages are low, personal freedom threatened, no trade unions and so on. Hitler has to show the German people all this is worthwhile and he can only achieve this by demonstrating to them that Germany is going to be a world power again. Throwing off the shackles of Versailles will make him popular. Well, perhaps not popular, but at least tolerated."

"I still don't see where Ribbentrop comes in."

"Generally he is, as you say, a prat, but there's one thing he's good at and that's socialising. He likes going to parties and rubbing shoulders with so-called important people. So he's cultivating his acquaintances among those members of our establishment who think a strong Germany would be a good thing."

"I've heard that argument before; world economic recovery needs a strong Europe and a strong Europe needs a vibrant Germany."

"And Hitler believes a strong Germany," Richard continued, "needs colonies and those German territories taken from them at Versailles; the Polish corridor, parts of Czechoslovakia, though that's never been part of Germany, but there's more than three million German-speaking people living there. You can see him making a move to grab Austria at some stage."

"You're saying he'll use these so-called allies in our establishment to get what he wants. Anyway who are these allies?"

"Ever heard of Cliveden?"

"Yes, it's a big house near Windsor. The Astors own it."

"That's right and they regularly have weekend gatherings of the rich and powerful."

"What's wrong with that?"

"Nothing if they'd stick to eating cucumber sandwiches, drinking tea and playing tennis but they're not. They're starting to poke their noses into foreign policy and maybe trying to influence it."

"Who are these people anyway?"

"You know, of course, that the Astors own *The Times*?"

The Astors were both Americans. Nancy was a Tory MP. Amongst the regular visitors to Cliveden were Lord Lothian, who, when he was Philip

Kerr, had been Lloyd George's Personal Secretary, and Geoffrey Dawson, Editor of *The Times*. Other visitors included Lord Londonderry, rabid anti-Semite and friend of Hitler, and various past and present cabinet members including Samuel Hoare, Lord Halifax and Anthony Eden, the Foreign Secretary.

"The Astors hate the Russians, and their allies the French, and they admire, if not love, Hitler's Germany. Above all things they worship the British Empire and think the government should put all its efforts into keeping the Empire strong and not interfere in European business. Lothian totally supports this and is using Dawson, through *The Times*, to let the world know that this is the view of the British government. You've already seen how Dawson tried to back track over the Guernica business so the Nazis wouldn't be upset. There'll be more of this, I promise you."

"How do you know all this Richard?" I asked.

"Through our source in the German Embassy."

"And how the hell does he know it?"

"Because the Downing Street Press Office is beginning to send stuff to the German Embassy, not state secrets of course, but sort of 'what do you think of this idea?' and so on, and most of these ideas seem to originate at Cliveden."

"But that's treason!"

"In theory, yes, but there's no evidence yet that Chamberlain's directly involved. More likely his personal adviser, Horace Wilson, is drip-feeding stuff to the Germans and of course nobody in the government knows there's an anti-Nazi agent at the Embassy. The only person who knows about him is Vansittart at the Foreign Office. He reckons the Germans are hell-bent on war. Any intelligence he gets his hands on he feeds fellow sceptics like Winston Churchill."

"How much of this can we print?"

"None of it at the moment. First of all there's no need and secondly the game hasn't really started yet. All that's happening at the moment is that Chamberlain's sitting by while Hitler and Mussolini flatten Republican Spain. He doesn't care about that. Spain's not important. Everyone thinks that Franco will win and, when he does, he'll say thank you to Germany and Italy and politely ask them to leave. Sounds awful I know but our government will have achieved its aim of keeping the conflict inside Spain and Hitler will have achieved his of keeping Spain free of Communism, and had some war practice as well."

"But what about Italy?"

"Nobody takes Italy seriously, probably including Hitler. They're no threat to anyone. As soon as Franco wins, Mussolini will set off to find some other defenceless country to bully."

"You've really thought this through Richard."

"That's because I think there's serious danger and everybody should know that. I'm preparing you so that, when the time comes, you'll understand the issues and know what's at stake. I'm British and proud of it and Britain has given a home to Inge and my children, keeping them away from those bastard Nazis. I'm doing what I can."

"Thanks Richard. I'll wait to hear from you."

"Just one more thing Roger. Somebody's keeping an eye on you and we desperately need to protect Harry and his source in the Embassy. When the balloon goes up it won't take the Gestapo long to work out where the stuff is coming from and they'll plug the leak and then we're snookered. Think of some smokescreen you can throw up which suggests you've got another source of information, even if it doesn't exist."

"OK, I'll give it some thought. Thanks a lot Richard."

Nobody suspicious had come into the pub while we had been talking so I left and walked straight back to the office. Ben was waiting for me. I told him about my meeting with Richard.

"Sound's promising, Prof, and exciting, but it makes me bloody angry to hear about this sort of shit. It could be dangerous, you know. Sure you want to follow it up? There's plenty of football to write about."

"No I want to follow this story. It could be a big one."

"OK, what about this smokescreen?"

"Not sure. I think I'll go up to Cliveden at the weekend and have a sniff around. Something might occur to me then."

CHAPTER FIFTEEN

A Day in the Country

"Like the sweet apple which reddens
upon the topmost bough"
DANTE GABRIEL ROSSETTI

It was early October. It had been a fairly routine week. Nothing much had happened since my return from Paris. Parliament had been in recess, the war in Spain continued to go badly for the Republic and Steer had written an article in *The Spectator* confirming his conviction that German aircraft had attacked Guernica.

By now, everyone was certain of German guilt over Guernica and this helped to swing public opinion against Franco. That is everyone except our government who continued to place their trust in the totally ineffectual Non-Intervention Committee. As far as I could judge, the French and British remained completely uninvolved while turning a blind eye to German, Italian and Russian presence in Spain. The Russians more or less acknowledged that they had people there while the others, defended by Ribbentrop, claimed that they had only volunteers. Ben told me that he'd heard that Eden had even offered not to complain about the Italians as long as Mussolini persuaded the Germans to get out. It looked as though Steer was right: the most likely outcome to this terrible war was a victory for the Fascists.

I'd heard nothing from Richard but saw a lot of Jane at weekends. We were growing closer. We were ideally matched, with similar interests and beliefs. Since she'd first surprised me after our night out watching *Things to Come* we'd had many discussions about the international situation and the threat to world peace.

Jane and I usually had dinner together on a Saturday night then either took in a film or went dancing. This particular October Saturday we decided to eat then head off to the local Palais. We'd both had a fairly easy week, so we felt full of energy.

After our meal we began talking. She said how well I seemed to be doing at the paper and had enjoyed reading my articles, especially the features about the Jews in Germany, Guernica, The Paris Exhibition and George Steer. She asked me when I could next expect to see my name under a headline.

I'd already told her about the encounter at Waterloo and, though she was concerned, urged me to keep on writing about what I believed to be true. She also knew, by this time, about my meetings with Richard, so I had no problem with what I was planning.

"It seems there's some sort of unofficial Foreign Office plan to do a deal with Hitler," I started.

Then I gave her a full account of what Richard thought might be going on at Cliveden; the Astors, the politicians and *The Times*. I knew she could be trusted, so I let her know about the source in the German Embassy and how, if anything happened at Cliveden, I'd be one of the first to know, after Vansittart at the FO.

After that I explained the need to protect the source in the Embassy and the necessity of putting up some kind of smokescreen.

"I thought I'd go up to Cliveden, hang around the nearby villages and ask a few questions. That way anything that came out might be thought to have originated with someone at Cliveden, a member of staff for example. What do you think?"

"Sounds sensible, but you're not going to get inside the house."

"Yes, I know that but I don't actually have to get any information, that'll come through Richard. Just appear to be getting some."

"Mm. When are you thinking of going?"

"I thought next Saturday."

"Great. I'll come with you."

"Now hang on," I began, "this could be a bit dodgy. You know what happened at Waterloo."

"I understand that but what can they really do to us apart from threaten? It's not Germany is it? They can hardly march us off to a camp or bump us off."

"I suppose you're right."

"Anyway, a man on his own wandering about the countryside is bound to raise suspicion, but what could be more natural than a boy and girl enjoying a day out away from the city?" she asked.

"All right, we'll give it a go next weekend. I'll find out where it is and how we're going to get there and we'll set off on Saturday morning."

I got up, paid the bill and we set off for the Palais. Jane paid, and then we danced till it closed. The band wasn't exactly Henry Hall but it was good enough. She was coming to Sunday lunch so I saw her home and kissed her goodnight. I walked home then told my mother about our planned outing. She said she'd pack up some sandwiches for us and would have dinner ready when we got back.

Cliveden seemed to be near both Burnham and Taplow, small villages not far from Maidenhead, so I plumped for Taplow for no other reason than it sounded more attractive. We made an early start on the Saturday and set off for Waterloo armed with our sandwiches. It was a dry, but chilly, autumn day so we both wore hats and coats. At Waterloo we caught the tube across town and arrived at Paddington with plenty of time to spare to catch our train to Windsor where we would change for the last leg of our journey to Taplow.

We used the spare time to have a quick coffee in the station buffet which was full of people and smoke, even though it was a Saturday. We chatted happily. For us it was a bit of an adventure and we planned the day ahead.

We decided not to go to Cliveden that day but spend the time wandering around Taplow, perhaps calling in at a café or pub to chat with the locals. We got on the train to Windsor and, rather like schoolchildren on an excursion, ate our sandwiches during the forty five minute journey. At Windsor we changed platforms and waited for the Reading train which would drop us off at Taplow.

The train was on time and, like the Paddington train, was pulled by a steam locomotive. We were more used to the electric trains that ran in and out of Waterloo.

It was fifteen minutes to Taplow and we arrived just after noon. The ticket collector directed us to the village which turned out to be further from the station than I thought. By now the sun was shining and the temperature had risen, so the short walk into Taplow was pretty good. We strolled hand in hand and twenty minutes later spotted a church spire then, just around the corner, a village green. There was a general store but it was closed because it was Saturday. There were a few houses dotted around the edge of the green. After London, and even our town, it seemed incredibly quiet. There wasn't a car in sight.

We had a good look round which didn't take long. The village green was on a bit of a slope, so no chance of playing Cricket. We looked at the church, St Nicholas, read the inscriptions on the War Memorial then spotted a pub, so we headed there.

The pub was called The Oak and Saw. We walked into the bar. There were a few Saturday lunchtime drinkers, a group of four men sitting at one table and a middle aged couple at another. There was an alcove just to the right of the bar where the occasional thudding noise suggested a game of darts was taking place. A large cheerful looking red faced man stood behind the bar.

"Good afternoon. What can I get you?" he asked.

"A pint of bitter and a half of shandy please."

I'd heard that if two strangers walked into a bar in the north of England or Scotland, all conversation would stop and if there was a piano it would instantly fall silent, like in a cowboy film. Here it was different. Everyone carried on as if we weren't there but it didn't stop the barman, or perhaps he was the landlord, from asking

"New round here are you?"

"No, we're not from round here," I said. "My girlfriend and I fancied a day in the country."

"From London are you?"

"Yes, well, south-west London actually but I work in town."

"We ain't got much round here but something we've got which you haven't is clean air and daylight. I've 'eard its night all day long in London."

I laughed. "It isn't as bad as that but there's pretty awful fog at times."

"That's called smog ain't it?" he asked.

"That's right."

I collected the drinks, thanked him and paid for them.

Jane was at a table next to an elderly lady I hadn't noticed when we arrived. You wouldn't find a woman drinking alone in a London pub but here in the country, I supposed, it was different.

Just as we were taking our first sips, the old dear piped up.

"From London are you?"

"That's right. South-west side," I replied.

"I 'aven't been in London since before the war. What's it like?"

"You wouldn't recognise it," said Jane. "It's busy all the time."

"It was when I was last there. The streets were crammed with buses and carriages, most of 'em pulled by 'orses. I nearly got killed crossing the road."

"There's still some horses about but now it's mostly motor cars, motor buses, trams and trolley buses. Did you use the tube?" I asked.

"What's the tube?"

"The underground railway."

"Not likely. You wouldn't catch me going down holes in the ground."

"Do you live in Taplow?" asked Jane.

"No, I'm from the big 'ouse just up the road, Cliveden."

Both of us could feel a slight flutter of excitement but neither of us showed it and we carried on sipping our beer slowly. Her glass was empty, so I asked her if she wanted another.

"That's very kind of you young man. I'll 'ave a port and lemon if you don't mind."

While I was fetching her drink I heard Jane ask,

"I've heard of Cliveden, big country house isn't it? What took you there?"

As I was returning I heard her telling Jane she'd been born there. Her mother was a cook and her father a footman.

I put the drink in front of her.

"Thank you ducky. Cheers. I was just telling your young lady I was born at Cliveden. When I grew up they gave me a job in the kitchens and I've been there ever since."

"Are you married?" asked Jane.

"Never met anyone who took me fancy. Still I'm 'appy enough. It's a grand place and I get treated OK. I like to come to the village of a Saturday. It's me only vice."

So far the old dear, whom I reckoned was in her sixties, had told us plenty about herself but asked nothing about us. That's the way we wanted to keep it so Jane continued

"Who owns that place?"

"The Astors, Americans you know. They bought it not long after I started working there."

"What are they like?"

"Yer don't see much of 'is lordship. 'Er ladyship runs the place. She wears the trousers. Mind you she's not often there during the week. She's an MP you know. They've got another smart place in London. Even so, there's plenty to do during the week. I'm lucky to 'ave some time orf of a Saturday cos the weekends are very busy."

"Oh?" queried Jane.

"Yes all sorts of important visitors; kings and queens, dukes and duchesses, businessmen, MPs, cabinet ministers, the lot."

"Any of them there now?" Jane asked.

"She's there but not many visitors. She said next weekend's gonna be very busy; all sorts of important people turning up."

"You must have seen some top people in your time there," I said.

"We've 'ad the Foreign Secretary, Anthony Eden, Lord 'alifax, that bloke that writes *The Times*, 'er usband owns it, *The Times* I mean, then there's

Lord Lothian. Don't like 'im, 'e's a cold fish. Mr Churchill used to come before the war but 'e 'asn't been for years. She 'ates 'im, you know."

"Who hates him?" I asked

"'Er ladyship. Mind you it's an enormous place. Room for forty guests. 'Ere I'd better be orf. I'll be late back. If I stay nattering to you any longer I'll be giving away state secrets."

We both laughed, I hoped convincingly.

"You ought to take a look at the place. It's worth seeing. It's only an 'alf hour walk up the road, less you got a car."

"No we came on the train and we're due back soon", said Jane. "Perhaps next week."

"Well if yer do, pop in 'ere first. I 'ave enjoyed chattin to yer. Thanks for the drink."

"Pleasure. How are you getting back to Cliveden?"

"On me bike. See yer."

We'd never asked her name but the barman told us it was Milly. We stayed a bit longer, finished our drinks and strolled arm in arm back to the station to catch the train back to Windsor. We had plenty of time before our connection was due so we had a tea basket each in the refreshment room: cup of tea, bread and butter, an orange and a bun.

It wasn't long after four when we reached Paddington so we crossed London again to Waterloo and just before six entered my house where, as my mother had promised, dinner was waiting for us.

CHAPTER SIXTEEN

Conspirators

"The treachery of the intellectuals"
JULIA BENDA

"Odd name for a pub that."

"What?" I asked.

"The Oak and Saw."

"Funny you should say that. I thought the same so I asked the barman about it while you were in the ladies."

"What did he say?"

"Oh, nothing much, but he did think it was the only pub in England with that name. There were a lot of trees round Taplow so they've probably been sawing down oak trees for centuries," I suggested.

Jane and I were doing what thousands of English middle class couples were doing that Sunday afternoon, wandering hand in hand through the park after Sunday lunch. There were babies being pushed in prams, dogs on leads, children playing with balls and old couples sitting on benches, watching what was going on around them. It was a scene being repeated in parks all over the country, with everyone dressed in their Sunday best uniforms. But not everywhere, I thought, and maybe not for everyone.

We had an excellent Sunday lunch: roast beef and Yorkshire pudding. It was always that or roast lamb and mint sauce, or roast pork and apple sauce. Jane's parents had asked us about our outing and we told them about the train journey, the Oak and Saw, Milly and tea on Windsor Station on the way back but nothing, of course, about our reasons for going there.

"So how do you think it went?" Jane asked

"I think we achieved everything we'd hoped for. We showed our faces, found out a bit of useful information without giving the game away, ate our sandwiches, the beer was good and we had a nice tea on the way home. And we enjoyed ourselves, don't you think?"

"Course we did but it'll be a bit different next weekend. Two weekends on the trot. Eyebrows will be raised when they see us again."

"That's the whole point," I reminded her. "To raise a bit of suspicion to deflect attention away from Richard and his source."

It was almost dark by the time we got back to Jane's house for the traditional end to the English Sunday: sandwiches, jam tarts, sponge cake and lashings of tea. We listened to the radio with Jane's parents. Sunday was never a great night's listening. It was mostly religious broadcasts, *The Week's Good Cause*, and classical music. Nevertheless it was fairly relaxing, so we chatted quietly and dozed. I left, and found myself at home by nine.

At the office the next day I got the chance to give Ben an account of my visit to Taplow. He didn't exactly leap to his feet with excitement but listened to what I had to say before responding.

"Well done, Prof. Off to a good start but there's no evidence that there's anything suspicious going on; just a bunch of toffs having weekend get togethers that's all. What's funny about that?"

"Nothing, but it's useful to know who goes there."

"Agreed," replied Ben, "and if we get anything from your pal at least your Saturday jaunts will divert attention away from him to your, er, Milly was it?"

"Yeah. Milly couldn't stop talking."

"And you're off again next weekend?"

"Think so."

"Do you reckon you'll get anything else out of Milly?"

"I'm sure of it. Couple of port and lemons and she's anyone's."

Ben laughed. "You know what pisses me off. Those bloody aristocrats think anyone working for them is either deaf or stupid or both. They don't pay a scrap of attention to what they say in front of the servants. They believe the working class are too thick to understand what's going on in what they call the real world. Still, handy for us. Right, off you go to the Old Bailey and see how those bent coppers on trial are getting on."

"Who says they're bent?"

"The jury will. Mark my words."

For once Ben was wrong and not guilty verdicts were returned late on Thursday. I wrote the trial up on Friday morning, and then thought about the weekend.

We made an earlier start on that second Saturday and luckily caught a through train from Paddington, so we were in Taplow just after opening time at the Oak and Saw. The bar was empty when we arrived but as soon as we sat down with our beers Milly walked in

"'Allo dearies. Back again?"

Jane said, "We enjoyed ourselves so much last Saturday we just had to come again and anyway we thought we'd wander up and have a look at Cliveden later."

"It's not a bad day for it," Milly replied, "but you won't get near the 'ouse. Still you can see it from a distance and the grounds are lovely."

I bought Milly a port and lemon and after one sip she was off.

"There's quite a gathering there this weekend. Apart from 'is lordship and 'er ladyship, the Foreign Secretary's there."

"Eden?" I asked.

"Yes 'e's an 'andsome young man, plays a lot of tennis you know. That foreign sounding gentleman 'oo works for the government used to play with him all the time but 'e doesn't come no more."

Vansittart, I thought. Not surprised he's not at Cliveden but what was Eden doing there? He was hardly likely to be a friend of the Astors.

Milly carried on.

"Funny thing, just after breakfast a great big black car flying them 'orrible German flags—you know, swastikas—turned up. I didn't like the look of the man 'oo jumped out the back seat. Slimy looking if you ask me."

I guessed that would be Ribbentrop. Things were getting very interesting.

"Not long after ten there was a phone call for Mr 'Enderson."

Britain's ambassador in Berlin, Sir Neville Henderson. Something was definitely up.

"Johnny announced, 'Call from Berlin for Sir Neville', 'e didn't say 'oo it was."

"Who's Johnny, Milly?" Jane asked.

"One of the footmen."

"How do you know all this?" asked Jane.

"I keep me eyes and ears open and, what I don't see or 'ear, someone else always does, like Johnny with that phone call."

I bought Milly a second port and lemon. I could hardly ask for a receipt. I just hoped Ben would believe me when I gave him my expenses.

"Just before I left to come down 'ere Johnny told me about the row."

"Row?" Jane asked.

"Yes they were all shut in the library when Johnny 'eard shouting. 'E couldn't exactly 'ear what was goin' on but 'e did 'ear the Foreign Secretary shout 'no' a few times."

I risked a question.

"Who's there altogether Milly?"

"Well apart from 'er ladyship and 'is lordship there was the usual crowd; Lord Lothian, Lord 'Alifax, Mister 'Enderson, though he 'adn't been there much before, Mister Eden and that bloke from *The Times*."

"Geoffrey Dawson?" I asked.

"That's 'im and another Lord, Cadogan I think 'is name is. That 'orrible German had gone by then."

"You must be good at remembering all those names and faces," Jane said.

"We always know 'oo's coming. There's lists. Lists for bedrooms and lists for meals. There ain't much that goes on upstairs that we don't know about downstairs," said Milly, tapping her nose with her finger.

We both laughed and Milly joined in. I glanced at Jane and we got up to go. No point in pushing our luck.

"Nice to see you again Milly," I said. "We have to go now. We're going to stroll up to Cliveden."

"Right-oh dearies. I'll probably pass you on me bike."

It took us about half an hour to reach Cliveden. The road was pretty quiet, just a couple of pairs of nineteenth century cottages on its edge. It was mostly uphill so we were a bit tired when we reached the gates. Milly was right. There wasn't much to see. The grounds were vast and beautifully kept and, in the distance, was this huge rectangular building in what appeared, from where we stood, to be white stone. I could just make out a number of large black cars parked in front of the house but I would have needed binoculars to see if any of them were flying swastikas. Besides, Milly had told us that Ribbentrop had already left.

We could just make out an impressive fountain in front of the house with an ornamental figure leaning over it. In the woods we spotted some kind of lodge. That was it really. We walked back to Taplow, waving to Milly on the way as she was panting up the hill on her bike, caught the train back to Windsor, had tea in the refreshment room (cake this week instead of a bun) and made our way home via Paddington and Waterloo. It had been an eventful and, we thought, useful, day and we were pretty pleased with ourselves.

After the weekend I again told Ben about our latest trip to Taplow and Cliveden. He listened attentively, nodding a few times.

"Good stuff Prof, but there's no story there, not yet anyway."

"Why not?"

"What's odd about the Foreign Secretary and another cabinet minister getting together with our ambassador in Berlin and the German ambassador?"

"Looks a bit sneaky to me. Why couldn't they do it during the week in Whitehall?"

"Just because it's the weekend, it doesn't mean the government stops running the country. I bet Chamberlain's at Chequers now dealing with matters of state, not fishing."

"But what about the Astors and Dawson? What do they have to do with all this?"

"Probably nothing," Ben replied. "The Astors were the hosts and Dawson edits the paper Astor owns. He's just a friend."

"But we know they were all in this meeting together and whatever was said Eden didn't like."

"Look Prof, I smell a rat just like you do but until you can find some hard evidence there's nothing we can print. So it's back to the grindstone for the time being me lad. Here's something you might like. The film guy's off sick so how would you like to cover for him tomorrow night?"

"Fine. What is it?"

"There's a new picture palace opening in Leicester Square on the site of the old Alhambra. It's another Odeon. There's some kind of do on, so here's a couple of tickets. Take your girlfriend."

"Great. What's the film?"

"Oh, um, *The Prisoner of Zenda* I think. Just get out your suit, go along, watch the film and write up the occasion and the movie next day, OK?"

"Smashing. Thanks."

I telephoned Jane and we arranged to meet at Lyons in the Strand before the film. She was pretty excited. The event itself was star-studded with well-known faces everywhere. I caught sight of the stunningly beautiful leading lady Madeleine Carroll wearing a silk evening dress that I could never hope to afford to buy Jane. Her blonde hair, for which she was famous, looked wonderful. Jane was much more interested in the hero, Ronald Coleman. He was handsome with a pencil thin moustache and a twinkle in his eye. *The Prisoner of Zenda* was great. It was a superb adventure story with an implausible plot but nobody cared. This was truly movie magic. I'd read the book when I was a boy but hadn't caught the silent film fifteen years before. The only slight disappointment in the casting was Douglas Fairbanks Junior as Rupert of Hentzau, who was not quite villainous enough for my liking. I'd have preferred Basil Rathbone. Still, it didn't spoil our enjoyment and we had a great night.

I wrote it all up the next day and got the thumbs up from Ben who passed it to the entertainments desk. Then I turned my mind back to what I was coming to call, in my own mind, the Cliveden conspiracy. I hoped something would soon turn up to justify my suspicions.

More evidence did turn up and sooner than I thought. By the usual roundabout route via my father, I got a message from Richard that he had something for me.

We met on the Embankment, not far from Temple Station. I got there first then saw Richard striding towards me looking excited. It was the last Friday in October and was getting colder by the day, so we were both wearing hats and coats. We shook hands and Richard began.

"Harry got word to me that there was a big pow-wow at Cliveden last weekend."

"I know. I was there."

"You were there?" he said incredulously. "What? At the meeting?"

"No. Near Cliveden."

I told Richard how Jane and I had sat in the Oak and Saw, letting Milly spill the beans, and about our stroll up to Cliveden.

"So you know who was there but not what was said."

"That's right."

"Well the telephone call your cook mentioned was from Goering. As far as we can make out, the fat Nazi has been trying to get Henderson to persuade Halifax to visit Germany to attend an international hunting exhibition."

"Why Halifax?"

"Didn't you know, Roger?" Richard said with more than a hint of sarcasm. "He's a very important person in England. He's Master of the Hounds. Just the man to visit a big hunting jamboree."

"What's Goering got to do with it?"

"He's a hunting, shooting, fishing type himself, enjoys killing things, so it's only natural that the invitation to Halifax should come from him. So far so good. Nothing odd there but then we come to the crux of the matter. While he's in Germany Goering's going to arrange for Halifax to visit Hitler and other Nazi big wigs for talks on the, er, international situation."

"But that's not right, Eden's the Foreign Secretary. He should be talking to the Germans."

"Of course, but Hitler doesn't like Eden I'm told, nor for that matter does Mussolini, hates him I believe. Eden doesn't care much for them either. Halifax would be the better bet for Hitler; much more compliant."

"That's obviously why Eden was so upset at Cliveden last weekend," I said.

"Quite. Anyway I hope you'll agree with me that your readers should know in advance that a cabinet member is setting off for unofficial talks with Hitler."

"Course I do. When's all this going to happen?"

"Couple of weeks I think. Halifax hasn't actually said he's going yet."

"And what's on the agenda for these talks?"

"No idea yet, but either before, during or after, if these talks happen Harry will find out."

"Thanks Richard. I'll knock something up and run it past my boss. See what he thinks."

"OK Roger. Try to persuade him that this is really important. If he won't print it, someone else will."

To say I was disturbed by Richard's revelations was an understatement. That my government was sending out feelers to that tyrant Hitler in the guise of a visit to a hunting exhibition filled me with dread. My government in secret talks with the man who was persecuting the Jews and had approved the murder of innocent women and children in Spain was something everyone should know about.

I went back to the office and put together what I thought was my best piece yet. I finished it the following morning and gave it to Ben. The next day he gave it back to me covered in blue pencil marks.

"Too much emotion in there Prof. Give it a bit of a rewrite and I'll see what we can do."

I did what Ben asked and he took it up to the Editor. I heard nothing for three days.

"This is really hot stuff, Prof. I like it, and so does the boss, but it's not going to be printed."

"Why on earth not?" I asked, with barely concealed disappointment.

"Owners have spiked it. Apparently Number Ten didn't like a piece recently in our daily and they're scared of upsetting the government. Besides we don't actually know yet whether or not Halifax is going to Germany."

"But surely we're not here to placate the government are we?"

"No, we're not," Ben replied. "But the PM's Press Office could play nasty with us and keep us out of important briefings and that's what's frightening the owners. We wouldn't be able to print up-to-date news and our circulation might drop, then advertisers might jump ship and so on. Anyway that's it. Accept it and move on. Don't give in. We'll beat the bastards eventually."

I got in touch with Richard and told him what had happened when we met in my father's office. I felt I'd let him down.

"No you haven't," said Richard. "You just write the news not publish it. There'll be other chances, I promise you, but I must tell Harry so he can use another contact."

Three days later Halifax's visit to Germany was the lead story in *The Evening Standard*.

CHAPTER SEVENTEEN

Scooped

"He delivered them into the hands of spoilers"
JUDGES 2.14

Between my trip to the cinema and *The Evening Standard* scoop there were all sorts of rumours flying about: Germany wanted her colonies back, Hitler was turning his attention to Austria and Mussolini supported the German demand for colonies. This campaign was being orchestrated in the Nazi press and Eden stood up in the House of Commons and told the Duce to mind his own business—not in those words, but his intention was clear and he received a standing ovation.

Then came the *Standard* story which we, along with every other paper, ran the following day. These were followed by denials, presumably originating from Number Ten, before Simon, the Chancellor of the Exchequer, confirmed in the House that Halifax was indeed going to Germany but that the visit was entirely unofficial although he may possibly meet senior Nazi politicians.

That same evening, November 12th, a shocking leader appeared in the *Standard*. It welcomed the talks, said that Germany's foreign policy was her own business, unless it directly affected us, and we should be focusing our energies on strengthening the Empire and let the Germans and Italians sort out Central Europe. It even suggested that we should recognise Italy's conquest of Abyssinia and praised Chamberlain for bringing a new realism and business-like attitude to our foreign policy.

As *The Standard* was owned by Lord Beaverbrook, this came as no surprise.

I decided that, over the weekend, I had to see Richard, so on Saturday morning I sent my brother round with a note, assuming he wasn't under suspicion and therefore wouldn't be followed. Richard replied suggesting a Sunday morning stroll in the park might be a good idea, so we met at eleven.

Richard had been closely following events both in the press and through Harry. He was as angry as I was.

"These idiots are just playing into Hitler's hands," he began. "He gets his papers to make all the right noises then sits back while Chamberlain and his cronies make offers to quieten him down."

"What kind of offers?" I asked.

"Hitler's made a song and dance about Germany's lost colonies but he's no more interested in colonies than he is in conquering the moon—well, not yet anyway."

"So why's he making such a stink about colonies?"

"To frighten Chamberlain. He knows that half of the cabinet and most of the public think the Empire is the most important institution on the planet. So Chamberlain tells the Fuhrer, through Halifax, that he can have a free hand in Central Europe if he backs down from asking for colonies. That's the gist of what Halifax is going to tell Hitler next week."

"I bet that'll put the wind up the Austrians," I said.

"And the Czechs and the Poles and anybody else who stands in that lunatic's way. They're playing into his hands."

"Where did all this come from?"

"The German Embassy, of course. Ribbentrop's dancing with joy. Makes up for his failure to get us to join Hitler's anti-Russian club. That's obviously what they were talking about at Cliveden last month."

"But Eden was there. He's not part of this surely?"

"Harry reckons that Halifax and Henderson duped Eden, got the Astors to invite him along for a game of tennis then started planning foreign policy. When he bellyached about it in the cabinet later, Halifax would say 'but you were there'. Guilty by association."

"But surely the PM wouldn't tolerate foreign policy being decided during a weekend tennis party?"

"I doubt he likes it but, if it suits his purpose, he'll somehow swallow his distaste. Anyhow, think you can get this printed tomorrow?"

"I hope so. I'll certainly try. I'll type it up this afternoon so I can get it on my boss's desk first thing in the morning. Mind you this whole business is leaking like a sieve so I doubt we'll get an exclusive."

"That doesn't matter. The more papers it's in the better. Anyhow here's something else for you, but not from the usual source."

Richard told me that he'd met an old friend of his, a Roman Catholic priest, who'd just come back from Germany. Hitler, it seemed, was not just anti-Jewish but anti-Christian as well and was conducting a systematic campaign to destroy the churches in Germany. Priests were being accused of sexual abuse, being thrown out of hospitals and religious teaching in schools was under severe threat.

He then recounted to me a story of a young woman at a dance somewhere in Southern Germany who was told by a soldier to take off the crucifix she was wearing round her neck. When she refused, the soldier tore it off. Her husband intervened and the soldier shot him dead on the spot. Naturally the soldier got off scot free.

I was pretty shocked but I was getting less and less surprised by reports of this kind of barbaric behaviour. Richard told me the priest's name and I promised to pass the story to Ben the next day. I thanked him then went home. I spent the afternoon typing up the stories, and put them on Ben's desk first thing on Monday morning.

Later that day Ben told me that my piece on the Halifax 'mission' was going ahead but the article about the attacks on the German churches had been passed to our sister daily paper. The Editor felt that it was sufficiently important to get national, rather than just London, coverage. What he said made sense and I was content with his decision.

The Halifax trip to Germany proved to be the turning point in press focus on foreign policy. The Spanish Civil War had been the main topic of interest for almost eighteen months. It had become a matter of which foreign ally would prevail and it looked like the support that Franco was getting from the Germans and Italians would, in the end, prove decisive. The war was so bloody in terms of lives lost that most accepted the winners would be so exhausted they would play no part in any forthcoming war, if there was to be one. Having another Fascist dictatorship in Western Europe no longer seemed threatening. The war would limp on to its inevitable, tragic conclusion.

The German and, to a lesser extent, the Italian, problems now became the chief causes of concern. The press was split on the best way to deal with them. The majority of newspapers supported Chamberlain's efforts to appease the dictators but a significant minority called for urgent rearmament and preparation for war. I wasn't sure where I stood with all this. Any attempt to avoid bloodshed had to be applauded but, on the other hand, the deterrent of us having a strong defence could be just as effective.

German soldiers marching with Franco in Spain and Nazi bombers killing innocent citizens, including women and children, began to harden my views about the threat that the dictators were posing to peace-loving nations like our own. I felt I had a duty, as a journalist, to tell the readers about my concerns and suggest to them the best way of avoiding war through collective security. The last thing our government, and the French, should do was to back off and let Hitler and Mussolini have their own way.

Halifax set off for Germany and was back at the beginning of the following week. Chamberlain refused to give details of the talks but admitted they were useful. He scoffed at speculation in some sections of the press that a deal had been done over colonies such that Hitler would stop bleating about them and in return we would let him have a free hand in Eastern Europe.

I suppose the PM hoped it would rest there, but he was wrong. Ben was keen that I keep in touch with the government's foreign policy so off I went to the House to have lunch with Philip Noel Baker. I asked Baker what the MPs thought about Chamberlain's statement on the Halifax visit.

"Most on the government side are toeing the party line," he told me, "though there are some exceptions; Churchill, Duff Cooper and Eden."

"Eden?" I asked.

"Yes. You already know that he wasn't keen on Halifax going to Germany in the first place and, from what I hear, he said so in cabinet. He wasn't without support either. In fact even the PM wasn't sure he wanted Halifax to go but he was finally persuaded by Kingsley Wood."

"How did he manage that?"

"Told Chamberlain that putting out peace feelers to Germany would help him win votes if there's a General Election next year. Most people still want peace. Don't forget Chamberlain wasn't elected by the country. Baldwin was, in 1935. If the PM could win an election it would be a real boost for his appeasement drive. He'd claim to have the country behind him, which he can't do now."

"So how's the cabinet split?"

"Halifax, Hoare, Simon and Wood on the PM's side, with Eden and his friends on the other."

"How's Eden taking all this?"

"Badly, I'm told. First you get the PM involving himself in foreign affairs then he finds himself pushed into a corner while Halifax goes off and chats with Hitler. And of course Eden thinks we should be trying to detach Italy from Germany and he's got Van on his side on that one."

"What about your side?"

"Tricky. They all agree that Hitler is a barbarian and we should have nothing to do with him but as for going to war, there's the problem. A year ago we were championing the peace lobby. You know my views on war Roger but even I'm beginning to think that we're not going to stop Hitler with offers of peace and the odd concession. But that's not a vote winner. Most of the country supports the PM not because they've any love for Hitler, but they're terrified of another war which, with the growth of air power, will be ten times worse than twenty years ago. The womenfolk believe that there will be many more husbands and sons not returning from a new war than there were in 1918."

"I can see your difficulty. How are you going to tackle it?"

"Our leader, Clem Attlee, has got guts and he'll say what he thinks is right, even if it does cost us votes. You'll hear plenty from him while this business lasts."

My piece on the cabinet split appeared in Friday's paper but I was upstaged by *Reynold's News* a couple of days later when they introduced the world to 'The Cliveden Set'.

They identified Cliveden as the hotbed of pro-Germanism in Britain, listed the conspirators and even added a further leak from the Halifax-Hitler talks: Hitler had asked us to recognise Franco as the legitimate leader in Spain.

Ben told me the next day that he had read the piece and liked it. He even thought they might get away with it. Apparently Goebbels didn't read *Reynold's News* so wouldn't be complaining to Henderson about it.

Things quietened down for a while. I spent a lot more time with Jane. We saw Paul Muni in *The Life of Emile Zola* (not bad) and Will Hay in *Oh Mr Porter* (very funny). The days closed in. Sunday afternoon walks became shorter and it seemed pointless returning to Taplow.

We talked about work and the relative success we were enjoying. Often we chatted about the films we'd seen and enjoyed, but the clouds of war brooded heavily over us both. Although we were growing closer by the day, neither of us seemed ready to make any kind of commitment to one another because of the uncertainty of the political situation.

The prospect of war terrified us both. Jane was a political activist of sorts and had taken part in a peace march. I was four square behind standing up to the dictators but felt that the best way to do this was to present a united front with our allies to Hitler and Mussolini and warn him to back off or else. Jane and I agreed on this. But what would happen if Hitler didn't back off?

Attlee's promised attack on the government's foreign policy came just before Christmas in the Commons. He reminded the House of the threat to world peace in Europe and the Far East, called for an end to Non-Intervention in

Spain, re- emphasised his support for the Spanish government and said that making a few concessions to Hitler wouldn't remove the war atmosphere. He strongly objected to our colonies being used as bargaining tools and called for collective security through strength of arms and alliances to counter the threat of Fascism.

I paid close attention to what was going on. I glanced down the chamber and saw a collection of mostly men, dressed in almost uniformly dark suits. True, there was a tiny smattering of women but they played no part in the proceedings. Some of the front benchers sat back in their seats and rested their feet on the tables in front of them. Phillip had tipped me off about Attlee's speech so I made sure I was there to hear it and Chamberlain's reply that followed. The government benches were packed and the members, slouching back in their seats, let out periodic grunts of approval.

Chamberlain responded by calling for press restraint. Despite looking old and frail, he still appeared very determined. He continued by saying that he would have no part in setting up a group of powers to oppose Germany and reminded the House that "different countries had different methods of managing their own affairs." Defending non-intervention, he claiming that it had prevented the conflict spreading beyond Spain's borders.

The opposition, small but vociferous, made occasional groans of disapproval but Chamberlain ignored these and went on to say that the last six months had seen a lessening of tension in Europe by keeping the Spanish Civil War inside Spain and that the efforts of his government had done much to contribute to this reduction in tension.

The London fog was closing in and I felt fairly miserable as I walked back to the office. Chamberlain struck me as vain with great self-belief in his mission to ensure world peace, whereas Attlee seemed open and honest. But who would provide this collective security? France? Of course. But what about Russia and the United States?

"How was it, Prof?" Ben asked as I walked back into the office.

I told him of my views on Chamberlain and Attlee and the call for collective security, refused by Chamberlain. I said that the Prime Minister's statement on press restraint sounded like a threat to the freedom of the press. In some ways it was this that had most disturbed me. The cut and thrust of political strife across the House was what I'd expected, but to hear our Prime Minster asking us not to tell the truth or express our opinions about what was going on in Europe was a step too far. "What next?" I asked Ben. "Full press censorship?"

Ben shrugged his shoulders.

"You're right, Prof. I don't like the smell of this at all. Anyway, go on then write it up. We'll run it tomorrow evening."

My piece appeared on Christmas Eve. I was very proud of it and so were Jane and my parents. We had a wonderful Christmas. My mother was first up on Christmas Day to prepare lunch and then she took a break while we opened our presents which comprised clothes and books, apart from my brother who excitedly opened a huge pile of additions to his Meccano set. After a long lunch, we all dozed through the King's Speech while John disappeared to complete his model of the Forth Rail Bridge with Meccano. The next day the four of us went for a walk before a cold turkey lunch and, after we'd spent the early part of the afternoon taking another nap, Jane joined us for Boxing Day tea, followed by an evening of radio and cards.

I was back at work on the Tuesday after Christmas, feeling pretty pleased with myself. True I had misgivings about the government's foreign policy but my career was on the up. The smog was awful but didn't dampen my spirits at all.

On my way home through the murk, my arm was seized and I was dragged into an unlit doorway near Waterloo Bridge.

CHAPTER EIGHTEEN

Battered and Bruised

"This is a London particular . . . a fog, Miss"
CHARLES DICKENS

"Now then Mr Martin. You've been a naughty boy again."

I peered through the gloom. I recognized the voice so it came as no surprise to see moustache-face staring at me below his hat. Next to him was somebody I hadn't seen before; a short thickset man, bare headed and wearing a belted fawn-coloured raincoat. I remained silent.

"Come on sir, you've been upsetting Mr Chamberlain again, making all those nasty suggestions in your grubby little newspaper."

He spoke quietly, his lips hardly moving, and stared straight into my eyes. My heart was racing but I managed to ask.

"What are you talking about?"

"You know what I'm talking about. Here's our Prime Minister trying to make friends with Adolf so we won't have to go to war again and there's you and your mates telling people the krauts are up to no good and what's more printing a whole pack of lies."

"How do you know they're lies?" I gasped.

He ignored my question and asked instead.

"Where did you get all that rubbish from? Somebody's been telling you something or else you'd have nothing to print."

"I've no idea what you're talking about."

I was about thirty yards away from the throng making its way home in the smog. There was the usual rush hour traffic feeling its way through the blackness and even though it was virtually at a standstill, the noise was deafening. There was no point in shouting out, nobody would hear me and, even if they did, I doubt they'd come to my rescue. Nor was there any mileage in making a run for it. Moustache-face's sidekick was blocking my escape route.

He was getting annoyed with me. "Come on sir, do I have to spell it out for you? You've been writing stuff about confidential meetings. We could make things really unpleasant for you," he said, his voice dripping with menace and never once taking his eyes from me.

"So they weren't lies after all."

"Very clever, but it doesn't alter the fact that you've been having a go at the government and telling your pathetic bunch of readers about stuff that's none of their business. Now where did you get your information from?"

"The same place that all the other papers that printed those stories got it from. Why don't you ask them?"

"Oh we will sir, don't you worry, but now I'm asking you."

"A journalist never reveals his source and especially not to a couple of men who accost him in the London smog."

"I can see I'm wasting my time, I'm gonna have to get my pal here to have a word with you."

"I've nothing to say to him either," I said.

"You haven't quite caught my drift. My pal here doesn't say much. He's a man of few words. More a man of action you might say. Now where did you get all that shit about Lord Halifax from?"

Would they really attack me? I'd no idea, but I was pretty frightened by now. I could give them Milly but they'd soon find out she knew nothing. Under duress, she might just remember our little chats in the Oak and Saw but it wouldn't be long before they realized she wasn't the source. Besides they might arrange for her to have the sack and I didn't want that on my conscience. On the other hand, there was no way I was going to give them Richard or Harry, so I decided to tough it out.

"I've nothing to say."

"Very well sir, my pal here is gonna have to teach you a lesson then perhaps you'll learn to keep your nose out of things that don't concern you."

This obvious threat spurred me into action. As the other man started to move towards me, I dropped my head and charged at him, hitting him just below his chest. He let out a cry of surprise and fell backwards against the wall.

"Get the bastard!" moustache-face shouted but, before either of them could react, I was off, sprinting down Stamford Street, away from the station. I knew I could outrun moustache face but wasn't sure about the other guy. There was still plenty of traffic about, most of it crawling in the fog or stationary. Then, as I dodged in and out of the cars, I had a bit of luck. I heard a shout, glanced round, and saw the other guy sprawled on the pavement. I didn't wait to find out what happened to him but carried on running towards Southwark Street. Near London Bridge Station, I looked round and saw a bus approaching slowly so I leapt on while the bus was still moving. The conductor gave me a funny look and asked me where I was going.

"Elephant and Castle," I said hopefully and he took a ticket from the rack. This was my second piece of luck. I had a vague idea where I was. By the time the bus reached The Elephant, I had got my breath back and recovered some of my composure. I stepped onto the pavement and caught the next bus which was heading to Clapham Junction.

I knew plenty about London's transport system and I walked briskly into Clapham Junction Station and caught the next train home. I said nothing to my parents but ate my tea and listened to the radio for a while then went to bed. Sleep didn't come easily and, as I tossed and turned, I thought to myself that I had got away with it this time but, I wondered, for how long? They knew where I worked and, probably, where I lived. The next confrontation wouldn't be long in coming.

I was pretty much on edge when I went to work the following day. I told Ben what had happened and he was livid. He said he was sure this was all part of Chamberlain's press muzzling campaign and suggested to me that

I didn't write any controversial stuff for a while. I wasn't having that. A fat copper and his thick looking sidekick weren't going to stop me doing my job. Ben smiled at me but warned me to keep my eyes peeled.

For a couple of days I did, looking over my shoulder wherever I went and taking care to avoid dark corners. Then, on my way home on New Year's Eve, they reappeared with reinforcements. There were three of them this time; the same two as before and a tall guy in black jacket and black trousers. It was too dark to make out his features but they didn't waste time with words. Two of them grabbed me and dragged me down the steps towards the South Bank. For a moment a terrifying thought passed through my mind that they were going to throw me in the river but, at the bottom of the steps, they started punching me. They started on my face then kneed me in between my legs. Some crazy instinct persuaded me to fight back and I drove my elbow into the eye of the thug in black clothes. The last thing I remembered was something hard striking me on the back of the head. I must have passed out.

I remember waking up in a large well-lit room full of beds with people lying in them. I vaguely recollect a nurse sitting on my bed telling me I would be all right but that I should get some rest.

The next time I came to I realized how much pain I was in. I could feel my testicles were badly bruised but the worst thing was a shooting headache and awful stinging in my mouth. I opened my eyes and there, sitting alongside the bed, were my mother, my father and Jane. I smiled weakly and croaked a hello to them. My father called to the nurse and told her I was awake.

The nurse arrived and told me I was going to be OK. My bruises would soon disappear. The largest was the size of an egg on the side of my head beside my right ear. I asked about my mouth and she said I had had a couple of stitches on my tongue and on the inside of my cheek, as well as two loose teeth. I'd be fully recovered within a week.

The nurse told me I was in St Thomas Hospital near Waterloo and I had been brought by ambulance after a policeman had found me unconscious down by the river near Waterloo Station. He was coming back in the morning to take a statement from me.

Despite those reassurances my parents and Jane looked very worried. The nurse left, saying they should let me sleep as soon as possible.

"Thanks for coming," I said. "How did you get here?"

"In the car. The roads were clear until we hit the smog," my father replied.

"How on earth did you find me?"

Jane explained: "The hospital telephoned your parents then your mum telephoned me and here we are."

"How did they know who I was and where I lived?"

"Probably from your wallet," Jane said.

"Um. Where are my clothes?"

"I'll look for them," my father said. "Why do you want them?" he added. "You can get them when you're ready to leave."

I was in a pretty bad way physically, but my brain was working overtime.

My father left briefly then came back with my clothes. I asked him to check my pockets. There was no sign of my wallet.

"That tells us why you were attacked," said my mother. "Did they get much?"

"A few pounds that's all. What time is it?"

"It's four in the morning," my mother replied.

"Good God, it's almost twelve hours since I was attacked."

"Look Roger," my father began, "Nurse said you must get some rest. We'll head off home then I'll telephone the hospital in the morning and find out what's happening. If the doctor says you can come home, I'll fetch you straight away."

"Thanks," I said, "there's just one thing. Could you give Ben a ring at the office please and let him know what's happened and say I won't be in the office for a day or so?"

"Of course," he said, then he squeezed my shoulder before my mother and Jane took turns kissing me on the forehead.

The nurse woke me at eight with a cup of tepid tea which was about all that I could manage. I lay in bed for about an hour thinking about my ordeal of the previous day, wondering what damage I'd managed to inflict on the bastard who'd attacked me, hoping I'd broken something and that he was suffering even more than me. I felt pretty sore but, apart from my mouth, no worse than a couple of occasions on the rugby field when I was at school. I thought, with some trepidation, what might have happened to me had I not followed my instincts and fought back. I knew exactly why I had been the victim of the violence but was determined that it wouldn't stop me from doing what I believed to be right.

The doctor arrived and gave me the once over. He told me that I was suffering from concussion but that I must have a hard head because it wasn't too bad. Nonetheless I wasn't to go back to work before I was checked out by my own doctor. I had to return to the hospital in a week or so to have the stitches removed from my mouth and he advised me to have my loose teeth checked out by my dentist. He smiled encouragingly, then left saying he would arrange for my father to come and collect me.

I washed, got dressed and gingerly made my way to the entrance hall and, while I was waiting for my father, Ben turned up. He was wrapped up against the end of year cold. He came towards me, told me to stay seated, and then began.

"Happy New Year. What's the other one look like Prof? Worse than you I hope."

"Dunno, but I doubt he'll be at work today."

Ben laughed. "Well that's something. What did the Doc say?"

I told him about the concussion, the stitches and my teeth and that I didn't think I'd be coming back to work until my own doctor had given me the all clear.

"Take as long as you want and if there's anything me or the paper can do for you, just say so. We look after our own people you know. Have you spoken to the police yet?"

"No. Somebody's supposed to come and take a statement this morning but nobody's shown up yet."

"Tell him everything that's happened and tell him why. Was it those two bastards from that business earlier in the year?"

"The two from before, plus some tall guy in black. They stole my wallet."

"Mmm, well tell the police everything. They probably won't believe you when you tell them what you think the motive was but, stuff it, tell 'em anyway. They'll say the stolen wallet was the reason for the attack."

"Right, I will."

"This appeasement business is really going to be stepped up now. I reckon Chamberlain'll do anything to get his way, not that I think for one moment he gave the orders to attack you."

"Who did then?"

"I'm not sure yet but we're going to do some digging round. I suppose it could have been the Germans; there's a rumour going round that the Gestapo tried to assassinate one of *The Manchester Guardian* lads in Paris a bit ago, but I doubt if they'd try that here. Our secret service is keeping a close watch on our Nazi friends. More likely it emanated from Number 10 indirectly. Anyway I'll see what I can find out and let you know when you get back. 'Allo, looks like your friendly neighbourhood copper. I'll be off and don't forget to let me know if there's anything you want. Take care of yourself Prof. Oh, and read these."

He gave me a small pile of typewritten sheets.

"Thanks Ben."

I stood up and walked over to the policeman, introduced myself. He was PC Rees. I told him about the attack, the threats and what I thought it was all about. He slowly jotted it all down in his notebook. I gave him what I thought was a pretty good description of my assailants.

I asked him how he'd found me. He told me someone had called the local Police Station and told the desk Sergeant that a young journalist from *The Globe* had been beaten up by the river and was still there, lying unconscious. Whoever had rung the station hadn't left a name but the Sergeant said it sounded like a young man. After I'd been found, the policeman had called for an ambulance. At the hospital, he telephoned *The Globe* and I was identified from his description of me.

He told me to call in at the local police station when I went back to work. He took my number so he could phone me at home if he had any further questions. I could tell he didn't believe what I said I thought were the motives behind the attack and it was obvious that this wasn't going to be a major investigation by a team of plainclothes officers.

I felt sure I knew why I'd been attacked, but who was the good Samaritan and how did he know I worked at *The Globe*?

I was turning this over in my mind when my father arrived to take me home.

I spent the next six days recovering from the attack. My bruises diminished, my mouth began to heal and I ate endless rice puddings, tapioca and semolina. I devoured every word in the newspapers, read a couple of Agatha Christie novels and let my mother wait on me hand and foot. If I hadn't, she would have been annoyed.

Jane came round every night after work, Richard and Inge came to see me and soon I was ready to return to Fleet Street. The day before I was due back at work I remembered the sheets Ben had given me. They were copies of a news sheet called *The Week*, typed (not printed) in brown ink. They looked distinctly unpromising. But, in this case, looks proved to be misleading.

CHAPTER NINETEEN

TRUTH

"Political language . . . is designed to make
lies sound truthful and murder respectable."
GEORGE ORWELL

The Week had made a tremendous impression on me and I was looking forward to talking about it with Ben. As I travelled into London that second Monday in January 1938, I thought about my own personal position. Was I in danger and who was posing a threat to me? The policeman at the hospital probably thought I was a bit paranoid. My mother and father no doubt thought I was the victim of a street robbery and maybe Jane thought the same, although she probably had a fair idea of the risks I was taking. But Ben, for certain, knew what was going on. Would I be allowed to continue challenging the government's foreign policy in print? Was it treason to suggest that my own government was closing ranks with a tyrant to try to prevent the spread of Communism? Was Stalin as bad as Hitler? Reports coming out of the Soviet Union certainly suggested that that might be the case.

When I reached the office Ben called me in and said we needed an hour together to 'sort me out' as he put it so we sat down together with a cup of tea and he began.

"First things first Prof, how are you?"

"Physically I'm fine, my mouth's still a bit sore but it's healing up nicely."

"And mentally?"

"I suppose I'm still a bit shaken but I'm eager to carry on where I left off, if that's what you want."

"That's good. Now look, I had a long chat with the Editor about you and we're both very pleased with your first year here and your foreign policy stuff is great. Not only is it good to read, but it fits in with the owners' views of things. On the other hand we're not in the business of getting our staff threatened and beaten up."

"Any thoughts on who's responsible?" I asked.

"It's either the Gestapo or Number 10."

"You're joking. Surely the government doesn't go about organizing the attacking of journalists who don't toe their line?"

Not directly of course, no, but Chamberlain's sidekicks are fully behind the PM in this appeasement nonsense. Some papers have had stuff suppressed and others, especially *The Times*, have been told what to write."

"How many other journalists have been attacked?" I asked.

"None that I'm aware of," Ben replied.

"Why me?"

"You're expendable. A young journalist making his way up the ladder. You're not a public figure like some of them. Not yet anyway."

I understood this well so I didn't feel slighted by Ben's comment.

"Chamberlain's determined to press on with this appeasement stuff and remove the two main obstacles to his crusade: the Foreign Office and the press."

Ben then told me that Vansittart, the top foreign policy adviser to the government had been promoted to another post out of harm's way. Lord Cadogan, who had been present at the October meeting in Cliveden, had taken his place; a man much more supportive of Chamberlain's views. He also reminded me that Sir Eric Phipps, our man in Berlin, had been transferred to Paris and replaced by Neville Henderson, another Clivedenite. Phipps had been warning of the threat of Hitler for years but Henderson was a keen appeaser. He was a regular visitor to Cliveden as well. Ben also told me that he was pretty certain that Ribbentrop had insisted on this.

"So where does Eden stand in all this?"

"Not sure. Hate to ask you this, Prof, but maybe you can get some info on this from your contact. Are you up for it?"

"Of course."

"Then take care for heaven's sake. I doubt if they're on to him yet. That much you learned from your latest visit from them."

"I will, but you still haven't told me who's doing Chamberlain's dirty work for him."

"He's brought in a creepy bloke called Horace Wilson as his chief hatchet man. I've told you about him before. He used to be an important industrial advisor to the government and knows bugger all about foreign policy but he'll get the job done. In other words, get shot of all opposition to the PM."

"But—"

"Hang on, I haven't finished yet. Wilson's fetched on board a guy called Joseph Ball. Another nasty piece of work. Ball used to be a secret service agent. He was the one who placed a source in Odham's Press and he organized phone tapping of Communists and so on. He's even placed moles inside Labour Party HQ. You can bet your bottom dollar he's got a bunch of mates in the Secret Service or Special Branch who'll do his dirty work for him, like beating up ambitious young journalists who say rude things about the government. That's the triumvirate. Chamberlain says he wants something done, Wilson decides what's to be done and Ball sees to it that it is done. It's just a tiny bit like, note I said tiny, what goes on in Germany." Ben was getting angry now.

"Ball's a close friend of Chamberlain's of course. They go fishing together."

"Have you read *TRUTH*?" Ben asked.

"Never heard of it."

"Take a look at this."

Ben handed me a magazine about fifty pages thick. It looked far more professional than *The Week*. Ben sat patiently while I flicked through it. There were reviews of music, films, a racing report, various articles including a short story, a crossword and pages of advertising. It looked rather innocuous and I said so to Ben.

"Don't judge a book by its cover, Prof. Ball's behind this, you can bet on that, even though you'll not find his name on the staff list. Most of the political stuff in it consists of insults to the government's enemies, dressed up with the odd lie, and praise for Chamberlain and his mates. *TRUTH* is an anti-Semitic, pro-German filthy rag. Anybody who opposes appeasement is Jewish, Bolshevik and anti-patriotic or, most likely, all three. It's a sort of aggressive reply to *The Week*. We'll talk about that in a minute."

"So Chamberlain's got no idea what's going on?"

"No, of course not. He must have read *TRUTH* of course. This guy Ball is having a go at *The Yorkshire Post* now. Arthur Mann, the Editor, is no friend of the PM's foreign policy either and regularly says so in his paper, so Ball, who has some official position in the Tory Party, is trying to persuade *The Yorkshire Post*'s owners, who are all landed gentry in the Conservative Party, to sack Mann."

"Could that happen to us?"

"Never, not as long as the present owners are in charge. They hate the Fascists and believe that we should be lining up with like-minded countries like France, America and Russia, to oppose them. We're all for collective security along with a big rearmament programme. That's the only way to stop another war."

"But surely," I protested, "we're already rearming?"

"Chamberlain deserves credit for that at least." Ben replied, "He did start the ball rolling when he was Chancellor of the Exchequer but it's not enough, and it's not being done quickly enough."

"But why's he rearming at all?" I asked.

"A show of force, nothing else; warning the Nazis there's a big strong country on the other side of the English Channel ready to take them on if they try anything. OK, Chamberlain doesn't want war; he's terrified of it, and so are most of the British people. You can't blame him for that."

"No."

"But even with our rearmament we're still weaker than Germany. They've got three years' start on us. The PM seems to think that a few planes and our Navy coupled with one or two concessions will keep Hitler quiet. In any case it'll be air power not sea power that'll be decisive in the next war."

"You seem certain there'll be another war," I said.

"There will, unless we stand up to Hitler now, that's the message from this paper," Ben replied. "By the way did you read those copies of *The Week* I left with you?"

"Yeah."

"And?"

"Well, I was pretty amazed. They seem to have been warning us about the Nazis for years."

We discussed some of the stories I'd read in *The Week*. More than four years ago they published a story about the 'new' Germany's approach to married life, quoting the example of a wife who'd been told to quit her job and get on with home building and child rearing. The couple had, as a consequence, decided to divorce so she could keep her job. Then they carried on living together and were arrested for immoral behaviour.

There were mentions of government threats of suppression, questioning of the editorial independence of *The Times* and, of course, attacks on the Cliveden gatherings. There was even the odd witty contribution such as Churchill's alleged reply when he was asked why the then Prime Minister Stanley Baldwin was delaying the appointment of a defence minister: "Mr Baldwin is seeking a personality less brilliant than his own and this Herculean task has naturally absorbed all his energies."

The Week dealt with serious matters but there was plenty of sarcastic humor and even the odd joke like Hitler's predecessor as German President, Hindenburg, excusing a visit he made to a Nazi prison camp by telling the SS guards that he'd only come to chat with his old electors.

The biggest scoop I read about in *The Week* was a report of a meeting that preceded Halifax's infamous trip to see Hitler the previous November. According to *The Week* Lothian, Henderson, Londonderry and Goering had met in Berlin to plan the agenda for the Halifax visit.

"How the hell does he get away with it?" I asked.

Ben replied, "If any one threatens the news sheet with legal action the Editor, who's called Claud Cockburn by the way, tells them to go ahead. He says he only prints the truth and, if anyone did prove otherwise, he's got no money to pay off any damages. So nobody bothers."

"But where does he get his material from?" I asked.

"He seems to have impeccable sources, especially in Germany. In this country journalists like you and I tip him off. If our papers are threatened with suppression of a piece, or it's based on dodgy evidence, one of the lads tells Cockburn about it, who prints it, and then our papers run the story claiming, of course, it's in the public domain because it's been in *The Week*."

"Very clever."

"If you get some info that for some reason or other we can't print take it to Cockburn but, for heaven's sake, check with me first."

"What? Take it to his office?"

"No, he holds court in the Café Royal."

"By the way Prof," Ben continued, "there is something else. We're not going to give you a by-line for the time being to try to protect you from unwanted attention. You can publish under a pseudonym. Try and come up with a suitable name. Any feature not likely to upset them can go out under your actual name."

"OK. That should confuse them. Is that it?"

"Yup. Carry on with your normal stuff and get in touch with your contact. Rumour is that the next big story coming out of Downing Street will be about Eden. See what you can get about him and take out a subscription for *The Week*. It's only twelve bob a year. Goebbels reads it, so I've heard. Then go and have a chat with Cockburn."

It crossed my mind, on the way home that night that everyone was playing for high stakes. I trusted Ben and everything he said made sense. As far as I could judge Eden was the only figure of influence left in the government to question Chamberlain's policies. Surely he couldn't remain Foreign Secretary, could he? I decided it would be a good idea to get some background on the Foreign Secretary's position. So the next morning I went into the office and had a word with Richard.

I think he'd assumed I'd keep a low profile for a while and wasn't too keen to put me in further danger. I persuaded him otherwise and he promised to get in touch with Harry as soon as he could. I told him I was particularly interested in anything about Eden and he promised to do what he could.

Four days later a note came from Richard asking me to meet him in Leicester Square the following lunch-time. I was back in business.

CHAPTER TWENTY

The Freedom of the Press

"Governments always tend to want not really a free press but a managed or well-conducted one."
LORD RADCLIFFE

Richard was waiting for me when I reached Leicester Square. It was a cold, dull January day and we were both heavily coated and hatted. I wasn't cold, however, having had a roundabout trip from the office to avoid being followed. I'd been in and out of tube stations, on and off buses, and up and down back streets. The normal brisk fifteen minute walk had been replaced by a trip lasting almost an hour.

I apologized for my late arrival and explained the reasons.

"Very wise, Roger. How are you?"

I told him I was OK and determined to carry on where I'd left off after Christmas. My writing under a *nom de plume* amused him but he agreed it was a sensible precaution. I said that I would file controversial stuff under the name Philip Case. We walked together along Coventry Street to Piccadilly Circus then doubled back down the Haymarket and across Trafalgar Square to the Strand, talking as we went.

"Doesn't sound too suspicious," Richard continued, "how did you come up with that?"

"No idea," I replied, "just put together a couple of reasonably common names. Probably safer than adopting some sort of grand sounding title like Truthseeker. They'd soon smell a rat with that. Anyway what's the latest?"

"Not a lot really. My German friends believe that Hitler will make some sort of move this year."

"What makes them think that?"

"Whatever Hitler wants to achieve, and nobody's sure just yet what that is although I can guess, he needs the German people on his side. They're pretty fed up with low wages, control of the press, suppression of decent films, plays and music, uniforms everywhere, people being beaten up in the streets and friends being dragged off to camps and prisons. There's only one way he can keep control and that's through popularity."

"And how's he going to do that?"

"By getting the Treaty of Versailles overturned and grabbing back those bits of Germany lost in 1919. Marching into the Rhineland went down well with a lot of the Germans. Plenty of them still feel humiliated by having their land pinched from them in 1919 but it's almost two years since Hitler's done anything. One thing's certain: he's got a plan and we'll soon find out what it is."

"I'm sure you're right," I said, "but I can't write about speculation. We're more concerned about what Chamberlain's government will do if and when Hitler does make his move. To a lot of us he seems to be mounting a sort of pro-Germany campaign and getting rid of those not on his side."

"There's rumours flying about that he's fallen out with Eden and of course he's just got rid of Vansittart who both hates and mistrusts Germany. There's plenty of people who'd like to see Winston Churchill in the cabinet but, by all accounts, there's not much chance of that happening."

"Interesting that, Harry told me the other day that a fellow called George Steward is a regular visitor to the German Embassy."

"The Number 10 Press Relations Officer?" I asked incredulously. "Who does he meet there? Ribbentrop?"

"No, Ribbentrop thinks himself far too important. Besides Harry reckons he's on his way back to Germany soon, having failed to persuade Chamberlain to join in Hitler's anti-Russia crusade. No, the guy Steward meets is Dr Hesse, the Press Attaché. By all accounts he was in and out of the Embassy all the time during that Halifax business in November. That's about it for now. Sorry there's not more."

"Not at all," I protested, "there's plenty there. I'll talk to my boss and a couple of colleagues about this Steward and Hesse thing and see what they know and I'll go and see my friendly MP and find out what the Westminster rumour mill makes of Eden. Thanks Richard."

Back in the office, I gave Ben a brief account of my meeting with Richard. He seemed concerned, especially about the link between Number 10 and the German Embassy.

After I'd finished he seemed preoccupied for a while then gave me some stories to chase up. Shortly afterwards he left his office and went to see the Editor. Then the pair of them left the office together and I saw neither of them again that day.

Several days passed but not much happened. Rumours of a rift between Chamberlain and Eden persisted but news coming from Whitehall was strangely thin on the ground.

At the end of the week I was called to a meeting upstairs. I was shocked when I walked into the meeting room to find so many there. As well as Ben both Editors were present, ours and *The Daily News*, and senior journalists from both newspapers. I was pretty embarrassed to be in such company but I was put at ease by our Editor, who said, "I've asked Roger to attend the meeting because he's got excellent contacts and has come up with some decent stories for us."

The distinguished gathering murmured their assent. Then the Editor-in-Chief of our daily took over.

"I've called you here because some of us feel there is a serious threat to our editorial independence and that threat appears to come from the government. Roger over there has already been beaten up for writing the truth, even if the police thought it was a straightforward street robbery, and I've every belief that the instructions for the beating originated in Number Ten Downing Street, though not, I hasten to add, from the Prime Minister.

People in the room turned to me in sympathy and several swore under their breath.

"I'm not saying," continued the Editor-in-Chief, "that we're all under threat of physical violence from these people. I'd guess this was an isolated incident designed to teach a young pup a lesson. What appears to be happening now seems far more sinister, no disrespect to you Roger."

He then explained how he had pieced together what he described as a conspiracy to muzzle the press. Chamberlain was hell bent on doing a deal with both Hitler and Mussolini so that he could avoid leading Great Britain into a war with either dictator. Chamberlain felt, evidently, that the Halifax talks with Hitler before Christmas had established some kind of understanding with Germany and he was now anxious to do a similar deal with Italy. The PM had little faith in the League of Nations and was taking on the role of keeping Germany and Italy quiet himself. He reminded us that Chamberlain needed to remain popular or he'd lose the next election. If he followed policies that the press didn't like and they said so, he'd be out on his ear. He had to have sympathetic newspapers so he'd try to control them in order to shape public opinion.

"What an arrogant, vain man he is," a voice intruded.

"Quite," replied the Editor. "Chamberlain sees two obstacles to this; the Foreign Office and the press. He's already dealt with the FO by getting rid of Van now he's after us."

"Excuse me," I interrupted, "but how has he dealt with the Foreign Office? This is all a bit new to me."

"Up to Christmas there were regular news briefings from the FO's press man, Rex Leeper, whose boss was, of course, Vansittart. Our people got a load of useful stuff from Leeper and, occasionally, Van organized the odd leak for us. Now Van's gone, booted upstairs and Cadogan, who's taken over, is keeping a much tighter rein on Leeper. So the supply of news is drying up."

"Our other source of news is the Downing Street Press Briefings from our friend George Steward, whom Roger here has already identified as having friendly, probably too friendly, relationships with the German Press Attaché, Doctor Hesse. Steward briefs the various papers' Lobby Correspondents and the stuff coming from him is virtually useless. Steward tells us only what Chamberlain wants us to hear and no more. One of the young lobby lads asked Chamberlain what he thought of the Nazi treatment of the Jews and Mussolini's bullying and the PM expressed surprise that such a professional journalist was susceptible to Jewish Communist propaganda. Off the record of course."

He paused to take a sip of water, but before he continued Ben interjected.

"But what is his obsession with controlling the press? Surely the PM can carry on without worrying what the papers have to say about him?"

"Normally that's true, but dealing with the dictators is different, especially Hitler. He hates reading anything nasty about himself in the papers. Of course, there's nothing said about him in the German papers because there's no freedom of speech. Anyway, if he doesn't like what he reads in our newspapers Chamberlain reckons he could go into a sulk and call off talks."

He then told us what we already knew about how Goebbels scoured the English newspapers every day and, if he found anything he thought the Fuhrer wouldn't like, he'd call in Henderson and read the riot act to him.

"So you can see Chamberlain feels he needs to control the press so he can continue to court Germany unhindered."

"Mind you, you've got to hand it to the PM. He's got himself nicely set up. He's almost a sort of mini-dictator himself. As far as foreign policy is concerned he ignores the cabinet and operates a sort of inner cabinet of four. He makes all the decisions after discussing the issues with his fellow appeasers: Hoare, Simon and, of course, Halifax. Their links to the German government are through Henderson, another like-minded soul, to Goebbels and Hitler and through Steward to Hesse at the German Embassy. I'm not sure how that works. Maybe Roger's contact will get some more on that for us."

He looked at me and smiled and I nodded.

"Any questions so far? I haven't quite finished yet but, if you need clarification on anything I've said, now's the time to ask."

One of the senior journalists asked.

"Apart from keeping information from us and having the odd young journalist beaten up, how's he going to control what we print?"

"Good question. No idea yet. He may not have to. The cabinet gang of four has already got four papers on board: *The Times*, *The Express*, *The Mail* and *The Observer*. He may feel that's enough."

"Those three represent less than a third of the total circulation of daily papers in this country. What about the rest?"

"Well *The Times* is regarded abroad as the sort of semi-official mouthpiece of Her Majesty's Government and Dawson is a close friend of Halifax so that's OK. Garvin *The Observer* Editor is a member of Nancy Astor's set so he's on board and Beaverbrook will take the *Express* wherever he wants to and they've got the biggest circulation. Incidentally, keep this quiet for the time being, but you know Beaverbrook and Hoare are as thick as thieves? Beaverbrook sees Hoare as a future PM and would expect a leg up himself into a cabinet role if Hoare ever reached Number Ten. And we all know about *The Daily Mail*."

The Editor drained his glass, looked round the room, then said, "You know nobody in this country wants war and, if any paper opposed a government policy that appeared to be geared to avoiding war, it might become unpopular, circulation figures might drop and we could lose advertising revenue. Now some newspaper proprietors are as rich as Croesus, but ours aren't, so they're feeling a bit uncomfortable at the moment."

"Are you saying we should kowtow to the government line just so the papers won't lose money?" *The Globe* Editor asked.

"No, I'm not but I am warning you of what's going on out there. There's no threat at the moment to our editorial independence but things could change and the blue pencil might be working overtime. If that happens I shall resign."

There was a chorus of "So will I".

"Thank you and thanks for listening. These papers remain dedicated to opposing Fascism. Get out there and send that message to the readers. And, er, don't worry too much. Hitler is a total shit and a barbarian and sooner or later he'll behave so badly that even Chamberlain will have to stand up to him. Not a pleasant prospect I know, but there we are. Right, back to work."

After work, Ben had treated some of us to a pint in the Wellington. We talked about what we'd heard in the meeting and its implications. The general reaction was one of anger, not to the Editor or the owners, but to the government whose attempts to manipulate the press had echoes of what Hitler had done in Germany. At the end of the day the message was, don't write anything that Hitler won't like.

I began to wish I was still sitting in the cold and dirty press box at Clapton Orient on Saturday afternoons but immediately dismissed the thought. I asked myself how many twenty-three-year-olds got the chance to tell more than half a million readers what was going on in the world and what they should feel about it? No, I was lucky, privileged even, and I wasn't going to let anyone down. Besides, I loathed Fascism and was determined to carry on doing my small bit to oppose it.

Someone asked Ben if he'd heard from any other papers about the views of their staff. He said that he was pretty sure that most journalists were up in arms, except in those openly pro-Fascist papers like *The Daily Mail*, but couldn't do much if their submissions were suppressed. He'd heard that there was a fair bit of unrest even at *The Times* at Dawson's compliant attitude to Chamberlain's foreign policy.

Ben walked with me to Waterloo. He said he wanted me to concentrate on Eden and see if there was a story there; senior minister being excluded from Chamberlain's inner cabinet, rumours of discord etc. Nothing too controversial; just the facts and my interpretation of them. It seemed to me that Eden was the one surviving obstacle to Chamberlain getting his own way over appeasement. I told Ben I'd go down to the Commons and hopefully hear from Philip Noel Baker about what the Westminster grapevine was saying about Eden and also about what the Members thought of Chamberlain's foreign policy.

"Of course," said Ben, "you Cambridge boys must stick together. Just kidding Prof. He's another really useful contact you've developed. Go and see him as soon as you can."

So I did.

CHAPTER TWENTY ONE

Exit Mister Eden

"The Times has made many ministries."
WALTER BAGEHOT

The top brass had put me in the picture about how the appeasers planned to achieve their goals. Their one last obstacle was Eden, the Foreign Secretary. Funnily enough it was Eden who'd coined the term appeasement in dealing with the dictators a couple of years earlier. Anyhow, he had to go. That much was clear.

It seemed like a good bet to see what Philip thought of this so we had tea at the Commons. We chatted for a while about the 1938 sports events. The British Empire Games were about to start in Australia and later in the summer there were European Athletics Championships in Paris and Vienna.

For both of us, the biggest sporting event of the year was the Ashes Test Matches against Australia. The Aussies held the Ashes and had the formidable Don Bradman as their star batsman. We had a good team too, with young tyros Len Hutton and Denis Compton expected to score plenty of runs, and spin bowling genius Hedley Verity spearheading a strong home bowling attack.

Eventually we got down to business and talked about foreign policy. I told him about the worries that many newspapers had about the government's attitude to the press.

"My colleagues reckon Chamberlain's got a plan to silence the papers and the FO but he still has to get rid of Eden before he can fully implement his plan."

"How long Eden will last is anybody's guess." Philip replied.

"Will Chamberlain sack him?"

"Very unlikely. Chamberlain needs to present a united front both to his own party and the public at large. He's not going to achieve that by kicking out a senior minister. No, my guess is that he'll make it impossible for him to stay."

"How will he do that?"

"By pursuing a policy directly opposed to Eden's. Of course if Eden does a U-turn and supports him, then Chamberlain's won. There'll be no opposition to his plans."

"Do you think that'll happen?"

"Not a chance. The two have been at loggerheads since Halifax trotted off to cozy up to Hitler in November. Besides Eden's not a bad bloke and he generally sticks to his principles. He can be weak at times but, by and large, he's a good Foreign Secretary and his ideas are good for the country."

Philip sipped his tea and continued.

"The Halifax business we both know about and that seems to have encouraged the PM to improve relations with Mussolini. Eden doesn't have a problem with that but only after the Duce pulls his troops out of Spain. Mussolini won't have that and Chamberlain won't press it. It seems that our PM is so keen on doing some sort of deal with Italy, he's even prepared to recognise their conquest of Abyssinia."

"Then there was the matter of the US peace initiative. Their President Roosevelt offered to head up some kind of world peace conference. Eden was all for it but Chamberlain wasn't. He probably doesn't want anyone else seizing his moment of glory when he delivers European peace."

"But be warned Roger, Eden has a strong sense of loyalty. He won't speak against the government while he's in office, so there's no scoop for you there. If he goes then that's quite another story."

"Thank you Philip. It seems like Eden will be out sooner rather than later."

"You're right, Roger. See you at the cricket?"

I left having agreed to spend time with Philip at the Oval Test and went back to the office and wrote a piece, "EDEN'S DILEMMA", under my new name. Ben liked it and it appeared in the following evening's paper.

Matters reached a head during the next week. First, Eden spoke at Birmingham and went as far as he could in supporting the Prime Minister. He denied that there was a rift between them and accepted that, while the British believed in democracy, we shouldn't necessarily be antagonistic towards those who thought differently. He too was after a lasting peace but said we shouldn't sacrifice principles for quick results. He finished by supporting the League of Nations, an organization which Chamberlain had consigned to the dustbin of history. Philip was right; Eden was keeping his views to himself, for the time being at least.

Later in the week, also in Birmingham, Chamberlain spoke of his aim of peace and added that we were making great progress in rearmament and we would soon be so powerful that we would have an even stronger voice in the councils of Europe.

Despite all this fairly meaningless hot air, the rumours of a rift between the two just wouldn't go away. Naturally, *The Times* denied these. Then on the Saturday morning Richard gave me a great story which we ran in that evening's paper.

Harry had got hold of the details of a Whitehall meeting involving Chamberlain, Eden and Count Grandi, the Italian Ambassador. This was the PM's first step in his appeasement of Italy but Eden was having none of it and told both men that talks couldn't proceed before Italy withdrew her troops from Spain.

Chamberlain's henchmen then put the boot into Eden, circulating rumours via *TRUTH*, and other sources, that Eden was exhausted, close to a nervous breakdown and ready to go. It came as no surprise that Eden threw in the towel over the weekend and resigned. It was a sad day. I shared Noel Baker's view of Eden as a decent man, firm in his beliefs, and it seemed a terrible shame that the last obstacle to a policy of which many were uncertain was removed so unceremoniously.

The next seven days were fascinating as the nation's press gave their views on resignation. Our editorial spoke of Great Britain's humiliation and surrender to Italy and our daily described Eden as a realist. *The Times*, *Telegraph* and *Express*, of course, supported Chamberlain as did the *Sketch* and the *Mail* who said that Eden was divorced from reality. *The Manchester Guardian* praised Eden for sticking to his principles and *The Daily Mirror* suggested that the PM is now free to throw himself at Mussolini's feet and say, "we yield everything—we ask nothing", a sentiment echoed in the columns of *The Daily Herald*. Arthur Mann, the besieged Editor of *The Yorkshire Post*, praised Eden for his commitment to the League of Nations and noted that the former Foreign Secretary was hated in both Rome and Berlin. *The Evening Standard* backed Chamberlain.

This was the biggest news story since the Halifax trip to Germany and, despite the fact that Eden made a characteristically low-key resignation speech in the Commons, he became a national hero and when he spoke in his constituency in Warwickshire at the end of that momentous week he received a prolonged standing ovation. There was no sign of a man on the verge of a nervous breakdown. My worries returned. The man was at the top of his game and seemed to be the last man able to question Chamberlain's foreign policy inside the government. Who can stop the PM now? I asked myself, before he gives Hitler carte blanche to carry out his land grabbing in Central Europe?

According to Richard, who had again heard from Harry, there was jubilation at Eden's departure in the German Embassy. No doubt there was a similar celebration in Foreign Offices in Rome and Berlin. The story refused to die and fuel was added to the fire when Winston Churchill entered the fray.

I was at home the night before Churchill's intervention when Ben called me on the phone.

"Best bib and tucker, Prof. Churchill's giving a foreign policy speech at the Constitution Club tomorrow and you're invited. One o'clock kick-off, so you can walk down from the office."

I thanked Ben and told my parents. They were delighted, not just because it was another feather in my cap but also because they were both great admirers of Churchill.

"He's the sort of man we need to stand up to Hitler," my father began. "He knows how dangerous the Nazis are. Eden's not the type to kick up a stink, too much of a gentleman, but Churchill is. Let's hope the country listens."

What did I know about Churchill? I remembered Blunt telling Maurice Dobb and me in that restaurant in Cambridge almost two years ago that Churchill had warned the Commons about the Nazi threat as long ago as 1932 before Hitler seized power in Germany.

I must confess I had mixed feelings about Churchill. He'd done some good things in government, especially before the war, but all the evidence suggested he was now past it and plenty in the country saw him as a political maverick, always calling for more arms and seeming to relish the chance to take on the Germans again.

I walked down The Strand into Northumberland Avenue and left my coat in the cloakroom of the Constitutional Club. There was quite a crowd at the lunch, everybody older than me, though I did recognise a couple of journalists in their thirties. I was dressed in an immaculate dark blue suit, white shirt and my Trinity tie, which earned some nods of approval from the gathering.

All the talk over lunch was of Eden. I said very little but those at my table were generally supportive of the stance that he had taken. The lunch was lavish and, at the end of it, Churchill lit up one of his trademark cigars which took an eternity for him to smoke.

Eventually he rose unsteadily to his feet. He was wearing a brown three-piece suit which hardly fitted him and he'd dropped food and cigar ash on to his waistcoat. It was not a promising beginning but for the next forty-five minutes everyone in the room listened to him with rapt attention.

Churchill didn't as much speak as growl but he was a brilliant orator and raised and lowered his voice to maximum effect. He started by attacking the government's foreign policy, which he thought was muddled. Then he praised Chamberlain's financial management when he was Chancellor in Baldwin's government. This, he said, had enabled us to re-arm but, he warned, this had not gone far enough. He believed that Britain was not

a war-like country but others were, sadly, so we had to rapidly increase
our armaments. Eden, he said, represented the spirit of resistance to the
dictators and he deplored his being forced out of office. He concluded by
telling Chamberlain that he had no chance of detaching Mussolini from
Hitler or of forcing Germany and Italy to withdraw troops from Spain.

A standing ovation followed. I was as intoxicated by his words as the
rest and I felt that there was some hope that Hitler and Mussolini would
be stopped in their tracks before they plunged Europe into another war.
That was, of course, if Churchill became a member of the cabinet where
he could exert some influence.

I wrote the piece up, handed it to Ben who skim read it then pronounced
himself satisfied and promised it would be in the following night's paper.
Then I went home and looked forward to spending the weekend with my
family and Jane. My role at the newspaper was changing; I was no longer
the odd job boy covering football, films, court cases and lost dogs but a
fledgling foreign and diplomatic correspondent. I felt pretty pleased with
myself. All that was missing was a bigger salary.

The Eden saga rattled on over the weekend. My favourite Sunday paper
Reynold's News savaged the government over the Foreign Secretary's
resignation and accused Chamberlain of selling out to Italy. They forecast
that he would soon follow Hitler and Mussolini in recognising Franco as
the legitimate ruler in Spain. The paper had reminded the PM that Italy
had bombed our sailors and sunk our ships in Spanish waters and said
that any talks with the Italian dictator were ridiculous.

They then rounded on the Cliveden set and accused them of inducing
Chamberlain to plunge the dagger into Eden and then, still dripping with
blood, thrusting it into the League of Nations. *Reynold's News* identified
the usual suspects as the chief conspirators then added Hoare and Simon
as hangers-on. They reported that the Italian press had been calling for
Eden's resignation since early February. "Cliveden Uber Alles" the paper
concluded before calling for a General Election. How do they get away
with it? I asked myself again.

Obviously the government's press control machinery was not yet in full swing because, early the next week, I penned another article, similar to the one published that morning in our daily, which suggested that some papers were agreeing with the government but pointing out that, if Chamberlain continued to court the dictators, we would be playing into their hands. I said that we should be allying ourselves with the European democracies, Russia and the USA against Hitler and Mussolini. To do this, we needed a more broad based and energetic government.

The Week, however, had the last word. They too accused the German and Italian governments of prompting Eden's resignation. Eden, they said, was now aligned with Churchill. Then came their scoop; they knew of a German agreement with Italy over the future of Austria. The next installment was about to begin.

CHAPTER TWENTY TWO

Anschluss

"The concessions of the weak are
the concessions of fear."
EDMUND BURKE

Hitler appeared to be sitting pretty at the beginning of March 1938. He had assumed total control over his army, whose senior officers he had seen as a potential source of opposition to him. We already knew from *The Week* that he had been given the go ahead by Mussolini to interfere in Austria. Halifax had assured him that Britain would not obstruct his plans for Eastern Europe, as long as he carried them out peacefully.

The Fuhrer's chief opponents in the British government, Eden and Vansittart, had gone. The French were in disarray, with regular changes of government of varying political colours demonstrating their instability. Germany had a strong army, a large and threatening air force, as well as growing strength on the sea. For Hitler it was the perfect time to emphasise his patriotism to the German people and seek their approval by smashing another part of the Versailles Treaty that so infuriated him; the prohibition of the union of Germany and Austria.

This was the gist of an article I wrote under the pseudonym of Philip Case and its publication sparked further interest from the shadowy figures that had threatened and beaten me. Ben told me that an elderly man had presented himself at our reception desk and asked to speak to Mr Case.

The receptionist, primed by Ben, had said that Mr Case was a freelance who didn't work at the office. She also refused to give details of his address and telephone number but did volunteer to give the mysterious caller's contact details to Mr Case. Not surprisingly he refused. The threat was there, however, and I was grateful to Ben and the paper for their support and protection.

Austria was one of several countries created at Versailles in the aftermath of the war. Previously she had been part of the Habsburg Austro-Hungarian Empire whose defeat and collapse in 1918 had led to the setting up of Austria and Hungary, both independent countries. The Union of Austria with Germany, the Anschluss, was expressly forbidden at Versailles, even though almost everyone in Austria was German speaking.

Hitler himself was an Austrian and his great enthusiasm for the Anschluss was long known. *The Week*, heaven knows how, had a year earlier reported on a secret meeting between Goering and an Austrian General called Strauss, one of many Nazis who had been active in Austria for a number of years. I wished I had their sources.

Hitler now used his propaganda machinery to stir up trouble in Austria. He claimed that most Austrians wanted the Anschluss. To test this, the Austrian government announced a referendum so that the citizens could vote yes or no to unification with Germany. Ben and I discussed this at the beginning of the second week in March.

"We're going to have to tread carefully here, Prof. Did you see that stuff in our Daily this morning about the press? Evidently that sod Ribbentrop is about to re-appear."

"What, as ambassador?"

Ribbentrop had returned to Germany earlier in the year to become Foreign Minister.

"No, no," replied Ben, "as a personal emissary of the Fuhrer to ask for moderation of the British press."

"What a bloody nerve. Mind you, it does suggest that Hitler's planning something."

Ben went on. "Quite. Anyway, our man's stuff this morning was headed 'HANDS OFF BRITISH PRESS' and he pointed out that Britain was a relatively free country with a free and independent press. How long that'll last is anybody's guess. He compared ours with the Nazi press which he described as a gigantic official gramophone."

I chuckled. "From what I've heard he's right."

"Course he is," said Ben. "He had a crack at *The Times*, calling it Germany's friendliest witness in this country. Then he warned the government not to ask us, the press that is, to engage in self-imposed censorship, so that they can pursue their peace-at-any-price policy without us upsetting the Fascists."

"Hm, I can see that upsetting Number Ten. Looks like he's gotten away with it."

"For the time being anyway."

"By the way," I continued, "I've done the piece on Austria."

I outlined the background to Ben; Versailles and so on.

"I thought I'd add a bit about the further advantages to the Germans."

"What are they?" asked Ben.

"They've got a lot of iron ore deposits and a smallish steel industry; useful to the Germans for manufacturing tanks, planes and guns. Then, of course, there's the poor old Jews."

"Yeah they must be living in terror themselves. What do you think'll happen to them?"

"Who knows?" I replied, "but there's plenty of them, including lots of wealthy bankers and industrialists and so on. Hitler would love to get his grubby hands on their assets."

"What about the referendum, or plebiscite, as they call it? Who do you think'll win?"

"No idea," I replied. "If it was taking place in Germany, Hitler would rig the results as he's done with elections in the past, but here he can't guarantee the result."

"Right, add a bit about Chamberlain's statement in the House last week. You know, he didn't see any threat to Austrian independence and believed that Germany recognised their full sovereignty, then the bloody hypocrite's parting shot about the League of Nations having to give consent to the Anschluss."

"That'll certainly put the cat amongst the pigeons, along with the hands off British press article."

"Right, get on with it Prof. We'll sit back and see what happens."

We didn't have long to wait. The next Friday German troops marched into Austria, cancelled the plebiscite, forced the Austrian Chancellor to resign, then set up an all- Nazi government. The Austrians were helpless to respond.

To be fair, both to our government and the press, there was universal condemnation of Germany's action. Even *The Times* headed its piece "AUSTRIA SURRENDERS TO FORCE" and suggested that a fair vote on Austrian independence had been planned, with the likely outcome of most Austrians saying 'No' to unification with Germany.

The cabinet met in emergency session on the following day and instructed Henderson in Berlin to protest strongly to the German government. France did likewise and Halifax told Ribbentrop that our government deplored Germany's action.

The attacks on Germany continued into the following week. The ever reliable *Reynolds News* obviously had a correspondent in Vienna because they were able to report on uniformed Nazis attacking and robbing Jews in the streets. They blamed Chamberlain for abandoning the League of Nations and causing the crisis. It was, they said, the first fruits of the anti-Eden policy.

Everybody was anti-German; the use of overwhelming force, fear of the result of the plebiscite, a blow to appeasement, the latest and worst demonstration of German foreign policy. Abuse was poured on the Nazis from all quarters.

Reports then began to flow in from Vienna about the most appalling atrocities committed against the Austrian Jews. They were arrested, for no apparent reason, beaten in the streets, their property seized and prominent and wealthy Jews were marched off to camps. Vienna was completely under the control of Nazi thugs and criminals. Synagogues were set on fire. It seemed like a concerted effort was being made to drive the Jews out of Vienna at one fell swoop. The Jews in Germany must be next, I thought. I was so relieved now that Richard had got his family safely to England before they too became victims of these utterly distasteful actions.

I made certain that I kept in touch with what was going on by regularly frequenting the pubs where the press boys gathered. Some said their articles were printed as submitted, others said their stuff had suffered the indignation of the blue pencil, while some even said that their contributions had been thrown out by editors for no apparent reason. The general view was that the Nazis were a race of barbarians who would cause a second world war sooner or later and many thought that their owners and editors were being got at by the government.

All this blue penciling and spiking was very disturbing. How on earth were British citizens supposed to form their own views if the government denied them access to the truth? After the initial pouring of scorn on Germany, editors and owners appeared to be backpedaling, perhaps under instruction from the government. My suspicions deepened when I was sent to the Commons to hear Chamberlain's assessment of the situation.

He started well, severely condemning the German action, and said that her actions had come as a severe shock to all those interested in preserving European peace. He called for a fresh review of defence requirements, which went down well, and then said, "we must consider the new situation quickly, but with cool judgment", and added that this was not the time for hasty decisions or careless words.

He then went back on the offensive reporting that Henderson's angry note to the Nazis invasion of Austria had met an unpleasant response from Berlin, telling us to mind our own business and warning us of the dangers of interfering. Chamberlain refuted this, saying that, as both Austria and Great Britain were members of the League of Nations, we had every right to intervene as a fellow member. The PM was good at playing the League card when it suited him.

It all felt rather feeble to me. Lots of table thumping and anger but no real indication as to how the PM was going to stop Hitler doing as he pleased. I felt slightly more encouraged when the Leader of the Opposition,

Clement Attlee, stood up and said that Eden had been proved right and the house of cards of appeasement had collapsed. He called for a return to the principles of the League of Nations; collective security. It was a pity, I thought, that he wasn't the Prime Minister. I was sure he'd take a tougher line with the dictators.

Attlee, bald and bespectacled, looked more like a bank manager than a politician, but he was beginning to make an impression on me.

Chamberlain's response to the Anschluss seemed to me to be pretty weak and it soon became clear that we would sit back and do nothing. The PM's reference to the League of Nations had a pretty hollow ring to it and it was obvious that neither he nor they would take any practical steps to restore Austrian sovereignty.

Once the Germans had established total control in Austria, Hitler made his triumphant re-entry to the country of his birth. According to reports, crowds lined the roads on which he travelled, cheering him every inch of the way. Some newspapers, notably *The Times*, *Express* and *Mail*, saw this as a sign of the Fuhrer's popularity and suggested that, after all, union with Germany may well have triumphed in the plebiscite. They did, however, question the use of force. Prior to the crisis, *The Times* had declared itself in favour of the Anschluss and so, with the gentlest of slaps on the wrist for the Fuhrer, they let him get on with his own affairs.

Our government was predictably delighted. Halifax declared that we must recognise that the Austrian state had been abolished as a national entity and would be absorbed in the German Reich. Retrospective action, he said, would be useless.

Then, a few days later, Chamberlain made a speech in the Commons in which he praised the press for the restraint they had shown over the Austrian crisis. He, paradoxically, paid tribute to the freedom of our press. He said he was finding more and more support for his handling of the Austrian crisis.

Well, if certain of our national daily and regional papers were going to show restraint, ours certainly weren't. I wrote a piece attacking the government for its 'restraint.' Hitler, I said, had been encouraged by us to go ahead, knowing from his talks with Halifax that we would do nothing.

Hitler equated appeasement with weakness. What should we have done? Gone to war? Probably not. Austria was hardly accessible by land and we lacked the resources to mount any form of airborne attack. In any case the British people were dead set against war and wouldn't have supported action against Germany who had only taken what was theirs anyway, according to what I now called "some sections of the government press".

I said that we should never stop reminding Hitler that he was wrong and we should be allying ourselves with France, USA, the Soviet Union and any other like-minded countries and telling Hitler, in no uncertain terms, that if he took one more step against a democratic country, he would face devastating consequences for Germany.

"This is hot stuff, Prof," said Ben on reading my article. "Let's hope we can get it in print. The word is that the government is going to increase the pressure on the press to play ball, so a lot depends on how our people respond to this. By the way, have you read *The Week* this week?"

"Not yet, no."

"Claud's spoken to a 'high official' and he quoted him as saying that for the first time he envisages us suffering the same fate as Austria."

"Vansittart?"

"Probably. I mentioned this because I think it's time you made contact with Cockburn. I reckon we're going be gagged and we need to find an outlet for the stuff your sources are producing. I'll find out when he's next at the Café Royal and you can slip down and see him. Just establish contact for the time being. Oh, and take the usual precautions."

"Sure."

"I suppose you've worked out what's next on Hitler's agenda?"

"Of course, Czechoslovakia. I heard Archibald Sinclair in the House demand that we should support France if she felt bound to honour her treaty with the Czechs when Hitler came calling there."

"And," continued Ben, "according to *The Week* our people in Prague have told the Czech leader Benes to give in to all possible German demands. Heaven knows where he gets his intelligence from, but it's bloody reliable. It looks as though the Czechs are next in line for the high jump."

CHAPTER TWENTY THREE

The Week

"All great truths begin as blasphemies."
GEORGE BERNARD SHAW

I set off to see Cockburn one chilly Wednesday morning towards the end of March. Ben knew I was going and advised me to make sure, again, that I wasn't followed. He'd found out that Cockburn would be at the Café Royal, one his regular haunts, on that morning. I knew where it was, although I'd never been there, and organized myself a confusing route.

Before I met with Cockburn, I took the trouble to find out as much as I could about the man himself and the news sheet that had brought him a small amount of fame but a large degree of notoriety.

Cockburn was the son of a diplomat, born at the British Embassy in Peking. His father had retired to Tring in Hertfordshire where Claud became great friends with Graham Greene, the novelist, whose own father Charles was the headmaster of the school in Berkhampstead which both boys attended. From there he went to Oxford and the university later awarded him a travelling scholarship and he had spent time in both Germany and France in the late 1920s.

It was in Germany that he met a man who was to have an enormous influence on him, Norman Ebbutt, Berlin correspondent of *The Times*. I knew of Ebbutt, of course. He had been a constant thorn in the Nazi side during the early years of the Third Reich. Goebbels eventually lost patience with *The Times* correspondent and he was expelled from Germany in 1936 for criticizing Hitler's policies towards the German churches.

I was told by some of the boys on the street that Ebbutt was Cockburn's mentor and none had been surprised when, in 1929, Cockburn, barely older than when I embarked on my career, became a full time writer for *The Times*. Evidently there was, at the time, a story circulating in Fleet Street about a competition amongst *The Times*' staff about which of them could concoct the most boring headline. Cockburn had won with his "SMALL EARTHQUAKE IN CHINA. NOT MANY DEAD."

Later that year he became *The Times* correspondent in New York and was there during the Wall Street Crash. In 1932 he had married an American journalist but threw over his job with *The Times* the following year, returned to England and established *The Week*. Two years later he combined his editorial work on *The Week* with work as a journalist at *The Daily Worker*, the Communist daily newspaper.

I'd read most copies of *The Week*, as indeed had many of my colleagues who found it an extremely valuable source of information.

Impressively he had predicted the Rhineland occupation in March 1936 and even told his readers that Hitler had been reassured by Lord Londonderry that Great Britain and France would do nothing when the German troops marched in. Long before the first shots were fired, *The Week* had prophesized the start of the Spanish Civil War and the later German and Italian involvement in it.

So I felt pretty well prepared for my meeting with Claud Cockburn. I hadn't made an appointment because I'd been assured that none was necessary. At the Café Royal he held 'open house,' so I was a little surprised when I walked in to find a man I knew to be Cockburn sitting at a marble topped table with a single companion. Nervously I approached their table when Cockburn jumped to his feet and extended his hand.

"Mr Martin? Good to see you."

I was flabbergasted. How on earth did he know who I was?

"I can see you're wondering how I recognized you." He tapped his nose with his right index finger. "I make it my business to know about every journalist on Fleet Street, especially those who support the cause. I've been following your progress closely and keeping an eye on you. I believe you've had a spot of bother."

I couldn't understand how he knew about that and I was a bit mystified and wasn't sure what to make of his last couple of comments. I let it pass and then Claud turned to his companion.

"Let me introduce you to Negley Farson," he smiled.

I knew of Negley Farson. He was the London correspondent of *The Chicago Daily News* and chairman of the Foreign Correspondents' Association. Farson gave me a warm handshake. Standing together all three of us were of similar height and Farson and Cockburn appeared to be about the same age, mid-forties, although I knew Cockburn to be only 34. Claud was losing his hair and this, together with his thick horn rimmed spectacles, made him look older than he was. By contrast, Farson had a full head of hair, thick but with a hint of grey. He had a rugged, lined and lived-in face which, I guessed, reflected his adventurous travelling life. He had, I also knew, an excellent reputation as an angler and I wondered if he could teach our Prime Minister, a keen angler himself, a thing or two about fishing.

There was a bottle of red wine and two glasses on the table and Cockburn summoned the waiter to fetch a third glass but I quickly declined, choosing a coffee instead.

"Not a proper journalist yet then Mr Martin?" began Cockburn.

"No. A bit early in the day for me, and please, call me Roger."

"Thank you."

We sat down and the two of them drained then quickly re-filled their glasses. Cockburn had a reputation of being a heavy drinker, but not a drunk, and Farson also looked as if he could handle himself. Claud offered me a cigarette, which I politely declined, and then the two of them lit up. My coffee arrived and the waiter was dispatched to empty the ash tray.

The pair of them had quickly made me feel at ease and my nervousness began to evaporate. I decided I would start the conversation.

"Claud, I'm very familiar with *The Week* and have read practically every copy but what made you start it up?"

"Easy. The papers only print stuff they can verify. I print rumours, gossip and some material that the other papers won't print for fear of upsetting the government, or other governments come to that. I didn't much like the way *The Times* was going. Not the reporters—most of them were very straight and professional—but the Editor Dawson was always interfering with his wretched blue pencil. Things were bad enough in 1933 when I packed it in but they're worse now and I'm sure will get even worse as the year goes on. I wanted to print stories that told the real truth about what was happening in the world."

I asked him why it was printed on buff coloured paper in brown ink.

He laughed. "You've obviously heard the one about how *The Week* looks as if it's written on lavatory paper."

I smiled and nodded.

"Three reasons. One, cost. I haven't got that much money and depend on handouts from friends. This was especially so at the beginning so I couldn't afford a glossy printer which brings me to reason two. If I get sued for libel, a distinct possibility I'm sure you'd agree, the complainant would also target the printer as well. No printer: therefore, one less person to sue. And thirdly, looking as if it's been printed on lavatory paper does draw attention to *The Week* and people now subscribe to it for its content not is appearance."

We discussed staffing at *The Week* and Claud told me he had dozens of staff, none of whom got paid a penny.

"The office, which is hardly bigger than a large cupboard, is on Victoria Street and a happy band of volunteers put *The Week* together; you know, typing, stapling and so forth. I don't have journalists, just sources like Negley here. They're more than happy to pass stuff on, particularly if their papers won't publish it. And I get plenty of stuff from MPs, especially the younger Tory set who think Chamberlain's foreign policy is harebrained, as well as diplomats here and abroad."

"You're making me feel a bit of a fraud. I thought I had some good sources but nothing like the stuff you're getting," I said.

"You're not a fraud Roger, just a young journalist making his way in the profession. That's where I was when I started at *The Times*. Besides I've read your articles. They're good and you've obviously got sources of your own."

We paused while they refilled their glasses and lit fresh cigarettes.

"Do you sell many copies?" I asked.

"We do now, we've over 40,000 subscribers. You can't buy it in the shops or at street corners. We send it out by post. The annual subs are going up to sixteen shillings a year next month. The first issue had only seven subscribers but two things happened that gave us a big boost in circulation. I don't suppose you remember the World Economic Conference five years ago."

"I do. I was about to start at Cambridge."

"So, you'll remember it all came to nothing, as we'd predicted in *The Week*. After it was all over Ramsay MacDonald called a press conference in the basement of the Geology Museum to defend his part in the fiasco. You should have seen him surrounded by skeletons. You couldn't tell the difference between the poor old fellow and some of the exhibits."

We all laughed.

"So MacDonald says some bad press was to blame and holds up a copy of *The Week* as an example of this. Everybody was on their feet rushing to the front to jot down the address and subscription rates. Circulation shot up after that. Then the Rhineland business began to persuade folk that Hitler was a threat. We'd been saying it for years but after the Nazis crossed the Rhine people began to sit up and take notice. Negley's met Hitler you know."

"Good heavens," I replied.

"It's true," Negley explained. "Didn't get much out of him, mind you; just the usual claptrap about the injustices of Versailles and how everybody is ganging up on Germany. He did take a fancy to my son, however. He's blonde you know. Adolf described him as a perfect Aryan specimen."

"Negley's far too modest. He was in Petrograd when the Russian revolution started and outside the picture house in Chicago when John Dillinger, the gangster, was shot," said Claud.

"I didn't actually see him shot but I did see his body being taken away. Of course Claud's seen a bit of action too."

Claud then told me about his involvement in the Spanish Civil War while a fresh bottle of Burgundy and another cup of coffee were ordered. He'd initially been there as *The Daily Worker* correspondent but later fought in the Republican militia.

"I eventually became *persona non grata* with our Foreign Office and couldn't get back there. I had the last laugh though. There was a meeting of West European TUC leaders about Spain in London. I attended as an interpreter, in disguise of course, false whiskers and so forth, then published details of the so called secret discussions in *The Week* and *The Worker*."

We all laughed again but Claud quickly stopped us.

"It's a real tragedy, Spain. I'm not too optimistic about the outcome. It looks as though we're going to have another Fascist dictatorship in Europe."

"That's exactly what George Steer told me," I said.

"Of course, you've met Steer. I remember your stuff from Paris last year."

I recounted the tale of my trip to Paris.

"Good chap, Steer," said Claud, "man after my own heart."

"Mine too," Negley said. "Did you know, Roger, that Claud here has been on one of those hunger marches?"

"No."

"Now tell Roger, Claud, about your trip to Hamburg."

"Really Negley, Roger didn't come here to hear about that sort of thing."

"I'll tell the tale then," said Negley.

Negley told me how Claud had travelled to Germany on a false passport and rescued two children of a communist worker who had fled to avoid arrest. Claud's fake passport wasn't too convincing so he hadn't dared risk using hotels and had spent his time in Germany on sleeper trains zig-zagging his way through the country.

"Right," said Claud, "enough of these silly stories. What more do you want to know Roger?"

"How on earth do you get away with it?" I asked, referring to *The Week*.

"With difficulty," Claud replied. "My phone is tapped and both the office and my flat are under constant surveillance from shady characters in the security services."

"How do you know?"

"There's always men digging the road outside and, besides, I've got sources in MI5 and Special Branch, as well as my own team of snoopers. The government can't sue me, or rather won't, because I've no money so it's not worth it, and, of course, all our mail is opened. I write what people want to read: rumour and gossip; some facts that the local press won't print. We've got all sorts amongst our subscribers. They like the fresh perspective it brings. After all, I've been abroad for so long I can look at what's going on here from a different point of view from those who've lived here for donkey's years. I don't believe I've got too many enemies; Chamberlain's lot, the Cliveden Set, the Fascist dictators perhaps but plenty of support from people I feel have been shaken out of complacency by *The Week*. Did you know Ribbentrop wrote to the government and asked that for *The Week* to be suppressed?"

"No."

"They wouldn't play ball, bless 'em. Ribbentrop's a horrible man."

Claud was a Marxist and a member of the Communist party of Great Britain. He'd witnessed the Wall Street Crash first hand when he was in New York and it led him to realize that capitalism was in decay and there's dreadful inequality of wealth and opportunity in the so-called civilized world.

"Frankly, I hate the British class system even though I'm a product of it. I try not to let my politics affect my judgment as far as foreign affairs are concerned but being labeled a Communist is a bit of a handicap. What about you?"

"I'm a socialist and I believe in the democratic process," I replied, "and I'm not sure Communism as practised in the Soviet Union is the way forward."

"You could be right, but that doesn't make Communist principles necessarily unworkable. Were you in the Socialist Club at Cambridge?"

"I was, yes."

"So you know Maurice Dobb?"

"He was my tutor and, I suppose, political mentor."

"Fine fellow, Dobb. There has been some funny business with the Cambridge socialists. The party had a powerful cell in it but some of the leading lights have jumped ship and joined the other side. Guy Burgess has tagged on to the Anglo German Fellowship. By the way Negley, I'd advise you to keep your son well away from Burgess. And Kim Philby has just been decorated by Franco in Spain. Most odd. That's enough about me. What about you and how can we work together?"

I told him about Ben, of whom he knew, and the worry that the government was beginning to interfere with the freedom of the press. I let him know that I'd developed some useful sources, but obviously wouldn't reveal names, which he unhesitatingly accepted, and said that I too felt that I was under surveillance, telling him about my warning and my beating.

"I can guess who was behind that," said Claud. "I'll see what I can do to help."

"Thank you," I said, not really knowing what he meant.

"I would suggest," Claud continued, "that anything you get you use, unless your people blue pencil or spike it, in which case pass it on to me and I'll publish it. If you get something that's a bit vague, not too much evidence, pass it to me and I'll print it as fact rather than just rumour."

"Isn't that a bit risky?"

"Not at all. I'll publish, the government'll deny it, and then we'll know it's true. Never believe anything until it's been officially denied."

I'd heard that one before, but I laughed nevertheless.

Negley chipped in: "The story of the spring and summer is going to be Czechoslovakia. Hitler's already making noises and you can bet your bottom dollar that Chamberlain and his men are already trying to work out how they can avoid trouble over the Czechs. All our efforts need to be focused on trying to find out how he's going to achieve this and, if we don't like it, try to stop him."

"Right Roger, it's been a pleasure meeting you and I'm looking forward to working with you. Get whatever you can. Try to develop new contacts and remember, never underestimate the effectiveness of a straight cash bribe. Above all take care of yourself."

"Thank you, I will."

I shook hands and left them to finish off their second bottle of wine (or was it the third? I couldn't remember). My head was buzzing with thoughts, ideas and worries as I made my way back to the office in a daze.

CHAPTER TWENTY FOUR

Back to Taplow

"Honesty is a good thing."
DON MARQUIS

Ben listened attentively that afternoon when I told him of my meeting with Cockburn and Farson. Of course he knew of the American and was aware of his close links with *The Week* and its Editor. There was no doubt in my mind that he rated both Cockburn and his news sheet very highly, Communist or not, and it was equally obvious that he shared this view with many of his colleagues on our paper and others.

"You've made another good contact there, Prof," he began, "and the arrangement you've come to with him could be useful, if not to us then certainly to the anti-Chamberlain cause."

"Why not just to us?" I asked.

"Let's see. Remember what he said to you. He publishes stuff that the other papers daren't use, especially if it's not totally backed up by fact and in the present climate, we all have to be pretty careful. No good upsetting the PM as he embarks on the great peace mission."

"OK, I understand. What do you want me to do next?"

"First, down to the Commons tomorrow. There's going to be a foreign affairs debate. Could be interesting to hear what Chamberlain has to say. Then I think it's time you did a bit more sleuthing, Prof. How about taking your girlfriend for another nice day in the country on Saturday?

See what you can pick up at the pub in Taplow. You might need to grease a few palms. Grab twenty quid from petty cash and offer some of it to the cook, what's-her-name."

"Milly."

"Yeah, and if she can get anything, there's a tenner each for her and the footman if they can pick up much else that might be useful. Mind you if she hasn't got any info just stick to buying her the odd port and lemon."

"OK," I laughed, "I'll head up there on Saturday morning and I'll write up the Commons debate first thing on Friday for the evening paper."

I gave a lot of thought both to my meeting with Cockburn and to what Ben had said. Claud's sources were clearly impeccable and he was performing a vital service in keeping his forty thousand readers up to date with what was really going on. My own paper, and our daily downstairs, were calling for Chamberlain to commit to defend Czechoslovakia if she was attacked by Germany. We were a bit of a voice in the wilderness, but how long we'd be allowed to express that kind of opinion was anybody's guess. This was why *The Week* was so important. Cockburn didn't have to keep any owners sweet. He was the owner and not subject to editorial interference. And Claud couldn't give a damn about being sued, or losing advertising revenue. There wasn't any.

The last Thursday in March saw me back in the Commons to listen to the foreign affairs debate.

Chamberlain covered his backside with his opening statement that he was about to express an attitude, rather than outline policy. He looked, as usual, old and frail, dressed in his immaculate three piece suit and white shirt with winged collar and a conservative blue tie.

When he spoke, however, he was not as feeble as he looked and there was a steely determination in his voice which suggested to me that, although he claimed these were only his opinions, he was going to make damned certain that they became policy.

The House was packed when he announced that there would be no fresh commitment to Czechoslovakia. There were groans from the opposition benches and several none too convincing 'hear hears' from the government side. He told the Members that we should continue to increase our arms. This resulted in murmurs of assent from both sides, but that the prime objective of our foreign policy remained the maintenance and preservation of peace but, he added, that did not mean that we would not fight if we had to.

The PM then went on to admit that he had lost confidence in the League of Nations but saw merit in trying to nurse it back to health.

Chamberlain then got to the crux of the matter. He reminded everyone that we were committed by treaty to France and Belgium and, if either of those countries were attacked, we would immediately come to their aid. On the other hand, he continued, France was bound by treaty to defend Czechoslovakia's sovereignty and, if we agreed to support France in the event that she defended Czechoslovakia, the decision to go to war with Germany would be taken out of our hands.

Although I could more or less follow what he was implying, I made a mental note to find out more both about these treaties and about Czechoslovakia herself.

Czechoslovakia, continued Chamberlain, was not an area of our vital interest, unlike France and Belgium. He believed that now was the time for all the resources of diplomacy to be enlisted in the cause of peace and he noted, with pleasure, that the German government were satisfied with the steps currently being taken by the Czech government to meet the demands for the German minorities in Czechoslovakia. What was that all about? Another mental note.

Chamberlain then reminded the House that the Spanish conflict had not spread outside the Spanish borders, thanks to non-intervention. We were just going to let the Spanish Republic die, I thought. The PM reminded the Members that we had taken in some Spanish children who'd been displaced by the conflict.

He then turned his attention to Russia who had recently called for a peace conference. Chamberlain thought this would aggravate the present situation, or I thought, steal his thunder, and he believed that Russia's only interest was in getting as many states as possible together to create a buffer against Germany.

Any slumbering Members were rudely awoken by the roars of laughter (particularly from the Members of the opposition) in response to the PM's next statement: that Germany wanted peace. Talks with Italy, he said, were going well and he believed Italy's promises about the withdrawal of their so-called volunteers from Spain. Cue more cynical laughter. Talks with Germany were also going well, Chamberlain added.

He finished by talking about rearmament and stated that we must be strongly armed for defence and counter-offence. He indicated that the air force and air defence were especially important and that we must build new factories to increase our production capacity.

There was a disappointingly muted response to all this with only Attlee, who suggested that Mussolini was a liar, saying much. Perhaps, I thought, the Members were all keen to get out of the Commons as quickly as possible so that they could head for their clubs for dinner.

As I trudged back to the office along the embankment, I reflected on what I'd heard. As far as I could judge, Chamberlain was opting for diplomacy, not war, and as the League of Nations was in no fit state to conduct this diplomacy, he would step in to carry out these duties. He did recognize that we had to negotiate from a position of strength, therefore the rearmament programme was essential, but overall he was prepared to abandon Czechoslovakia, just as he and Baldwin had abandoned Spain.

I had invited myself to Jane's house for tea that night and, when I arrived, I apologized for neglecting her. She was aware of how busy I was and, in any case, was hard at work herself preparing for her accountancy exams so hadn't had a lot of time for leisure. I asked her if she fancied another visit to Taplow on Saturday and she said she did. I got the impression she was just the tiniest bit excited by the prospect. I promised to take her to the cinema the following weekend. We agreed to meet at the station at nine o'clock that Saturday morning.

Although it was officially spring, it was still cold on that Saturday when we met. We made the usual journey into Waterloo, then took the Bakerloo line to Paddington and, finally, the train to Taplow, changing at Windsor where we had a cup of coffee. It was about half past eleven when we walked out from Taplow Station heading for the Oak and Saw. I'd explained to Jane during the journey that this wasn't quite the same as our previous visits and that I was going to offer Milly money if she could get us some useful information.

"Don't worry about Milly. She loves talking. The people up at the house think the servants are too stupid to realize what's going on," Jane said. "They've no idea that someone like her would have any interest at all in politics, foreign or otherwise."

Jane was right, of course, so I was fairly optimistic when we stepped into the bar of the Oak and Saw which, for that time on a Saturday morning, was fairly busy. I glanced about the room and there, to my immense relief, was Milly, alone at a table nursing a port and lemon. Jane left me to join her while I went into the bar to order the drinks.

By the time I joined Milly and Jane with the drinks, Milly was in full flow. She thanked me for the drink.

Jane said, "Milly was just telling me what a busy weekend it is up at the house."

"Oo yes," Milly said, "there's a right gathering up there."

I thought it best to let her carry on without interruption.

"'Is Lordship and 'er Ladyship are both there and the usuals; Lord Lothian, Lord 'Alifax and Mr Dawson and another paper man, Garvin I think 'is name is.

"I know of him," I said, "He's editor of *The Observer*. It's a Sunday newspaper."

"Well, I wouldn't know about that," said Milly, "if I ever read a paper of a Sunday its *The Pic*, and sometimes in the week I 'as a look at *The Mirror*."

"Do you like those papers?" Jane asked.

"I'm not much of a reader really but they're alright. I do like the cartoons and some of the pictures. I never read the sport. Can't stand football."

We both laughed. "What about politics?" Jane asked.

"I've always voted Tory, even when Lloyd George was Prime Minister. That nice Mr Baldwin knew 'ow to run the country. I wish 'e was still Prime Minister. I can't stand Mr Chamberlain. 'E looks like death warmed up.

Ooh that reminds me. 'E's up at the 'ouse too."

"Who?" I asked.

"Mr Chamberlain. 'E turned up first thing and since 'e got 'ere they've all been locked away in 'is lordship's study."

"I wonder what they're talking about," I said.

"'Aven't a clue," replied Milly. "Johnny'd know though. 'E's been in and out all morning with teas and coffees and biscuits. Do Mr Chamberlain good, a packet of biscuits. 'E needs fattening up."

We laughed again and Milly continued.

"They're a right lot, full of their own importance. 'Er Ladyship treats the staff like dirt. 'Is lordship's not so bad mind you."

Jane steered the conversation towards where we wanted to be.

"Do you think there'll be another war, Milly?"

"I 'ope not. I lost a cousin in France in 1917 and lots of people I know from the 'ouse had relatives killed in the War. Some of them that survived died of flu in 1919. I was reading in the *Pic* last week that Mr Chamberlain should stand up to 'Itler."

"If he doesn't," I said, "we could well find ourselves in another war with Germany."

"'Ow's that?" asked Milly.

"A lot of people think if we keep giving way to Hitler, he'll think we're weak and it'll be our turn soon. Once he's grabbed all the bits of Europe he thinks are his, he'll then attack France, if they haven't already turned on him first, and, once he does that, we're in it. We'd have to fight on France's side."

"I never thought o' that," Milly said. "What do you think Mr Chamberlain should do about it?"

"Stand up to Hitler over Czechoslovakia. Your Mr Baldwin's already sat back while Hitler sent troops into the Rhineland. Mind you, that was part of Germany at least. Then, Chamberlain did nothing when he grabbed Austria. Czechoslovakia's next then Poland then probably France and Belgium. Then he'll turn his attention to Russia, but we'll be in it by then."

"You should have guessed by now, Milly," Jane said, "Roger's a journalist and lots of the journalists don't trust Hitler; they think it's time to stand up to him."

"What paper do you work for?"

I told her. She'd heard of it but never read it.

"We think everybody in the country should know what's going on, and if Chamberlain and that crowd up at Cliveden are cooking up some scheme to let the Germans walk into Czechoslovakia, we think they should know that too."

"I'd 'ate to live in Czechoslovakia," said Milly, "sitting in your 'ouse waiting for 'Itler and 'is thugs to march in."

"They will," said Jane, "unless someone does something about it."

Milly drained her glass and I went for a refill. When I got back I asked her: "I don't suppose you could have a word with Johnny when you get back and see if he's picked up anything on this Czechoslovakia business could you?"

Milly sat in silence, staring at her glass, thinking about the implications of what I'd told her. Eventually she took a deep breath, looked up and said: "What the 'ell. Ooh I'm sorry. I've no love for Mr Chamberlain or 'er Ladyship or that stuck up Lord Lothian and *The Sunday Pic* says we should stand up to 'Itler. I'll speak to Johnny tonight. See what 'e's 'eard."

"Thanks Milly. Do you think you could be down here tomorrow and let me know what's gone on?" I asked.

She thought for a moment.

"They all go to church of a Sunday morning. I could get the lunch going, then cycle down 'ere to meet you while they're in church. The other cooks can get on with the lunch. This place'll be shut. Where shall I meet you?"

Thinking quickly, I told her the railway station, although I'd no idea whether or not the trains would be running on Sunday morning.

"What time?" I asked Milly.

"Half past eleven," she replied. "Do you think I'll get into trouble for this? I wouldn't want me and Johnny to get the sack."

"No chance," I said, "None of them would believe that a cook, or a footman, or anybody else on the staff for that matter, would have any interest in what they're talking about. No, they'll think one of their own has spoken to the press. When Chamberlain gets back to London, he'll be telling some of the other ministers what's been going on and there'll be plenty of suspects."

"That's good," said Milly.

She sat with us for another half hour then headed off back to Cliveden. Jane had cleverly steered the conversation back to day-to-day things and Milly seemed to have forgotten the grim forebodings of the earlier part of the conversation.

After Milly had left, we had another beer then walked back to the station. I was disappointed to find there wasn't a train on the Sunday that would get me to Taplow in time for the meeting with Milly. I thought quickly and suggested to Jane that she head off home and I'd spend the night at a hotel in Windsor then come back here by taxi.

I still had the money that Ben had given me. Milly would have been insulted if I had offered her a bribe.

Jane, of course, had a better idea.

"Do you think your mum and dad would fancy a Sunday morning spin?"

"Possibly."

"You're sailing pretty close to the wind now. You're actually getting hold, you hope, of details of confidential conversations, if not state secrets. A man on his own arriving here, chatting to an old lady, then riding back to Windsor in the same taxi looks a bit suspicious and, anyway, you could be putting yourself in danger, not to mention Milly. On the other hand what could be more ordinary than a group of townies having a Sunday drive in the countryside and stopping in a beautiful village to ask an old lady on a bicycle for directions to some place or other?"

She was right of course.

"OK. I'll ask my dad when I get back. I'll have to tell him what's going on, but he's already a sort of co-conspirator, what with carrying messages to Richard."

When we got back, Jane and I shared the telling of the day's events with my mother and father. They were both sympathetic to our views, although a little worried about the risks I was taking. But they were delighted to be asked to play a part in all this and agreed to the Sunday morning outing. My mother said we'd have a late lunch. John would be left in his room to build stink bombs or whatever he did up there.

My father planned the journey like a military operation. Taplow was about thirty miles from where we lived. He allowed plenty of time to get there and suggested that, if we looked as if we were going to arrive early, we'd stop en route to stretch our legs. We wouldn't be rushing it. My mother wouldn't allow my father to drive too fast.

The weather was good. It was a fine spring morning when we set off and we made good progress, stopping in Maidenhead to stretch our legs, as my father put it, and drew up at the rendezvous about five minutes early. Milly herself appeared a couple of minutes later, a bit breathless after her cycle ride. I introduced her to my parents and told her they were fully aware of what was going on.

The five of us stood outside Taplow station, seemingly having an innocent conversation. Johnny had indeed picked up some very useful information.

We were all correct. The only item on the agenda was Czechoslovakia. It seemed that the main problem was that Hitler wanted parts of Czechoslovakia to become part of Germany. Lothian was all for this but, according to Johnny, Chamberlain wasn't too keen and suggested that we should talk to Hitler and try to persuade him that the Germans living in Czechoslovakia might be given certain rights. Milly said that Johnny had told her that if Hitler didn't agree to this, most of the others, except the PM, thought that we should give Hitler the German parts of Czechoslovakia anyway.

This was useful and very disturbing. I thanked Milly, and we said we would be back to see her soon. She said she wouldn't be thanking Johnny for us because she hadn't told him that she would be passing his tit bits on to anyone else. With that she set off to pedal back to Cliveden.

I again realized that I had nowhere enough knowledge to properly understand the situation in Czechoslovakia and I made bringing myself up to speed about that a priority for the next week. We got home safely, had our late lunch, listened to Godfrey Tearle playing King Lear on the radio, and then went to bed early, ready to face the week ahead.

CHAPTER TWENTY FIVE

Czechoslovakia

"A quarrel in a far away country between
people of whom we know nothing."
NEVILLE CHAMBERLAIN

I made certain I got to the office early that Monday morning. The weekend's events had left me exhilarated, but I was not altogether sure that I knew what I was talking about. I knew where Czechoslovakia was but had little real understanding of its importance to the European situation. Nonetheless, I decided to write up what I had learned at Taplow and briefly explained this to Ben.

Ben seemed interested in what I had to say and congratulated me on my subtle approach to finding out what was going on. He told me that our daily was continuing to attack the government over its handling of foreign policy.

I spent several hours putting the piece together, suggesting that Chamberlain was seeking advice from non-professionals like Lothian, the Astors and Dawson, rather than relying on guidance from the experts in the Foreign Office. I had no idea where Halifax, who had replaced Eden as Foreign Secretary the previous month, stood in all this but assumed that he was prepared to follow his Prime Minister's lead, at least for the time being.

By lunchtime I'd finished, dropped the article on Ben's desk, and left for the pub where I hoped to find some colleagues who would help me to understand the Czech situation.

It turned out better than I'd hoped and, by two o'clock, I was back at my desk with at least an inkling about the importance of Czechoslovakia. The general view in the pub was that the government should stand up to Hitler and not let him march into Czechoslovakia like he had Austria a couple of weeks earlier. Having said that, there was, as yet, no real indication that Hitler had any intention of attempting to grab hold of Czechoslovakia, but when I said this to one hardened old cynic from *The Manchester Guardian* he advised me to learn more about central Europe. Then I would see that, as far as the Nazis were concerned, Czechoslovakia was a ripe piece of fruit just waiting to be picked.

On my way back to the office, I again felt like a wet behind the ears schoolboy, which I almost was, and I knew I would have to do some research of my own to make sure I really knew what was going on. The other journalists said that Hitler was just taking a breather after his Austrian triumph before turning his attention to the Czechs; the next item on his shopping list.

I was mulling over this at my desk, preparing to spend the afternoon going through both of our papers' archives when Ben called me in.

"Good stuff this, Prof. Well done," he began, holding up my article for me to see, "but we can't publish it."

"Why on earth not?"

"It's not my decision, it's the Editor's. He's had a chat with the powers that be and they've been told not to upset the government for the time being. No one knows what Hitler's going to do next. We need to keep this stuff until he shows his hand, which he will, I'm sure you'll agree."

I nodded and he carried on.

"The stuff you got from Cliveden is sketchy at best and we've only the word of a cook and a footman that Chamberlain is planning anything. I know the whole thing looks fishy, but why shouldn't the PM spend a relaxing Saturday with his pals like Halifax at the home of the Astors? She is after all a Tory MP. They could have been planning an angling outing or chatting about domestic politics."

"But—"

"Hang on Prof. I smell a rat as well, but it's not quite time to start a campaign on this one. I think your friend Cockburn might be interested. Why not nip over and tell him about your weekend in the country. I think you'll find him in Farson's office in Bush House."

"How do you know?"

Ben tapped his nose.

So off I set to Bush House. It was located at Aldwych, at the top of the Strand, and was less than ten minutes' stroll down Fleet Street but, as usual, I took precautions and followed a roundabout route, arriving there about forty minutes after setting off.

It was a vast building and I had some difficulty in finding Farson's office but, after a couple of false starts, I got there. As Ben had predicted, Claud Cockburn was there with his American friend, both looking as if they'd enjoyed a good lunch. Farson's office was thick with smoke and there was a scattering of papers, pens, pencils, a telephone and a typewriter on his desk.

"Roger, good to see you again so soon," said Negley, rising from behind his desk with an outstretched hand.

"Yes, indeed," said Claud, and he too greeted me warmly. "What have you been up to?"

I told them both about my visit to Taplow, the conversation that Jane and I had had with Milly, my return the following day and Milly's information that she had got from Johnny.

"That's very interesting, Roger," said Claud, "and it confirms what I've got from another source. Thank you very much and congratulations on the way you've handled it. Smart move that, turning up with your girlfriend. She sounds sharp. What does she do?"

"Yes, she is on the ball. She's finishing off her accountancy studies."

"Really?" said Claud. "I'd get her to look after my money, if I had any."

All three of us chuckled.

"Then the family outing on the Sunday. Very shrewd. Sounds like you're pulling a good team together, Roger. What about Ben Rogers? What does he make of all this?"

I explained how the Editor had spiked the piece and how Ben had advised me to bring it to him.

"He's dead right. I can certainly use this. Now, if you'll excuse me, I must dash. I've got to finish off Wednesday's edition. Now you've confirmed what I suspected, a nice little piece on the Astors and their merry men needs adding to very quickly. If you're not in a hurry, stay and chat with Negley for a while. I'm sure he can find you a cup of something. Must go. Thank you very much and please keep in touch."

With that he was gone. Negley left to organise coffee for us both and, when he returned, he sat down and looked me in the eye.

"Claud's a great guy, Roger, brilliant journalist, witty, modest, unassuming but, whatever you do, don't think this is some kind of game. It's a deadly serious business and Hitler's the biggest threat to peace this planet's ever seen. He'll stop at nothing to get what he wants and your Neville Chamberlain's just the same. He may look like a useless old man but he's ruthlessly determined to get his way with this appeasement business. That puts the likes of Claud and you British newspapermen in danger because Chamberlain's guys will do all they can to shut you up. You've already had a couple of run-ins with them and if you carry on like this it won't be the last time you're under threat."

Negley paused then drank some coffee before continuing.

"You go to the movies, Roger?"

"As often as I can." I explained to Negley that I had stood in as film reviewer on the paper from time to time.

"What do you make of the newsreels?"

"To tell you the truth, they irritate me a bit. I sometimes get the impression that they're either not telling the whole story or taking sides, particularly over Spain."

"You're dead right. Did you know *Movietone* is controlled by your man Northcliffe? His *Daily Mail* paper seems unlikely to stand up to Hitler, doesn't it?"

"Hardly."

"The movie companies see the newsreels as part of the evening's entertainment. They don't want to put the fear of God into the audience about war, Hitler, Mussolini, Japan or whatever. They pay to be entertained not frightened. The public would stop coming if they don't enjoy their evenings."

"Yes I can see that."

"But the audience still believes what they see and they're not getting the true picture about what's going on. Ever see footage of Jews being persecuted in Germany in the newsreels?"

"I seem to remember seeing something when I was at school, just after Hitler came to power."

"But nothing since, eh Roger? The newsreels are under strict orders not to show any Jewish stuff in case they upset Hitler. Ever seen our newsreel *The March of Time*?"

"Occasionally," I replied, "it seems pretty good to me."

"It is but you haven't really seen it! In the States, you get shown all about Germany: the good and the very bad. Here you just get to see the good. Anything nasty about Germany and Italy is censored."

I said I was beginning to realise that.

Negley resumed. "So far your newspapers have mostly been left alone but we both know that might not last. I'm not suggesting it'll ever be as bad as the censorship in Nazi Germany, but any interference in the freedom of the press is a really intolerable thing which is why *The Week* is so important. You'll find that out when you read Wednesday's issue."

I then asked Negley to tell me what he could about Czechoslovakia and for the next forty-five minutes he gave me the whole story. Together with what I had learned in the pub that lunchtime, I was now beginning to see just how deep the Czech problem might be.

I thanked Negley and walked back to Bouverie Street. I had plenty of time before I left for home, so I went to the archive room where back copies of both of our papers were kept. I read up on all references to Czechoslovakia then trawled through some back issues of *The Times*. Now *The Times* might appear to be playing a sinister role in the appeasement programme, but as a public record of events it had no equal.

It was gone ten when I left the office, feeling much better equipped to write about Czechoslovakia than at the start of the day. It was after eleven when I arrived home and I'd been so absorbed all day I'd forgotten to eat. My mother made me a ham sandwich, I had a cup of tea then fell into to bed exhausted.

I hardly seemed to have fallen asleep when it was time to get up, but I arrived at the office on time and told Ben about my afternoon at Bush House, the likelihood that the next day's issue of *The Week* would have some good stuff in it about Cliveden and Negley Farson's take on things. I'd gotten over my disappointment at having my Cliveden piece spiked and asked Ben if I could put together something about Czechoslovakia. He agreed to this, but warned me to deal in facts. Let the readers draw their own conclusions by reading between the lines. We both knew that this was going to be the big story of the summer of 1938. So I sat down and wrote it.

Czechoslovakia was a made up country. It hadn't even existed before 1918. The winners of the war, notably France, the USA and ourselves, had met in Paris over a long period of time and eventually came up with the Treaty of Versailles. It was a long and complicated series of documents which, amongst other things, told the Germans they couldn't station troops in the Rhineland, forbade the Germans from uniting with Austria and gave part of Germany to Poland so that the Poles could have access to the Baltic Sea. The former German port of Danzig was declared a free city, managed by the League of Nations. Germany was effectively cut in two with East Prussia separated from the rest of the country by the so-called Polish Corridor to the Baltic.

Even as the treaty was being signed, many experts were already sensing that the Germans would eventually want to do something about their loss of territory. The Rhineland and Austria had already been dealt with. Poland should be next but Hitler seemed to have pushed it down the agenda for the time being. Why? The area governed by the new state of Czechoslovakia had never been part of Germany, so why did Hitler have any interest in it all? What justification did he have for poking his nose into

Czech affairs? The simple answer was there were more than three million German speaking people living within Czechoslovakia's borders.

The new Czech state had a mixture of nationalities living within its borders as well as the Germans who were living next to the frontier of the Reich. Under these circumstances, it operated quite well as a modern democracy.

But the Czechs were no fools. Despite their success they knew they were vulnerable and began to plan for a second future. They made defensive treaties with other countries including France and, later, the Soviet Union who said they would support the Czechs if France did the same. Now I could understand Chamberlain's reluctance to commit to the Czechs. If France defended the Czechs so would the Soviet Union and we would be duty bound to join in. Without a treaty with the Czechs, we would only have to fight if France was attacked directly.

The area of Czechoslovakia where the German speaking peoples lived was called the Sudetenland and here the Czech government built a series of massive fortresses to protect themselves from German attack. Their western border with Germany was straddled by the Bohemian Hills, providing superb natural defences. Also in the Sudetenland was the Czech city of Pilsen which housed Europe's biggest armament factories: the Skoda works.

Czechoslovakia had everything Hitler needed; rich mineral deposits, Europe's best armaments factories, natural and man-made defences and three million German speaking people. It was a perfect buffer to the hated Soviet Union. He needed an excuse to intervene and the Sudetens provided it.

Henlein, the Sudeten German leader, had already written to Hitler complaining about the treatment of the German minority in Czechoslovakia. Henlein said that all the best jobs were grabbed by Czechs and the Sudetens didn't have a voice in the Czech parliament. Hitler didn't bother replying. Austria was top of his agenda. Then, on the day after my visit to Bush House, Henlein called for the German speaking peoples in Czechoslovakia to be allowed to manage their own affairs within the Czech state.

Later that evening Richard Walker called at my house to say that he had heard from Harry that Henlein had met Hitler in Germany on the previous day. Was it a coincidence that the day after he met the Fuhrer, Henlein was calling for some form of independence? Almost certainly not. The stage was set for the next installment of Hitler's plan but he was taking an incredible risk going up against the last remaining democratic state in Central Europe which was heavily armed, well defended and had treaties with two major powers. I thought there were only two possible outcomes; a German defeat at the hands of a combined Czech/Soviet/ French force or Hitler backing down and losing face. I reckoned without Chamberlain.

CHAPTER TWENTY SIX

The Shame of Not Knowing

"Give me not poverty lest I steal."
DANIEL DEFOE

Thursday morning found me in Ben's office reading the latest edition of *The Week*. Claud had certainly not disappointed us.

Starting off with a small boast, the Editor informed the readers that he had to raise subscriptions to eight shillings for six months and sixteen shillings for the full year from the end of April. This, he informed us, was because the demand for news not normally available was growing at such a rate he had to print more pages.

Claud also pointed out that Lady Astor had written to our sister daily the previous week denying the existence of the Cliveden set. I knew of this letter so it seemed doubly odd that the whole gang of them, including Chamberlain, had gathered there the previous weekend.

The Week then turned to the weekend's events. The news sheet claimed that the chief item under discussion was the desertion of Czechoslovakia, adding, and this I didn't know, that the Prime Minister would tell France that we would not support her if she honoured her treaty with the Czechs. Hitler, of course, would be rubbing his hands with glee. The British were keeping to the promises made by Halifax the previous November. Claud then reported on the PM's recent fishing trip with Lord Londonderry, Hitler's closest ally in Britain. He concluded by describing the Cliveden set as 'Hitler's Fifth Column' and the Cliveden House itself as 'the Schloss.'

"Doesn't pull his punches your friend Claud, does he Prof," Ben began, "and you played a part in that. You must feel pleased."

"I suppose so," I replied, "but I would rather we weren't talking about deserting countries and preparing for war."

"Still, the cat's out of the bag now. Believe you me this story's going to run and run. Hitler obviously wants to get his grubby paws on Czechoslovakia, for the reasons you said in that good piece last week. It'll be interesting to see how he does it without sending the whole of Europe up in flames. How do you think he'll go about it?"

"Haven't a clue, but he won't make a move if he thinks the French and Russians'll stand up to him. He needs to be certain that the French won't have a go at him. Once he's achieved that, he knows the Russians'll stay out of it because they'll only make a move if the French do."

"And where do we come in?" Ben asked.

We don't. Halifax and Londonderry have already told Hitler that as long as he drops his demands for colonies we'll give him a free hand in Eastern Europe."

"Mm," mused Ben, "I'm not so sure about that. We're going to have a nervous and interesting summer. Now then, Prof, I want you to have a crack at something else."

"Oh what's that?"

"Housing."

"Housing? I don't know anything about it," I protested.

"You didn't know anything about Czechoslovakia a couple of weeks ago now you're our resident expert."

I laughed. "Hardly."

"The point is that you've got yourself clued up on foreign affairs pretty quickly. A clever bloke like you can do the same with housing, I'm certain."

"What exactly do you want?" I asked.

"Both our papers have been conducting a campaign for better housing since the end of the war. We're not the only ones, of course. Remember Lloyd George's 'homes fit for heroes' promise in 1919? Well, you probably don't, but you must have heard of it."

"Yes."

"I'd like you to find out how we're doing in keeping that promise."

"OK."

"I don't mean reading up and coming up with a pile of facts and figures. I want you to go and see for yourself."

"Where do you want me to go?"

"How about Wandsworth?"

"Why Wandsworth?"

"Because everybody tells me that the housing there is pretty awful but the local council are trying to do something about it. There's some spanking new flats just opened up. Get yourself down there tomorrow, visit the shitty houses first, chat with some of the residents then do the same at the new flats. Write a nice piece and compare the two, do some background mugging up and put some stuff together on how we're doing in getting rid of the slums."

The word slums gave me a jolt. I knew about them of course. I'd just read George Orwell's *The Road to Wigan Pier* but that was about the north of England, a foreign country to me. Surely it couldn't be like that in London. I said as much to Ben.

"You'd be surprised Prof. Anyway go see for yourself. By the way, don't wear your best suit. You wouldn't want it ruined."

I got off the train at Wandsworth Town on the following morning. I was lucky the train stopped there on its way from home to Waterloo. Ben had given me instructions so I had a pretty good idea of where to go.

As soon as I stepped out of the rather scruffy station, I knew I was entering a world about which I knew precisely nothing. This wasn't my home town, nor was it Cambridge, nor Paris, or even central London. This was working class Britain: dull, smoky, down at the heel and utterly depressing.

I made my way to the streets where Ben had told me some of London's worst slums were. I passed a Victorian school en route, bright and well lit inside but dour and dirty red bricked outside. The first houses I spotted

were a block of back to backs with a brewery next to them. The brewery
was belching smoke and noise, with a dozen or so men busily loading
barrels of beer on to carts, at the front of which stood an expectant off-
white horse waiting to set off on his delivery round.

I looked at the houses, all of them completely run-down with old
newspapers blocking out the windows, doors hanging off hinges, roofs
with dozens of tiles missing. Not one of them looked to be inhabited so I
assumed they were awaiting demolition.

I wasn't going to get much copy here, I thought, so I set off in search
of some inhabited houses. After a few steps, I was astonished to see an
elderly woman step out through a front door in one of the houses and
proceed to belt the living daylights out of the wall next to the door with a
mat. All sorts of filth flew out of the mat and I thought to myself that the
whole house would fall down if she carried on much longer.

I took a few deep breaths and walked up to her and introduced myself.
As luck would have it she was an avid reader of our paper and she knew
of our campaign for better housing for the London working class. She
invited me in and offered me a cup of tea which I accepted, thinking that
to refuse would set me off on the wrong foot.

Her name, she told me, was Chrissie and she'd lived in this house all
her life and her parents, now both dead, had lived there before her. She'd
married after the war but her husband had died of TB in 1925 when she'd
been left a twenty-six-year-old widow, with four children, two boys and
two girls, to bring up on her own. I quickly did some mental arithmetic
and was amazed to realise that she was barely forty, although she looked
at least fifteen years older. She had steel grey hair, immaculately combed,
a thin pale face with blackness around her eyes and was dressed in a green
cardigan and brown skirt, both of which were clean but had clearly seen
better days.

Chrissie then told me all about her living conditions. What she said
filled me with horror but she did it in such a matter of fact way that I was
even more disturbed than I might have been had she shouted, moaned
and complained.

I could see for myself that her house was falling to pieces. I could hardly believe that anyone could survive, let alone choose to live there. To start with the room in which we were sitting was almost pitch black and I could hardly make out Chrissie's features as I peered into the gloom. What little light there was came from a small window which she told me she covered with newspaper at night. There was a feeble coal fire burning which filled the room with smoke. Chrissie explained that the chimney was blocked. The walls were infested with insects and appeared to be moving. What passed for a dining table was perched on wedges because the floor was uneven and sinking. The wood in the window frames was rotten.

There was another small table with a bowl on it where Chrissie said she did the washing up and the laundry. There was no garden to dry the laundry, like at my parents' house, so she explained she had to spread them around the room, adding to the dampness. In the summer, she said, she sometimes hung them in the street when the sun broke through the industrial gloom.

I couldn't see a tap and, when I enquired, Chrissie told me there was one outside which was shared between the four houses in her block, just like the toilet which was in a shack propped up against the brewery wall and didn't flush properly. Everything: eating, washing of clothes, plates and people, was done in this one tiny room.

Then we went upstairs, taking care to avoid the holes in the steps, to the one bedroom where five people slept. We could just about get into the room where there was an old iron bedstead about four foot wide which had been immaculately made up with worn sheets and a threadbare blanket. Most of the rest of the room was taken up with a mattress on the floor and an ancient chest of drawers, which was against the wall under another tiny, rotting window.

Chrissie said the four children slept head to toe in the bed and she made do with the mattress. The bed and mattress were fairly comfortable, she claimed, but they were often kept awake at night by the constant scurrying of rats, one of whom had woken her a week or so previously when it ran across her face.

I was glad to escape from this and we gingerly made our way back downstairs to the other room. I asked her how she made ends meet and she told me that she did odd jobs like taking in washing and mending clothes. Three of her four children were working: the eldest boy in the brewery and the two girls as assistants in local shops. The youngest boy was still at the Elementary School that I had passed on the way to Chrissie's house.

She went on to tell me that there were no cupboards in which she could keep food. Anything left lying about would be eaten by the rats, so she went shopping every day. She had just about enough money to get by. The rent was low and she reckoned that this gave the landlord the excuse not to bother with any repairs to the houses. It wasn't just that the houses were old, they'd been built in the 1850s, but they had been very badly built.

Chrissie, however, thought she'd been lucky. Even though her husband had died young, all of her children had survived and she hoped they would reach adulthood. Plenty of her neighbours, she told me, had lost one, two, sometimes even more children to the diseases that flourished in these foul conditions: TB, bronchitis, pneumonia, diarrhea and others. Yes, she felt very lucky.

I asked her about the new flats that the council had built and she told me she was on the waiting list to move to one. The hovel she was in was due to be demolished in the next year. Obviously, she was looking forward to that and, though the rent was likely to be higher, she thought her health would improve and she'd be able to earn more with extra work. She wasn't really that worried about money; she just wanted to get out of this hell hole and the sooner, the better.

Chrissie had brains, guts and determination and I was sure she would cope, especially when she moved into her new flat. Nevertheless, I was glad to escape from the slums and ten minutes later I was standing across the road from the council's new flats.

The flats were a kind of sparkling grey from the outside. There were five floors and at each of the top four levels were balconies where I could see tables and chairs and pots and plants. In front of the building was a stretch of beautifully cut grass and, every ten yards or so, smart black waste bins.

I approached an old man in dungarees who was sweeping the path leading up to one of the entrances. I introduced myself and he told me that he was the caretaker of one of the blocks of flats. There were a total of five hundred flats and, when they were all occupied, two and a half thousand people would have moved there from the slums.

He offered to take me to see one of the flats. He was sure Mrs Cave was in. He telephoned the doorbell and, a few seconds later, a dark haired middle-aged lady appeared. I introduced myself and she invited me in.

The flat was beautiful; plenty of space, freshly painted white walls, a living room which had a dining table in the corner, a kitchen, two bedrooms and a bathroom. It was warm in each room with bags of light and, of course, electricity.

Mrs Cave had moved from a slum house about six months ago. She shared the flat with her husband, a postman, and her two children, a boy and a girl, who were both at school.

For Mrs Cave, for me and for anyone with two eyes in their head, the contrast with slum life couldn't have been greater. Here were families, not living in squalor and disease, but in clean, well looked after and well-furnished homes with constant hot water and with room outside for the children to play in safety. There was a far smaller chance that anyone would fall ill with some life threatening disease but, above all, a place where they could live like human beings.

I thanked Mrs Cave and made my way back to the station. All kinds of thoughts were rushing around in my head but, more than anything, I felt a deep sense of shame. I was ashamed that, until that day, I knew nothing of these slums; it was just a word I'd read in the newspapers. At my grammar school, at Cambridge, and in my smart middle class semi-detached post war home, nobody ever talked about the slums.

I thought how the situation in London was better than in other parts of the country. We were always being told that the south-east of England was recovering well from the worst of the depression. How much worse might it be in South Wales or North East England or Clydeside where there were still millions out of work?

And what was the government doing about all this? That same government that seemed to spend most of its time trying to pal up with those revolting tyrants Hitler and Mussolini. A morning trip to Wandsworth and a quick read of *The Road to Wigan Pier* wasn't enough. I needed to know more. And what was Chamberlain doing about it, I asked myself in anger. Precisely nothing, I guessed.

Of course I was wrong.

CHAPTER TWENTY SEVEN

Not Quite What I Expected

"Money is like muck, not good
except it be spread."
FRANCIS BACON

The late spring and early summer started quietly. The Australian cricket team arrived and all sports fans were looking forward to the Test series starting in June. The Aussies held the Ashes and had their champion in Bradman but we had our own star players, including Walter Hammond, who had been scoring runs for fun in Test Matches for more than ten years. I planned to take some holiday time to watch one of the games.

Then there were holidays. The papers were full of adverts for trips to Germany. Perhaps I'd take one with Jane. Then again perhaps not. We'd stick to Bournemouth or Torquay or the Isle of Wight, or maybe even Blackpool. Perhaps we'd bump into Gracie Fields or George Formby.

Thinking about Blackpool reminded me that it was in the north of England, not far from Orwell's Wigan. I wondered what it was like to live up there. Was it all like the slums of Wandsworth? This brought me back to my eye-opening trip to that part of London and the shame I felt. What was the government doing about lousy housing? And especially our Prime Minister, Mr Chamberlain?

During my last few months at Cambridge and since I'd started working, I'd followed the line that the dictators in Italy and Germany were bad people and that our government should be standing up to them and making sure that they kept themselves to themselves and stopped threatening other countries.

Without giving it too much thought I'd jumped onto the bandwagon, shouting insults at Germany when she marched into the Rhineland, seized Austria and now threatened Czechoslovakia. Like all other journalists I was angry at the government's attempts to control the press and hated the cinema newsreels with their biased and inaccurate coverage of the Spanish Civil War which favoured Franco. I disliked the way they played cheerful music over footage showing tens of thousands of uniformed Germans carrying banners and torches at the Nuremberg rallies.

The people I'd spoken to—Dobb, Farson, Cockburn, Ben Rogers, Jane and Richard, even my parents—all seemed to think like I did—or rather I thought that they did. It was time to do some thinking for myself and I started by finding more about our bogeyman, Neville Chamberlain, the man who was offering his hand in friendship to Adolf Hitler, the biggest tyrant since Attila the Hun.

I spent a couple of days in between routine work finding out all I could about the PM. I talked to colleagues, spent a couple of hours with Philip Noel Baker and read the back issues of just about every newspaper I could lay my hands on. I was quite surprised to find that, far from being a weak leader with a peace-at-any-price mission, he seemed to be a tough, determined man of the people, with the best interests of the country as a whole as his chief aim in life.

For a start he was as old as he looked, nearly seventy. He came from Birmingham where he had been a successful businessman and a popular and effective Lord Mayor, improving the lot of the working class. He'd only been an MP for twenty years and had won his seat in 1918, campaigning on a social reform platform. It wasn't long before he became a minister, Post Master General in 1922 and Minister of Health a year later, a job he kept till 1929, apart from the short spell when Ramsay Macdonald's Labour Government had been in office.

Chamberlain hated war. His close cousin Norman had been killed in the

1914–1918 conflict. He mistrusted alliances. He believed that those we'd made with France in 1904 and Russia three years later had done nothing to prevent the war. In fact, these alliances had made sure it happened, he had claimed.

Chamberlain became Chancellor of the Exchequer when the National Government was formed in 1931 and stayed at the Treasury until he became Prime Minister in May 1937.

Evidently, he was a tough Chancellor. The country was in deep trouble in 1931 and was almost broke. He deserved some credit for improving our financial position although I doubt that the unemployed, who'd had their benefits cut, or the police officers, nurses and teachers whose pay had been reduced would agree.

I remembered seeing Chamberlain on a cinema newsreel a few years previously; leaning back on his chair, with a grin on his face, telling us that other countries were amazed at our financial recovery. He obviously enjoyed being seen to be successful.

It was Chamberlain himself who started to tackle the housing problem. Lloyd George, Prime Minister during the second half of the war, had talked about building 'homes fit for heroes' but had done nothing about it. So it was left to Chamberlain to initiate the big slum clearance and house building programmes. He'd had some success, but there was still a lot to be done.

Philip Noel Baker told me that he admired but did not like Chamberlain. He said that the Prime Minster had a strong sense of duty and was obviously a born social reformer, but he was a bit of cold fish and didn't socialise much. He didn't like criticism, was easily flattered and found it difficult to judge the mood in both the House of Commons and the country as a whole. However, Philip believed that at heart Chamberlain had a social conscience and liked him for it. That very week, the PM had told the House about the urgent need to build more schools, houses and hospitals.

The picture I was getting wasn't what I expected. The PM was definitely not your typical Tory, more a reforming Liberal or, dare I say it, a socialist, a bit like me in fact. I was a bit confused though. How could he reconcile spending almost three hundred million pounds on armaments in 1937, rather than using the money to demolish slums and build more houses?

I was beginning to become convinced that improving the lives of ordinary Britons was his aim but he couldn't do it until he'd dealt with Germany. OK, we had to negotiate with Hitler from a position of strength, hence the arms bill. I'd buy that, but war would have been even more expensive in terms of lives lost and the scrapping of the PM's social programme. So war had to be avoided.

I put together this pen picture of Chamberlain and his dilemma and handed it to Ben. He was in his usual garb: rolled up sleeves, open necked shirt and braces. He read my piece, looked at me and said, "Falling in love with our beloved PM are you Prof?"

"Not at all," I protested. "Just trying to give a balanced view of things and ask some relevant questions."

"Just kidding. This is very good. You've obviously gone to a lot of trouble here. I'm sure they'll like it in Downing Street."

"That's not why I wrote it. I just wanted to show that there are two sides to everything. Turns out Chamberlain's not quite the weak man we thought him to be."

"I hate to pull the age card on you Prof," Ben continued, "but I'm old enough to remember when old Neville was performing all these good works, and quite popular he was too. He was even on good terms with some of the TUC boys, but its one thing building schools, houses and hospitals and another dealing with maniacs like Hitler. Anyway, it's not all spot-on in this country; just ask the dock workers on Tyneside or in Glasgow or the coal miners in South Wales. You've seen what it's like in Wandsworth."

"I bet there's a lot more of that up north. Things might be looking up in St Albans and Guildford but it's not so great in Tonypandy and Jarrow. Anyway, you're right, he's made a start. Let's see how he gets on with Hitler."

"So you'll print it?" I asked.

"Don't see why not. Right, I've got some jobs for you. Our film guy has left so I want you to fill in for the time being."

"But—" I began.

"It's OK. It's only temporary. We'll be getting someone else soon. I thought you liked films?"

"I do," I replied, "but I'm a bit hooked on this politics stuff. I wouldn't want to give it up."

Ben's response was reassuring.

"I don't want you to. There's only a couple of films to cover for the rest of this month. The rest of the time keep your eyes on this Czechoslovakia business. It's starting to kick off now. Your contact could come in useful. Still seeing him?"

"Yes. He works for my father. I'll pop in and have a chat with him tomorrow."

"Good. Off you go Prof. Keep up the good work."

The next day I went to work with my father and spent time with Richard. I hadn't upset my watchers for quite a while and I was pretty sure they'd given me up as a won cause. They'd be even more certain when they read my piece on the PM later that day.

Richard seemed pleased to see me.

"How are you Roger?"

"Very well, thanks. And you?"

"OK, but I've got a bit of bad news."

"Oh?"

"Our friendly German in the embassy has been posted to the Hague."

"Do you think they're on to him?"

"No. It's normal in their line of work to get shuffled about between embassies and he's done his four year stint here. From what he said to Harry, our secret service is sending a man to Holland to keep in touch. He'll still be getting useful intelligence coming across his desk."

"That's no use to us though is it? The secret service isn't going to pass this stuff to us."

"Hardly," replied Richard, "but the good news is that he's passed the Harry contact to another member of the embassy staff who's even more senior. He's totally reliable and hates the Nazis."

"I hope you're right. I wouldn't want Harry to end up floating in the

Thames."

"No, he won't. I'm sure it's safe. I just hope it's useful. There is something for you I got from Harry yesterday. I was going to get your father to let you know, but now you're here you might as well have it."

Richard then gave me an up-to-date summary of the Czech situation. Henlein had been told by Hitler to demand more from the Czechs than they could possibly agree to and the Fuhrer had promised to send 'trained personnel' into the Sudetenland to stir up trouble.

"Same old pattern from Hitler," Richard said, "just like Austria. March in and save the persecuted German citizens."

"So Chamberlain's wasting his time with all this appeasement stuff?" I asked.

"No, not necessarily. As long as he makes it clear to Hitler that Britain and France won't stand by while he attacks the Czechs."

"But why should we care?"

"Because if we don't, who knows who's next?"

Richard then told me Harry might have something else and he was meeting him later that day. He asked me to call in the next morning.

That turned out to be a false alarm and he called my father to tell me the meeting was off. The tell-tale clicks on the telephone had disappeared. I took this as a sign that whoever was listening in had either developed a more sophisticated method of eavesdropping or stopped tapping the telephone. I guessed the latter.

So I didn't have to rush the following morning to catch the preview of *The Adventures of Tom Sawyer*. It was a really good film, a welcome relief from slums and the threats of war. It was in colour too, not that this was all that unusual, but this print looked especially good. The film had great nightmare sequences in the caverns. It was an excellent ninety minutes of entertainment.

I had a spring in my step as I walked back to the office. I did my piece on Tom Sawyer then put together an article about how Hitler was starting to pull strings in the Sudetenland and went home.

CHAPTER TWENTY EIGHT

Spiked

"Political speech and writing are largely
the defence of the indefensible."
GEORGE ORWELL

Czechoslovakia was the country on everybody's lips during the early summer. It completely overshadowed everything, including the start of the cricket season. The weather was mostly dry, the wickets hard, and the Australians took full advantage of it in the county games.

They won four and drew three of their first seven matches. They never looked like losing. Ominously, Bradman was in terrific form, racking up double centuries against Worcester at New Road and MCC at Lords. He scored hundreds against Surrey and Hampshire and only failed at Northampton, where he scored two.

The first Test was due to start at Trent Bridge in Nottingham on June 10th and, in normal circumstances, an awful lot of people would be looking forward to it. But these weren't normal circumstances. Europe seemed to be on the brink of war; well, not actually on the brink, but about to take a giant step towards it. Chamberlain hadn't threatened the Germans and didn't want the press doing that either, a fact that I became acutely aware of when Ben called me in just before lunch on the day after my trip to the movies.

"Tom Sawyer sounds good Prof," he began. "That'll be in tonight's paper.

Do another one for us please. *Convict 99* on Friday?"

"Sure. Usual place?"

"Yup. Eleven o'clock start. Now that other piece. Afraid it's going in the bin."

I wasn't surprised.

"Go on," I said.

"It's not that it's a bad piece. In fact, it's bloody good and I'm sure the tip-off is right. It's just that all the big white chiefs at the papers have had a three-line whip from Number Ten. Lay off the krauts. It seems the PM thinks that if Hitler thinks we're being moderate, he'll be moderate. Load of rubbish, of course, but for the time being we're under orders to behave ourselves. It doesn't help that our daily is the most unpopular amongst the jackboot brigade. Goebbels says we're the worst of the lot and Henderson agrees with him."

"What's he got to do with it?" I asked.

"Every time there's an article in the English papers telling the readers what a bunch of shits the Nazis are, Henderson has to trot along to the Ministry of Propaganda and tell the poisoned dwarf that we don't represent the views of the government. Henderson has difficulty in persuading Goebbels that we have a free press, unlike them. I doubt he mentions that last bit to the nasty little fella. Anyhow, for the time being, we're gonna do as we're told. If things go too far, we'll think again, but keep digging, Prof."

"Ok."

"At the moment," Ben continued, "our papers' policy is to support the Czechs. I doubt we'll get into trouble for saying that, but once we actually start threatening the Nazis we'll upset that prat Steward. He's already had a word with the owners about that piece we did saying that if Britain deserted the Czechs, Hitler would take it as a sign that he could have carte blanche with other countries. You know, Poland, Belgium, France, then who knows?"

"By the time he's mopped that lot up we'll be right in it. Our policy—the papers', I mean—is that, if we stand up to the bastard now, he'll back off. But we have to tread carefully. We don't want any more of our staff being beaten up by Chamberlain's hatchet men."

"Right, I get it," I replied. "Softly softly for the time being."

"Exactly. Now what I'd like you to do for the next few weeks is to keep an eye on the nationals, see how they're handling this, especially Dawson's rag. I've a feeling he's getting preferential treatment; stuff that the other papers aren't getting. I reckon *The Times* is acting as the government's unofficial mouthpiece."

Chamberlain couldn't have been too pleased with Churchill's latest outburst in Manchester. The old warhorse didn't mince his words and spoke about the war-lust of the dictators, called Germany a Nazi tyranny, pointed out that Italy was a spent force and nothing like the threat of Germany. He trotted out his usual call for rearmament and alliances to encircle Germany, whom he said was an aggressor, and stated his belief in the League of Nations. He finished off by pointing out that Russia had a part to play in all of this.

I still wasn't sure what I made of Churchill. He'd been a good Home Secretary before the war but had made some blunders when he was in charge of the Admiralty during the war. He wasn't much of a Chancellor of the Exchequer during the twenties, as far as I could judge and had been violently anti-Communist since Lenin's revolution. Churchill had been warning everybody about the threat of the Nazis for six years. He seemed to have decided that they were worse than the Russians.

Lots of people called him a warmonger and it was hardly surprising that he had been kept out of the cabinet for almost ten years. One thing was for certain: he'd be top of the list in Hitler's little black book.

Meanwhile, in Czechoslovakia, Henlein was calling for autonomy for the Sudeten Germans. He wanted them to run their own affairs inside the Czech state, a bit like Switzerland or, if say, Scotland stayed inside the UK and collected their own taxes and made certain laws of their own. It didn't seem a bad idea. Even Churchill, in another one of his speeches, this time in Bristol, seemed to agree with it.

So, of course, did the Germans, but they also wanted the Czechs to tear up their treaty with Russia. That would be useful if the Germans did march in. They'd have one less opponent to deal with. The Czechs had no intention of doing that, and who could blame them?

The Czechs took all this in their stride. Their President, Benes, promised to look into making concessions to the Sudeten Germans: greater representation in the Czech Parliament, more jobs in the civil service, greater acceptance of the German language and so on, but nobody had the right, he said, to tell Czechoslovakia to change her foreign policy.

The Times (or was it Chamberlain and Halifax?) supported the Sudeten grievances and told the Czechs to make concessions. The Sudetens, like *The Times* and Her Majesty's Government, were seeking a peaceful outcome. To be fair, Dawson did accept that, once the Sudetens got what they wanted, the various other racial minorities in Czechoslovakia would start kicking up a fuss and asking for their slice of the cake.

But things were looking up. The peaceful Sudetens were asking for certain rights and the Czechs were prepared to look into giving them. Great, no war then. It helped me as well, as I was becoming increasingly worried about my country spending its hard earned money on guns rather than schools, hospitals and houses. We all reckoned without Hitler.

The Fuhrer wanted Czechoslovakia. He wanted her minerals, her agricultural land, her armaments factories and her military defences. He wasn't going to get any of that with everyone agreeing on a peaceful solution so he used the German press to orchestrate his own outcome.

Suddenly, the Nazi papers were full of reports of anti-German atrocities in the Sudetenland. Germans were being beaten up and arrested by Czech police for no apparent reason. Even Czech children were alleged to be getting in on the act by telling anti-German jokes in school.

Hitler responded by moving troops towards the Czech border, the German press telling the world that there was nothing sinister in this. The troop movements were part of normal manoeuvres. The Czechs called up a hundred thousand reservists and the French chipped in saying that they were ready to stand by their treaty with the Czechs. It was 1914 all over again and war became a strong possibility. We had obligations to France and, if they became involved, we'd have to fight alongside them.

Where did all that leave me and my family and Jane? I'd probably be

called up to fight and be killed in some muddy trench. Jane and my mother
and father would probably be bombed to bits in their beds.

So I wasn't in a great mood when I set off to watch *Convict 99* and my
mood was hardly improved by the film, which starred Will Hay. Now, I
liked Will Hay and some of his films that I'd seen before like *Oh Mr Porter*
and *Ask a Policeman* were very funny. His usual sidekicks, Moore Marriott
and Graham Moffatt, were with him, but it just didn't come off.

As I hurried back to the office to write a bad review, I asked myself
whether my mood was affecting my judgement of the film. I hoped not.
I'd be a lousy journalist if it did.

The Czech crisis fizzled out, for the time being anyway. Troops drew back
from the border and Benes promised a Minorities Act which would look
after the interests of the various races living within Czech borders. They
would be 'equal amongst equals' said the Czech President. Local elections
were soon to be held in Czechoslovakia and proper discussions would be
held with the minorities when elections were completed in early June.

The Times reported that both our government and the French were
urging restraint on both sides and Henderson told Ribbentrop, now
German Foreign Minister, that Chamberlain was confident that the Czechs
would give the minorities what they wanted. *The Times* added that all this
tension might have been avoided if the Czechs had tried to deal with the
minorities' grievances earlier but, I added in my summary, before Hitler
and the Nazis there were no grievances.

Ben seemed OK with my newspaper watch then packed me off to
Chingford to listen to Churchill's latest outburst. I must say I had a sneaking
admiration for the old fella. He looked about six stone overweight, smoked
like a chimney and, from what I'd heard, drank like a fish. Yet here he was,
in his mid-sixties, running around the country like a man half his age
spreading his gospel to all and sundry. He must truly believe in what he
was saying, I thought, or else why go chasing all over the shop when he
could have been at home knocking back a brandy or puffing on a cigar?

Churchill was in good form. He said he remained hopeful of a peaceful
solution and added that the reason for the relaxation in tension was

that Great Britain and France had stood, side by side, in supporting Czechoslovakia. This pleased me and everyone present but I didn't like the next bit when he called for even greater rearmament. The German Air Force was more powerful than ours, and moving further ahead, and the German Army was far stronger than the French. We might have got away with it this time, he added, but the matter wasn't over, by any means, and we'd need a far stronger team to hold the Germans off in future.

I didn't care too much for this. Hitler's bluff had been called. Benes had agreed to concessions and the Nazis had backed down. Yet, at the back of my mind, was a nagging worry that Richard had sown when he said that Henlein had been told by Hitler to ask for more than he would ever get from the Czechs.

My father told me that Richard has some important information. I telephoned Richard and we agreed to spend the next day together watching cricket at the Oval where Surrey were playing Warwickshire.

I called Ben first thing the following morning and told him where I'd be. Richard and I travelled to the match together and, after buying a scorecard, a cup of coffee and hiring a cushion, we settled down in a quiet corner of the ground where we couldn't be overheard. What he told me was the most frightening thing I'd ever heard in my life.

CHAPTER TWENTY NINE

The Hossbach Memorandum

"Dictators ride to and fro upon tigers
which they dare not dismount."
WINSTON CHURCHILL

"I'm not sure you're going to be able to use this Roger," Richard began. "In fact, I know damn well you're not, but just knowing about it will help you to interpret Hitler's actions. When you've heard what I've got to say I'm sure you'll agree that Harry's new source in the German Embassy sounds like he's going to be a goldmine."

Any interest I had in the cricket vanished straight away and I looked at him and nodded for him to continue.

"I wasn't sure I was going to give you this, knowing that it couldn't be printed, but reading the papers over the past couple of weeks makes me think they believe the crisis is over; Sudetens ask for concessions, Czechs say OK, and everyone settles down happy. But they're kidding themselves."

He paused for a moment, then continued.

"Just before Halifax went to Germany last November, Hitler called a meeting at the Reich Chancellery in Berlin. Apart from the Fuhrer himself, present were Goering, representing the Air Force, von Blomberg the War Minister, von Fritsch the Army Commander in Chief, Admiral Raeder of the Navy, von Neurath the Foreign Minister before Ribbentrop and a Colonel called Hossbach. He's Hitler's Military Adjutant and it was his job to take the notes and write them up later in the form of a memorandum."

"Neither Harry nor I know where the leak has come from but, when I've gone through the memorandum, the possible source of the leak might become clearer. It is, of course, ultra secret. Tell me, Roger, have you ever read *Mein Kampf*?"

"Good heavens no. I don't suppose my German's good enough."

"Well, perhaps you should because it contains all the clues about Hitler's behaviour and his plans. That's where this meeting started, I say meeting but it was really six men listening to the Fuhrer while he talked for more than four hours, with a summary of Mein Kampf."

Richard then gave me a synopsis of what Hitler had said. He had begun with his well-known desire for extra living space beyond existing borders for the eighty million Germans. To achieve this, Hitler had said, meant taking risks and he thought that set-backs were inevitable. Germany's chief opponents, he said, were France and Great Britain and that opposition should be overcome by force. Hitler, it seemed, particularly hated France because of his own experiences in the war and because of the humiliation that he considered Germany suffered at Versailles. He was seeking revenge over the French and recognised that attacking them meant Britain would be bound by treaty to come to their aid. He then pointed out that both countries were re-arming and his aim was to defeat them sooner rather than later and in any case before 1945 when both countries might have become too strong.

Hitler had continued by saying that France was in the throes of internal political strife and that might render them incapable of honouring their treaty obligations to Czechoslovakia which, along with Austria, was his immediate top priority.

Surrey were batting and I was vaguely aware of wickets falling, although neither Richard nor I took a scrap of notice and our scorecards remained blank.

Hitler hoped that Poland would remain neutral and that France might become involved in a Mediterranean war with Italy. We'd have to become involved with that as France's ally and Hitler thought that would leave him free to deal with Austria and Czechoslovakia. He also recognised the long term but not immediate threat from Russia. He finished his lecture by ordering attack plans against Austria and Czechoslovakia to be drawn up instantly.

"Now this is where, Roger, you might get a clue as to where all this incredible information has come from because, when the Fuhrer paused for breath, Blomberg, Fritsch and Neurath told him that Germany wasn't ready for war. Within a couple of months, all three had been sacked."

"So you think one of them has spilled the beans?" I asked.

"Definitely. Probably Fritsch."

We paused to eat our lunch and buy a drink. I needed the break to take all this in.

Play resumed after lunch and Richard and I carried on our discussion. This time I led the way.

"Do you think Chamberlain knows all this?"

"Almost certainly," replied Richard. "I can't believe the Secret Service haven't been able to get hold of it."

"Then why's he continuing to cosy up to Hitler?"

"Who knows? Perhaps he doesn't believe it or maybe he thinks he can persuade Hitler to change his mind or he could be trying to buy time until we're strong enough to face up to Germany. I know as little about Chamberlain's motives as you."

Another wicket fell, the first after lunch, and we politely clapped the outgoing batsman up the pavilion steps, then Richard continued.

"One thing I'm certain of, Roger, is that Chamberlain and France must stand up to Hitler now. If they do, war might just be avoided or, failing that, maybe there'll be just a short war."

"Go on."

"If Germany marches into Czechoslovakia, France would most probably tell Hitler to get out. Since France and the Czechs have a treaty, any refusal by Hitler would result in France declaring war on Germany. Then France, and Czechoslovakia's other ally the Soviet Union, would honour their treaty obligations and Hitler would be facing his nightmare scenario of a war on two fronts."

"What, France attacking German occupied Czechoslovakia from the west and Russia from the east?"

"No, don't be daft. Think of the geography. France can't attack German occupied Czechoslovakia without passing through Germany. France will have to attack Germany's western front. That might just be enough to deter Hitler."

"What sort of resistance will the Czechs put up?" I asked.

"Pretty stiff. They've got a well-trained army, strong fortifications and the Bohemian mountains as a natural defence and, with the French sniffing up his rear end, the Fuhrer won't find it easy."

"What about the Russians?"

"There's a bit of a problem there. Their army's not strong; Stalin's had most of the top officers shot and they won't easily get permission from the Poles to march across their land. Stalin would probably have to content himself with bombing German troops and artillery in occupied Czechoslovakia."

"Still," I said, "Hitler's position won't look too good with Czech troops and Russian bombers on one flank and French, and probably British, troops on the other. He'll probably lose won't he?"

"More than likely and that's where Fritsch, Blomberg and Neurath come in. A defeated Hitler would almost certainly be kicked out by his own army. In fact even if Hitler doesn't attack Czechoslovakia he may well be kicked out. The German people and the army will see him for what he is: a bully, all bluster and no action. There's only two ways that Hitler can win this one: either by attacking the Czechs and everyone else stands back and lets him get on with it, or by negotiation."

"Negotiation?"

"If Chamberlain and the French can persuade the Czechs to give ground then Hitler gets what he wants without firing a shot."

"Surely that won't happen will it?" I asked.

"Let's hope not. Britain and France must stand up to Hitler now. Hitler can't tell France to mind her own business, it *is* her business; she's got treaty obligations with the Czechs, and we're allied to France, so it's our business too. In any case, Czechoslovakia has never been part of Germany, so Hitler can't play the injustices of Versailles card."

Richard made a very convincing argument and he spoke with the angry conviction of a man who saw war on the horizon.

"So Chamberlain and France confront Hitler now, end of story." Richard said and then fell quiet.

That was it really. It was a fine afternoon and we caught up with the cricket. Surrey struggled against the spin bowling of Hollies and Paine, who took four wickets each, and reached 173 for 9 at the close with only Barling, who made 56, topping fifty.

We hardly exchanged a word on the way home. We hadn't fallen out but we were both overwhelmed by the implications of Richard's view.

As we went our separate ways Richard said.

"I hope the newspapers don't back Chamberlain if he does try to do a deal with Hitler."

"They won't, I'm sure," I replied, "as long as they're free to say to say what they think."

I was pretty shaken by what Richard had told me. Did I believe it? Of course I believed Richard. Did the Hossbach memorandum really exist or was it just something cooked up by Hitler's opponents in Germany to discredit the Nazis and lead to their overthrow? I had no idea nor, I suspect, did Richard, but there was a horrible logic to Hitler's planning if he really was hell bent on war. The best way, I thought, was to follow events closely and see if I could spot any clues as to Hitler's motives and what he might do next.

For a short while there was calm. The Czech local elections passed off peacefully and proposals from the Czechs to placate the Sudetens were published in a draft Nationalities Statute. Our newspapers, led by *The Times*, seemed to think this would do the trick.

In this lull before any possible storm I settled down to follow the cricket. The first Test at Nottingham was a high scoring draw on an easy wicket. Bradman scored a century and the match petered out into a draw. Ten days later at Lords the match was very close and the Aussies only escaped with a draw after yet another match-saving century from Bradman.

The calm in Czechoslovakia was too much for Hitler to bear and in the middle of July the Nazi press were at it again, accusing the Czech government of mobilising its troops near the German border. There were also more reports of Czech persecution of the Sudetens.

Our papers reported the news and commented on it. The German papers did what they were told by Goebbels and there was no way of knowing whether their stories were true or false. Hitler used the press to get across to the world what he wanted, sometimes backing this up with one of his four-hour speeches.

So, towards the end of July, the German press reported that Hitler was anxious for peace and good relations with Britain and France but this would only come about if there was a satisfactory outcome to the Czech problem.

What was this satisfactory outcome? I wondered. If the Hossbach Memorandum was to be believed it was the removal of Czechoslovakia from the map of Europe and its replacement with a province of Germany. I didn't think Hitler would say this but he did tell the British and French to mind their own business and the best that we could do was to tell the Czechs that they couldn't rely on our support. Hitler had already dismissed the Czech government's efforts to do something for their minorities, confirming what we already knew, that he would continue to tell the Sudetens to demand more than the Czech government would, or could, ever give.

Tension rose again and few noticed or cared when the third Test in Manchester was rained off without a ball being bowled. It rained a lot in Manchester but not in Leeds, where the next match was, and a close and exciting game helped us to forget all about Czechs and Germans, for a short while at least.

England had batted first and were bowled out for a modest two hundred and twenty three. Australia didn't do much better. Of their total of two hundred and forty two, Bradman made one hundred and two. Where on earth would they be without him, I asked myself.

The wicket was playing tricks and England were tumbled out for a feeble one hundred and twenty three in their second innings, with Bill O'Reilly taking five wickets. The Aussies needed just over a hundred to win and lost five wickets in getting them. They went one up in the series with one match to play. So the Ashes were gone, but perhaps we could square the series at the Oval?

I had a pretty routine couple of months, covering domestic stories, following the cricket reports on the radio and taking Jane to the cinema. We'd seen *A Slight Case of Murder* and re-runs of *A Farewell to Arms* and *The Scarlet Pimpernel*. Only the last, with Leslie Howard as Sir Percy was up to much. The new film guy had arrived so I wasn't asked to do any more reviews.

Chamberlain wasn't doing too much about Czechoslovakia, apart from calling for restraint from both sides, so I decided to go down to the House and see Philip Noel Baker to hear his take on things. I knew that Philip had been to Czechoslovakia in the spring, so I thought an interview with him would be useful.

Philip seemed pleased to see me. We chatted about cricket for a while, then athletics—Sydney Wooderson was running some fantastic times for the mile. Philip said that Wooderson was taking on the mantle of Britain's great tradition in that event. A tradition, I reminded him, that was partly based on his own achievements.

Then he told me about his visit to Czechoslovakia. I suppose I wasn't greatly surprised to hear that most of the Sudetens he'd met were dead against Hitler interfering in their affairs. Quite a few, including some Jews, had lived in Germany before the Nazis came to power and had left to avoid persecution. He agreed that there were some genuine grievances, but he was sure that the Czechs would sort these out with the new laws they were proposing.

I asked him what he thought Chamberlain would do next.

"He hasn't done anything so far, Roger, apart from asking the papers to keep quiet and the odd speech in the House urging moderation. Perhaps he thinks the whole thing'll blow over; anything for a quiet life. It's the summer recess soon. He's probably planning a fishing holiday."

"Surely you don't believe that?" I protested.

"Not really. I'm just getting more and more cynical about the whole business. The Czechs seem to be doing all they can to meet the Sudeten demands but whatever ground they give it's never enough for Hitler and Henlein. Most of the cabinet are fed up with the Nazis. Even Halifax has come to realise how bad they really are. He's had a bit of a row with the PM by the way."

"Oh, really? What was that about?" I asked.

"He, Halifax that is, thinks it's time we did something to sort this mess out so he's asked Lord Runciman to go over there and act as mediator between the Sudetens and the Czechs. Neville doesn't like the idea."

"Why not?"

"He thinks it'll steal his thunder. He sees himself as a one-man League of Nations trying to save the world from war. Sorry, I'm being cynical again."

I didn't know much about Runciman. He had been, I vaguely remembered, a cabinet minister a year or two back. So I asked Philip about him.

"Surprised at you Roger, he's a Trinity man after all; mind you, that was in the last century. He's a tough old sod, which is good for dealing with that lot over there but he's quite ancient, and I'm not sure he's got the stamina for this sort of thing."

"So why is he going to Czechoslovakia? Is he representing the government?"

"Good heavens no. He's unofficial, doing it as a personal favour to Halifax. Huh, it would be quite a feather in the Foreign Secretary's cap if he could bring an end to this nasty affair. That would really put Chamberlain's nose out of joint. Oops, there I go being cynical again. Seriously though, Roger, I hope he succeeds. War's the last thing we want or need. But I'm not very optimistic. They're a really bad lot, these Nazis."

We arranged to meet at the Oval Test then I reported back to Ben who suggested I keep an eye on the Runciman mission, as it was being called, and write some pieces about Londoners' reaction to Runciman's attempts to sort out the crisis.

Runciman set off at the beginning of August and started an endless round of meetings with the Czech government and the Sudetens. He soon got down to what he saw as the crux of the matter: the Sudetens wanted total control of their own affairs while the Czech government were only prepared to give them limited control, whatever that meant.

Runciman had only been in Czechoslovakia for a little over a week when the German press, or should I say government, decided to intervene.

CHAPTER THIRTY

Records and Threats

"I couldn't bat for that length
of time. I'd fall over."
DENIS COMPTON

Three-tenths of the Czech population was German speaking and the Czech government were offering them three-tenths of the representation in the national parliament as well as giving them the chance to run their own affairs in the Sudetenland. It seemed fair enough to me and was probably OK with most of the Sudetens themselves.

But obviously this was not enough for Hitler whose henchman Goebbels now organised another anti-Czech campaign in the Nazi press. A Sudeten worker was murdered, the Germans claimed by a Czech, and, for the first time, the Germans began to hint that the Sudetens would be safer in an enlarged Reich.

Whether Hitler was on his holidays or not I don't know, but things calmed down when the fifth Test was played at the Oval. Rather strangely, it was decided to play the match to a finish rather than call a halt when the normal four days were up. It wasn't exactly all to play for: the Aussie win at Leeds meant that they retained the Ashes, but, for England, there was a Test Match to be won and a series to halve. It had rained the day before but it was dry and cool when the match started on the Saturday morning. England won the toss and chose to bat. Jane was with me and we sat and watched every ball without a thought or mention of Czechoslovakia, accountancy or even the cinema. Like all the spectators in the packed ground, we were totally absorbed with a fabulous display of batting from Len Hutton and Maurice Leyland, both of whom were unbeaten with big centuries when England ended the day on 347.

The weather improved on the Sunday but there was no cricket of course. Instead, it was the traditional Sunday lunch, this time at Jane's house, followed by the usual walk in the park. Then it was back to my house for tea with my family, followed by an evening listening to the radio. All the talk was of the cricket; even my brother seemed to be taking an interest. We all wondered whether Hutton or Leyland, or maybe even both, could bat on and make a really big score.

Jane had to work on the Monday but I spent the day with Philip. The day was fine and warm and Hutton batted all day and was unbeaten on 300 at the close, by which time the England innings had topped 600.

Queuing at the Oval tube station, I cynically observed to Philip that, if Australia batted like England, only the outbreak of war could bring an end to this particular game of cricket. Most of the chat, however, was about Hutton and whether or not he could break Bradman's World Record Test innings of 334 which he'd scored at Leeds eight years previously.

Hutton, not Hitler or Chamberlain, was the centre of attention throughout the country on that Monday evening. Just for a while worries about war were pushed to the back of people's minds. Even folk who'd never heard of Hutton before the match started talking about him and whether or not he could break the record.

He did it just before lunch on the next day and was eventually out for 364. It had taken him 13 hours and 20 minutes, the longest innings in first class cricket history. England's score of over nine hundred was too much for Australia who were twice bowled out cheaply on the Wednesday to give England a massive innings victory.

The vast crowd happily trooped out of the ground just after four o'clock. Any win against Australia was worth celebrating. I had the tiniest pang of conscience. I felt we'd all been behaving rather like Nero, fiddling while Rome burned. Maybe that's what we were doing, but the match, and especially Hutton's record, lifted the nation's mood, albeit temporarily.

I spent some time on the day after the Test Match talking with Richard at my father's office. He'd been in touch with Harry who'd got some useful stuff both from his new contact in the German Embassy and his old source in The Hague.

"Things are going to come to a head in the next month," Richard told me. "Hitler wants the whole Czech business wrapped up by the beginning of October."

"What do you mean 'wrapped up'?" I asked.

"Germans in, Czechs out, of the Sudetenland."

"But he's not asked for that."

"Not yet, but he'll be speaking at the Nuremberg Rally in a couple of weeks. We'll know more then," he replied.

"But surely we're not going to stand by and let this happen?"

"I bloody well hope not!" Richard said, quietly but emphatically. "Now's the chance to put Hitler on the back foot; stand up to him and he might fall over, you never know. Where's Chamberlain by the way?"

"On holiday, fishing I believe."

"Typical, the world's on the verge of war but it'll have to wait until the British government's had its summer holidays."

"He's probably waiting to see what Runciman's come up with," I protested.

"Runciman, what good's he done?" Richard asked, but, before I could answer, he carried on. "I'm sure he's a capable diplomat and he means well but he's not made a scrap of progress since he went to Prague, that's almost a month. The Czechs won't give way. Perhaps the Sudetens would if they weren't being egged on by Hitler."

"Any news from Berlin?" I asked.

"Oh, the usual rubbish in their press. Hitler wants a peaceful solution but can't wait much longer and it's almost time for the autumn army manoeuvres. Guess where they're taking place?"

"The German-Czech border?"

"Of course. Anyway, Harry's going to concentrate on the German Embassy. It's only a stone's throw from Downing Street. The German press have been criticising our papers. Despite Chamberlain's efforts they're still mostly anti-German. If he tries to get involved with this Czech business, he's got to have the press and the people behind him. That's where our old friend Steward comes in, making sure the Germans like what they read in our papers. You can expect more efforts from Number 10 to keep you lot quiet."

Back in the office Ben told me he wanted me to go to Epping Forest to listen to Churchill.

"The Czechs are preparing for the worst, Prof. There's even talk of them dismantling their industrial plant in the Sudetenland and shifting it further east to keep it out of Hitler's grubby hands. It'll be interesting to hear what Winston's got to say."

Churchill was in good form, perhaps a little less bellicose than I'd expected. We were at Theydon Bois, a village in his Essex constituency, and he started off by warning us that Europe was moving towards a climax. He didn't believe that war was inevitable but there was danger to peace and he called for the manoeuvring Germans to move back from the Czech border. He pointed out that the noises coming from the Nazi press were similar to those which preceded the seizure of Austria.

Churchill believed, however, that the Czechs and the Sudetens could come to an agreement as long as outside forces, the Nazis of course, kept their noses out. He said that, if Germany invaded Czechoslovakia, we'd be asking "whose turn is it next?" He doubted the German people wanted war but finished by asking whether the man at the top in Germany wanted peace.

Reading between the lines in Dawson's rag, there was a hint that we might leave the Czechs in the lurch.

The Nazis raised the stakes. Hitler attended the troop manoeuvres and food, animals and vehicles were requisitioned by the Germans. The Berlin press reported more Czech 'atrocities.' War seemed likely. Then the Russians had their say. They would stand by the Czechs, if the French did so. They promised air support.

I set off home in a gloomy mood that evening. I'd been writing in support of the Czechs and telling the PM and France to take a tough line. It looked like that would soon be put to the test. There was a youth, I suppose an oldish teenager, lounging on the corner of Fleet Street and Beauvoir Street. I didn't usually notice people, but I was sure I'd seen him before, but couldn't place him.

The youth appeared to be clean and was wearing working clothes: green jumper and grey trousers. I thought perhaps he was a messenger with one of the papers. He turned away as I looked at him. I hurried on down Fleet Street, but he was still niggling at the back of my mind. Where had I seen him before, I wondered.

I forgot all about it when I found Richard waiting for me at home. He told me that Steward had been to the German Embassy twice that day, carrying his brief case on both occasions. Why was that? We both wondered. The next morning we found out.

CHAPTER THIRTY ONE

Mightier than the Sword

"Who live under the shadow of a war,
What can I do that matters?
STEPHEN SPENDER

The newsroom was in bedlam when I walked in the next morning. I hadn't read anything on the train, they were usually too packed for that, so I was totally unprepared for the anger that swelled round the office. One of the older reporters thrust a copy of the morning's *Times* in my hand.

"Read that, Prof," he said. "That'll get you going. The bloody *Times* is telling the government to give the Sudeten bits of Czechoslovakia to the Nazis."

I sat down at my desk and rummaged through *The Times*.

"Read the leaders," my colleague instructed me.

I did. The main thrust was that the solution to the Sudeten problem was to hand over to Germany those parts of Czechoslovakia where the majority of the population was German speaking.

Was this the first time that anybody had suggested this, I asked myself. To my knowledge, neither Hitler nor Henlein had asked for this but it was certain that they would now.

Ben, like everyone else, was livid.

"It's one thing, Prof, supporting the government when you think they're in the right but it's quite another suggesting a solution to the problem when the government hasn't got the guts to put forward the idea themselves."

"Do you think that's what's happened?" I asked.

"Course it is. Chamberlain's hardly likely to announce to the world that the Czechs would be well advised to give away a large part of their land to the Nazis is he? What would the French think? And what about the poor old Czechs? No, he hasn't got the guts to come out with it, so he's got *The Times* to do his dirty work for him. Ben leant on his desk, took a deep breath then continued.

"I don't know what's worse, having the press attempting to run the country, like Beaverbrook's trying to do, or have the government dictate to the press like Chamberlain's doing to *The Times* and one or two other tame rags."

I'd not seen Ben as angry as this and he looked at me.

"Remember what I told you when we first met Prof. Our job is to report the news and comment on it. Thank God our owners are not like that creep Astor who uses the pathetic Dawson to suck up to Chamberlain and do the PM's bidding. It's getting like bloody Nazi Germany."

The next week was total chaos. The German press rejected the latest Czech proposals but, not surprisingly, were all for *The Times'* ideas. The French again announced that they would stand by their treaty with the Czechs and there were reports, probably exaggerated, of more anti-German 'incidents' in the Sudetenland.

There was enormous tension in Prague and plenty in England as well. Our press was pretty quiet except, of course, *The Week*. Claud brought out a special edition on what was now being called The Notorious *Times* Leader.

On the morning of *The Times* piece, I'd nipped down to Bush House and told Negley Farson of Steward's furtive visits to the German Embassy. Claud was nowhere to be seen but the message obviously reached him because he accused Number Ten, through Steward, of submitting the article to the German Embassy for approval before publication.

The Week had its usual dig at the Cliveden Set and named A.L. Kennedy as the journalist who had written the leader. He'd been assisted, Claud said, by a bunch of minor stooges, yes-men and careerists who were hoping to earn themselves a place of honour at Cliveden.

Halifax denied he knew of the article before publication but his friend, Editor Dawson, must have known and approved. According to *The Week*, the German Embassy had contacted that snake Ribbentrop who was, of course, delighted with *The Times'* proposal to give away a large chunk of sovereign territory to the Nazis.

Claud's article finished off by telling us, and where he got this from I'd no idea, that our government had told the Czechs to negotiate on giving up its territory to Hitler or we, and France, would abandon them.

Not much happened for a week. The government distanced itself from *The Times* article, although there were plenty who believed Claud's version of events. The world settled down to await Hitler's latest rant from Nuremberg.

The Fuhrer, true to form, started off by hurling abuse at Communists and Jews, accusing them of a plot to encircle Germany. He then turned his attention to the Czechs, saying that life for German people there had become unbearable and miserable. He described the Czech government as warmongers who wanted to annihilate the Sudetens and bomb German towns and industry.

Hitler then read out an almost certainly fictitious list of atrocities against the Sudetens and called for an end to oppression by giving them the right to self-determination; in other words, the right to vote themselves into Germany.

We didn't get to know what Chamberlain thought of this but our press were fairly muted in their reaction. *The Telegraph* described Hitler as disagreeable, *The Daily Mail*, not surprisingly, supported the Sudetens and both our daily and the *Express* said the speech had deepened anxiety. *The Daily Herald* recognised the menace in Hitler's words and called for more arms and a stronger treaty with France and a new one with the Soviet Union. Arthur Mann reminded us, in *The Yorkshire Post*, that the only argument that Hitler understood was force.

The Times on the other hand, while asserting that a lot of what Hitler had said was rubbish, repeated its call for self-rule, although this time it did not call for outright secession.

Mussolini now joined the party and said that secession should go ahead as soon as possible. Whether or not it was this that woke up Chamberlain we'll never know but the next day he announced he was off to Germany to see Hitler.

So the old chap, complete with rolled umbrella, flew to Germany to talk with the Fuhrer at his country retreat at Berchtesgaden, a sort of German Cliveden as far as I could make out. Like the whole country, I was relieved. Chamberlain would make Hitler see reason.

What was said we didn't know. He came back the day after seeing Hitler then closeted himself with Halifax and company to decide what to do next. The French were summoned to London to hear about what had gone on. Henlein called for secession and so did *The Times*. It was the only solution, they both said.

The Czechs responded by banning the Sudeten Nazi Party and we talked with the French over the weekend. The football season carried on as normal but nobody paid a scrap of attention to the results and we waited, with bated breath, to see what would happen next.

White smoke was seen coming out of the Downing Street chimney on the Monday and on the Tuesday we learned from *The Times* that the predominantly German-speaking areas of Czechoslovakia were to be handed over to the Germans. Evidently some formula had been agreed with Hitler whereby areas with a high percentage of Germans would be handed over by the first of October. Other areas with fewer Germans, would vote on their future. Czechoslovakia was neither Germany's to take nor ours to give away.

Nobody thought about asking the Czechs what they thought of this, but they did plead with the French and us to reconsider the proposals. The Soviets again said that they would come to the Czechs' aid if the French did the same. Chamberlain was due to fly to Germany on the Wednesday to see what the Fuhrer thought of the Anglo-French plan. The German army paraded through Berlin but were greeted by small, less than enthusiastic crowds. The German people did not want war.

The evening before Chamberlain flew off to Godesberg to meet Hitler, Ben asked me to write something about the Czech crisis, asking what we should do and what the ordinary people thought of it all.

"Leave it till the PM gets back from his latest jaunt, Prof," Ben said, "then put together a summary of this whole horrible business."

"Think it might be blue-pencilled or spiked?" I asked.

"That depends on two things," he replied. "What happens at Godesberg and what you say. Having said that, there hasn't been much interference from Number Ten lately so a nice balanced argument that comes down on the side of the Czechs should be OK."

I laughed then set off home. The youth I'd seen before was hanging around outside the office which disturbed me a bit. He glanced at me before quickly looking away and carried on smoking a cigarette. I walked to the station, checking from time to time that he wasn't following me. He wasn't. Who the hell was he, I wondered. A policeman? No, far too young. Perhaps he really was a messenger boy who worked on the street and his periodic appearances were just a coincidence. It worried me though. I thought it might be part of the plan for me to keep my mouth shut. Surely they wouldn't stoop so low as to use the youth to follow and check up on me? Would they?

I was still a bit concerned when I got home and my mother noticed it straight away.

"Are you all right dear? You look a bit down in the dumps."

"Pressure of work I expect," my father chipped in.

"I'm fine," I said. "We're sitting back waiting for something to happen and all I'm writing about is stray cats and burglars. These things don't seem very important at the moment"

"That'll be it then. You're a bit uptight about Hitler and his antics," my father replied. "I'm not surprised. Everybody feels the same way. Let's go out and have a pint after we've had dinner. Do you good."

I agreed, ate my dinner and we set off for the pub. My father fetched a couple of pints from the bar then asked me what I thought about the situation. He didn't need to tell me what situation to which he was referring.

"I'm not sure really. I bet there's not a single British person in his right mind who wants war. Even Churchill, who keeps being accused of being a warmonger, is always telling us how we can guarantee peace. The big thing is that he and Chamberlain have different views as to how this might be achieved. I'm more worried about giving away parts of Czechoslovakia to Germany. That idea started with *The Times*. Without that, the two sides might still be talking about how to improve the Sudetens' lot, without involving Hitler."

"You're probably right, Roger, but, from what I've seen and heard about that Nazi brute, he won't give up easily," he replied. "Anyhow, changing the subject, how's Jane? Haven't seen her for a week or two?"

"She's great, but we're both very busy so we only get to see each other at weekends. We're off to see *The Adventures of Marco Polo* at the Regal on Saturday."

"Talking of cinemas," my father said, "have you seen the new Odeon at Shannon Corner?"

"No, what's it like?"

"Magnificent. I bet it's the smartest picture palace in the country."

"You haven't seen the Odeon Leicester Square," I told him.

"Well the smartest outside the West End. Anyhow back to Jane. Your mother and I were wondering whether you two were making any plans?"

This was getting a bit embarrassing so I decided to make him feel a trifle uncomfortable as well.

"What sort of plans?" I asked.

He stared at his beer then mumbled something about a more permanent arrangement than we had at present.

I decided to rescue him from his discomfort.

"Oh, you mean wedding plans? No, we haven't discussed it. I'm twenty four and she's twenty three. Bit young yet, don't you think?"

He recovered then said.

"Of course in usual circumstances you'd be right, Roger, but these aren't normal times. Who knows where we'll all be in twelve months' time?"

I loved Jane and was sure she loved me too and there was probably some kind of unspoken understanding between us that, one day, we would get married. But I hadn't the slightest intention of rushing her down the aisle and into the marital bed on the off chance that we might be blown out of it by a German bomb a day or so later.

I didn't tell Dad that. I just reassured him everything was OK between us. We finished our drinks then went home.

The next day Chamberlain flew to Germany and came back empty handed. When he set off everybody knew he was confident that Hitler would accept the Anglo-French four point plan which called for armies on both sides to stand down, an international commission to supervise the exchange of populations, a declaration from Hitler that he would keep the peace while the new arrangements were put into place, and Britain and France would guarantee the new Czech frontiers.

The rumour mill was working overtime on Chamberlain's return. The story was that the PM presented the plan to Hitler then leant back in his chair and smugly told Hitler that we were giving him everything he wanted. It was rather like that piece of newsreel film when, as Chancellor, our Prime Minister had told the nation what a wonderful job he'd done in solving our economic problems.

This time Hitler wiped the smile off his face. He banged the table and said this would not do. Whatever happened, probably an interpreter or some functionary had leaked the details, Chamberlain came back with egg on his face.

Hitler was demanding more territory than he had at Berchtesgaden, and he wanted it straight away. Other countries bordering Czechoslovakia should have a bit of what was left. Naturally, Hitler changed the rules so that he could have more of the best bits; the Czech fortifications, the Skoda munitions works and as many mineral resources as he could lay his hands on. Those Czechs who didn't want to live in the Third Reich should get out immediately and leave behind foodstuffs and livestock, he said. If the Czechs didn't give way, Hitler's troops would march in and seize the territories for the Reich.

The French immediately rejected Hitler's so called Godesberg Memorandum. So did the Czechs, of course. A deflated Chamberlain told the navy to get ready for war. The French and Czechs began to mobilise and call up reservists. All domestic air travel in Czechoslovakia was suspended and British residents there were advised to return home.

It was July 1914 all over again. This time, though, war was an even more dreadful proposition.

Chamberlain appeared to have given up the ghost and the papers poured scorn on Hitler and Germany. I wrote the article that Ben had asked for and urged Britain and France to stand firm. The previous day Richard had told me that, if we called Hitler's bluff, the German army would overthrow him. So now was his opportunity. Harry's source in the German Embassy had sneaked into Number Ten by the garden gate and told Halifax this. It's inconceivable that Halifax didn't pass this on to the PM so now was his opportunity. "Please don't back down, Mr Chamberlain," I urged in my article. Now was the chance to get rid of the wretched Fuhrer.

I was happy with my article which appeared on the Saturday evening, but was outdone by the following day's *Reynolds News* which, under the headline "MUST WE ABANDON CIVILISATION?" called Hitler a madman, said that the Empire had told the PM to end this surrender and accused him of isolating Britain and France in world opinion. Stand firm and war was not inevitable, they concluded, and then called for Chamberlain to step down.

Philip wrote to *The Times* and said that the responsibility for any war was Hitler's alone. He refuted claims in the Nazi press that it was Czech stubbornness that was taking us to the brink.

Churchill joined the fray the following day. He insisted that our government must tell the Germans that any move against the Czechs would constitute an act of war, not just against the Czechs but against their allies France and the Soviet Union and us as well, bound by treaty to France.

Gas masks were issued to the general population and trenches were dug in Hyde Park. Public buildings were sandbagged to protect them from bombs. More than thirty London hospitals were set up as clearing stations in the likely event of heavy bombing casualties. Panic swept the country.

War seemed certain. The only thing that could stop the inevitable was Hitler backing down. Nobody thought that was likely. There seemed to be no chance that Britain and France would retreat from their position. As far as the press was concerned, the gloves were off. Everybody, except *The Times*, was calling for the allies to face up to their responsibilities and stop Hitler.

If the stakes hadn't been so high, it would have been fascinating to watch this game of bluff and counter-bluff. Who would back down first? Hitler or Chamberlain? Then, while the PM was mumbling his way through a foreign policy speech in the House on that last Wednesday in September, he was handed a note. Hitler had invited Chamberlain for further talks in Germany on the following day. Daladier of France was invited as was, presumably as peace broker, Mussolini. We had our answer: Hitler would back down.

Hitler wasn't ready for war, I thought, and would do all he could to avoid it. One of our boys came back from the Commons and said that most of the members had stood and cheered when the PM announced he was off to Germany. Then he said to me that he was afraid that Chamberlain would interpret this enthusiasm to mean that he should do anything to avoid war and not stand up to that bastard Hitler.

Well, we'd soon see. He was off the next day, enthusiastic crowds cheering his plane into the sky. What would he return with? Peace with honour or peace with disgrace? Or war? We'd shortly find out.

CHAPTER THIRTY TWO

*M*unich

"The hand that signed the paper felled a city."
DYLAN THOMAS

The whole country, probably the whole world, was on tenterhooks that Thursday and Friday in late September. The big four—Hitler, Mussolini, Chamberlain and Daladier—worked feverishly into the small hours to try to save Europe from war. Of course, the Czechs weren't invited. Why should they be? It was, after all, only their country that was being carved up like a turkey with all the choice bits being given to Hitler on a plate to go alongside the Rhineland and Austria.

What would he want for dessert? Poland? France? Belgium? Us? The Soviet Union? One thing was certain. He'd need to have several more courses before his appetite was satisfied. My hope, and that of many others, was that Daladier and Chamberlain would say no. But it wasn't to be. They gave Hitler everything he wanted without a shot having to be fired in anger. No doubt the Fuhrer danced a little jig of delight as soon the two leaders departed. He'd huffed and puffed but hadn't had to blow the house down. This grabbing other people's land was easy, Hitler must have mused, when you have to deal with feeble politicians like our Prime Minister. Mussolini probably clamped his hands on his waist, pushed out his chest and thrust his head upwards, thinking about another triumph for the Fascist revolution.

For a few days after Chamberlain's return the whole country, probably the whole continent, expressed its joy at the prospect of peace with an outburst of celebration usually reserved for Coronations and other state occasions. Just for a moment, I was caught up in all this. What was the fate of one small state, cobbled together by the peacemakers in 1918, compared to European peace? How many slum dwellers could now be rehoused and how many new jobs would be created?

On his arrival at Heston Airport, Chamberlain held up a scrap of paper which he claimed meant that the German and British peoples would never go to war again. He'd triumphed at Munich, we were told, and he'd even managed to drag a few concessions from Hitler. The Fuhrer had insisted at Godesberg that the claims of other minorities in Czechoslovakia, Poles and Hungarians, be dealt with but he put these to one side, for the time being. He couldn't care less about them. He'd got what he wanted: Czech heavy industry and fortifications, rich mineral deposits, the Skoda arms factories and a land buffer against Soviet invasion. Now there were three and a half million extra Germans, the youngest and fittest of whom could march with his ever growing army.

Non-German Czechs were to leave the Sudetenland immediately. Chamberlain did manage to persuade Hitler to allow them to take their foodstuffs and livestock with them. An international body would be set up in those areas not predominantly German to decide their future. The rump of Czechoslovakia was left defenceless although Britain and France did agree to guarantee the new Czech borders. What would happen if Hitler tried to grab the rest of Czechoslovakia? Presumably we'd go to war to defend them. Nonsense, said Chamberlain. There will be no war because the Fuhrer had given his word that he has no further territorial claims to make.

And we believed him because we wanted to. When Chamberlain's plane landed at Heston just before six on that damp Friday evening, the Lord Mayor of London was there to greet him, along with cabinet ministers, ambassadors and hundreds of cheering citizens. He made a brief speech, was handed a letter from the King then set off on a triumphal journey to London, like a Roman General returning to collect his baton of victory from the Emperor.

Thousands lined the route into London despite the rain. Just after seven he reached Buckingham Palace where he joined the King, Queen and Mrs Chamberlain on the balcony to wave to another vast, cheering throng. The rain abated briefly then the PM was off to Downing Street where he found another enthusiastic gathering who were undeterred by the return of the drizzle. He told them he had returned from Munich bringing "peace for our time". That was it. He'd done it! There wouldn't be another destructive war. They weren't celebrating in Prague. One-third of their country had just ceased to exist.

The national press were almost unanimously in favour of the Munich settlement. Our Editor told us to back off for the time being and acknowledge Chamberlain's achievement.

The Times had a field day describing the Prime Minister as heroic and had great pride in him for achieving a settlement which would avoid a world-wide conflagration. They heaped praise on him for settling 'the Sudeten question.' Not surprisingly, they reminded us, that they'd always thought that the loss of the Sudeten lands to Germany was inevitable and blamed the Czech government for not sorting it all out earlier. But they reserved their greatest eulogy for Chamberlain. Had he not been so resolute, they said, war would have broken out. He had achieved the impossible; an agreement with Hitler that our two peoples would never go to war with one another again.

Unlike *The Times*, which had been one of the architects of the Czech betrayal, the other papers were not quite as enthusiastic, but did seem relieved. There was a story floating round our office on the Saturday afternoon that the editor of *The Daily Telegraph* had toned down his piece after the Home Secretary Sam Hoare had intervened. Even *The Manchester Guardian*, whose chief foreign correspondent had survived an assassination attempt by the Gestapo in Paris a year or two back, were quiet, saying that Munich offered respite and hope.

I still had doubts as I set off home that night but generally I was like the rest of the population: happy that war had been avoided. Jane was due for lunch the next day. I went to bed assuming we'd all reluctantly be supporting Chamberlain.

I read my favourite newspaper *Reynolds News* over Sunday breakfast. They were far from pleased with Munich. They'd obviously been talking to MPs because they claimed that many of the members were stunned by Chamberlain's new role as national hero and were alarmed by Britain and France's surrender to force. The whole world, according to the paper, spoke of a great betrayal and they accused Chamberlain of giving in to Hitler's demands. This, they said, amounted to national dishonour. As a footnote they reported that the League of Nations Union had cancelled a mass rally at the Royal Albert Hall because they wouldn't promise not to criticise the government.

I still wasn't sure how *Reynolds News* got away with it. Every other paper was more or less backing Chamberlain, with varying degrees of enthusiasm, yet here was a newspaper, read by half a million people every Sunday, which unremittingly attacked the government's foreign policy. I was quite certain that, if a German paper behaved like this, the Editor would end up in a concentration camp.

Still it was good to see that we retained some freedom of the press but their views stirred some further uncertainty in me and by the time we sat down for lunch I was beginning to feel just a bit ashamed of my silently cheering for Chamberlain on Friday.

Munich was the main, the only, topic of conversation over lunch. My mother, unusually for her, lead the way announcing she was delighted that her sons wouldn't be killed in action, her husband's store wouldn't be bombed to smithereens and she and Jane wouldn't have to stand by and watch while jackbooted Germans goose-stepped down the High Street.

I'm sure it was a view being expressed over hundreds of thousands of Sunday lunch tables all over the country. My father agreed with my mother but I remained silent in my growing shame. My brother too was quiet. I don't suppose he'd given it much thought and who could blame him? I could sense Jane shifting about in her seat and she looked as if she was about to explode.

"How can you sit there saying nice things about a man who's just given away the only decent country in Eastern Europe to a gangster?" she began. "Do you realise that Czechoslovakia is the only state in that part of the world that's got a proper democratic government. She's surrounded by dictatorships—Germany, Poland, Hungary and Russia—yet flies the flag of freedom."

"But it's none of our business," interrupted my mother.

"Of course it's our business," said Jane, her voice rising. "Hitler won't stop now until the whole of mainland Europe is under his thumb. Who's next? Poland, of course. Then it'll be France, then us. We're a democracy. The people decide what's best for them. The dictators make the rules up as they go along and woe betide anybody who doesn't obey them. All Chamberlain achieved at Munich was to help Hitler on his way."

The room was in shocked silence and my mother excused herself to put the kettle on.

"What do you think, Roger?" asked Jane.

I admitted that I had been enthusiastic about Munich at first, especially because I believed there were more pressing things to spend the nation's money on than war. Now, I admitted, I was confused.

"Then let me know when you've decided whose side you're on," said Jane angrily.

There was no Sunday walk; it was raining anyway. Jane left early and I spent the rest of the day in miserable thought.

Ben called me in first thing the next morning and told me he wanted me at the Commons on Tuesday to report on the Munich debate.

It wasn't up to much. The Prime Minister, wallowing in his new-found fame, boasted of his taming of Hitler. The government backbenchers, no doubt threatened by the Whips, backed him and there were occasional hollow cheers.

Duff Cooper, First Lord of the Admiralty, showed some guts and resigned in protest at the Munich agreement and Eden was rather lukewarm about the whole thing. Attlee, more impressive each time I heard him, described Munich as a victory for brute force, the defeat of democracy and the destruction of a gallant people.

Back in Czechoslovakia the Germans marched in and the non-Germans left in their thousands, many of them towing their possessions in hand carts. Foreign correspondents found plenty of Sudetens who were horrified to wake up and find themselves in Germany. They claimed they wanted self-determination, not to be part of Hitler's Reich. Meanwhile the dismantling of Czechoslovakia continued. We needn't worry about the new Czech state, *The Times* told us. Britain and France would look after them.

Ben told me that Chamberlain's gang were stepping up their efforts to control the press. Hoare had banned the latest edition of the American newsreel *The March of Time* because he didn't like the way the Yanks reported on Munich. Fresh attempts were being made to oust Mann from the editor's chair at *The Yorkshire Post* and the BBC were told to stop broadcasting anti-government material in their programmes. Hoare even asked for the contents of some of these to be submitted for his approval before broadcast.

None of this made a scrap of difference to Claud and the latest edition of *The Week* was a classic. He began by saying that Chamberlain had turned all four cheeks to Hitler, but did acknowledge the PM's problems.

"Mr Chamberlain was in a very difficult position," Claud wrote. "He thought that the only alternatives were war and a shameful betrayal. To make sure he was right, he chose both."

By the middle of the week the euphoria over Munich was fading. People were reminding themselves what a brutal lot the Nazis were. It was time to take stock of my own situation. I needed a fresh perspective. I took the day off and went to see Maurice Dobb at Cambridge.

Anthony Blunt was with Maurice when I arrived. I was a bit surprised. I thought he'd left Cambridge to become art critic for *The Spectator* magazine. I wasn't that disappointed though. Although I disliked him, I had a certain amount of respect for him and he had a keen mind.

"Well, Roger," Maurice began. "You're doing well. I've read some of your stuff. Very good. What do you think about Munich?"

I admitted to my initial enthusiasm and my more recent growing doubts.

"I can understand that," said Blunt. "Nobody in their right minds wants war. Notice I said right minds. Hitler's not. He's a lunatic. I've told you that before."

"Chamberlain was in a difficult position," continued Maurice. "He needn't have got involved or he could have backed down or stood up to him."

Blunt picked up the thread. "But he couldn't not have become involved because of the various alliances. I'm sure you know all this."

I nodded then Blunt continued.

"Chamberlain believed until mid-September that all the Germans wanted was self-determination for the Sudetens. He'd no idea that the Germans were going to grab it for themselves."

"So that left him with two options—call Hitler's bluff or give him what he wanted. He chose the latter because the French weren't keen on war, no surprise there, and he really believed he could bring peace to Europe."

"What about Russia?" I asked.

"Stalin's in a bit of a mess. He's got rid of his best generals in his purges. His air force is getting stronger. If he'd fought, it would have been very reluctantly."

"So Chamberlain did France and Russia a favour? Neither wanted to fight."

Maurice re-joined the debate.

"Yes that's probably true, Roger, but Munich's done with. What matters now is that we stop bowing and scraping to Hitler, stand up to him whenever he threatens some poor defenceless country and prepare ourselves for war, because war there certainly will be. Russia is certainly not the country I visited in 1930. As Anthony has pointed out, they're hardly in a position to wage war. They need to sort out their own problems. I wouldn't bank on them just yet."

"Do you think the PM thinks war is inevitable and gave in to Hitler at Munich to buy time to prepare for it?" I asked.

"That would be the charitable view, but I doubt it," said Blunt. "He's got this unmovable belief in his ability. He really does believe he can save the world from war."

I decided to explore further. "Do you think the German people want war?"

"Probably not, but they won't get to make that decision," replied Blunt. "Have you been to Germany, Roger?"

"No."

"Then you should," Maurice said. "Make up your own mind about the country and the people. Guy Burgess was here last week. He's with the BBC now, you know. He's been to Germany and didn't like it one bit, apart from the Hitler Youth of course."

Both men sniggered.

"He couldn't say so to his employers at the time, he was working for the Anglo-German Fellowship you remember, but he told me how much he hated it. Anyway go and see for yourself," said Maurice.

I told Ben about Maurice's suggestion and he said he'd talk it over with the Editor. A couple of days later he came back to me.

"Right Prof, you can go and we'll pay for it, but you're to make all the arrangements yourself. I'll see you get all the necessary cash but you book your own transport, hotels etc. Keep the receipts just to make sure the accountants are happy. You're going as a tourist, not a reporter."

"Why's that?"

"Our daily's not popular over there. You'll be in a lot of trouble if they find out who you work for. Don't even take your press card. When they ask you at the border why you're visiting Germany, and they will, say you're a tourist. Maybe give 'em some flannel about wanting to see the wonderful new Germany. Most of their uniform types are as thick as pig shit, I'm told. They won't spot your sarcasm. How's your German?"

"Not bad."

"And your memory?"

"OK as well."

"Good. Remember everything you see and hear but don't write anything down. When you get back you can give us the full picture of what's going on over there."

"Right. Got it."

"When are you planning on going?"

"I thought in about a month or so. Second week in November."

"Fine. Make it a four-day trip, two days travelling and two days sightseeing."

"OK. Thanks Ben."

"And Prof, for God's sake come back in one piece."

CHAPTER THIRTY THREE

The Lion's Den

"I have been a stranger in a strange land."
EXODUS 2.22

The month before my trip to Germany passed uneventfully. The Nazis continued to march into Czechoslovakia, using an out of date population census to grab more territory than had been agreed at Munich. Chamberlain did nothing. He'd got what he wanted—peace, but at a high cost—and he now turned his attention to courting Mussolini.

Il Duce, as he called himself, was still piling troops and aeroplanes into Spain where the civil war was moving towards its predictable and awful ending: victory for Franco. It was all very depressing, Fascist Germany, Fascist Italy and soon Fascist Spain, not to mention undemocratic regimes in Poland, Hungary and the Soviet Union. France and ourselves would soon be the only democratic governments left in Europe, except for smaller countries like Belgium and Netherlands and those in Scandinavia. But was it worth going to war for? I was still undecided.

What I did decide was that I would go to Berlin. It was the heartbeat of the Nazi regime and I was sure I would learn more about the new Germany there than anywhere else. I bought myself a *Bradshaw's Continental Rail Guide* and told Ben I planned to leave on the afternoon of Monday November 7th. It was an overnight journey and I would arrive in Berlin on the following morning. I reckoned two and a half days was enough. I didn't want to stay longer than I had to, so I would start my return journey on the Thursday afternoon, reaching London in time for tea the next day.

Bradshaw's, helpfully, carried adverts for Berlin hotels so I booked a room at the Excelsior, near Anhalter Station. The ad claimed it was the largest hotel in continental Europe. It sounded like a Berlin version of London's Regent Palace. I'd have preferred to stay at the Adlon, Berlin's best known and most luxurious hotel, but I guessed the paper wouldn't run to that sort of expense.

Completing these arrangements, I realised, meant that I was now committed to going and I began to grow nervous. I knew from others who had visited Berlin that it felt as though it had a sinister cloud hanging over it. Still, I would see this at first hand. There was no point, at this stage, in reaching conclusions.

Thanks to Ben, I was able, at least for a short while, to put my worries to the back of my mind. He had somehow obtained tickets for Jane and I to attend the premiere of *Pygmalion* and I reviewed *The Adventures of Robin Hood* and *The Lady Vanishes* for the paper. All three films were great entertainment and gave me brief—but nonetheless welcome—relief from my growing concerns.

My apprehension wasn't helped by regular sightings of the mysterious youth and just about every night I spotted him on my way home. Even more worryingly, he began to turn up at Waterloo from time to time. He'd got himself a winter coat and a flat cap but I had no trouble in recognising him. It made me even more uncomfortable when I realised that he wasn't really making any attempt to avoid recognition. His persistent presence felt like a threat and these regular appearances were now much more than a coincidence. But, try as I might, I couldn't come up with any explanation for his behaviour and so every day as I headed for home I became a bag of nerves.

Despite Chamberlain's best efforts, the country settled into gloom and despondency. The Munich euphoria hadn't lasted long. After telling me of her strong disapproval of Chamberlain's retreat at Munich, Jane calmed down a bit. Neither of us felt that Hitler was worth destroying our relationship for and she was understanding when I told her I was going to Germany to see for myself.

The weekend before my trip we went dancing and then followed the usual Sunday ritual. The dining table chat was much less heated than after Munich. Jane sensed my unease but reminded me that I was doing the right thing in making up my own mind about Germany. Her insistence that she believed that I was right to take a close look at Nazi Germany gave me the strength to face up to what I believed were my responsibilities. She wished me a good trip, but warned me to be careful. A colleague of hers had been harassed by the police on a recent visit.

Ben repeated the warning on the morning of my departure.

"Just watch your step, Prof," he began. "Behave as if you've come to talk to our new friends. You know, 'what's life like in the wonderful new Germany' and all that shit. Don't even think about criticism or you'll be on the next train home. Remember, don't write anything there. Keep it all for when you've crossed the border on the way home. If you've got anything worth printing, phone it through from Brussels when the train stops there for a while."

"OK, but what if I've got some stuff that'll upset the government? Still want to hear about it?"

"Definitely. It's not your job or mine to decide what goes in the paper. The Editor can sort that out."

"Is he still under pressure?"

"As far as I can make out, Chamberlain's mob are stepping up their efforts to keep the press in line but so far, touch wood, they've left us alone. By the way did you see that stuff from Sinclair?"

Sir Archibald Sinclair was a Liberal MP who wasn't too keen on appeasement.

"No," I replied.

"He made a speech in Aberdeen attacking the government for trying to control the press and censoring BBC programmes and the film newsreels. Anyway, tell it as you see it. I'll deal with the Editor."

I caught a cab to Victoria and arrived early enough to grab a cup of tea and a sandwich at the buffet. I climbed aboard in good time, took my light reading, an Edgar Wallace novel, from my suitcase, then settled down in an empty compartment. Just before the two o'clock departure time, the door slid open and a smartly dressed middle-aged man joined me. He nodded at me pleasantly, threw his case on the rack then took his seat. We sat in silence as the train puffed its way out of London.

As we were speeding through the fields, farms and villages of Kent, I asked him if he was going to Berlin. No, he told me, he would be getting off in Cologne in the early hours of the next morning. He spoke excellent English but, I explained to him, this was my first visit to Germany so would he mind if we spoke in German. I needed the practice.

He smiled, made a small laugh and introduced himself, in German, as Thomas. He was, just as he looked, a businessman and he'd been in Manchester buying textiles for the clothing business which he managed in Dusseldorf. Thomas had a round, slightly pale face with his thick black hair oiled almost into his scalp. His trip had been successful and now he was looking forward to re-joining his family in the Rhineland. I asked him how he found England. A fine country, he told me, although Manchester he found a little damp.

"You appear to have two Englands," he said.

"How do you mean?" I replied.

"Plenty of people seem wealthy in the south but poor in the north. In Manchester I saw many without jobs, but in London everyone seemed to be working."

"How does that compare with Germany?" I asked.

"In Germany, all the men work," he said, "except for the old, the ill and the Jews. And, of course, the young married women stay at home to bring up children to serve the great new Germany."

There was a fair amount of sarcasm in his reply but I decided not to press it and the train soon pulled into Dover and we headed together for the cross channel ferry. The destination this time was Ostend and Thomas and I drank beer in the bar and made small talk until the boat docked in Belgium. It was dark by now as we walked to the Berlin-bound express, which was surprisingly empty.

We dined together in the restaurant car. I told Thomas that my father was a store manager, a business that he had some familiarity with, and that I'd been to Cambridge. I explained that I was going on a short visit to Germany, because I'd heard so much about it but had never been, and that I was looking forward with pleasure to seeing it for myself.

"You may not find too much pleasure in Germany today, Roger," Thomas said. "It is, in many ways, an unhappy country. Of course, we're better off financially than we were ten years ago, but it's a country living in fear; afraid of what Hitler might do next, afraid of speaking its mind and terrified of the police, the Gestapo, the brownshirts and the SS. Still you must make up your own mind. Two days in Germany should be enough time for you to get a feel for the new Germany."

At the end of the meal we shook hands and went to our sleeping quarters. I wouldn't see him again but, as I began to doze on my bunk, I thought about what Thomas had said. Was he a typical German? I asked myself. I'd soon find out.

I fell asleep but was woken up by a banging. The train had stopped. I looked at my watch. It was almost one o'clock. A voice shouted in German that everybody should leave their bunks and wait in the corridor with their papers.

There were two of them; a policeman, or a customs officer, in a dark green uniform and a man slightly older than me in a belted fawn coloured raincoat and hat. The uniformed man politely asked to see my passport. He examined it closely then handed it to his plain clothed colleague who read it for what seemed an eternity and then asked me in heavily accented English, "And why are you in Germany, Herr Martin?"

I told him I'd come for a short holiday. I'd never been to Berlin and I'd heard it was a great city.

I was sweating a bit despite the cold night but I could see little point in getting into a prolonged argument with this man whom I presumed was from the Gestapo. I repeated I was here for a holiday, would be staying at the Excelsior Hotel in Berlin and would be returning home on Thursday afternoon.

"Where are you sleeping?" he asked.

I pointed him towards my bunk and he instructed the policeman to take a look in there and fetch my suitcase, which they then proceeded to search.

They didn't find anything and I thought I was in the clear but he continued with his questions.

"Who will you be meeting in Berlin?"

I told him that I didn't know anyone in Berlin and hadn't made any plans to meet anyone.

"Are you Jewish?" he snapped.

I told him I wasn't.

"If you were, you would not be welcome in Germany. A Jew has just committed a great crime against our country. He has shot one of our diplomatic staff in Paris."

I told him I was sorry to hear that but that it was news to me, which it was. He stared at me in silence for another thirty seconds or so and then handed my passport back to the uniformed officer who took it into my sleeping area and stamped it with a big, black swastika. Then they both left.

I took off my jacket and trousers and lay on my bunk. My heart was racing. I was suffering from a dose of that fear that Thomas had spoken about. I lay awake for an hour and felt the train slowing down so I lifted the blind and saw we were in Cologne. I didn't see Thomas, but I assumed he'd got off and wondered what kind of a life he'd got to look forward to. At least I was only there for a few days.

I must have fallen asleep as soon as we'd left Cologne because the next thing I remembered was more banging and a voice shouting "Berlin in ten minutes!" I washed and dressed quickly. I'd missed breakfast but felt reasonably refreshed when the train pulled into Friedrichstrasse Station, not long after eight o'clock.

CHAPTER THIRTY FOUR

Berlin

"Architecture is the art of how to waste space"
PHILIP JOHNSON

The first thing I did after I clambered off the train was to head for the station buffet. I found it easily. It was, I thought, the same as station buffets all over Europe, packed with people on their way to work, smoky and noisy. I collected a large milky coffee and three hot rolls and made my way to a seat in the corner. I was starving after sleeping through my breakfast and I wolfed down the rolls and sipped my coffee which was weaker than I was used to. The rolls were soft and warm. I'd have preferred bacon and eggs, but that didn't seem to be an option.

About five minutes into my breakfast, I was joined by a man of about fifty. He had a pinched face and was well on his way to losing what was left of his thin, greying hair. He smoked while he drank his coffee and didn't seem too bothered when the ash spilled on to his scruffy winter jacket. Several times he stared at my suitcase, eventually plucking up the courage to start talking.

"Have you just arrived in Berlin or are you just leaving?" he asked.

"Just got here," I said. "I've come from England."

"Ah, England, a fine country. Gave Czechoslovakia to the Fuhrer so we wouldn't have another war."

I managed to refrain from saying that it wasn't ours to give away in the first place. Instead I asked him if he was on his way to work.

"Yes, a printing works about five minutes from here."

"Do you like it?" I asked.

"OK I suppose. At least I've got a job. After the war, I was in and out of work for ten years till the Fuhrer came along. Now I've had steady work for more than five years."

"You're one of the lucky ones then."

"How do you mean?" he asked.

"Well, in England we still have lots of people unemployed, though things are picking up," I replied.

"There's no unemployment in Germany. If people aren't working in places like I am, or on the land, the armaments' factories and so on, they're in a uniform: Army, Navy, Luftwaffe, Police, SS, SA, trains, trams."

I looked round the room and saw four men in brown shirts with swastikas on their arm bands shouting while they slurped their coffee.

"Then, of course," he continued, "there's the young women. Many are married so they stay at home and bring up their children to serve the fatherland. This is their duty. Those who are not married work like the men."

There was a hint of sarcasm in his voice but I ignored it and carried on.

"How many people are employed at your printing works?"

"Oh about fifty. There's plenty of work printing party pamphlets and notices announcing new laws."

"What kind of laws?" I asked.

"Mostly telling the Jews where they can and can't go and what they can and can't do, not that there's much left for them to do anyway. Funny thing is, there are several Jews working with me. They're very good at printing. Still, I reckon they're for it now."

"Oh?"

"Haven't you heard? A Jewish boy has shot one of our diplomats in Paris and the Fuhrer's own doctor is flying to France to look after him. God help the Jews if he dies."

I said I'd been told something about it at the border but didn't have the full details.

"It's all in the papers. Buy one and read all about it. Anyway I must go. Where are you staying?"

I told him the Excelsior at Anhalter Station. He seemed impressed. He told me to take the S-Bahn to Anhalter then walk into the hotel from the station. He offered to show me to the ticket office and, on the way, he put a hand on my arm and said, "You have to be careful what you say in Germany. The Gestapo are everywhere and there are plenty of people in Berlin who would report you to them if you said anything rude about Hitler and his government. Take my advice. Have a quick look round Berlin then get back to England as soon as you can. Germany's not a nice country. Maybe one day it will be again. Good luck my friend."

I thanked him, bought a ticket and headed for the S-Bahn. This was a bit like the tube in London, only above ground. They had their own underground as well, the U-Bahn. It seemed an efficient transport system. It was a short ride to Anhalter and I booked in at the Excelsior. It was very large and modern and was connected to the station via a tunnel. My room was clean and light with a bed, a chair, table and lamp, and a washbasin. I was on the fourth floor and through the window I could see across to the north and west of the city. In the distance was a vast expanse of green which I guessed was the Tiergarten, Berlin's equivalent of London's Hyde Park.

I took a bath at one of the hotel's two hundred or so communal bathrooms, and then sat down to read *Angriff*, a German newspaper I'd bought in the hotel lobby.

It was all there. A seventeen-year-old Jew called Grynsban had indeed shot a German diplomat called von Rath, in Paris on the previous day. Grynsban had been born in Hannover. His parents had come there from Poland some time before. The paper said that the Fuhrer had generously allowed Polish Jews to return to their homeland and Grynsban didn't like it when his parents were forced to leave the Reich, so he'd taken his revenge on the diplomat.

The newspaper then went on with an anti-Jewish rant, saying that Jews in Germany could expect an outburst of anger at this outrage. Whether von Rath would live or die wasn't clear, but he'd been shot five times and was said to be in a weak condition.

It was after eleven by now and I decided that the best way to see Berlin was on foot. The centre of German government wasn't far away so I could look at that, then walk up the Wilhelmstrasse to the Brandenburg Gate and find some lunch. The weather was good for walking—dry, cool and cloudy—but not much chance of rain as I walked towards the government area. There were plenty of cars on the roads, though not as many as in London, but in the area near to the Wilhelmstrasse the pavements were teeming with people hurrying towards, or in and out of, a host of grim looking grey stone buildings.

Plenty of these people were in some kind of uniform. In fact, it was the large number of people walking about in uniforms of a huge variety of colours and styles that had first struck me as I emerged bleary-eyed from the train three hours earlier. That and flags. There were flags billowing in the breeze everywhere, most of them blood red with a menacing black Swastika on a white background in the middle.

I'd bought a street map of central Berlin in the hotel so I was able to identify Himmler's building next to the Gestapo Headquarters in Prinz Albrecht Strasse before turning up Wilhelmstrasse, passing Hitler's private office, Goering's Aviation Ministry then the incomplete building of the new Reich Chancellery, next to the existing Chancellery which was on the opposite side of the road to Goebbels' Propaganda Ministry. All the buildings had three things in common; they were all covered in the usual Swastika flags, each was guarded by black-uniformed, black-helmeted and white-gloved soldiers and all of the buildings, without exception, were ugly.

This was the centre of Nazi power. Hoards strutted about with an air of self-importance. There was no happy chatter amongst the crowds as you'd find in London or Paris. I continued my journey up the Wilhelmstrasse, passing the British Embassy en route before reaching the famous street of lime trees, the Unter den Linden. I turned left and approached the Brandenburg Gate, which was a magnificent structure, and briefly examined the ruins of the Reichstag, the German Parliament, which had remained untouched since the fire of 1933. The Germans had no use for a parliament building; after all, they had no democracy. When Hitler wanted to play at democracy, he dragged the Reichstag members into the Kroll Opera House and shouted at them.

Retracing my steps eastward towards the Unter den Linden I passed, for the second time, the Adlon Hotel. I looked at my watch. It was well past lunchtime, so I decided that, even if I couldn't afford to stay there, I could manage a snack lunch so I strolled into the hotel dining room.

The dining room was very plush. An old waiter with a kind face showed me to a table. Most of the lunchtime diners had gone but a few remained: a pair of black-uniformed SS men at one table, a well-dressed elderly couple at another and a pair of worn out looking men in expensive looking, but crumpled, suits at a third. The last two were speaking English, or to be more accurate, American.

The menu was pretty pricey so I settled on a bowl of soup with bread. The old waiter took my order with a beam on his face and returned a few minutes later with a deep bowl, in the middle of which was what appeared to be a hollowed out half loaf of brown bread filled with, and surrounded by, steaming vegetable soup. It was a meal in itself and I clearly wouldn't be needing a second helping. It was delicious and I followed it with an excellent cup of coffee. It was by now mid-afternoon and I left the hotel feeling pretty pleased with myself. I could boast that I'd eaten in the Adlon, even if I hadn't stayed there.

It was still a decent afternoon as I walked east along the Unter den Linden. I paused and spent a short time looking at Humboldt University; I'd heard of that. One of my friends at Cambridge had spent a year studying there. Then I made my way to the Berliner Dom, their cathedral. It was squat and domed but far less impressive than either St Paul's Cathedral or Westminster Abbey.

Eventually the graceful promenade of the Unter den Linden gave way to ordinary streets with shops, offices, small bars and cafes and, behind them, a sprawl of four- and five-storey tenement blocks. The streets were busy with Berliners doing some last minute shopping before heading home.

Some of the shops, I noticed, had a white Star of David painted on their windows. These were Jewish properties and non-Jewish Germans were discouraged from shopping there. They were less busy than the other shops but not totally deserted. This was the real Berlin, I thought, not the tourist city of the Brandenburg Gate, the ruined Reichstag or even the government quarter guarded, as they were, by black-uniformed SS sentries.

Every lamp post, spare space on walls and other suitable spots had loud speakers attached to them. Earlier I'd noticed that there were radios in many of the public places like the station buffet, the hotel lobby, and the Adlon dining room. The Third Reich meant to ensure that their citizens were kept fully up-to-date with everyday events.

I strolled around some side streets and came to Berlin's Town Hall, the Rathaus, and then came across a rather inconspicuous looking building with a Star of David above the entrance.

I tried the door, found it open then stepped inside a beautiful synagogue. An elderly Jew approached me and nervously asked me what I wanted. He was, I guessed, the English equivalent of a church verger and he visibly relaxed when I told him I was an English tourist.

The interior of the building was magnificent, with high painted ceilings and superbly decorated walls. What I presumed was the altar was covered with wonderfully coloured cloths and tapestries. It was breathtaking. The elderly Jew told me that it had been a place of worship for more than two centuries but, he added in a low voice, God knows for how much longer. I was slightly disturbed by this last comment but didn't feel either brave or confident enough to prolong the conversation, so I thanked him and left.

I rejoined the main street then found myself at a corner of the Alexanderplatz, one of the great squares of east Berlin. The whole area was crowded with people and trams. I chatted to a woman at a stall selling various types of sausage and she told me that the large grey building dominating one side of the square was the Police Headquarters, the Alex as she called it. The Wertheim Department store was another of the features of this drab, but somehow impressive, square.

The S-Bahn station overlooked one side and below was the entrance to the U-Bahn. There was a cinema, several bars and a number of small restaurants as well as a dance hall. The woman, rather bravely, told me that the cinema hardly ever showed any interesting films anymore and none of the music played in the dance hall was up to much but she did recommend a decent restaurant so I headed across the square for dinner.

It was a small establishment, but quite crowded. A notice on the door announced that Jews were not welcome. I was shown to a table and given a menu by a matronly looking woman. There were some odd sounding items to choose from; pig's knuckle and sauerkraut didn't appeal to me much, so I settled for the pot roast.

At the table next to mine a young couple were talking loudly in agreement that something had to be done about the Jews and I learned that the German diplomat was still clinging on to life in Paris. The radio was blaring out music, probably Wagner, before the broadcast was interrupted by a rant from someone from the Ministry of Propaganda. The announcer informed us that von Rath was still alive but added that it was now time for all true Germans to confront the Jewish threat and take action.

I didn't like the sound of this at all so I quickly finished what turned out to be quite a small meal, paid my bill and left. I went down to the U-Bahn and bought a ticket for the Potsdamer Platz. When I got there I walked back to the hotel, dropped my overcoat in my room and went down to the bar.

I recognised one of the two men in crumpled suits I'd seen in the Adlon dining room. I walked over and asked if I could join him. The waiter fetched me a beer and I introduced myself.

He was called Bob and had been in Berlin for six months as correspondent for a San Francisco newspaper. I told him I'd met Negley Farson a couple of times and that really broke the ice.

"Negley," Bob said. "What a great guy. He gets everywhere. I'm surprised he hasn't turned up here. London's a bit tame for him."

"He's doing a great job in London," I replied, explaining Negley's links with Claud Cockburn and *The Week*.

"Now that's what I call a paper!" Bob exclaimed. "Tells it as it is, not, from what I've heard, like some other of your English papers."

I decided I could trust him and admitted I worked for *The Globe*, and then mounted a rather feeble attempt at supporting our papers.

"That's true to an extent," I replied. "But not all our papers are licking Chamberlain's backside. My paper tries to print the news as it happens and aren't afraid to say what we think. Not everything gets in. Some of our stuff does get blue-pencilled or spiked after the owners and the editors have been leaned on by Chamberlain's henchmen."

"Thank God it ain't like that in the states. We think the Nazis are a bunch of shits and tell the public so on a daily basis. You've only got to spend a few weeks in Berlin to see what an inhuman lot they are."

"I've only been here for a day and I'm getting the same picture," I told him.

We chatted about the plight of the Jews and the attempted assassination in Paris. We had another beer and Bob told me he was often in the Adlon. Lots of foreign journalists gathered there, he said. It was a good place for gossip as well as to drink and play cards. It was also handy for the Wilhelmstrasse where press briefings were given at the Propaganda and Foreign Ministries. He said these were mostly hot air and half-truths, sometimes downright lies and hardly worth attending.

I suddenly realised how tired I was and I excused myself for an early night. We agreed to meet on the following evening in the bar. When I reached my room I hardly had the strength to take my clothes off but I managed, flopped into bed and fell asleep straightway.

I slept like a log and it was almost nine o'clock when I came round. I washed, shaved and dressed quickly, hurried down to the lobby, bought a copy of *Angriff* then went for breakfast.

Bob wasn't there. He didn't strike me as being much of an early bird and I wasn't surprised. Over the usual breakfast of coffee and rolls I read the paper. It contained the most appalling diatribe of racial hatred I'd ever read.

Describing Grynsban as a Jewish murder urchin, the paper carried pictures of the young Polish Jew alongside one of David Frankfurter, another Jew, who had murdered a Swiss Nazi in 1936. Beside these two were photographs of Winston Churchill, Duff Cooper and Clement Attlee.

Above the pictures was the headline "JEWISH MURDERERS AND INSTIGATORS". *Angriff* continued by saying that things were going too well for Jews in Germany and called for a final settlement of the Jewish problem.

I was pretty shaken by this and, over a second cup of coffee, I thought about what I should do. As a tourist, my first instinct was to jump on the next train home, but, as a journalist, I knew I should stay at least until my scheduled departure just after lunch on the following day.

So I decided to stay. The hotel concierge recommended a stroll down Leipzigstrasse, where there were many fine shops, and then a walk through the Tiergarten. He thought I should go to Berlin Zoo but warned me to watch out for the famous gorilla who regularly urinated over onlookers. Finally, he said, I should spend some time on the Kurfustendamm or Ku'damm as it was better known. Here I would find some of Berlin's finest shops, theatres, cinemas and restaurants.

So I spent the day walking. Leipzigstrasse did indeed have some fine shops, some with Stars of David on the windows, and the Tiergarten was beautiful. The Zoo was the best that I'd been to. The old gorilla must have been off duty but I did come across an ancient lioness who turned her back on me and sent a stream of piss in my direction before retreating back into her cage.

I had a sausage and beer lunch in the Zoo Station buffet where the radio was constantly calling for action against the Jews. This brought a mixed reaction from the customers. Some looked sad, others happy, and the rest didn't seem to care.

The Ku'damm was a fine street with splendid stores, a beautiful new cinema, impressive theatres and loads of fashionable restaurants. I ate in one of them: meatballs, potato pancakes and red cabbage. The radio announced that von Rath had died in the afternoon and repeated its call for action against the Jews.

I decided it was time to go. I walked to Zoo Station, caught the U-Bahn to Potsdamer Platz where I changed to the S-Bahn back to the hotel.

Bob was in the bar when I got there. He bought me a beer and carried on drinking his whisky. He looked glum and said he was glad he wasn't a German Jew and he felt horribly afraid for them. We decided to skip any more political talk and spent the rest of the evening discussing the merits of Baseball against Cricket, Rugby against American Football, who would play Scarlet O'Hara in the forthcoming film *Gone with the Wind* and whether or not Jimmy Cagney was really a gangster.

I got to bed about eleven. I was glad to be going home the next day and, with that thought, fell asleep.

CHAPTER THIRTY FIVE

Kristallnacht

"The terrorist and the policeman both
come from the same basket."
JOSEPH CONRAD

I'd no sooner fallen asleep before something woke me up. I glanced around the room and saw a glow through the curtains. I slipped out of bed, switched on the light and glanced at my watch. It was one o'clock in the morning. I could hear doors opening and closing in the hotel and feet running in the corridors. I opened the curtains and was astonished to see fires all over Berlin. Had there been an air raid? Unlikely, I thought.

I dressed quickly and went down to the lobby where I found Bob in hat and coat ready to go out.

"Go and grab your coat, Roger," he instructed. "This we must see."

"See what?" I asked.

"Looks like the Nazis are taking it out on the Jews. See the fires?"

"Yes."

"They're synagogues, I'm told. Most of Jewish Berlin is going up in smoke. Anyway, go and get your coat. Let's see what's going on."

I went back upstairs, thinking that a tourist would lock himself in his room and mind his own business. But I wasn't a tourist. I was a journalist. Ben would never forgive me if I missed this story. Perhaps, more importantly, I would never forgive myself.

Bob and I headed out of the hotel and into the street. The station seemed quiet, just a few goods trains shunting about. We could hear fire engines in the distance but where we were seemed calm. Bob suggested a brisk walk towards Potsdamer Platz. The closer we got the louder the noise. We could hear shouting, marching feet and breaking glass.

We walked towards the shops on Leipzigstrasse and caught sight of a group of men in ordinary clothes systematically smashing the windows of the few remaining Jewish shops. Some were pouring petrol through the broken windows and setting the shops alight. There was no sign of the police or the fire brigade. There was a small gathering of onlookers. What they made of it all, I couldn't say.

"Come on," Bob said, "let's get over to the Ku'damm and see what's happening there."

"But it's the middle of the night," I protested. "There's no trains or trams. How the hell are we going to get there?"

"Walk, if necessary. Maybe we'll pick up a cab on the way."

So we set off towards the Brandenburg Gate and crossed the Tiergarten, pitch black but for the glow from the fires. We were lucky and flagged down a cab that took us to Zoo Station. The nearer we got, the greater the bedlam. As soon as we reached our destination, we headed for the biggest fire we could see. It was a synagogue. A large group of men were making a bonfire of books and various Jewish artefacts. The synagogue was ablaze and, in the light thrown by the fire, we could see the men urinating over the still unlit bonfire. They sounded drunk and their bladders must have been full because they emptied endless streams of piss over the pile.

"They'll never light it after that soaking," I whispered to Bob.

On cue, one of the louts produced a can of petrol, poured it over the mountain and, with a whoosh, hundreds, maybe even thousands, of years of history was reduced to ashes. A huge cheer went up from the hooligans, most of whom seemed to be men in their twenties, thirties and forties.

A fire engine was standing by and doing nothing. Bob asked the fire officer why he didn't put the fire out and was told they were under instructions to ignore Jewish fires but make sure the flames didn't spread to neighbouring Aryan properties.

"Come on," said Bob, "this must be a Jewish district. Let's see what they're doing to the poor inhabitants." We didn't have to wait for long to find out.

Around the corner from the synagogue, groups of people; old and young men, old and young women and children, were standing huddled together, mostly in pyjamas and nightdresses, watching in horror as groups of thugs dismantled their homes. We could hear windows, mirrors, crockery and washbasins being smashed to smithereens. Books, clothes, food, everything in fact, was being thrown into the street. Furniture was being reduced to sawdust.

Several police were in evidence but they stood by and did nothing—probably, like the firemen, under orders not to interfere. Women were screaming, children were crying and the Nazis were celebrating. Then the Jewish men were rounded up. Some were allowed to collect their clothes, but most remained in their dressing gowns and pyjamas. The makeshift placards, identifying them as *Juden*, Jews, were hung round their necks and they were marched off by the gangs to heaven knows where.

"I've seen enough for now," Bob said. "The station buffet should be open soon. Let's go and get some breakfast." Bob, the hardened journalist had obviously seen plenty of horrors in his time, though I doubt any as monstrous as the acts we'd seen carried out.

I felt utterly drained, tired, sick and ashamed that I was a member of the same human race as the beasts who had carried out these atrocities. I hardly felt like eating but thought that a cup of German coffee might bring me round a bit.

On the way back to Zoo Station we passed a small group of young men who were enjoying themselves kicking a naked old man in the gutter. I began to feel sick but managed to keep it down and we reached the station buffet just as it was opening.

People on their way to work were beginning to arrive. We sat down to coffee and rolls and looked round the room. Groups were congregating at tables. Some were shouting that the Jews were getting what they deserved while others, heads lowered over their drinks, were speaking in low voices. They were presumably expressing opinions they didn't want their neighbours to overhear in case they were denounced to the Gestapo.

"That looked pretty well organised to me," said Bob. "I reckon those bastards were brownshirts out of uniform, acting on orders."

"Whose orders?"

"The party's. I'll ring the Adlon later and see if there's any news about what's going on elsewhere in Germany."

We had a second cup of coffee. It was light by the time we left the buffet. Bob headed for a bank of telephones and came back ten minutes later.

"As I guessed, every city and town in Germany and Austria is conducting a pogrom against the Jews. This has definitely been organised from the top."

"Hitler?" I asked.

"He'll have given the go ahead but the planning would have been done by that club-footed shit Goebbels and the organisation by Himmler and his police. I bet they've had something like this in mind for a while. Von Rath getting shot provided them with the excuse they were looking for."

More screaming, shouting and sounds of destruction led us to the Ku'damm. The pattern of violence was being repeated. Some of Germany's, and Europe's, finest stores were Jewish owned and these were now being reduced to rubble.

Many of the marauding groups had now armed themselves with axes and proceeded to smash every window of every Jewish shop in the Ku'damm before marching into the stores to work on the goods. Furniture, clothing, kitchen and bathroom ware, even corsets, were totally ruined. We saw a couple of soldiers in grey uniforms try to reason with the barbarians but they were warned off with the threatening raising of axes.

Uniforms appeared mid-morning, the Hitler Youth, and they started to enjoy playing their part in the wanton destruction. We watched as a group of four youngsters, all of whom looked younger than my brother, marched into a Jewish owned café, led by an older teenage boy. They proceeded to break every table, every chair, every glass, every cup, every saucer, every bottle; anything they could break, they did break.

One group of Hitler Youths were marching smartly up the middle of the Ku'damm carrying a banner, *Deutschland Erwache Juda Verrache*:

"Germany awake. Perish Judah".

Crowds of shoppers had gathered to watch the brave young men of the Third Reich do their worst. Some looked confused. Others were sad. No one was cheering. Their passive reaction was a measure of the grip of terror that the Nazi regime held over the ordinary citizen.

"Seen enough Roger?" Bob asked.

"To last a lifetime," I replied.

"Let's go back to the hotel."

I told him I had to be at the Friedrichstrasse Station by three. My train left at four.

We passed another poor old Jew, crawling on his hands and knees, being booted about by the SA who by now had put on their brown uniforms. Watching this and sitting on a nearby wall enjoying themselves immensely were five little boys in uniform, cheering and giving the Hitler salute. Their uniforms were the only resemblance to English Boy Scouts.

Further up the street a Jewish woman was being hosed down. "That's how to treat vermin," announced the courageous brown shirt who was leading the attack. Just before turning for the station we saw another elderly Jew, from his dress apparently a rabbi, being harassed by another group of Hitler Youths, some of whom were pulling his hair while others tried to set fire to his beard.

It was a relief to get back to the hotel. I packed my bags and said my farewells to Bob.

"May see you in the war," was his parting shot. I couldn't have coped without him and I told him so.

I settled my bill. The Manager thanked me for choosing the hotel. He asked me not to judge all Germans on what I'd seen today. I nodded and said goodbye.

I reached the station with plenty of time to spare. I went into the bookshop and bought a plain writing pad. Glancing through the magazines, I spotted a copy of *Der Sturmer* which Richard had told me about. It was an anti-Semitic rag which carried pages and pages of lies about the Jewish people. The cover showed a blonde haired young girl lying in the sunshine while an unshaven scruffy Jew with a ludicrously big nose, sprouting nasal hair almost down to his top lip, leered at her from behind a tree, presumably preparing to rape her. I didn't buy a copy.

I settled into my compartment and was soon joined by a family of four; a smartly dressed middle-aged couple and two teenage girls. I helped them with their luggage, and then we sat in silence till we reached Hannover.

Pulling out of Hannover, I told them I was English and had been visiting Berlin for a few days. I guessed they were Jewish. They told me were leaving Germany to join other members of their family in Amsterdam. They were leaving the train in Brussels. They must have thought they could trust me as the handsome dark haired father told me that he was a doctor, but his list of patients had shrunk to almost nothing as the Nazis had passed a law which forbade Jewish doctors from treating Aryan patients. They were Germans, as had been their parents and grandparents before them. The Doctor had fought for Germany in the war. I told them a little about myself then invited them to join me in the dining car. They refused politely. There were no laws against Jews using dining cars, the doctor explained, but they wouldn't be welcomed there.

I ate a small meal of pork and mashed potato. It was all I could manage. I washed it down with a glass of beer. The train was drawing into Cologne by the time I returned to my seat. I was still boiling with rage at what I'd seen in Berlin. I knew I wouldn't sleep but I wanted some rest before writing my article after we'd crossed the border so I left for my berth.

I was wide awake when we reached the border at Aix-La-Chappell, or Aachen as the Germans called it. A voice instructed passengers to assemble on the platform with their luggage.

There must have been about a hundred bleary eyed people who climbed from the train in the small hours of that cold November morning. There were two grey uniformed soldiers, each with a rifle slung over his shoulder, organising us into an orderly queue.

I was about half way down the queue. In front of me was an obvious-looking businessman in a smart overcoat with an expensive looking suitcase at his feet and in front of him were the Jewish doctor and his family. Both he and his wife appeared very nervous and the children still looked half asleep.

At the head of the queue a small table had been set up, behind which sat a customs officer. On his right there was another soldier, also armed, and on his left stood a tall bare-headed man with close cropped fair hair wearing a knee length black leather coat.

The column inched forward without incident until it became the turn of the Jewish family.

"Your papers!" barked the customs officer.

The doctor handed over what were presumably passports, train tickets and exit visas. The customs officer glanced at them and then handed them to the leather coated man who almost shouted at them.

"Your papers are not in order. They are out of date."

The doctor protested but leather-coat cut him off.

"New laws have been passed and these papers were issued before these laws came into force. You will return to Berlin immediately. We shall provide the transport."

The doctor's wife and his daughters began to cry and the doctor stepped forward and raised his arms in protest but was stopped by the soldier who hit him in the back with the butt of his rifle. The doctor staggered but stayed on his feet.

"Take them away," leather-coat ordered, "and search their luggage before they join the transport to Berlin."

The two soldiers who had been controlling the now silent and stunned queue moved forward and prepared to take them towards the station buildings, but leather-coat had the last word.

"You are all under arrest for attempting to leave the Reich without the correct papers. You will be questioned when you reach Berlin. At the very least you will be required to assist other members of your race with the cleaning up of the appalling mess which you Jews left on the streets yesterday. Take them away."

The businessman's papers were given a cursory glance. Then he left to join the train and it was my turn. I had no reason to be nervous but I was terrified, though I tried very hard not to show it. The customs officer flicked through the pages of my passport then handed it to leather coat that stared at me and said.

"And how did you enjoy your visit to the Reich, Herr Martin?"

I pretended not to understand and asked in feeble German whether any of them spoke English. All three shrugged their shoulders and shook their heads.

For one crazy moment I thought of telling them that I thought Germany was the most revolting country I'd ever been to, but common sense took over and I told them I'd found it very impressive.

He shrugged his shoulders again, shut my passport and handed it back to me. I picked up my suitcase and walked back to the train. I wasn't too pleased with myself for not making my views clear. I wished I'd said more, but I was saving that for when I was safely over the border into Belgium.

I went straight back to my compartment and began to plan what I would write. An hour later the train reached Liege, safety, and civilisation, and I made my way to the restaurant car.

I pulled out the notebook I'd bought in Berlin and, over a steaming cup of coffee, began to write. I knew that I had to keep control of my emotions to make the piece effective. I felt a deep sadness at the fate of the doctor and his family and a great depression at the probability that a majority of Germans were as horrified as I was at the barbaric behaviour of the Nazis towards the Jews. But most of all I was livid with Chamberlain for seeking friendship and peace with a man so obviously determined to brutally suppress opposition to his vile regime.

It wasn't just the way the Nazis treated the Jews that so troubled me though that was bad enough. There was war in the air. Uniforms, public speeches, propaganda, conscription, a growing air force and a bigger navy. There would be war all right, sooner or later. We had to stop them. My mind was made up.

After a couple of false starts I got going and, by six o'clock, when the train reached Brussels, I'd finished. The train wasn't scheduled to leave Brussels 'til nine so I found a telephone and called the paper. It took a while to get through but eventually the phone was picked up at the other end.

I'd never been in the office outside of what I thought of as normal hours and it had occurred to me that it might be deserted in the early hours of the morning. Common sense told me that, with first editions being on the streets soon after noon, there was bound to be someone about.

The phone was answered and I asked to be put through to a copy typist and slowly read my piece over the phone, remembering to say stop and paragraph in the appropriate places. When I'd finished, I asked if it could be put on Ben Rogers' desk. I thanked her, hung up and went to the buffet for breakfast.

The train left Brussels on time and we all got off for what turned out to be a choppy crossing to Dover. It was twenty past four when I bought the evening paper on the concourse at Victoria. I didn't need to search the paper for my story. It was the main story on the front page under a thick, black headline:

THESE ARE THE PEOPLE CHAMBERLAIN
WANTS FOR OUR FRIENDS

And underneath, a sub-headline in smaller letters:

CENTURIES OF JEWISH CULTURE DESTROYED
NAZI GERMANY'S NIGHT OF SHAME

A photograph of a burning synagogue accompanied the piece, probably the work of a freelancer, which was there above my article, printed word for word. There was no blue pencil this time.

I felt a sense of satisfaction, but also of immense sadness that so many lives had been destroyed to enable me to get my big breakthrough.

My mother, father and brother were waiting for me, clutching the paper, when I got home. Their response when I walked in was a mixture of pride, sadness and relief. I explained to them that, after a sandwich, I wanted to sleep. We would talk about it tomorrow as I had been awake since the start of the pogrom forty hours previously. I was exhausted. I telephoned Jane to assure her I was OK and asked if she'd come round about noon. She said she would, so I ate my sandwich, undressed, crawled into bed and slept.

CHAPTER THIRTY SIX

Realisation

"It is necessary only for the good man
to do nothing for evil to triumph."
EDMUND BURKE

I must have slept for more than ten hours. I woke up mid-morning, dressed, then went downstairs where my mother had a cup of coffee waiting for me. I refused breakfast, saying that Jane would be around soon.

There was a pile of newspapers and when Jane arrived spot on twelve she'd brought some more. My mother made us both a big plate of bacon, eggs, sausage, tomatoes and fried bread. As I ate the food I found my energy returning and, after we'd knocked back a couple of cups of tea each, I felt ready to tackle the papers.

My father was at work and my brother was spending the day with a couple of school friends so the three of us had the place to ourselves and we ploughed through the pile.

My mother and Jane both said that my article on the Jewish pogrom in Germany was the best that they'd read. I thanked them, though I knew in my heart of hearts that I had a long way to go before I matched the efforts of the more experienced foreign correspondents. Still I felt some degree of satisfaction, although I was desperately unhappy that these atrocities had given me my big chance.

Every newspaper totally condemned the Nazi actions. Not one offered a single excuse. All described the Nazi behaviour as barbaric. I wondered what Chamberlain and his team would make of the British press view of a country with whom he wished to live at peace. One thing was obvious: any attempt by him to tone down the press attacks on Germany had failed miserably. I looked forward to the next day's *Reynolds News*.

The phone rang. My brother announced he would be staying for tea at his friend's house. My father got home just after five and told us that Richard and his family would be joining us for Sunday lunch. Jane was invited, of course.

We had a tea of veal, ham and egg pie with salad followed by pear tart and then Jane and I set off for town to see a re-run of *Captain Blood* at the Regal. Errol Flynn was in it and we both felt that, if it was half as good as *Robin Hood*, we were in for a treat.

We arrived in good time for the supporting picture which, to our horror, turned out to be a documentary, *Chamberlain, Man of the Hour*. It soon became clear that the censor's scissors had been idle on this one as we were treated, if that's the right word, to an unrelenting heap of praise piled on the Prime Minister who had pulled the world back from the brink of war and promised us "peace for our time".

Neither Jane, nor I, nor, judging by the frequent groans, the audience, were impressed by this so it was a relief when it finished and the lights went up. The mood lightened when the organist appeared and kept us entertained for twenty minutes.

I joined the queue for ice creams while the adverts were on and, when I got back, Jane told me there'd been one for my father's store. Then it was the news, which told us nothing, then the trailers for next week's films, none of which seemed to be very appealing. I put my arm round Jane. She settled her head onto my shoulder and *Captain Blood* began.

I don't know whether it was what Jane wanted but it was certainly what I needed and for an hour and a half I escaped to the world of pirates and the Caribbean, heroes and villains and spectacular adventure. The cast was the same as in *Robin Hood*, Flynn being joined by Olivia de Havilland and Basil Rathbone. It was the same director too, Michael Curtiz—a man who knew how to make a movie. It was a great evening and, as I walked Jane home, we chatted about exciting films, dashing heroes, sneaky villains and beautiful women. There was no mention of Chamberlain or Munich or Berlin. I kissed her goodnight and set off home, feeling in a much better mood than I had been at the start of the day.

Reynolds News didn't let me down the next day. It blasted Hitler, tore into Chamberlain and called for a change in government. The lunch party had assembled by half past twelve. There were nine of us, like the last time, but this didn't bother my mother, who was not only a good cook but a brilliant organiser. We ate our way through tomato soup, roast pork, crackling and apple sauce, jam roly poly and custard, and finished off with a coffee. The chat was traditional Sunday lunch stuff: football, the radio, how the children were doing at school and *Captain Blood*. The boys left for my brother's room, no doubt to continue their scientific education, while the adults took their second cups of coffee to the lounge.

"You had a pretty rough time then, Roger?" Richard began.

"Yes. It was awful," I replied. "I was frightened for most of the time but luckily an American reporter from San Francisco called Bob took me under his wing and showed me the ropes. He knew where to go and what to do and what not to do when you got there."

"You were very lucky to have him with you," my mother chipped in, and I agreed that I was.

Then my father joined the conversation.

"I see Goebbels has been telling the world that it was a spontaneous outburst of anger at the Jews after the murder of that diplomat in Paris."

"Huh! Spontaneous my foot," said Richard. "The whole thing was organised by the Nazi hierarchy from start to finish."

"How do you know that?" Jane interjected.

"Harry, Roger knows who he is, told me his contact in the German Embassy had it from the highest authority that Hitler had given Goebbels the green light and Himmler had ordered the brownshirts to begin the attacks just before midnight."

"I guessed the brownshirts were behind it," I said, "even though they were in their ordinary clothes. Mind you, by lunchtime they'd given up the pretext and put their uniforms on."

"What time did you leave Berlin?" Richard asked.

"Four o'clock."

"Not long after you left the whole thing came to an abrupt halt. There was no spontaneity about it. The pogrom stopped when Hitler, Himmler and Goebbels gave their orders."

"What baffles me," said Jane, "is why the Jews? What have they done to deserve this awful treatment?"

"I've been acquainted with Jews all my working life," said my father, "and they're no different from the rest of us, but a lot of them fled to other countries to escape from persecution in Russia in the last century. In many of the places they've settled, they've been labelled as Christ-killers because, supposedly, they stood back and did nothing at the Crucifixion. Anti-Semitism has been rife throughout Europe for almost two thousand years."

"But Judaism is one of the world's oldest religions," I protested. "Christianity evolved from it."

"You're right, Roger," my father added. "But not everybody thinks like we do."

"But it's different in Germany. Hitler hates the Jews because they're Jews, not because he thinks they're so-called Christ-killers. In fact he hates all religious groups. No, with him it's a racial thing. They're not fair-haired and blue-eyed like his wonderful Aryans. He's got a manic obsession about racial purity." Richard paused for a moment. "And of course he's jealous of them. Many of Germany's most successful businessmen and most brilliant scientists, doctors, lawyers, artists, musicians and so on are Jewish. Some of the wealthiest people in Europe are Jewish and Hitler would love to get his filthy paws on their money. To cap it all, the other target group for Hitler's hatred, the Communists, have strong Jewish influence. Lenin was a Jew, after all."

Jane asked how the Jews were treated in other European countries.

"In some places very badly," said Richard. "Not as bad as we've just witnessed in Germany, but the Poles and the Hungarians treat them like dirt. Even the Czechs weren't happy when Jewish refugees flooded in from the Sudetenland last month."

"But at least in England we treat them like human beings," said Jane.

"To an extent that's true," my father said, "but not everyone loves them here. Look at Moseley and his blackshirts."

Jane nodded, conceding the point, but pressed on.

"OK, but he's not really got much support has he? I've seen his paper *The Blackshirt* and read one of his pamphlets, *Keep Alien Jews Out*, but he's never won a single seat in parliament and only one local council seat. Moseley doesn't seem to be much of a threat."

"He's not," agreed my mother, "but he's still a nasty piece of work. He'll never get my vote."

Inge, the only Jewish person present, who had been listening quietly up to now, joined the discussion.

"Wherever you get minorities some people show dislike for them. Thankfully in Britain it's only a few who complain about the Jews. Most people don't pay a scrap of attention to the blackshirts or any of the other lunatic organisations."

"Lunatic's the right word," said Richard. "Tell me Roger, have you ever come across this bloke Ramsay?"

"I know of him but I've never heard him speak in the Commons. What about him?"

"He makes Moseley look like a moderate. He's strongly pro-German and anti-Jew. There's others like him as well who believe that Communism is the real threat and that all Jews are Communists. We're back to the old chestnut of fascism being a bulwark against Communism. Ramsay's even tried to introduce anti-Jewish legislation in parliament."

"So he's an MP?" my mother asked, incredulously.

"Yes, believe it or not."

"Which party?"

"Tory."

"I'm surprised they'll have him," my mother said.

My father looked at her.

"Mary, that's the price we pay for democracy. I'm sure we'd all prefer that to National Socialism."

"The trouble is," my mother continued, "the British people are mostly decent and they believe that everybody else is like them. Its only when people like you, Roger, tell them what's really going on in Germany that they realise that everyone isn't like us."

There was a murmur of agreement. I'd been mostly quiet and understood that Jewish people wouldn't be persecuted here, as they were in Germany and elsewhere, but it still didn't answer the real question that was buzzing around in my head.

"So Richard, where do you think this all leaves us in terms of our relationship with Germany?"

"No change," he replied. "Hitler's not yet broken his word over the rest of Czechoslovakia and he's not threatening anyone else."

"But the man's a barbarian," I protested. "What about the Jews?"

"What about the Jews?" Richard asked. "How the Nazis treat their subjects is their business not ours."

I was getting pretty agitated by now and I sat forward and looked Richard in the eye.

"Are you saying that we should stand by and let the Nazis walk all over the Jews?"

"No, I'm not saying that Roger. I'm saying there's nothing we can do about the Jews inside Germany but we could get together with other decent countries like France and the United States and offer them new homes and lives here. There'll be some opposition from idiots like Ramsay and Moseley, but the British are a reasonable lot. They'll look after them but the people and the Empire would not support a war with Germany over its treatment of the Jews."

Richard continued with his argument.

"We should only go to war if we're attacked or threatened with attack. Hitler persecuting the Jews is not a threat to us. Hitler grabbing land that doesn't belong to him does, because we could be next. Chamberlain will either have to declare war the next time Hitler goes country grabbing or wait for him to attack us."

"What do you think he'll do?" Jane asked.

"Go to war at the first opportunity," Richard said.

"Good God," said my mother. "Why on earth should he do that?"

"Because if he waits till Germany attacks us it'll be too late. The Nazis will be too strong. They'll have overrun other countries and snapped up their natural resources. They'll have built more battleships, bombers, fighter planes and trained more soldiers. Hitler's not ready for a full-scale war just yet. It's all bluff. If only that fool Chamberlain had stood up to him at Munich, Hitler might have been kicked out by his own army by now."

"Still there's one thing," I added. "Last week's pogrom in Germany has shown everyone what a vile lot the Nazis are. If we do go to war, the whole country will be behind the PM. They loathe Hitler and his sidekicks."

On that sombre note my mother left the room with Jane and Inge to make tea. My father, Richard and I settled down to discuss Saturday's football.

I gave a lot of thought to our Sunday afternoon chat and, by the time I reached the office on Monday morning, I felt I'd resolved my uncertainties about appeasement. Chamberlain was wrong at Munich and from now on we had to stand up to the Nazis.

I'd seen what the Germans were capable of and I felt certain they wouldn't stop at persecuting the Jews. Hitler aimed to dominate Europe and that probably included us. Why else were so many people strutting about Berlin in uniform, I asked myself. And why was Hitler building so many new planes, launching new ships and pushing so many young men into military service? He was planning for war alright and I thought back to Blunt's words more than two years ago in that Cambridge restaurant when he said that, wherever there was hate, there would be war. I'd seen the Nazis first hand. War was inevitable, I concluded.

Richard was right, of course; we couldn't declare war on the Nazis because of their dreadful mistreatment of the Jews but I believed their behaviour gave a clue as to their ultimate goal. Berlin was infested with uniforms and this together with the violence of the pogrom, Hitler's rantings and his aggressive actions in Austria and Czechoslovakia left me in no doubt about his ultimate intentions.

Ben was pleased with the stuff I'd written about Berlin. I even got some grudging acceptance from some of the older hands and this I sheepishly acknowledged.

I asked Ben if he thought that the pogrom might turn Chamberlain against Germany but he thought quite the opposite. Yes, he admitted, public opinion was now fiercely anti-German but the PM would probably now double his efforts to avoid upsetting the Nazis because he'd placed his faith in the Munich agreement and that war would be avoided.

Ben said the Prime Minister would have no illusions about how dreadful the Nazis were but he had his bit of paper that said there would be no war and he trusted Hitler to keep his end of the bargain. Unfortunately he still wouldn't tolerate anti-German stuff in the papers because that would upset Hitler and put the Munich agreement under threat.

"In other words Roger, watch it. Do some routine stuff for the next few weeks; football, rugby, some film reviews and so on. Oh, by the way, our daily's Editor is very impressed with you. He's asked for a loan of you on a temporary basis if anything comes up."

So it was back to run of the mill work. The awful business with the Jews in Germany rumbled on. It was now being called *Kristallnacht*, the night of broken glass. Facts and figures began to emerge. Fifteen synagogues had been burnt in Berlin alone and it was thought that ninety-one Jews had been murdered throughout Germany and a further three hundred had committed suicide. Thirty thousand Jewish men had been arrested and sent to concentration camps, without trial. That probably included the doctor who had been arrested at Aachen on my return from Berlin.

Millions of pounds of damage had been done and the Jews were forced to sweep up and replace the broken glass and the rest of the mess themselves. Then the government fined the Jews eighty four million pounds for the damage they'd caused.

New laws were swiftly enacted. Jews were forbidden to take part in all business activity and Jewish businesses were handed over to what the authorities laughingly called real Germans. They were barred from visiting theatres, cinemas, concert halls, art galleries and their driving licences were confiscated. Areas of towns and cities were declared off limits to Jews. Those who lived in these areas had to abandon their homes and move out. Ghettos were being set up in towns and cities all over Germany and Austria.

The German press attacked our coverage of Kristallnacht, saying it was none of our business and telling us we should sort out our own affairs before criticising the Reich.

Claud Cockburn in *The Week* called for the government to step down and let a Churchill-Eden coalition take over. *The Manchester Guardian* questioned whether a policy of appeasement was possible with what they called a barbarous apparition among modern governments and Churchill chipped in at the end of the month with a speech in his Essex constituency. He called the Nazis barbarians, demanded greater rearmament and warned that now the Czechs had been devoured and digested the rest of middle Europe would soon follow. Even the weekly edition of *Truth* accused the Nazis of barbaric behaviour.

All this left as nasty taste in my mouth, and the mouths of most of the British public. Chamberlain, it was rumoured, was soon to visit Mussolini hoping to woo him to our side in the event that we had to fight Germany. Fat lot of good that would have done. Italy only picked on people they knew that could defeat, like the badly armed Spanish Republicans and the Abyssinians. One puff from Hitler and they'd run a mile.

It was back to bread and butter for me. I went twice to see Brentford play. They were having a poor season towards the bottom of the league. I'm not sure whether it was my presence or not but I seemed to act as a lucky charm as both of the games I reported on they won 2–1, against Liverpool and Middlesbrough.

I had the opposite effect on Charlton. When I arrived at the Valley to see them play Wolves, they were third in Division One but they slipped up 4–0 against the Midlanders and dropped to seventh.

I went twice to Twickenham. Cambridge, to my delight, won the Varsity

Match despite Oxford being pre-match favourites. Just before Christmas I saw the Harlequins thrashed by Cardiff, with my old Cambridge hero Wilf Wooler in great form.

I reviewed some films for the paper. *The House of Rothschild* was OK but *Room Service*, with the Marx brothers, was not up to their usual standard. Jane and I saw the best film of the month, *The Lives of the Bengal Lancers*, starring Gary Cooper.

Just before Christmas, Ben told me that our Daily wanted me to travel up to Scotland to cover a by-election. The main, indeed only, issue at stake was the government's foreign policy.

CHAPTER THIRTY SEVEN

In the Bleak Midwinter

"Don't buy a single vote more than necessary."
JOSEPH KENNEDY

The Editor of our daily called me in the week before I was due to travel up to Scotland. He filled me in on the background; how the by-election was the result of the current Tory MP, the Duchess of Atholl, standing down to fight as an independent. He told me he could send anyone to Perth to report on the weather, the declaration, the candidates' reaction to the result and so on. He was sending me because he believed I could sniff out a good story; what the voters thought of appeasement, what they thought of the Duchess and were there any local issues to consider. I thanked him and left to mug up on the Duchess of Atholl.

Her constituency, Kinross and West Perthshire, was one of the largest in the country, in area if not in population, and she'd represented them in the Commons since 1922. Her husband, the Duke, was Chairman of the local Tory constituency party.

I soon found out that she had a mind of her own and wouldn't slavishly support party policy if she thought it was wrong. She'd fallen out with Baldwin's government over the self-determination for India bill. She supported the Spanish Republican Government and was a fierce opponent of non-intervention in Spain. She'd been to Spain herself the previous year and had written about her experiences in *Searchlight on Spain*. The

Duchess hated Mussolini and was angry when her party stood by while Il Duce gobbled up Abyssinia. She was no friend of Hitler and the Nazis and was totally opposed to the Munich agreement.

Munich was her present bone of contention and the by-election quickly became seen as a test of opinion of the government's foreign policy. This was the third by-election since Munich, with the government narrowly holding on to their Oxford seat but getting soundly beaten at Bridgwater.

Things had started moving in Perth about a month previously when the local Tory party voted not to adopt the Duchess as their candidate at the next General Election. An infuriated Duke resigned as Chairman, then the Duchess made a fiery speech in which she attacked Munich and Chamberlain's Spanish policy and said she was giving up her seat and would fight the by-election as an Independent.

The Tories in Perth adopted William McNair Snaddon as the government candidate. He was a wealthy landowner and his property was littered with tenant farmers. The Labour and Liberal Parties decided not to field candidates in case they split the anti-government vote, so it was a two horse race.

There were only three weeks of campaigning. Dawson of *The Times* was behind the government, of course, and published plenty of letters in support of Snaddon but few backing the Duchess.

Dawson, no doubt acting under orders, tried a little smear campaign, suggesting that the Duchess was a Communist. Some of her political opponents had already labelled her the *Red Duchess* and there were totally unfounded rumours floating about that she had received a good luck telegram from Stalin.

The by-election was clearly a big deal, especially for the government, and Chamberlain's machinery threw everything it could behind Snaddon. A dozen or so back benchers made the long trek north to speak on his behalf. Lord Dunglass, Chamberlain's Parliamentary Private Secretary, appeared at Perth as well as couple of cabinet ministers: Scottish Secretary John Colville and Ernest Brown, the Minister of Labour.

There seemed to me to be an awful lot of fuss about a by-election in a small constituency but the stakes were high: peace or war? One more setback for appeasement and the popularity of the PM's foreign policy would be seriously in doubt.

I liked what I read about the Duchess, but didn't know her at all. I went to see Philip and see what he thought of her.

"She's a tough old bird, perhaps I shouldn't say old. She's only sixty-four. I admire her greatly. If she doesn't like something, she says so even if it means upsetting her party."

"Would you say that was disloyal?"

"It's a difficult one that, Roger, but there are circumstances when you just can't support things you think are wrong. Like sitting back and watching the Spanish government being attacked by fascists or Abyssinia being overrun by Mussolini. And as for making friends with a tyrant like Hitler, well, you've said it all yourself."

"If you can't support your party then get out and stand as an Independent?"

"If you think the issues are really important, then that's exactly what you do. This by-election is bigger than Oxford and Bridgwater because, when they were held, plenty didn't know what Hitler was really like but now, thanks to people like you, everybody can see him for the bastard he is. I'm a pacifist, as you know, but there comes a time when you just have to stand up to people like Hitler. That's what the Duchess is doing and I wish her all the luck in the world."

We talked a bit more about other political issues before I left and headed for King's Cross to buy my rail tickets.

During the days before I was due to travel north, I followed the campaign closely in the newspapers. The Duchess' team had littered the constituency with posters calling for the voters to put country before party and advised them to send Hitler their answer. *The Times* described this as electioneering propaganda. Snaddon called for the public to show their approval for Mr Chamberlain and his perseverance in pursuit of peace.

I paid a flying visit to Bush House, hoping to catch Claud, but was unlucky. He'd just left. Negley, however, made me welcome, told me how impressed he'd been with my Berlin despatch and asked me what I was up to next. I told him about my imminent journey north of the border.

"Keep your eyes and ears open up there, Roger," Negley advised. "Claud's been picking up some nasty vibes about Tory election rigging. They'll stop at nothing to get a result, Claud reckons."

"And watch it," he added. "There's some dangerous people on the loose at the moment."

I assured him I'd follow his advice and thanked him. As I began to leave, he said, "Don't worry. We'll look after you."

I hadn't a clue what he was talking about but I smiled and set off back to the office.

I had booked a seat, there and back, on *The Flying Scotsman* and had found myself a room in The Station Hotel in Perth. I would be in the town for two whole days: Wednesday, which was polling day, and Thursday, when the declaration was due. All being well, I'd be back in London by tea-time on the Friday, the day before Christmas Eve. Then the weather took a turn.

The temperature dropped rapidly in the south on the Saturday, then plummeted again on the Sunday. Up in Perth heavy rain had fallen on the Saturday. Twenty-four hours later, it had turned to snow. By Monday the whole of the eastern side of Britain was blanketed in snow and gale force winds had led to a lot of drifting. That Sunday night was the coldest in London for three years and Monday's snowfall was the heaviest for some time. There were reports of accidents, blocked roads, abandoned vehicles with frozen radiators and considerable rail disruption. Points were frozen and lines blocked with snow. I began to wonder if I'd make it up to Perth.

My mother made a big fuss, making certain I had plenty of food for the journey, sufficient warm clothing and my wellingtons. I took some books to read on the train: *Unnatural Death* by Dorothy Sayers, featuring her famous sleuth Lord Peter Wimsey, and the Edgar Wallace classic, *The Four Just Men*, which I'd never read despite it being about since the beginning of the century. I'd also packed Evelyn Waugh's *Scoop*. George Steer had told me that he'd met Waugh in Abyssinia and didn't care much for him. Still, I thought, I'd give his novel a try.

Assuming there'd be delays caused by the weather, I set off very early on the Tuesday morning and reached Kings Cross with an hour to spare. I bought a couple of newspapers and had a cup of coffee in the buffet. As I came out of the buffet, there he was again: my almost permanent tail was loitering on the main concourse. He had a thick scarf wrapped round his neck and obscuring the bottom part of his face but I'd have recognised him anywhere. I wondered if I should approach him and ask him what the hell he was playing at, then I thought better of it. I reasoned he was hardly likely to follow me up to Scotland. I'd feel safe once I got on the train, so I walked down the platform to take a close look at the world's most famous train and tried to put him out of my mind.

The engine stood imperiously at the top of the platform, a brilliant green with gold lettering painted on it, LNER. Half way along the engine was a crescent shaped red badge telling us it was indeed *The Flying Scotsman*. There were several blazing braziers on the platform, making sure the water didn't freeze.

I joined the train, walked down the corridor and found my seat by the window—thankfully facing the direction of travel. I took the Dorothy Sayers novel from my suitcase, heaved my bag on to the luggage rack and settled into my seat. I was looking forward to the journey, which felt more like the start of a great adventure than a routine work assignment.

The train set off on time at ten o'clock and soon cleared the North London sprawl. I spotted Alexandra Palace as we sped northward and we were soon racing through the English countryside.

There wasn't a lot to see out of the window. Every road, every field and every rooftop was covered in snow. I read my book, exchanged small talk with my three travelling companions who were businessmen travelling to York and Newcastle. In less than three hours we were pulling into Grantham, surprisingly on time. There was a call for the first sitting of lunch as we left Grantham, so I strolled down to the restaurant car where I had an excellent meal of vegetable soup, fish, rhubarb crumble and coffee. By the time I'd finished we were pulling into York with its glass-domed roof covering half a dozen platforms. York was one of the great railway junctions where the East Coast line crossed lines carrying passengers to and from the Yorkshire seaside towns, the great industrial cities of the West Riding of Yorkshire and beyond to Manchester and Liverpool. We were now in North East England, the birthplace of the world's railways, and I was a little sorry that we weren't stopping at Darlington, where it had actually all began.

We were on time leaving York but there were then a series of hold-ups which meant that the train was over an hour late reaching Newcastle. By now it was dark and there was nothing to see but the glistening snow carpeting the countryside. Further delays north of Berwick-on-Tweed meant it was after seven when the train pulled into Edinburgh Waverley.

The train hung around Waverley for what seemed an eternity while carriages were taken off or added. By the time I stepped onto the platform at Perth it was nine o'clock, almost two hours late. It felt even colder than London. The ticket collector directed me to the hotel, which was next to the station, and I checked in.

The dining room was closed for the night but the cheerful lady on reception told me I could have a sandwich. Having already eaten lunch and afternoon tea on the train as well as my mother's packed food, I wasn't particularly hungry.

Walking up the impressive central staircase, I took the case to my room, had a quick wash and then went downstairs to the bar where a roast beef sandwich was waiting for me. I washed it down with a pint of beer, exchanged a few words about the weather with a couple of the guests and then went up to my room. After twenty minutes with Lord Peter Wimsey, I switched off the light and went to sleep.

More snow had fallen overnight and there was almost six inches lying on the ground when I looked out of my window shortly after eight o'clock. I had a first class Scottish breakfast, found a phone and telephoned everybody to say I'd arrived safely. I put on my wellies, scarf, coat, hat and gloves, then stepped out of the hotel into an absolutely freezing day; the day of voting in the Kinross and West Perthshire by election.

The barman the night before had told me that Queen Victoria had slept at The Station Hotel so I had a close look at it from the outside. It was a fine three storeyed sandstone structure. The entrance was below a gable and behind this was an octagonal tower topped with a spire.

I trudged through the thick snow and soon came across a church hall which was acting as a polling station for the day. I stood watching for a while as groups of middle aged and elderly men and women were driven up by car and ushered through the entrance. Several minutes later they re-appeared, climbed back into the cars and were driven off to be replaced, a short while later, by another small convoy. Then the whole process was repeated.

While the voters were inside, I asked the driver of one of the cars what was going on. He told me that Mr Snaddon had organised the cars to bring voters to the polls who would otherwise not have made it because of the weather. I asked him if The Duchess of Atholl was making similar arrangements for her supporters and was told that she didn't have many supporters and that those stupid enough to think about voting for her didn't have access to cars. The buses weren't running so a lot of the Duchess' supporters wouldn't be voting, not that the result would be any different, he told me.

I was beginning to get a bad feeling about this election, a feeling that was strengthened when I tramped up a street with a row of houses and a few shops. Several shops and houses had posters in their windows, "Red Kitty wants war", urging the people to vote for Snaddon. Another shop was open but the window was boarded up. I went in and asked the old dear behind the counter what had happened to her window.

"The swine put a brick through it," she told me.

"Who?"

"Snaddon's people."

"Why?"

"I put a poster up for the Duchess. Others have had their windows smashed because they're for her. I've even heard that folk have been warned not to shop at places that support the Duchess."

I thanked her and left. This election was beginning to have a familiar ring to those over the North Sea in Germany.

My feet felt like blocks of ice, so I limped back to hotel to put on some warm shoes and socks and ate lunch. The papers had arrived so I read *The Times*, which carried more accusations that the Duchess was a Communist. Most of the local papers appeared to be pro-Snaddon, or rather anti-Atholl, repeating the nonsense about her left-wing affiliations. One even reported that she'd been heard singing The Red Flag while another said she was ill and on the edge of a nervous breakdown. This, they claimed, made her unfit to serve as an MP. It was the same old accusation that had been pointed at Eden earlier in the year. One paper, Glasgow based, did support her and carried a plea from a John Dick to "defy the fascist hordes".

I asked the waiter who served me lunch why the papers were so against the Duchess.

"Because the lairds own the papers and the lairds support the Prime Minister," he informed me in a neutral tone.

Shortly after lunch I headed back to the polling station. The situation was much the same as in the morning. Cars continued to bring Snaddon supporters to vote although a couple did carry posters supporting the Duchess but these were outnumbered by about six to one. Some came to vote on foot and were handed leaflets by party workers urging them to vote for one side or the other. As it began to grow dark a loudspeaker van appeared, clearly booming out support for the Duchess. "A present from Lloyd George," one of the Duchess' workers told me.

It was a great pity that the weather wasn't better because Perth seemed a fine city, nestling on the banks of the River Tay. It wasn't like where I lived, which was much larger, and it was obviously a market town. My place, about three times the size, was a dormitory for London, a big shopping centre and the home of several aircraft factories.

I lived in a town which had some history, but Perth seemed to go back to the year dot. The skyline was dominated by the spire of St. John's Kirk which, I was told by a passer-by, dated back to the fifteenth century. I made my way there and found it just back from the river, equidistant from the two fine bridges, both of which were totally deserted.

Then I returned to the main street, which was full of shops but had very few shoppers. The buildings housing the shops looked to be from the previous century; three storeys of old grey stone but the weather was having a drastic effect on trade.

There wasn't much more I could do, so I returned to the hotel. After a ten minute battle through the thick snow, I had afternoon tea then a hot bath. I'd been frozen to the marrow but over tea I thawed out a bit. The bath completed the process.

After an excellent dinner, I settled down for an evening in the bar, hoping to strike up a conversation with someone who could fill me in on how the election was going. I wasn't disappointed.

The bar was crowded and soon after eight a middle-aged couple asked if they could join me. Introductions were exchanged. He was called Charles and his wife Rosemary. He had a full head of light brown hair and a considerable beard. His red face I attributed to the weather, rather than an excess of drink. His wife didn't say much at first. She was dark haired with pointed features and spectacles. She smiled at me as I introduced myself as a journalist up from London to cover the election. He was an accountant, living and working in Perth. I knew I had to tread carefully. They could be Snaddon supporters for all I knew, but it soon became clear that they were one hundred per cent behind the Duchess.

I told them about my discomfort with how the campaign had been conducted, and then Rosemary came in.

"And that's not the half of it. About the only straight thing about this rotten business will be the count. I don't think that even they would dare to fiddle that."

"Who are they?" I asked.

"The lairds and landowners."

"I can see that they've been providing cars to bring voters stranded by the weather to the polling stations. Nothing wrong with that is there?" I hazarded.

"If that's all they're doing I wouldn't mind, but some of the other things they're getting up to are despicable. Tell Mr Martin, Charles."

"I know a lot of tenant farmers through my work. They're totally dependent on the goodwill of the landowners. Most of them have had letters offering them lower rents No threats mind you, just a letter with a vote Snaddon leaflet with it. Some of those working on the land have been warned that a vote for the Duchess could mean they'll lose their jobs. Nothing in writing of course."

"Then there's the matter of *TRUTH*," continued Rosemary.

"What's that rag got to do with it?" I asked.

"Down in London, you can see through that sort of rubbish but poor cottagers up here are frightened by it. A copy of *TRUTH* has been posted through the letterbox of just about every house in the constituency. I'm sure you can guess what it said."

TRUTH, it seemed, was sticking to its tradition of making threats and printing lies.

Charles picked up the story.

"Most think that this by-election is being fought over the rights and wrongs of appeasement, and on both sides that's largely true. But Snaddon's people, the government, have suggested that the Duchess is a bad MP. They've accused her of chasing lost causes like the Spanish Civil War and not looking after her constituents. It's absolute rubbish, of course. She's been a damn good MP but the local party would have been powerless to force her out if they hadn't had piles of letters from constituents complaining about her. I was amazed when I heard about that. I talked to a lot of people who'd supported her in the past and not one of them had written to the local party. This might be the largest constituency in Britain, but really it's just one huge village where everybody knows everybody else's business. Where these letters came from I've no idea. They might even have been forged."

A chill ran through me. Bribes, forged letters, lies. Surely not in Britain?

"I'm sure you know about all that muck about her Communist leanings that's been thrown at her?"

"Yes, I do know about that," I replied.

"And," continued Rosemary, "you must have noticed how many big guns have come up here to support Snaddon, yet nobody's come north to speak for the Duchess."

"I had a word with her agent," said Charles. "He'd lined up Churchill, Bob Boothby and Duff Cooper to come up but they backed off when the

Tory brass told them that they'd be in trouble with their own local parties if they spoke up for the Duchess."

We came to the conclusion that the Duchess would lose. The unfair pressure put on the tenants, the lack of cars and the poor weather which would stop many voters making the polling stations, all looked to paint a bleak picture for the Duchess. Some of her poorer supporters hadn't voted because the weather had kept them home looking after their children, Rosemary added.

We agreed how desperate Chamberlain must be to keep his 'peace at all costs' campaign on track. He would hail Snaddon's victory as a triumphant confirmation by the people of the righteousness of his policies.

I slept late the next day. The declaration, or verdict as I preferred to call it, wasn't due 'til after lunch and there wasn't much more I could do. I made my way to the Town Hall for the declaration and caught my first sight of the Duchess. Slim and thin faced, she showed signs of the strain of the campaign and looked devastated when Snaddon was confirmed the winner. His margin of victory was just over one thousand votes. The turn-out was sixty seven per cent, six per cent less than the 1935 General Election. Would those uncast votes have made a difference, I wondered, sadly, as I made my way back to the hotel.

I read for a while before dinner then wrote my story, keeping nothing back. The hotel receptionist told me that London trains were running three hours late. A thaw was forecast, so things might be better in the morning.

After an early breakfast, I was at the station in good time for my train. We set off half an hour late. The best parts of the return journey were in daylight which lifted my glum mood a little. Through my carriage window I saw the fine walled town of Berwick-on-Tweed, the wonderful Northumberland coastline, Newcastle's iconic Tyne Bridge and the magnificence of Durham's Norman cathedral.

There were a few short delays but eventually we steamed into Kings Cross just before seven in the evening.

The tube took me as far as Holborn and I walked the rest of the way down

Kingsway to the office. The temperature was rising and the snow rapidly disappearing. A frosty, rather than white, Christmas was forecast.

My young shadow was hanging around Bouverie Street which gave me a bit of a scare, but I was working to a deadline and tried to dismiss his presence from my mind.

I hurried up the stairs to a deserted newsroom, anxious to write my article. I typed up my piece, took it into the Daily's office, handed it to the Night Editor and set off home.

It was the last working day before Christmas and Waterloo was packed with shoppers and office workers. Office parties had probably been in full swing since lunchtime and the workers looked as they'd been hard at it since then. There he was again, my shadow, as I approached the ticket collector. This time he looked at me and gave me a thumbs-up. As I walked along the platform, I looked back. He had vanished.

CHAPTER THIRTY EIGHT

There May Be Trouble Ahead

"What is a rebel? A man who says no."
ALBERT CAMUS

Christmas passed quietly. We had our traditional family lunch on Christmas Day and I spent Boxing Day at Jane's house. My piece about the Perth by-election appeared a couple of days after Christmas. It was more or less untouched. I was very pleased.

On New Year's Eve, I talked to Ben in the office. He told me that pressure was still coming from Downing Street to stop criticising the government's appeasement policies and tone back the attacks on Nazi Germany. But, Ben assured me, ours and our Daily would still carrying on printing the truth irrespective of whom it might upset unless of course the papers came under a vicious attack from the government.

"What do you mean?" I asked.

"Well those bastards Ball and Wilson are now directly threatening some papers, including ours."

"How?"

"I'm sure you realise, Prof, that papers don't stay afloat financially with the coppers our public pay for them. What keeps 'em in print is advertising."

"I understand that."

"Just glance through any edition of *The Globe* and you'll see that almost half of the space is taken up by adverts: a full page from Selfridges and Gamages, half a page from Bravington's Jewellers and ads for HMV, C&A, Booth's Gin, White Horse Whisky, cars, vans, cafes and Beecham's Pills. And they pay through the nose for these. If people don't like what they read in our paper they won't buy it, the circulation will drop and advertisers won't take up space, then we're up shit creek without a paddle."

"You've explained this to me before, but there's no evidence that our circulation is dropping is there?"

"No, in fact it's on the increase, but now that evil pair Ball and Wilson are telling the advertisers that our papers and others no doubt, are a threat to peace."

"How the hell are they doing that?"

"My dear Prof, half the Tory party have got their paws in big business, mostly through being members of Boards of Directors. All Ball and Wilson have to do is get some Tory MP who's on the board of one of our advertising companies to persuade his fellow board members that they shouldn't be buying space in our paper and that's it: no ads, no money, and soon no paper."

Ben then shot off on a tangent and his voice shot up a notch or two.

"You're a good guy, Prof, and it looks like you'll make a great journalist but, you're still a bit wet behind the ears."

I felt myself starting to blush but Ben paid no attention to this and continued.

"This country's run by the aristocracy and big business. I wouldn't accuse Chamberlain of sacrificing the country's interests for money making but that's what's happened with the Spanish Civil War. The PM's kept us out of it because he doesn't want the conflict to spread and most of the Tories have backed him, but not for the same reason; they want Franco to win.

"Surely not?"

"You might not know this, but it was a guy called Hugh Pollard— remember him sounding off in *The Times* about Guernica?—who organised the flight that brought back Franco from the Canaries in 1936 so he could get hold of troops in North Africa and start the war. Pollard was a toff and like plenty of his pals couldn't bear the thought of a left-wing government in Spain."

"Why not?"

"Simple. With the communists in charge all business assets would be seized and run by the government. Plenty of our people are involved with money-making in Spain. They'd lose the lot. I wouldn't be surprised if they weren't already in touch with Franco, promising to support him in return for them carrying on raking in profits."

I remembered George Steer saying more or less the same thing when I met him in Paris.

"I'm beginning to get the picture," I said. "That's why Fascism seems to be the lesser of the two evils to them. It doesn't pose a threat to the private businessman in the way that Communism does."

"Quite. Perhaps you can now understand why Ball and Wilson need to keep us in line. The Prime Minister thinks they're helping him to preserve world peace but really it's all about keeping the reds out and not interfering with the flow of cash into the businessmen's pockets."

"Chamberlain's really surrounded himself with a nest of vipers. But what if the MPs won't go along with getting at our advertisers?"

"Simple, one of the two turds, most likely Wilson since Ball likes to keep himself in the background, tells any MP who won't co-operate that pressure will be put on their local Constituency party to kick them out before the next election."

"I can believe that. Remember what happened to Churchill, Boothby and Cooper up in Scotland. They received the same threats. Anyway, how bad is this?"

"At the moment none of the advertisers are actually paying too much attention, but the deadly duo won't give up easily and things will get rougher."

"There is one person we've got on our side," I said.

"Who's that?" asked Ben.

"Hitler."

"Hitler?"

"Of course, that bloody guttersnipe will soon do something that'll bring an end to this appeasement nonsense, and then Chamberlain will have to face up to him or resign."

"You're probably right," said Ben.

After Kristallnacht few people harboured anything but a deep suspicion and hatred of Nazi Germany. Chamberlain's trip to visit Il Duce was scheduled for early in the New Year and Ben told me that the government's press office had arranged for all visiting British journalists to be accommodated in the same hotel. A full programme of cultural visits had been planned for them, presumably to keep them too well-occupied to indulge in mischief-making.

That same evening we all went to a party at Richard's house. He and I had the chance to exchange a few words. Even Hitler seemed to be respecting the holiday season. We saw the New Year in at midnight, but without any real optimism for 1939. Neither family nor Jane could see anything but a dangerous and depressing twelve months ahead.

From our papers' point of view the New Year started with a bang. The Editor had told Ben that Chamberlain had denounced us as "the most dangerous of the lot". We took this as a compliment.

Our status as the most dangerous member of the fourth estate was confirmed the next day when our Daily published an article by HG Wells in which the famous author described Hitler as a certifiable lunatic. It would be a patriotic thing if he were put away, he said. The gloves were well and truly off.

Various polls had been conducted during the closing months of 1938 which showed that less than twenty five per cent of those questioned supported appeasement. Our own papers polled our readers and found that eighty six per cent of those who replied didn't believe that Hitler had no further territorial ambitions. It was a small sample, but the hint was clearly there. Would Chamberlain respond to this? We would see.

There was some good news about Germany. After Kristallnacht a committee had been set up to raise money to bring Jewish children from Germany and Austria to live in England, until it was safe to return home. Stanley Baldwin, now Lord Baldwin, was chairman of the fund raising committee.

I'd not had a lot of time for Baldwin when he was PM; he was too much of a fence-sitter for my liking, but he did a great job raising money, so the fund soon reached half a million pounds. Trains had been leaving Vienna, Berlin and other German cities since early December and generous families had been waiting for them at Liverpool Street to take the children into their homes. The youngsters had had a long journey through the Reich, Holland and Belgium, then by sea to Harwich. What the scenes of distress must have been like on those German and Austrian platforms it was not hard to imagine. But at least the *Kindertransport*, as it became known, was something. Not a lot perhaps, but at least something.

There was growing unrest in the country. Despite Chamberlain's best efforts, the press were beginning to doubt the wisdom of the Munich agreement and the government's pursuit of friendship with the dictators. None were as hostile as our papers and *Reynolds News,* but, without doubt, there was diminishing enthusiasm for appeasement.

The Times, however, lived up to its reputation as the unofficial government mouthpiece by praising the Prime Minister to the heavens in its review of 1938. The year had been a great one for Britain, it concluded, with the PM bringing us 'peace for our time.'

A couple of days into the New Year I was chatting over these issues at the Café Royal with Claud and Negley. They both seemed pleased to see me again.

"You're doing well, Roger," Claud began "I read your stuff from Scotland. None of it surprised me, but all of it saddened me. Poor old Duchess."

"I always thought elections were totally above board in Britain," said Negley.

Claud said they normally were, but anything that involves Joe Ball stinks.

"He'll have been the one behind the bribes and threats. He's done it before. Lost Ramsay Macdonald a General Election back in the twenties. Got the good old *Daily Mail* to publish a letter from the Soviets to our Labour Party. Can't remember the details but of course it scuppered Ramsay's chances. Links with the Communists were bound to lose you an election."

Negley picked up the story.

"I remember that. The Zinoviev letter wasn't it? Turned out to be a forgery, I think. Don't suppose the *Mail* cared one way or another. Anything to support the right."

"Well that's Ball for you. Used to be in the Secret Service. And as for that rag *TRUTH*, I wouldn't wipe my backside on it. Lies would be a better title," said Claud. "Their latest outrage is to insult *The Daily Mirror* which, as you know, is no friend of the government. *TRUTH* called the paper 'the Jew-Infested sink of Fleet Street' Germany's got Goebbels and we've got Ball and *TRUTH*."

"And speaking of Ball, Roger, you need to watch your step." Claud continued "I think I've told you before that I've got sources in Special Branch and MI5 and the word is that Ball is stepping up his campaign against what he calls annoying journalists and anyone else who's against the government. You've seen what he did up in Scotland. Now he's tapping the telephones of Eden and his mates and telling Tory constituency parties to deselect MPs like Churchill, Boothby and Cooper. And, I'm led to believe, he's after discrediting journalists who attack appeasement."

"How's he going to do that?" I asked.

"Any way he can. Blackmail for example. You haven't got an illegitimate baby tucked away with a showgirl in Poplar have you Roger?"

"No," I laughed.

"We'll watch your step. He's not going to target a public figure like HG Wells but a young crusading journalist like you is just what he's after. Imagine the headline in *The Daily Mail*:

PEACE OPPONENT IS A SECRET OPIUM SMOKER

I laughed again, but Claud leant forward and looked me straight in the eye.

"I mean it Roger: watch it."

I'd already had a taste of what Ball's men could do with the threats and the beating so I took Claud's advice and I did watch it. Everything on the political front was quiet so I didn't write anything provocative for a couple of weeks, just routine stuff; local stories, court cases, football, the cinema, and so on. Controversial stuff I penned under my pseudonym, though, I guessed, the enemy had probably seen through that by now. I wasn't clear in my own mind whether or not I was steering away controversy or whether Ben was doing it for me. Claud's warning kept coming back to. He was someone I trusted implicitly. I reasoned that Chamberlain might be prepared to risk one last desperate throw of the dice and those toadies Wilson and Ball might try anything to make sure the old man had his way.

Nevertheless there was quite a lot of work and I was often in the office after six. One Friday evening, towards the end of January, I decided to drop into The Old Bell in Fleet Street for a pint before catching the train home.

CHAPTER THIRTY NINE

Fitted Up

"No! No! Sentence first—verdict afterwards."
LEWIS CARROLL

Surprisingly the pub was fairly deserted. There was the usual fug and, in one corner, three obvious journalists were drinking beer, puffing on cigarettes and having a fairly animated conversation about football. There was no reason for me to join them, so I didn't. I took my pint to the far side of the bar and sat down to read *The Globe*.

There wasn't much of interest in the paper. Roy Ullyett had his usual funny sports cartoon. I read the Dot and Carrie comic strip and glanced at the quick crossword. An advert for Craven A cigarettes claimed they helped to prevent sore throats, which made me chuckle. There was speculation about the next day's football matches, a report on the building of the new Waterloo Bridge, a couple of court reports that I'd written and, on the features page, a preview of Hitler's planned speech in the Reichstag at the end of the month. After about half an hour I drained my glass and left.

It was a cold and dry evening and I set off down Fleet Street and on to the Strand. As I was passing Somerset House a tall man wearing a brown raincoat and grey hat approached me, flashed a card under my nose and said, "Police. Come with me please sir."

"Why?" I asked.

"You'll be told when we get to the station."

At this, a black police car drew up to the kerb. The driver, a stocky man in a tweed sports jacket, got out and the two of them grabbed me, handcuffed me and literally threw me in the back of the car. I was too stunned to say anything and I sat in the back seat next to the man in the raincoat as the car sped towards Covent Garden.

I found myself in familiar territory, Bow Street. How many times over the past two years had I sat scribbling notes at the Bow Street Magistrates Court? I was hauled out of the car by the man in the raincoat and frog-marched up the steps into the police station. He pulled me towards the main desk behind which stood a large balding man, probably in his fifties, with the palms of his hands resting on the counter.

The man in the raincoat began.

"I'm arresting this gentleman for making an indecent suggestion to a young man in the York Place toilets. Book 'im please, Sarge, while I make a call to the Yard."

He removed the handcuffs.

"Right," replied the Sergeant, "let's have your details please sir."

"I've no idea why I'm here," I protested. "I didn't even know there were any toilets in York Place. You're making a big mistake!"

"Then I'm sure it'll all be sorted out sir. In the meantime, let's have your details."

The Sergeant, who was a Scotsman judging by his accent, wrote down my name, address, age and place of work then asked me to empty my pockets. I had a horrible feeling in the pit of my stomach and my hands were shaking as I put my keys, cash, watch and wallet on the counter. He made a note of my property, added the newspaper which by now I'd squeezed almost to pulp, then gave me a receipt which both of us signed. He kept the receipt. A young constable was summoned and he searched my pockets, which he declared to be empty. They made me take off my shoes and my braces and I handed them over.

The tall man in the raincoat reappeared, peered over the Sergeant's shoulder then said, "Ok Mr Martin, an officer is on his way over to interview you and he'll be bringing a witness with him. Meantime constable, lock 'im up."

My legs felt like jelly as the constable led me by the arm through to the back of the police station into a badly lit corridor where there were about half a dozen cells on each side. It was deafeningly quiet. He produced a bunch of keys, opened one of the cells and ushered me in. It was even gloomier than the corridor—freezing cold and stinking of urine.

"Look, this is all a big mistake," I said to the constable.

He ignored me.

"Can't I at least let someone know I'm here?"

"All in good time," he replied, gently pushed me into the cell and slammed the door shut behind me.

I peered through the semi-darkness. Against the wall was a scruffy looking bed with a wafer thin mattress on it. On top of the bed was a dirty, threadbare blanket. There was a toilet in one corner which I promptly used, my shattered nerves and full bladder following my pint getting the better of me. The toilet was full of thick looking dark yellow urine and, of course, didn't flush.

I carefully sat down on the edge of the bed and tried to figure out what was happening. My first thought was that they'd got the wrong man. They'd mistaken me for someone else. Briefly, I cheered myself up by reasoning that this would all be cleared up when the officer due to interview me and the witness arrived.

These optimistic thoughts lasted only a few minutes until I remembered Claud's warning. The police seemed so confident when they arrested me that I began to think that this was some sort of set up, an attempt to punish me for speaking out against Chamberlain's foreign policy. Surely they wouldn't stoop that low, I thought, but then I remembered the dirty tricks they'd used to topple the Duchess of Atholl, the tapping of phones and all the other nasty ways they'd been using to keep people's mouths shut.

But why me, I wondered, and then I remembered again Claud saying that I was expendable and I thought my arrest would serve as a warning to others who dared to speak out against appeasement.

I started wondering about the witness. Who the hell was he? Some stooge in police pay probably, prepared to tell lies about innocent people.

Then I remembered the mysterious youth who kept appearing in Fleet Street, Bouverie Street and Waterloo. The more I thought about it, the more I became convinced that it was him who'd pointed the finger at me. I could hear him telling the police that I had been staring and smiling at him whenever our paths crossed for quite some time. It would all sound very convincing to the magistrates and would end up with me going down for six months. My life would be ruined. I'd lose my reputation, my job and probably Jane.

Then I began to wonder when all this was alleged to have taken place. Not while I was in the office obviously, too many witnesses. When I was in The Old Bell perhaps? Would anyone remember me there? Certainly not the group in the corner. They were too tied up with their football. The barman? Perhaps.

I was chewing over these scenarios when I heard a key turning in the lock and my heart jumped. It seemed it was time for my interview and worry again began to flood through me. The constable stepped in, handed me my shoes and braces and asked me to follow him. I was terrified. We made our way back along the corridor to the main desk where the Sergeant was waiting. My possessions with a sheet of paper were in front of him.

"There seems to have been a mistake, sir. Please would you be good enough to check your property and sign the sheet if you're satisfied it's all there."

I did as he asked with a shaking hand.

"Thank you sir. You're not being charged. You're free to go."

I mumbled a thanks and walked out of the door. On the pavement outside the police station stood two men, one of whom I recognised with astonishment: Negley Farson.

He walked towards me with his hand outstretched, shook my hand warmly and put his left hand on my shoulder.

"Roger," said Negley, "glad to see you're still in one piece. Let me introduce you to Edward. He's a solicitor friend of mine."

We shook hands. He was tall, thin and very handsome, a bit like I'd imagine Anthony Eden would be in ten years time, minus the moustache. Edward ushered me towards a waiting car.

As we approached it another police car pulled up and out jumped moustache-face, followed by a short spotty-faced youth with a flat cap pulled down over his forehead. Moustache-face looked at me and his mouth dropped open. He was about to say something then caught Edward's eyes which were fixed on him with a steely glare. He turned away and walked into the police station.

Edward climbed into the driver's seat and Negley slid in alongside him. I got into the back seat and had another, even bigger, shock. Huddled in the corner, with the street lamps lighting up a mischievous grin, was my mystery youth.

"Roger, meet Joe," Negley said. "He works for Claud."

His handshake was firm and his grin spread from ear to ear.

"Pleased to meet you guv."

I assured him likewise, then asked, "Could someone please tell me what's going on?"

"You tell him, Joe," said Negley.

"OK guv. I do jobs for Mr Cockburn—running messages, taking mail to the post office and looking for coppers hanging round the office. He asked me to keep an eye on you in case you got into any bother."

I don't suppose I'd ever made a bigger error of misjudgement in my life, imagining Joe to be part of the set-up against me. We were driving towards the East End when Negley took up the story.

"As soon as Joe spotted you being arrested, he watched the car heading towards Covent Garden, guessed the destination was Bow Street then found a public call box and telephoned me. He couldn't risk ringing Claud because his phone's still being tapped. I called Edward. Joe and I were waiting for him outside Bush House, and then Edward drove us straight to the police station."

"It wasn't the first time you'd helped Mr Martin, was it Joe?" Negley said.

"It was a while before you spotted me, but I've been keeping an eye on you for more than a year. Remember when you ran away from those two buggers last Christmas? I tripped one of 'em and then 'e went flying. A few days later I saw 'em snatch you on the bridge. I'm sorry I couldn't 'elp you, but as soon as they'd gone I telephoned the cop shop and told the bloke who answered the phone where you were and where you worked. Didn't leave me name, of course."

Edward drove the car into a street of terraced houses in an area I didn't recognise but was obviously in the East End. We pulled up outside one of the houses.

"There you are Joe," said Edward. "You've done a great job tonight. Thank you very much."

"Yes," I quickly added. "Thanks for looking after me. I'm not sure where I'd be if it weren't for you. Thanks a lot Joe. Is there anything I can do for you?"

"No thanks guv. Mr Cockburn sees me alright. All in a day's work. Night all."

We said our goodnights and he was gone. It was just after ten. The nightmare had lasted less than three hours, but it seemed like a lifetime.

Edward said, "I'll drive you home, Roger. Your parents must be getting worried about you."

I said there was no need as the trains were still running but he insisted.

"I'm sorry to carry on a bit," I said. "I understand how you found out I was in trouble but how did you get me out of the police station?"

We were driving along the Embankment towards Westminster Bridge and Negley picked up the story with some relish.

"As soon as I heard from Joe, I telephoned Edward, who was fortunately still in his office in Lower Temple. He drove up to Bush House, collected Joe and me and then we concocted our story. I'd already called your office and they told me you'd left about six. Joe said it was seven when you were arrested so we guessed that the alleged incident, whatever it was, must have taken place between six and seven."

"But how did you know that I wasn't being arrested for something that was supposed to have happened earlier in the week or even earlier in the month?"

"Roger you're not on any wanted posters," said Edward, "and in any case they don't pick people off the streets for something that happened earlier. In those cases they arrest people at home or at work. It makes more impact that way."

"So Edward walked into the police station and demanded to know why his client, that's you by the way, had been arrested. The Sergeant gave us some details, so I told him that it was quite impossible that it was you because we were having a drink together in the Wellington between just after six and just before seven. You'd walked back to Bush House with me, and then set off home."

"Clearly a case of mistaken identity, I told the Sergeant," said Edward.

"So," continued Negley, "after veiled threats about losing his stripes and being back on the beat, he released you."

"You had a couple of strokes of luck," said Edward. "The Sergeant was a bit dim and it didn't occur to him to ask how we knew you'd been arrested and those idiots who set this frame up didn't let the Sergeant in on their plans. He's a decent copper."

I thanked them again and asked about a fee.

"Not necessary, Roger. I do work against bent policemen for free and there's plenty of them in the Metropolitan Police—though to be fair, most of them are OK."

"Edward defended a young woman charged with prostitution a couple of years back. Tell Roger about that."

"She was very good looking and one of the local bobbies in Euston fancied her but she wasn't interested. So he had her arrested and charged with soliciting. A couple of his friends on the force confirmed she was a well-known prostitute and she was charged. In court I produced several respectable citizens who testified to her good character and a doctor who confirmed she was a virgin and that was that. Case dismissed."

We all laughed as we drew into my road. Negley told me they wouldn't dare touch me now. They were too frightened of Edward. He urged me to keep up the good work. I invited them in, but they politely refused. I told my parents I'd been working late. I had a cup of tea, and then went upstairs. I undressed and got into bed and began shaking like a leaf. It was almost two hours before sleep rescued me from the horrors of the evening.

CHAPTER FORTY

The End of Appeasement

"Oh what is that sound that so fills the ear
Down in the valley drumming, drumming?
Only the scarlet soldiers, dear
The soldiers coming."
W.H. AUDEN

I never told my parents, or Jane or even Ben, about my horrible experience with the police. I had nothing to be ashamed of, but didn't want to worry them. I woke up on Saturday morning with an unpleasant jolt as I lay in bed and remembered my experiences of the previous evening. How would I respond to this latest threat? It didn't take me long to decide that nothing would change. I would carry on writing the truth as I saw it, backed up by compelling evidence. Besides I now felt I had powerful protectors in Edward, Negley, Claud and, of course, Joe.

I got through my work quickly on the Monday morning then set off to the Café Royal to see Claud. His table was crowded when I arrived. I was immediately made welcome then sat down with Claud's 'correspondents' and began to help them through several bottles of Burgundy.

The talk was all about Hitler and his speech to the Reichstag, scheduled for the following day. As they sipped their wine and smoked their cigarettes, cigars and pipes, speculation ran rife: Hitler would attack Poland, the Nazis would seize the rest of Czechoslovakia or they would enact even more draconian measures against the Jews. Nobody really knew anything but everybody was agreed he would do something and that 1939 would be as bad as 1938, perhaps even worse.

Eventually the crowd dispersed to their offices or their homes and I was left alone with Claud.

"Thank you Claud," I began. "Without your help on Friday I'd have been in deep trouble."

"It's Joe, Edward and Negley you should thank, not me. Damn fine fellow, Joe, he'll go far in the world of sniffing and secrets. After you'd blown the whistle on how Hitler was treating the Jews and then fingered Halifax, I had an instinct that you might attract attention. That's why I asked Joe to keep an eye on you. He's saved my bacon several times, spotting coppers trying to set me up or spy on me. Anyhow, you're one of us now, against the establishment. If you think they're wrong, you've got the guts to say so. Ball and his men probably see you and your papers as a lost cause now. They'll most likely concentrate their efforts on trying to keep the qualities like *The Daily Telegraph* and *The Manchester Guardian* in line."

"That business on Friday has made me realise just how desperate Chamberlain must be to stamp on anybody who opposes his policies. Whatever happened to the freedom of the press?" I asked.

"Don't be too harsh on the old feller. He's vain, arrogant, incredibly determined and I think totally misguided. But if he thought attempts were being made to frame journalists, he'd throw up his hands in horror. No, his real weakness is that he trusts Hitler. Sooner or later that Nazi monster will do something that'll destroy that trust. What or when I couldn't say, but it'll happen."

"When it does happen, what do you think Chamberlain's response will be?" I asked.

"He'll stand up to him, perhaps not very forcibly, but he won't back down again. There'll be no more Munichs."

I thanked Claud and left for home. The next day Hitler's speech gave no definite clues about his future plans except that they involved violence. He told his fawning audience that, if war came, it would be the fault of the Jews and the Bolsheviks and that any such war would result in the annihilation of the Jewish race in Europe. There may have been nothing new in all this but there was a hint of menace in the way he prophesised the future and then blamed everything on the Jews. What about his promise of peace that he'd guaranteed Daladier and Chamberlain at Munich? I asked myself. Again, Blunt's words about hate came back to me.

Chamberlain had meanwhile been to Rome and courted Mussolini. By all accounts he got nowhere and it didn't seem likely that Italy would side with us in a future war with Germany. More likely Il Duce would line up alongside his pal Hitler hoping, no doubt, for more cheap conquests like Abyssinia.

February was a month of waiting. What would Hitler do next? I covered some sport, mostly football but some rugby as well. It was almost as if the country was going through the motions, trying to carry on as normal but, deep down, a majority of the country knew that this was just an interlude before Hitler struck again.

I did some film reviews. There was not much worth writing home about except perhaps *Gunga Din*. Things were a bit more interesting in the courts. Various visiting Germans were either deported or jailed for ham-fisted attempts at spying. The police and security services appeared to be on war alert. The IRA set off bombs in London and other cities. These were a threat, no doubt, but seemed unimportant when compared with the danger from Germany. Some of the perpetrators were caught and locked up. There were an unusual number of bankruptcy cases.

Then, in a repeat of the Duchess of Atholl business, the Tory hierarchy attacked their chief opponent Winston Churchill. They attempted to persuade his constituency party in Epping to deselect him, but narrowly failed.

At the beginning of March, Hitler made his move. As usual events conspired to help him. The Slovaks decided they didn't want to be part of Czechoslovakia any more. They wanted their own state, Slovakia. Hitler saw his chance. He encouraged the Slovak separatists and called their leaders to Berlin for friendly talks. Richard had heard from Harry that, as soon as Slovakia had set up their own government, Hitler would grab the rest of Czechoslovakia. I passed this information to Claud who said it confirmed what he'd heard from his source in the French government.

There was the usual prelude to Nazi aggression. The Berlin press accused the Czechs of 'terrorising' the Slovaks. The Czech government sacked Slovakian ministers. Hitler invited the Czech President and Foreign Minister to Berlin to try and sort out the crisis. That same day Samuel Hoare, the Home Secretary and a staunch supporter of appeasement, made a speech telling the British people that we were entering a golden age of peace and prosperity. The following day Czechoslovakia disappeared from the face of the map of Europe.

The Germans marched into what was left of Czechoslovakia at six o'clock in the morning. Ben sent me to the Commons to hear what Chamberlain had to say about it. He certainly wasn't at his best. He talked about disappointment and betrayal but pointed out that Czechoslovakia no longer existed so we wouldn't be taking action. The guarantees we'd given at Munich no longer mattered. He then announced the cancellation of a forthcoming trade mission to Germany and of any remaining aid to Czechoslovakia. Hitler had no moral case to occupy the rest of Czechoslovakia and the brutality of the Nazis was now out in the open, he said.

It was a feeble effort from the Prime Minister and the next day one or two newspapers called for his resignation. A revived Churchill blasted the failure of Munich in a speech in his constituency. The whole world waited for Chamberlain's reply.

On a Friday evening in mid-March my family, Jane and I gathered around the radio and listened to the Prime Minister speaking in the Town Hall in his native Birmingham. What he said destroyed appeasement for ever.

With unconcealed bitterness in his voice, Chamberlain left Hitler in no doubt of our country's detestation of Nazi methods. He asked, "Is this the last attack on a small state or is it to be followed by others? Is this, in fact, a step in the direction of an attempt to dominate the world by force?"

He defended the Munich agreement, saying that he had trusted Hitler, but he would trust him no longer. Hitler, he said, had taken the law into his own hands.

He told his audience that we had accelerated our armaments' programme and we would now be doing more to ensure our nation's safety and finished by saying "I do not think anyone would question my sincerity when I say that there is hardly anything that I would not sacrifice for peace, but there is one thing and that is the liberty that we have enjoyed for hundreds of years and which we will never surrender."

At this point we heard a huge roar of approval from the audience and, when silence had fallen, Chamberlain's final words were an undisguised threat as he said, "Germany will bitterly regret what her government has done."

It was a bravura performance but, once the dust had settled, we all agreed that, apart from issuing some strong threats and warnings, he hadn't actually said he'd do anything. On the following Sunday, *Reynolds News* called for an alliance with the French and Russians to deal with the Nazis. They called Hitler a liar and a lout and demanded that the Prime Minister step down. The German press, predictably, attacked Chamberlain savagely.

All that remained was for Hitler to take some action to test Chamberlain's new found resolve and the Fuhrer duly obliged by turning his attention to Poland where a substantial number of Germans lived. Also there was the Polish corridor splitting Germany from its lands in East Prussia and, of course, the German City of Danzig being governed by the League of Nations. The Treaty of Versailles had certainly given Hitler plenty of reason to shout and scream.

The German press carried the usual stories about German women and children being beaten by Poles, and then Hitler grabbed a bit more territory. This time it was Memel, part of Lithuania. He was, perhaps, entitled to this which represented another Versailles blunder, and the handover passed without incident. The real significance was that if Hitler seized the rest of Lithuania, Poland would be encircled by hostile states; Germany to the north, west and south and the Soviet Union to the east.

The British Ambassador met with the Polish Foreign Minister. There were more orchestrated incidents in Poland then, on the last Tuesday in March, the German press issued a veiled threat against Poland by warning that any further mistreatment of German citizens in Poland could be harmful to the Polish nation.

Chamberlain now had two choices: to do nothing or to stand up to Hitler and back the Poles. On March 31st I walked to the Commons to hear him make a foreign policy statement.

The Prime Minister's statement was brief and to the point. If any country threatened Polish independence, and that threat caused the Poles to take up arms, we would give the Poles all support in our power. He'd spoken to the French government, who would take the same course of action.

So now the choice of peace or war was taken out of our hands. If Poland was attacked, we would fight on their side alongside the French. Just over two weeks after Hoare's golden age of peace and prosperity speech, appeasement was dead and buried and war, if not certain, was highly likely.

I had tea with Philip after the House had adjourned. I asked him how likely he thought war was.

"Very," he replied. "Hitler won't stop now and he doesn't believe Chamberlain will defend Poland."

"Do you think he will?" I asked.

"He has to now he's made the commitment to Poland. OK, he's guaranteed Polish independence, but not their borders. It gives him a bit of space to back down, but he won't. That's what Hitler doesn't understand. It's the difference between democracy and dictatorship. If Chamberlain attempts to wriggle out of this now, he'll be kicked out and replaced by someone else, probably Halifax, who'll see it through. It's not Chamberlain who's threatening Hitler. It's the British people."

"There's a heavy irony about all this," I said. "We let Hitler get away with seizing a country that had never been part of Germany yet we seem prepared to go to war over Poland, part of which was German before 1918."

"That's right, but the game's up as far as the Nazis are concerned. We now know that Hitler won't just be after Danzig and the corridor. If there's one thing we've learned from the Czech business a fortnight ago, it's that he'll try to get hold of the whole of Poland. He probably thinks there'll be another Munich and we won't have the stomach for war, but this time he'll be wrong."

"I suppose Churchill and all those crying for collective security were right after all," I said. "If we'd ganged up with the French and Russians against Germany we might not be dreading war now."

"As you know, I believed in international cooperation all along," Philip replied. "But it's too late for that now. War really is inevitable."

"And how do you feel about the prospect of war?"

"I dread it, but Hitler is a total megalomaniac and has to be stopped. In my own mind, even allowing for my hatred of war, this is the battle we have to fight. It would be the right thing to do."

"Will the Germans fight?" I asked.

"Of course they will," Philip replied, "but not for Hitler or the Nazis. For Germany. The one thing Hitler's given them is a sense of restored pride after the humiliation of Versailles. That's how he's gotten away with it. They're a very proud race."

"So are we. I'm sure we'll fight if we have to. Chamberlain's tried everything to avoid war: letting the Spanish Republic die, standing by while Austria and Czechoslovakia vanish from the map, using threats to keep his opponents in line, as well as underhand tactics to keep the press and his own party on side. He even managed to rig a Parliamentary by-election. Then there's Ball; our very own Goebbels. Well, perhaps not quite that bad. The one thing Chamberlain couldn't control was Hitler. He totally misjudged him and now we're all going to pay for it. How many dead this time, I wonder?"

"You're absolutely correct. It's a dreadful prospect for us but it's something we just have to do." We both realised there was nothing more to say, but a great deal to think about. Philip got to his feet with a sigh. "Good-bye, Roger."

We shook hands and I left the Commons and strolled across Parliament Square towards Whitehall. The inevitably of war with Germany had really struck home. Listening to such a decent man as Philip, who all his adult life had been against conflict, say that this was just something we had to do, convinced me there was no escape from the war to come. Just how important it was to confront Hitler was now totally clear to me, having heard previously ardent pacifist Philip Noel Baker sacrificing his long held principles.

Jane was in town on business and we were meeting at Lyons Corner House in Coventry Street before going home to see Robert Donat in *The Citadel* at that plush new Odeon at Shannon Corner. My thoughts meandered as I passed the Westminster Tube Station. I thought about the sporting winter coming to its end and the summer ahead. Wales had upset Ireland's Rugby Triple Crown hopes in Belfast and those two shared the Championship with England who beat Scotland. Wisden Cricketer's Almanack had just been published, reporting on Hutton's epic innings at the Oval and previewing the forthcoming West Indies tour. Would it take place? Did it matter?

I was shaken out of my day-dreaming as I walked up Whitehall by the approach of a familiar face: that awful copper with the moustache.

He looked as surprised as me because, for once, it seemed our meeting was purely co-incidental. It didn't stop the butterflies from seizing control of my stomach, however. I hesitated for a second and was just about to ignore him when he spoke.

"Are you well today, Mr Martin? Looks like you've had your way. We're gonna have another war. I expect you'll be joining up soon?"

I stared into his small black eyes. I was rapidly re-gaining my composure. There was a hint of a sneer on his mouth. I said just one short sentence: "Why did you do it?"

"You needn't worry about that sort of thing now, sir. We're all on the same side after all." I fixed my stare on him. He couldn't bring his eyes to meet mine. I said again, "Why?"

He looked up with a sickly grin.

"Just doing my job, sir. Ours is not to reason why and all that. I was only following orders."

I bored my eyes into his. He looked down at his shoes. I turned away from him without a word and strode towards Trafalgar Square.

EPILOGUE

This is what happened to some of the people who appear directly in this story.

Claud Cockburn continued to publish The Week until it was briefly suppressed at the outbreak of war in 1939. It resumed publication when the Soviet Union became our allies following the German invasion of that country in June 1941. At the end of the war he retired with his wife to her home town in the Irish Republic.

Here he wrote a number of novels including *Beat the Devil* which was filmed by John Huston with Humphrey Bogart in the lead. He also wrote for Punch, the Sunday Telegraph and was Guest Editor of *Private Eye* in 1963, contributing to the legendary satirical magazine until his death in 1981 at the age of seventy-seven.

George Steer completed his account of the Basque war in 1938. Entitled *The Tree of Gernika* it became accepted as one of the finest pieces of writing about the Spanish Civil War. In 1940 he joined the army and served in the campaigns to drive the Italians out of East Africa. In May 1941 when the Emperor Haile Selassie re-entered Addis Ababa in triumph, Steer was in the column of troops accompanying him. He had books published on these campaigns.

Later Steer, by now a Lieutenant-Colonel in the Intelligence Corps, was posted to India and was tragically killed in a motor accident in India on Christmas Day 1944. He was just thirty-five years old.

Maurice Dobb remained a peripheral figure at Cambridge and, because of his overt Marxism, was denied certain rights normally due to university staff. Some sort of grudging recognition of his intellect came when he was made of Fellow of Trinity College in 1948 but it wasn't until the late 1960s that his reputation as a great economist was fully accepted. The climax of this came when he was elected a Fellow of the British Academy in 1971. He died in Cambridge in 1976 at the age of seventy-six.

Philip Noel-Baker (the hyphen was added in the early 1940s) became a Cabinet Minster as Secretary of State for the Commonwealth in Clement Attlee's Post War Labour Government in 1947. In 1950 he was moved to the Ministry of Fuel and Power and removed from the cabinet. In opposition in the 1950s, the Labour Party was torn apart by the debate on nuclear weapons and Noel-Baker supported a multilateralist policy in direct opposition to the unilateralist policy favoured by the Labour left under the leadership of Aneurin Bevan.

Noel-Baker never again held a Cabinet post. His final term in Parliament was during Harold Wilson's Labour Government in the 1960s. His lifelong campaign for disarmament was recognised by the award of the Nobel Peace Prize in 1959. He was made a life peer in 1977 and died at the age of eighty-two in 1983.

Negley Farson continued to work as a Foreign Correspondent for the Chicago Daily News and eventually settled in England. He was one of the most famous adventurers of his day and became a prolific author of eight books recounting his experiences around the globe. He wrote a two volume autobiography, *The Way of the Transgressor* (1936) and *A Mirror for Narcissus* more than twenty years later but is best remembered for his classic book on angling *Going Fishing* (1946). He died in Devon in 1960 at the age of seventy.

Anthony Blunt was one of five Cambridge students who spied for the Soviet Union before, during and, in some cases, after the Second World War. The others were Burgess, Philby, Donald Maclean and John Cairncross.

Blunt worked for MI5 during the war but left when peace came to become Surveyor of the King's Pictures, a post he also held under the present Queen, Elizabeth II. He was knighted in 1956 but unmasked as a traitor in November 1979 and was stripped of his knighthood. He died in 1983 at the age of seventy-five.

Harry really did exist, although not under that pseudonym. There were also anti-Nazi sources in the German Embassy in the 1930s. The rest of the characters are fictitious.

ACKNOWLEDGEMENTS

I became aware of the Chamberlain government's attempts to control the media when I saw the disturbing documentary *Before Hindsight* on television more than 30 years ago. It dealt exclusively with the manipulation of public opinion through the cinema newsreels. The British Film Institute kindly allowed me to watch it again at their Library in St Stephen's Street, London. How the government tried to control the written press is brilliantly recounted in Richard Cockett's book *Twilight of Truth* (Weidenfeld and Nicolson, 1989). The best of the many books which I've read about Nazi Germany is *The Third Reich in Power* by Richard J Evans (Allen Lane, 2008), the second part of a magnificent three volume history of Nazi Germany. I read numerous books about the period generally, the best of which was *The Thirties* by Juliet Gardiner.

There were other sources, too numerous to be listed here, and I am grateful to the British Library, and the libraries of Durham and Bradford Universities, Durham County Council, and the Lit & Phil in Newcastle-upon-Tyne. The British Library Newspaper Library at Colindale was very helpful in making copies of *The Week, Truth* and National and London Evening newspapers available to me. *The Times* is available digitally.

I watched dozens of documentary films about the thirties. These can be seen at BFI Mediatheques at various locations in the UK including the BFI South Bank and the Discovery Museum in Newcastle upon Tyne.

I visited many of the locations in the book but learned a great deal more about pre-war London from The London Transport Museum, The Museum of London and the Imperial War Museum (London).

A number of people read the manuscript and were extremely helpful with their criticism, comments and suggestions: Neil and Liz Young, Damien Jarvis, Dr Lizzie Seal, Lynne Moores and Marianne Bevis. Thank you very much. Much of the typing was done by my friend Tamara Anderson. Thanks Tamara. You saved me a whole load of hassle.

Lightning Source UK Ltd.
Milton Keynes UK
UKOW06f1522170615

253660UK00014B/208/P